The Sol Empire Volume 3 Greed

Vic Broquard

The Sol Empire Volume 3 Greed
First Edition
Copyrighted © 2018 by Vic Broquard
ISBN: 978-1-941415-84-9

What isn't fictional is the work that Humanity and Inclusion (formerly Handicapped International) is doing to help those who have suffered:
http://www.hi-us.org

Published by:
http://www.Broquard-ebooks.com
Broquard eBooks
103 Timberlane
East Peoria, IL 61611
author@Broquard-eBooks.com

For Morgan and L. Ron Hubbard

Table of Contents

Chapter 1 Kidnapped

May 3, 2360, Chicago, Earth, Sol Empire

After years of floundering, I decided on my goals. I was happy with them, and they worked out for me and my family. But I forgot one critical detail: life, which sometimes insists on other plans.

While wrapping up some notes on my last missing person case, my phone rang in my second-floor Parker Skyscraper office.

"Molly Parkinson's Private Investigations and—oh!"

A foot tall, 3-d hologram of my daughter Nikita and son Matt appeared. The front of their grade school rose behind them.

"Mom, how come Dad's not here? He's really late. Should've picked us up ages ago."

"Have you tried calling him? I'm at work."

"Duh, Mom. Yeah. Like six times. His phone's off. Can we walk home? Lara can watch us."

"One second. Let me try him."

Several years ago, I splurged and bought each of us one of the expensive phones that also sent 3-d holo images of the caller. I put them on hold, dialed Sam's number, and got voice mail, meaning the device was off or didn't exist any longer. I didn't want to consider the second possibility. Since we four had telepathic abilities—those three being legal while I was an illegal telepath, I had another way to talk to Sam. Reaching out for his mind, I found it, and my stomach twisted. Drugged and only semi-conscious, his sluggish thoughts blurred.

"Kids. Walk home. Don't stop anywhere. Lock the doors and wait for Lara to get there. I'm texting her now. Bye."

I didn't wait for the kid's reactions. They could pick up my thoughts anyway, and I didn't want them panicking. I popped the clip on my Glock, verified I had seventeen rounds, slammed it back in, and cocked it. I dashed out of the office, texting General Beverly Blythe, my sister, for help.

A block later, I jumped onto the fast track lane of the MTES, Mass Transit Eco-moving Sidewalk. Ordinarily, I go slow and admire the sky through the transparent canopy. But today, I raced along, hoping I still had time to save Sam. New O'Hare Spaceport: the only place he could be. Seven years ago, a new industry appeared: black-market telepaths. Legally hired telepaths often made a million credits a year. But if you kidnapped one and got them off-world, you could make a fortune selling them to the highest bidder.

What can I say? During this past decade, Earth has turned into a very different place from the world in which I was born. Years ago, an alien race known as the Sixth Invaders nearly succeeded in conquering Earth, and by proxy, the Sol Empire. They did it by inventing a series of genetic mutation agents. One of these called the Galactic Doll Agent mutates the body into what the Sixth Invaders thought was the idealized body form for both males and females, based on their own physical forms. Breasts the size of a head, distorted feet that forced the person to wear tall heels, long hair, along with other minor changes turned women and men into gorgeous Galactic Dolls. But with men, a set of ribs dissolved, their voices rose, their Adam's apple vanished, and their body became indistinguishable from female Galactic Dolls, until you looked at their genitals. The Sixth Invaders managed to convert most women on Earth into Galactic Dolls.

Today, we're dealing with a side-effect. Children born to a Galactic Doll are themselves a Galactic Doll, male or female. That is, these genetic traits are dominant. Yes, we now have a partial cure that reduces breast sizes down to a manageable large size, and our feet can lie flat on the ground.

But that was their benevolent mutation.

In their society, females ran everything, so the Sixth Invaders wanted to force our men out of their positions of power, replacing them with women. Thus, they developed a very nasty genetic mutation agent, which we call the Armless Galactic Doll Telepath Agent. Yes, in addition to the Galactic Doll changes, their arms dissolve, but their pituitary gland enlarges, turning them into true telepaths— possibly a compensation for a difficult life.

Seven years ago, my sister Eve and a good dwarven friend Lara created a genetic cure that regrew the lost arms. However, the ruling corporations demanded that any arm regrow cure also remove their telepathic abilities. Why? If you see an armless Doll, he or she is a telepath. If you see someone with arms, they aren't a telepath. Silly, dumb, and impractical, because not everyone without arms is a telepath. Accidents and birth defects happen. However, in today's world, such babies and individuals are given the Armless Doll Telepath Agent so they, too, will fit the pattern. So why not just regrow their arms?

The side-effect of these armless Doll telepaths is that any children they have are also born as armless Doll telepaths. These genes are dominant over all others. Because both my husband Sam and I were one of these, our two youngest children are also armless Doll telepaths.

However, because of all the spiritual therapy I had prior to being injected with this agent, I had telepathic ability long before my body was mutated. After undergoing the cure to regrow arms seven years ago, my telepathy didn't disappear. Hence, I'm an illegal telepath. I just don't advertise my skills.

With the birth of our children, things got more complicated. When our daughter, Nikita, came, she insisted she wanted to be a telepath, begging us not to give her the arm regrow cure. Thus, Sam decided to remain an armless Doll telepath so he could show our daughter how to do things and provide moral support. A year later when we had our son, Matt, the laws had changed.

Since that time, any child born as an armless Doll telepath had to be raised as such until they reached the age of eighteen, at which time they could choose to have the cures or remain a telepath. Thus, Matt still is one, too.

Nikita is in second grade, while Matt is in first grade. And Sam always meets them at school, walking them home, just as he always walks them to school each day. Except today. Someone kidnapped him, presumably because he's an adult telepath.

I reached the edge of New O'Hare Spaceport. The place is gigantic. I flashed my PI badge as I raced on down the fast lane of the MTES system. My PI license provides me with many special benefits, one of which is an instant pass through nearly all security. The flashes I'd seen in Sam's hazy mind suggested he was being carried to the long-term parking area on the northwest edge, which is where I headed, now jogging. I spotted a green EMAC landing; it had a large blaster mounted in a topside turret. That had to be General Bev, my sister, other wise known as Kick-Ass among her fellow First Infantry Division soldiers.

As I jogged towards the various transport ships parked on the tarmac, I knew I had only one shot at rescuing Sam, so I had to pick the right transport to attack. Three were being serviced, last minute fuel top-offs and window cleaning. I guessed one of these held Sam. Which one? If I attacked the wrong one tipping off the kidnappers, they'd do an immediate power up and take off before I could get to them. As the distance closed, two crews didn't seem to be in a hurry, while one crew was moving as rapidly as possible, handing pre-flight checks.

I pointed to it, signaling Bev, and sprinted, while drawing my Glock. As I neared, two men looked up at me. I knew I'd picked the right transport because they drew weapons and fired wildly as they raced to the bay ramp. Me, I simply fired two rounds at each man, roughly aiming at their center of mass. One dropped to the ground, while the other man dropped his gun when my bullet struck his arm, spinning him around. I ignored his feeble attempts to retrieve his gun, figuring Bev would handle him.

I raced up the ramp, only to see men coming at me from either end of the ship. I saw five armless Dolls, presumably telepaths, strapped into their seats. One was my golden-haired Sam. They fired at me but I was a racing target. They missed. I shot while diving to the floor on my left side, placing two shots dead center. I hit hard and rolled out of the line of fire from the remaining gunman. Bev ran up the ramp, saw the man trying to get a bead on me, and fired twice. The man dropped like a rock.

"Save some for me," Bev said. She raced on towards the back of the ship, while I rose and dashed up front.

In a panic, the pilot raced through the obligatory pre-flight checks. I came up behind him, pressed my Glock to his head. "Power down or I'll shoot." Wisely, he flipped switches, powering the ship down.

"Clear back here," Bev yelled.

"Clear up front. One prisoner. You: get up. Walk to the bay doors."

I kept my gun on him. I had to, for he was a giant, nearly eight feet tall. One fist strike would probably kill me. Giants are that strong. And they were one of the two new immigrants to Earth.

Giants and dwarves had settled here as part of the Federation's bargain with us to stop the Sixth Invaders' invasion fleet from attacking the Sol Empire's fleet. The invading space fleet outnumbered us three to one, so Earth had little choice but to accept immigrants from two overpopulated worlds in order to get Federation protection. The giants came from Liatos-D, while the dwarves, including my friend Lara Axe-head, came from Dian-C. The dwarves were about four feet tall, but incredibly strong, because their world had heavier gravity than Earth's.

Bev took over for me. I rushed to Sam's side. His breathing and rolling eyes told me he was drugged. I checked on the other four. They, too, were oblivious. Just then, a dozen New O'Hare security guards rushed up, blasters drawn. Explanations time. I let General Bev do most of the talking.

The squad's captain recorded our discussions. At first, he seemed on our side. "Damned telepath kidnapers. We've been after them for months."

But then, he began probing a bit more. "So, Mrs. Parkinson, how did you know this was the kidnapper's transport, that your husband Sam was here?"

Bit by bit, he began to sense I must also have telepathy, for what else could explain the fact I ran straight to this ship out of all the others on the enormous tarmac. Soon, Galactic Medicine personnel arrived, whisking all five away to the Med Center for observations. The captain did allow me to go with Sam, while Bev headed back to her army EMAC. As I left with the medical personnel, I had an uneasy feeling about the situation.

At the Med Center, doctors quickly discovered they had been given a knock-out drug, so they injected the antidote into each person's leg. A half hour later, Sam was back with me, though he had a headache and felt groggy. His golden hair, which nearly touched his ankles, lay draped in his lap, a tangled mess in dire need of the hair/nail machine, which used air flow and static electricity to de-tangle and fluff our hair, compliments of the Sixth Invaders, who also provided dressing machines, and a chef/maid mechanical robot.

Sam preferred to dress like an armless Galactic Doll and not try to pretend his body wasn't one. This way, Sam avoided public embarrassment, since unless one looked into his panties, he appeared to be female. However, many such men cut their hair short and wore suits, although their bosoms were obvious, as were their high pitched voices. In fact like all male Dolls, he helped nurse both our children. He wore a yellow satin gown that encased his empty shoulders tightly, while flaring wide at his waist, a design made especially for us by another of my sisters, Leslie. Since all formal Dolls wore tall heels, even though he had this cure, he chose to wear them to work and when in public. Doing so brought far less attention to himself. Even after seven years as an armless Doll, Sam still felt ill at ease in public.

I helped him sit up, when another guard stepped up. "I'm here to take your statement, Mr. Kross-Parkinson. Please, begin at the beginning."

He recorded the conversation. Sam had been walking to the grade school to pick up our kids when someone came up from behind and stuck a needle into his neck. An arm caught him, preventing him from falling. After that, all was mostly a fog.

That formality done, with my arm around Sam, we headed home, taking the slow lanes of the MTES.

"What's our world coming to?" Sam said. "A man can't even safely walk his kids to and from school any more."

"It's this telepath mess. They obviously wanted to take five of you off-world and sell you to the highest bidder, making themselves rich. Damn scary."

"Thanks for saving me. See, lack of arms made no difference. I would have been captured either way."

He referred to our long standing discussion about him getting his regrown, though it would mean losing his telepathy. Sam picked up my thoughts.

"We've been over this a hundred times. As long as our kids want to be telepaths, I'm going to support them the best way I know how—by being one myself and showing them how to do things they have to do and being there for them. And wearing flats wouldn't have made any difference either."

I dropped the topic. "So how did work go today?"

Sam worked at the UIC campus library in the basement stacks where their real books were kept. The vast majority of the college students used electronic books, but rare individuals visited the stacks, sometimes just to smell the books. Sam had a photographic memory and was widely known as the "go-to man." He knew or could find nearly anything in the many floors of the stacks. Heck, I'd used his locating skills countless times while finally earning my gen ed degree.

"Pretty dull. Had one giant come down looking for information on our early corporations and who ran them. Mostly, I continued my own studies. Look, if our Nikita wants to be a linguist and an astronomer, I aim to help her do that. Matt wants to be a telepath, historian, and an astro-navigator. Cool that he wants to take up history like me, but I'm also studying all I can about how to navigate spaceships. It isn't too hard, so like I said months ago, I think it's a career Matt could do while being a licensed telepath."

"But Sam, they're only in second and first grades. They don't have to make those choices for nearly a dozen more years."

Sam chuckled. "Until they decide otherwise, I'm sticking to it and being there for them both. Shame none wants to be a PI like their mother. By the way, a huge thank you for saving my butt today. And the other four telepaths. I owe you. So were you at work when this happened?"

Mornings, I worked with another sister, Celeste, at our Spiritual Recovery and Healing Center, delivering therapy sessions to others. I considered this the most important aspect of my life and by far the most rewarding.

Afternoons found me running my local PI business out of the Parker Skyscraper, just outside the Loop. Evenings used to be devoted to my college studies, but now that I had my basic degree, I was between courses. Lately, I'd gotten used to being with my family each evening.

"Yes, I wrapped up my last missing person case. Kid ran away from home because their father wanted him to become a telepath. I reported the incident to the police and Galactic Defense, but did convince the teen to return home. GD will take action against the dad if he forces the teen to become an armless Doll telepath. What's our world becoming anyway?"

Via Celeste's pioneering efforts, our therapy erased all physical trauma, mental implants, and emotional trauma, too. I'd also shown the therapy worked on dwarves and even Sixth Invaders, where doing the latter brought about the peace treaty between us some seven years ago. In fact, I often treated the Sixth Invader's Sol Empire ambassador, Commander L'Grina, who just couldn't get enough therapy sessions. She had a voracious appetite for bad things happening either to her or done by her. Both types got erased by the therapy.

Home at last. Seven years ago, we moved into the mansion in Northbrook that Sam inherited from his parents, who had held high paying positions with Galactic University. In fact, Helen and Casper Hugo lived in the ritzy estate next to ours. Their two children constantly played with ours and went to the same grade school. So I wasn't surprised to see both Veronica and Fritz at our house.

"Dad! You're all right," Matt said, rushing up to Sam, pressing his body into Sam's. "Mom, did you shoot the bad guys?"

Fritz Hugo walked up, eager to hear my answer, his blue eyes opened wide. Casper probably saw us coming, because he joined us just as I answered Matt's question.

"Yes, I killed three of the five giants who kidnapped your father and four other telepaths. I'm not proud of killing them, but they gave me no choice."

"Sam, Molly, I'm glad you're both all right. Honestly, I'm beginning to think we should never have allowed those giants to immigrate here," Casper said.

Just inside, I saw Nikita and Veronica sitting on a couch. I saw Nikita running a therapy session on Veronica. Even from this distance, I could see her eyes were red.

"What's going on with Veronica? Did she get hurt?" I asked.

Casper looked over at his daughter, intently observing, a worried look on his face.

Matt said, "Some girls picked on her today, calling her a helpless freak. She started bawling. Nikita's fixing her up. Mom, tell us all about it. How did you find dad?"

"Ah there you are," said Lara, my dear dwarf friend. "Supper's in twenty. Casper, are you and your brood staying for supper?"

He laughed. "No, Helen would have my head. I came to make sure Sam and Molly are okay. Best let Nikita finish up before I take them home. So Sam, what happened?"

Sam began telling Casper and the eager boys what had happened to him.

By law, Nikita, Matt, Veronica, and Fritz had to remain armless Doll telepaths until their eighteenth birthdays because they were born this way. The ruling Council of the Senate issued this hard and fast law seven years ago. No exceptions. I suspect they did this so more children would remain telepaths, which these days had become a most profitable business. By eighteen, they would be far less likely to want to undo it—to give it up. For Nikita and Matt, this was fine, because both wanted to be telepaths. However, Veronica and Fritz hated being armless Doll telepaths, but legally they couldn't get the cures until they reached eighteen. I'd lost count of the number of times Veronica had come home from school crying. Fritz, too.

With the birth of our children, Casper had followed Sam's lead and hadn't gotten his arms regrown. Thus, the two fathers did their best to be role models for their kids as well as showing them how to do things and providing moral support.

Casper dressed in Leslie's male Doll apparel, kept his hair short, and tried to look as much like a male as possible, given that nothing could hide his high-pitched voice, large bosom, and feminine-shaped body. Sam, however, continued to wear the new style shoulder-tight, satin gowns and tall heels, when in public. His wavy golden hair almost touched his ankles. Anyone looking at the two men would know immediately that Casper was a male Doll.

Like all children, Matt and Fritz had been given the feet and bosom genetic cures. So had Veronica and Nikita. The boys wore jeans with Velcro fasteners, easy for them to manipulate. Their shirts were tight-fitting, colorful plaids, but had no sleeves and fit snugly around their shoulders. They looked like most boys their age, except for their lack of arms. As a result, they received far less teasing at school, unlike the girls. Of course, we all knew that would change when their bodies began to mature in just a few more years.

Veronica emulated Nikita in many ways. She kept her blond hair
waist length just like Nikita's dark brown, wavy hair. The two girls dressed similarly, as best friends were wont to do. Both wore the new style shoulder-tight, satin gowns similar to those that Sam wore. Veronica's was a light blue, while Nikita was partial to rich blues.

While Matt, Fritz, and Casper listened intently to

Sam's tale, I moved closer to the girls, listening in on their therapy session. A smile creased my lips. We definitely had four very precocious and intelligent children, far advanced for their ages of seven and six.

At a very early age, I'd begun giving them therapy sessions intending to erase any harmful effects birth might have had on them. Soon, they began running therapy sessions on each other, though these days, the two older girls usually ran sessions on their younger brothers as well as each other.

One day, Matt fell down and skinned his knees. Nikita returned him to the fall and ran him through it, even going earlier in time when he didn't become cheerful about it. Nikita was seven going on fourteen.

The four's IQs were measured in First Grade. Each had an IQ over 150, which put them into the elite First Grade class. I like to think I had an influence on them, too. At the time, I had decided to get a higher education and went to UIC, studying Gen Ed. I had to constantly look up the definitions of words I didn't know or hadn't bothered learning when I was in high school. So when my kids started school, I drilled into their noggins to stop and look up any word or symbol they didn't know. By second grade, Nikita was doing fourth grade work.

"Bang. Bang. Your mother comes running up, her gun blazing," Sam continued his tale, bringing me back to the present. "She killed two giants who were outside the ship getting it ready to take off. Then she and Aunt Bev came racing up the ramp into the ship. Bang. Bang. Two more dead giants."

The girls finished the session. She and a giggling Veronica joined us, also intrigued by Sam's story.

"Dad, that's what I want to be when I grow up. Bang. Bang. A security guard," Fritz declared.

That's not what Casper wanted for his son. I knew he hoped Fritz would take after him and become a top financial planner for a corporation.

I knew Veronica wanted to be a general like the famous General Beverly Blossom Blythe, but without arms, she knew she couldn't do that. Her school counselor wanted her to become a fashion model for Galactic Entertainment, but she wanted no part of that. I also knew the Hugo children's constant clashes with reality were the subject of many therapy sessions. Why couldn't the Council of the Senate see that not everyone should be forced to remain armless Doll telepaths until age eighteen?

Casper asked, "So Molly, think there'll be any repercussions on you? Killing three giants? Have they interrogated you about how you were able to find Sam so quickly?"

I knew what he was hinting ask. I was an illegal telepath. "Probably not. They questioned me and here we are. Supper time."

With that, Casper ushered his children out our automated front door, which operated like all exterior doors in most buildings.

"So Mom, when can we see Isabella's latest call?" Nikita asked.

"Yeah, when?" added Matt.

"Okay, let's do it now. I'll setup my computer. Remember, there's always that long time delay between us."

"We know, Mom," Nikita said, rolling her eyes. "One minute per every four light years away. Everyone knows that."

Heck, I didn't. We've bright kids. Our adopted twins were now twenty years old and into their seventh year as telepaths on board two deep space exploration ships. We were very proud of Isabella and Bernardo. Each had helped discover new civilizations and unravel their languages. I replayed last month's call from our twins. It helped form bonds between them and our two young children, adding proof the children could grow up to become valuable members of society.

"Incoming call from the Star Voyager for Molly Parkinson. Isabella Parkinson calling." A 3-d holographic image fluttered into existence. We saw a black haired young woman staring into her ship's long distance communication device. Both twins had grown so much in these past seven years.

"Hi Mom, Dad, Nikita, Matt. I've got some exciting news this time. As you know, I'm in college working on my degrees in astro-linguistics and astro-archaeology. You'll never guess what I've deciphered."

Her eyes shone. She bubbled with excitement. "Mom, I've deciphered the Fifth Invaders' script! Almost two hundred years ago, our explorers discovered their giant, hexagonal towers on the moon and recovered a pile of ceramic documents along with some mummified remains. So we know they were tall, thin aliens with grey skins. The unreadable documents didn't shed any light on where they came from. Well, I've been studying them and have cracked their writing.

"Unfortunately, the documents are only operational manuals that describe how to run their implant machines. From my translations, their implants worked much like those of the Sixth Invaders do today. What a let-down. But my thesis advisor assures me that I'll be able to get my doctorate because of this. Mom, I'm going to be an astro-linguist for sure. Next, they're having me look over the few surviving writings of the Fourth Invaders based on Mars. If I can crack their writing, I'll for sure have my doctorate.

"Oh, tell Nikita and Matt to study lots. There's so much you can learn. Knowledge is the key. Okay, telepathy helps. Over." Isabella giggled. Her excitement rubbed off on me when I first recorded her call. Sharing it with Nikita and Matt raised their hopes. Okay, I felt inspired and extremely proud of her.

After our response and time delay ended, Isabella and a young man appeared. "Mom, this is my boyfriend and fiancé. Owen Barker. He's an astro-geologist and has been helping me with college. He thinks I'll be able to get dual degrees, so maybe I'll also be an astro-archaeologist. We're planning to get married when I'm twenty-one and finish my degrees. According to the commander of the Star Voyager, we're due to land on Earth early next spring, so Owen thinks we'll be able to hold our wedding with all of you. I can't wait for you to meet him."

Both Isabella and Owen chatted about life on the ship and each other. He was six years older than she was. His home was originally LA.

When the recording finished, Nikita giggled. "Mom, it's only going to be another eleven months until they're here. Where are we going to hold her wedding? We need to plan everything. I can't wait to see her."

Matt raised his nose. "Ah, who cares about that. Play Bernardo's call, Mom. Please."

Bernardo's calls were all about his latest culinary recipes, that and his engagement to Wendy Lu. She was seven years older than Bernardo and the captain of the Path Finder's security team of six.

When that recording ended, Matt said, "Mom, since Bernardo is a chef, why can't you cook?"

I laughed. "I'm learning. Aunt Gail is teaching me. You're welcome to lend me a hand in the kitchen."

Matt wiggled his nose and giggled. "I can't find them anymore."

We all laughed. Recording the monthly calls from our twins had been one of my better ideas. Even though Isabella and Bernardo were gazillions of miles away, we still felt close. For security reasons, they couldn't reveal their current location within the galaxy.

Chapter 2 Repercussions

That night, I stole into Nikita's bedroom. As usual, Sam lay in the middle of her bed with Nikita on his left and Matt on his right, pillows beneath each head, his hair spread out over the top of his dress.

"And so the prince leaned over and planted a loving kiss on the sleeping princess's lips. That broke the evil queen's sleeping spell. Oh, there's your mom. We best get you both to bed or she'll paddle us."

"Oh, dad. Mom's not going to spank us," Nikita said. "Mom, can we get photographic memories like dad has? That would sure help us in school."

"I wish I had it, too. Just keep on with therapy sessions. Maybe it can happen. Me, I really struggled in college. Just ask your dad; he had to help me a bunch. Remember, if you don't know what something means, look it up. Now let's get you two tucked in. You've school tomorrow."

Matt wiggled out of bed, followed by Sam, who carefully avoided getting tangled up in his long hair. He bent over and gave Nikita a kiss on her forehead, then followed after Matt. She scooted into the covers, and I pulled them up before giving her a night kiss.

After we got Matt settled down, Sam and I sat beside each other in the living room. "Have I told you how much I love you?" I said, hugging him.

"Ah, you just want to hear a bedtime story, too. You know I've got them all in my head." We laughed.

The next day, while Lara whipped up breakfast for us, I helped the others get dressed and ready for school and work. While they could do these actions on their own, with my helpful arms, the process went swiftly. Today, however, Lara insisted on walking with Sam as he walked the four children to school. As they stepped outside and met Veronica and Fritz, Casper joined them.

"After yesterday, Sam, I'm coming too. Damned if I

could do much, but maybe they'll think twice if there's two of us."

"Appreciated, Casper. Lara is coming as well. Now we can relax."

"That's right, boys," the dwarf said, "because I'll rip their arms and legs off their bodies."

The four kids laughed.

Me, I headed to deliver my morning therapy sessions.

After lunch, as I walked up to the Parker Skyscraper and my PI office, six security guards swept around me. One said, "Molly Parkinson, you are summoned before the Senior Investigator and Senior Judge. Right now. Come with us."

"Can I lock my gun up in my office?"

I had an awful hunch where this was headed and wanted to preserve my antique Glock. At least they allowed me to do that before marching me down into the loop.

An hour later, the security guards marched me into an austere meeting room. The Senior Investigator sat behind a small desk, an open computer before her. Standing at her side was an armless Doll telepath, a male in this case since he had short hair and wore a grey suit whose shirt and jacket had no sleeves.

The telepath focused on me. I felt his mind touch mine for the briefest instant. He nodded to the Senior Investigator, who typed something into the computer. A Galactic Doll, she was definitely not the woman I'd recommended to this post seven years ago. Back then, many wanted me to take this position, but I declined, allowing my assistant, Major Airla Baker to assume the position. However, not long after that, I discovered she was one of the five human-looking robots—one programmed with laws to protect humans. She and I knew any telepath could discover she wasn't human. So I recommended another person for the post and Airla vanished. I presumed she'd changed her identity.

Robots. Five other human-like robots had not been programmed with the laws before they vanished seven years ago. Ten disappeared, but I suspected Airla Baker and the other four were around, helping as they could from the background. However, my husband Ted had been murdered when he began to unravel the secret of these ten robots. While many organizations investigated his murder, including Helen at GD, no real clues were ever found. His murderer had made a clean getaway. I'd never really had the time to investigate his death or the authority to do so. Instead, I focused on having our baby, Nikita, and surviving.

Finally, the Senior Investigator spoke. "Guards, take her next door to the Senior Judge."

That was it. That was all that was said. I had no trial, offered no excuses, just examined for a second by another telepath. A couple minutes later, the armed guards ushered me into another room, one floor above the investigator's office. The male Doll looked up from his computer, motioned me to have a seat before his desk.

"Molly Parkinson. You are hereby found guilty of violating Council of the Senate's Law Number Twelve. All telepath must be armless, but Dolls are preferred. Considering your lengthy service to Earth and the Sol Empire and your valiant rescue of five kidnapped telepaths yesterday, this court is inclined to show you some leniency. The Council of the Senate's prescribed penalty for this offense is a lifetime ban on current and future genetic mutation cures. However, having taken your history into account, I'm limiting the curative ban to the next ten years. You'll immediately be taken to the Med Center and mutated into a legal telepath. This finding will be a permanent part of your medical record, so that there is no way to circumvent this ruling. Take her away."

I didn't get the opportunity to say a word, let alone present a defense. I had developed telepathic abilities as a result of the thousands of hours of therapy, not because of some genetic mutation. What had happened to jurisprudence in our world? I had no idea it had gotten this bad. Well, perhaps some of this was my fault. I'd chosen to get advanced education and continue doing therapy instead of taking the suggested roles in the formulation of our new ruling bodies.

They shoved me into an EMAC. Five minutes later, it landed outside the Med Center, where a doctor walked up the bay ramp. Before I could say a word, he stabbed me in my neck with a syringe.

"Carry her inside," he ordered.

I blacked out.

Analytically, I knew my body would be in a mutation coma probably for a week or more. Further, once I woke up, Celeste would give me another therapy session, erasing the physical pain the body was about to endure, along with any words spoken around me while I was out. One thing I had learned from my own therapy and from delivering it to others is that words spoken around an unconscious person can negatively affect them, gaining force and power from the underlying pain, such as "she can't feel anything."

The trouble was that I wasn't unconscious or was I? I felt rather foggy and had even blacked out at first. Yet now I'm alert. Whoa. I am alert—not my body. I'm viewing it from a few feet above its head. It's in a coma. No doubt about that.

I watched medical personnel hooking it up to several machines. What a different experience this was turning out to be. Well, it was my own damn fault that I was here. I'd chosen to pursue my own goals seven years ago instead of doing what I could for Earth. In fact, raising my children, running my PI business, and delivering therapy sessions had occupied my time, along with getting my college degree in Gen Ed. I never could decide what I truly wanted to learn. Still, I squeezed these classes into my evening study hours.

Celeste here, Molly. Are you doing okay? I see you're awake and above your body.

Yeah, kinda spooky, but I'm not my body down there.

Good observation. I'll run you through this when you're out of the coma.

Thanks. Keep an eye on my family for me, will you?

And be careful they don't discover you're illegal too.

Celeste left. Soon, I got bored. Wham. A white cloud surrounded me, blocking all perceptions. As it lifted, I found myself walking on the MTES heading towards the Loop. Over head a light delta wing cruiser drifted along, its grey shape silhouetted against the cumulus clouds. Something hung from its bottom, a device of some kind. Gas vented from it, drifting down onto Chicago. People looked up, watching and wondering. The escalator moved me along. Then, normal Galactic Dolls and male Dolls slumped, collapsing onto the MTES, jamming the escalators, forcing an emergency stop. Comas.

Giants and dwarves walked up to where I stood, surrounded by comatose people. "You, get in." A giant pointed at me and then at an EMAC I'd not seen before. I didn't move, so he picked me up and deposited me inside. "Stay put." I watched as they collected up many dozens, putting them into other waiting EMACs. Where'd they come from?

Now I was moving. "Where are you taking me?"

No one answered, but through a window, I saw New O'Hare Spaceport coming up fast. I protested, but a giant laughed as he carried me into a deep space transport, put me in a seat, and fastened my four-point seat belt. Varoom. The transport lifted off.

Another giant appeared wearing a reddish uniform. "Relax. We're about to make the jump into hyperspace. In a few hours, you will be auctioned at our first telepath sale. Since you're already one, you'll fetch a higher price. These unconscious people will need adapting time before we can auction them at the second telepath sale. Relax. We're mutating all you Earth people, one city at a time. We giants are soon going to be the richest people in the galaxy."

I screamed, but my body made no sound. A fog drifted through the ship, but when it cleared, I was still floating a few feet above my comatose body down there in the Med Center.

Shit, what a hell of a vision! Again, I'd just had glimpse of the future. I had to change it. Worse, I must have really missed something these past seven years. I knew I had to do something, anything, to prevent this from happening. As I waited for my body to come out of its coma, I worked on what I could do about it. Unfortunately, by the time my body stirred, I still didn't have any real idea what I could do to change our future. Greed had overcome all good sense.

"I feel awful. Someone get the number of the EMAC that ran over me?"

Sam stood beside my bed, smiling. "Awake at last, dear. Celeste will be by tonight to give you a therapy session. Leslie's dropped off some clothes for you. Light blue, your favorite color, the style that encases shoulders tightly. Gosh, dear, you sure have the curves now."

I looked at my chest, saw two soccer balls, and groaned. "More of me for you to love. Get me out of here, please."

"Gotta get you dressed. I've laid the clothes on the dressing machine. Can you manage that? Or I can call for the nurse or I can try to help you."

"I'll try it myself. Thanks, love." I struggled to sit up, somewhat weak and in need of wholesome, solid food. I sat on the edge of the narrow hospital bed for a bit letting my head stop swirling.

"I forgot how big they used to be. Well, I managed to survive this once before, so I can do it again. Kids okay?"

"Yeah, they're fine. Can't wait to see you. I think they are really curious about how you're going to look. Watch it."

I'd tried to stand up, forgetting my feet had also been mutated. No longer did my feet lie flat, nearly causing me to fall over. I flailed my non-existent arms about and then started laughing.

"Forgot about the feet. My arms don't seem to work any longer."

Sam didn't quite know how to react and wisely said nothing, though he smiled. A frustrating struggle later, the machine zipped up my new dress, which fit my torso tightly. I slipped into the matching heels, silently thanking my sister for her thoughtfulness. When I carefully rose, my raven hair slipped down, nearly reaching my ankles.

He said, "Yours is now longer than mine. Guess I'll have some catching up to do."

"Or I'm getting it trimmed."

"Don't you dare," Sam teased.

We shared a passionate kiss, and he summoned the nurse. She took a new photo for my new ID card. I grinned at the age disparity: Real Age: 31; Biological Age: 21. I just added year to my life expectancy, but doctors now made widespread use of this rejuvenation property.

Then, we walked out of the Med Center. Yes, I took it very carefully. My balance was off, but from past experience, I knew I'd catch on with a little practice.

"Wow, mom. You look so different," Nikita said when we walked into our living room.

"Now you have another role model, dear. I look like a Galactic Doll."

"Hey, we're wearing the same style dresses. Just like dad is."

"Yes, honey. I didn't want to give anyone a cold shoulder."

Seconds later, they duplicated my jest.

"Mom!" Nikita gave me a grinning protest.

Everyone roared. Mission accomplished. I'd lightened the tense mood my children were in. Lara entered, chuckling as well.

"Good to see you're back, Molly. I was worried about you. So many phone calls. You'll need an hour to get through all the voice mails on your phone. Eve said to fill you up with nourishing real food the moment you came home, not the synthetic usual stuff. I've got a chicken dinner waiting for you. While you eat, you can tell us all about it. The kids want to know everything."

"Thanks, Lara. Don't know what we'd do without you. I think I could eat a bear."

The gang followed me into the dining room, where Lara quickly fixed my plate. Evidently, Nikita had texted the Hugo's children because Veronica and Fritz quietly stole into the room like a pair of door mice eager to hear whatever I said, as well as to see what I looked like.

"Hi Veronica, Fritz. Now I'm like you."

"Will ours get that big?" asked Veronica. Her eyes bulged; her brows raised high.

A glance at our kids told me they were also worried. I chose my words carefully.

"My body is now what is known as an original Galactic Doll. This is what we looked like when the Sixth Invaders implanted all women on Earth to get mutated into this curvaceous form, only they had arms. My feet are messed up, too. So I'll be wearing tall heels like Dad does, only I'll have to wear them all the time. Lara and Aunt Eve created a cure that reduces breast sizes to those of Sam, Casper, and Helen. They also created a cure for feet. When you four were born, we and your parents gave you each of those genetic cures. So no, you won't have breasts this huge, but they will be big like your dad and Casper and Helen. Your feet lie flat, but when you're older and if you want to, you can wear the tall heels just for style."

That satisfied the children who ran off to play. Okay, I lied to them—well, just a little. Years ago via nighttime drone flights, the Sixth Invaders had implanted everyone to believe all women should be Galactic Dolls, the original formulation. Via Celeste's connections with Galactic Medicine, I knew that Eve and Lara's cures for breasts and feet weren't widely accepted. Women didn't want to go against their implanted notions of female body form. Today, only ten percent of Earth's women had accepted both cures. However, among telepaths who were eligible for them, the percentage rose to nearly ninety-five, because those two cures made life more manageable. I wouldn't be eligible for ten years, thanks to our misguided justice system.

I noticed the calendar. Saturday. I slipped off my shoes and sighed. "Well, here I go again. Give me time to get back into the swing of things."

For seven years, I'd had hands again. Grief swelled over me, as I struggled to pick up the silverware and feed myself. I suppressed it, knowing Celeste would soon come. I needed to be well-fed.

That done, I headed to the bathroom. I felt incredibly dirty, filthy, soiled, but that was probably just an emotional reaction. Sam was a big help, using his feet to wash my back. Oh, how I loved baths, but Sam preferred showers. While he and I worked on drying me off, I told him of my dream.

"Sam, something terrible is going to happen. I had another future vision. While Celeste is handling me, call up all our friends. Let's hold a meeting tomorrow around one."

Touching my mind so she knew when to arrive, Celeste showed up just after I'd gotten dressed and my hair done using the two machines. Without further ado, she ran her therapy on me. Fortunately, I had pretty much faced it myself, so we were done in less than an hour.

"Okay. We'll end here. Now then, Eve and Lara want a private word with you. They have some news. Good, for a change. They're in your living room now."

"Hi everyone," I said, when Celeste and I walked in and took a seat on the couch beside Sam. Eve and Lara sat on the stuffed chairs across from us.

Eve said, "We've done it. We have made a huge breakthrough. As you know, most women haven't taken advantage of the breast reduction cure or the feet repair cure because of the implant that has them convinced they need to look like Galactic Dolls. The problem is their offspring inherit these same genes, becoming male or female Dolls as well. We've developed a sneaky way around the problem, that is, of their children inheriting these mutations. Our cure alters what is transferred to the fertilized eggs. While the parent's bodies remain as they are, children won't inherit the mutations."

"Wow, that's one gigantic very well done, you two," I said.

"But there's a problem. We can't get corporations to allow the cure. There's more. Based on what we've already done, we believe we can undo male Doll's voices and large breasts. They'd then appear more normal, though their bodies would still be somewhat feminine looking—no

Adam's apple, missing ribs, with prominent body curves. We've received corporations' backing, but the cure can only affect male Dolls and absolutely not armless male Dolls. That restriction is throwing the monkey wrench into our research, but we're keeping at it. Just try to invent a serum that detects which kind the patient is."

"Eve, Lara, well done. Any chance you can implement the women's cure so their children don't keep on inheriting the mutation? Finding normal looking men is going to be impossible in another half century, maybe less," I said.

Eve snickered. "We think alike. If we can aerosolize it, then it can be spread over the Earth and no one will know about it."

"Excellent. Let's work towards that for now. We've got a much more serious problem. I've had another future vision. A horrid one. The giants are soon going to be spreading the Armless Doll Telepath Agent over Chicago. Then, they'll gather us up and take us off-world to some kind of galactic-wide slave telepath auction. Over time, they're going to do this to all cities on Earth, until only giants and dwarves live here."

"Holly shit! That's really bad. How do we stop them?" Eve asked.

"Dunno, since these days, most all corporation security forces are filled with giants and a few dwarves," I said. "Holding a meeting tomorrow at one to discuss what we can do."

After they left, I spent an hour listening to my voice mails, each offering condolences and so sorry's for my mutation. Nearly everyone I knew had called. When I finished listening to them, I felt angry. What good did all the condolences and sorry's do for me? Nothing at all!

At least that wave of grief I'd felt earlier had been erased during Celeste's therapy session. Several lifetimes ago, I'd been a famous athlete, when I was in something called an automobile crash and lost my arms. The grief came from no longer being that athlete.

I spent the rest of the day practicing daily life

actions, hoping and praying I could pick up those skills once more and rapidly.

Late afternoon, I faced my first huge hurdle: making supper. I used to be able to make a cup of tea. Seriously, I never cooked, not before three years ago, not even when I was married to Ted—he just programmed the robot cook/maid to do it. Bev's spouse, Lieutenant Gail, is a world-class chef, and they often had us over for dinner. Since I had arms then, Gail took the time to teach me how to cook basic synth meals. For the last three years, I'd been doing much of the cooking for my family, though Lara often helped.

I just stood there looking at our kitchen. Nikita wandered in, looking for a snack.

"Oh! No snack. Mom, we really are cripples—disabled and handicapped—just like some kids tease me at school."

I turned and saw water building in her eyes. The shattered look on her face—I wanted to scream and kill the bastards who made these awful rules designed to make life horrid for those with telepathy in order to make a telepath obvious to anyone with eyes.

"Nikita, we aren't crippled, honey. But we do have to face challenges others don't. Cooking is one of them. From now on, you're going to have to learn to do some of these things for yourself and so are Dad and Matt. If we work together, we can do this."

"Can't you ask Lara to cook for us?"

I sighed. "Honey, while I'd like to do that, it's not fair to her. She's a top-notch geneticist spending long hours each day with Aunt Eve trying to invent more genetic cures for us. Wouldn't you rather have her doing that? Isn't that more important than cooking? Besides, given enough time, we can do it. Come on. You've watched me often enough."

"Yeah, but Mom, you had hands then."

"We still have feet and heads. Stop and think how."

Later Sam and Matt joined us. I said, "Good. You two can set the table for us."

"I'm sorry. Matt and I were playing kick ball. I forgot

about supper," Sam said.

"We all did. Sam, Matt, from now on, you're going to have to help me make our meals. If you're going to be independent, you can't starve to death. We're going to have to make some other changes around here too."

"But can't you just hire a cook?" Sam asked. "After all, we have lots of credits."

"Point taken." I glanced at the kid's faces and saw such expectant looks—the perfect solution.

"Sorry, Sam. In this crazy world of ours, we simply must learn to be independent. We can't afford to be dependent upon others for our basic needs. Especially when we could do these things ourselves. We just need more time to get them done. Now come on. Put your brains and feet to work. Set the table for five. Lara will be home soon."

I added, "And another thing. I used to gather up everyone's dirty clothes, wash them in the washing machine or the dry cleaning machine, and put them back in your drawers. That has to change. Each of you are now responsible for bringing your dirty clothes to the laundry room. I'll still handle the machines, but you'll have to come pick up your clean clothes, take them to your rooms, and put the away."

The kids groaned as if I'd just made them swallow something awful. Now I regretted doing all these things for them these past seven years. Live and learn. Because I had arms and they didn't—I felt embarrassed by my own thoughtlessness.

"Gracious me," Lara said, as she walked into the dining room and saw the table set and smelled dinner coming from the kitchen. "Molly, you didn't? Did you? How?"

"Hi, Lara. Yes, we did. We're not helpless, just challenged in different ways from others. It's all about how something can be done. Right Nikita?"

I so wanted her to get some needed praise, since she'd done her best to help me fix our supper. Her eyes shone.

After we finished supper, I made each carry their things to the sink, rinse each one off, and put them into the dishwasher.

"I liked it better when you did that, Mom," Matt whined.

Sam said, "Okay, kids, Mom. I've a big surprise coming for us all. Our own special three-wheeled bicycles. I ran into Fred, an engineering student I helped with his library research. He found these for me. They're supposed to be delivered around seven."

"We can ride a bike?" asked Matt. His face told me he simply didn't believe Sam.

An EMAC dropped off the four three-wheelers.

Okay, even I said, "Wow, Sam!"

Each one had two front wheels and one large rear wheel. We lay reclined and peddled. The gears protruded way out in front, while a long chain transferred the power to the single rear drive wheel. A tall center pillar held a push-controlled brake pedal and a gear shifting lever. Two bars on either side of the padded reclining seat allowed us to steer the front wheels simply by leaning into these bars, either right or left.

Each bike was painted a different color. Sam said, "Okay, see if you can figure out which one is yours?"

Nikita giggled, "Pink?"

Sam smiled.

"Dibs on the green one," Matt said.

"I get the brown one," Sam said. "And the bright red one goes to the hottest woman in Chicago."

Nikita giggled. A helmet came with each, color coordinated. First challenge: get the darn helmet on and chin strap tightened. Sam showed each of us how to manipulate the controls, and then we headed off down the sidewalk. Soon, we hit the Andreas Bike Trail that wandered around Potawatomi Woods.

An hour later, we returned, tired but elated. A whole new family activity opened up. That evening when we retired, I made sure Sam knew how valuable his contribution was.

Chapter 3 What to Do

The Sunday meeting went about as I anticipated. All my sisters and their families, my dear friends, and even the Hugo family attended, crowded into our living room, though Helen brought over some needed folding chairs. I told them about my fuzzy vision of the future, where some giants unleashed the Armless Doll Telepath Agent over Chicago, mutating millions of humans. The agent didn't affect dwarves or giants. Curses followed when I told them what the giant told me about selling us at the telepath slave auction and that they were going to do the same with all the cities and towns on Earth.

"Filthy greedy bastards!" said Bev.

"And to think I've hired dozens of these giants," said Helen Hugo, the CEO of GD.

"Trouble is," Sam said, "giants are strong. One of their punches would crush our ribs or even kill us. Only Molly's gun or Bev's blasters can stop them. And now Molly can't do that. What can we telepaths possibly do to stop them? I've been thinking about this since she told me. Frankly, I'm at a loss."

Casper chuckled. "Molly once knocked me out with a karate kick."

Instantly, I recalled how he'd kidnapped me. There in his bedroom, I'd executed a circle kick, ending his corrupt CFO career.

He continued, "But these giants are too tall for such a kick and so strong I doubt a kick would bother them. Sam's right. We telepaths are doomed."

Leslie spoke up, "But like why are they doing this? Corporations are like paying telepaths a million a year."

I said, "Before, fear of being mutated ran our leaders' lives. Now, if telepaths looked like everyone else, how could anyone know who was spying on whom? So out of fear, they've passed a law that all telepaths have to be armless Dolls. That's what I was charged with. But now a new attitude has entered the arena of inhumanity. Greed."

The group buzzed for a moment, as I let this simple word bounce around their minds.

"Yes, greed. At first, probably only a few men figured out they could kidnap a telepath and sell them off-world for a huge profit. Our corporations pay premium salaries for legal telepaths. Why spend a million credits when you might be able to pick one up on the black market for a third that? In my vision, giants provided the muscle behind the operation, but I think there might be more to it than a bunch of alien giants out to make a gargantuan profit."

"How soon is this going to happen?" asked Casper. "Can we flee somewhere? Take our families with us. I don't want Veronica or Fritz to become telepath slaves. Maybe go to Brussels, Tau Ceti, or Pylon, Epsilon Eridani? Can anyone fly a space transport?"

"Hey, I've been studying deep space navigation," Sam said. "Anyone with a nose can be a navigator. Super easy. Button pushing and star recognition are all that's required. Of course, recognizing the star patterns is challenging."

"Hold on. Casper, I have no idea when my vision is going to occur. If it's like the previous ones I've had and if we do nothing, then it will happen. It's sort of a glimpse at where we're headed."

"Like could we immigrate to other worlds?" asked Leslie. "I like don't want to be a telepath. My mind is like confused enough with my own thoughts."

"My Airliner can only take us to locations on Earth," Deanna said. "It's possible we might be able to get a commercial flight, but the law currently prohibits Galactic Dolls from immigrating to other Sol Empire worlds. Rightly so, since we would be introducing our genetic mutation onto their worlds."

"Couldn't we visit other Federation worlds and let this whole thing blow over?" Felix asked. "I don't want Sandee or Leslie or any of us to become slave telepaths."

Most thought we should make plans to take a trip, possibly to this Bela Prime, home of the Federation. A few thought we should go there and drum up support to prevent the making and kidnaping of our telepaths.

"Honestly," said Eve, "soon many worlds will know about Earth's telepaths. The genetic mutation agents are widely available. Even the emergency responder crews carry syringes of the stuff, ready to inject it into a critically injured or ill person to save their life by rejuvenating them into an armless telepath Doll. It's the strongest, most powerful rejuvenation agent to date. You can bet that in a decade, other worlds will have gotten their hands on these agents, if they haven't already, and will begin to make their own telepaths by kidnaping humans from all the worlds in the Sol Empire, not just Earth."

That was a truly sobering prediction. But as I suspected, most ideas centered on abandoning Earth. Lara and Eve suggested taking a trip to visit our Senior Ambassadors on Bela Prime, outlining what was happening, and having them make our case among the ruling elite of the Federation. I promised to look into how such a trip could be arranged. Amid many "I'm so sorry for you's," my extended family and friends departed.

As I said goodbye to Helen and Casper, the last to leave, Ambassador Commander L'Grina walked in.

"Molly, looks like I'm too late. I got tied up with some ambassadorial duties and couldn't get away on time. Wow, you look stunning. Except for your missing arms, you look like a perfect woman of our world. Oh, and that your skin isn't grey."

"Come on in. Thanks, I think."

Well, she had a bosom that rivaled mine for sure. Instead of her green officer's uniform, today she wore one of Leslie's satin gown designs that displayed her very curvaceous feminine form. She even wore matching tall heels.

"You look very good yourself, Ambassador L'Grina."

She twirled around, showing off her outfit. Her large smile told me I'd said the perfect thing. Lara offered to make something to drink. I took tea, while the ambassador took coffee. Sam joined us, adding his order to ours.

"So tell me what happened, Molly. How could they do this to you?"

I spent a half-hour telling her about the laws—made because of fear that telepaths would uncover secrets. Then, I told her about my vision of the future.

"So is this similar to what happened on the battleship Kanika when our space fleet was about to conquer yours?"

"Yeah, the same. I think ordinary greed lay behind this. Are telepaths that rare among other civilizations in the galaxy?"

"If by rare you mean could I count the known telepaths on one hand, then yes. I concur. Greed. It's universal. We've found greed present in every culture we've come across. I'd like to say my people are immune, but we aren't. Molly, I give you my sworn word, if these giants mutate Chicago and abduct humans to be sold as telepaths at some slave auction, then the Sixth Invaders will go after and destroy every giant on this world and their home world. I'll let Home World know about this today. We'll be vigilant. The giants aren't going to get away with this."

"Thanks, but they almost got away with Sam and four others. I stopped four of them with my Glock, but that cost me my arms. Now, I've no defense against them."

"It's not right, but I'm honor bound to abide by Earth's laws or leave. Still, I'll see what I can do. By the way, Sam is right. You don't need arms and hands to be a spaceship navigator, mostly great skill at identifying stars and patterns of them. When I first came to your world, I was a light cruiser pilot. Actually, I think you could even be a pilot, Molly. You're good with your feet. You should try it. I think you might like being a pilot. I certainly did. As Earthlings say, fat chance I'll ever see a cockpit again. Anyway, let me see what I can dig up on these giants. They have their ambassadors here, too. Let's stay in touch."

"Thank you. Let's. I'd shake hands with you, but I seem to have mislaid them this afternoon."

"Good one, Molly. Good one. Catch you later."

She rose and left. I bent over and bit down on her

coffee cup handle, then carried it out to the kitchen, returning for my tea cup. Life had just become more challenging once again.

Sam said, "Tomorrow, I'm looking into how I can become a navigator. I'll see what you have to do to get pilot training while I'm at it."

I laughed. "Okay, Sam, but I highly doubt I could pilot a star ship. Pretty sure they really need hands for that."

After tucking the kids into their beds, I sat in one of the plush living room sofas to think. If I'm being honest, I really didn't believe the big meeting would yield anything useful. But it wasn't a total loss; Sam had something to occupy his time: his investigation of what was needed to be a spaceship navigator and a pilot.

A plan of action. That's what I needed. A thread to pull. No, it was worse than that—much worse.

My stomach tensed up. It wasn't safe for Sam or the kids to be walking the streets. Plus, it wasn't for me either, not after this mutation. I had no way to stop a giant from abducting Sam, my kids, or me! One human? Maybe I could circle kick him, but two or more? Forget it. I truly was disabled; fighting back had been taken away from me. Had that been done on purpose?

Whoa! That hadn't occurred to me before. But what if those behind these abductions had gotten those in power to take me out of action? With arms, I killed giants who were kidnaping telepaths. Now I couldn't harm anyone, not really, and was a prime telepath to be kidnapped and sold at auction. Nausea swept through my gut.

I took a deep breath and slowly exhaled. Twice. Thrice. Finally, my nerves calmed. Someone wanted me out of the "stop them" picture and into the "slave telepath" option. They could grab me anytime I left my home and walked the MTES, which happened several times a day. I had been quite an active person.

I knew I needed some form of security personnel accompanying me. If he or she was human, they could easily be injected with a syringe and turned into one of us. I envisioned the guard walking or being moved along on the MTES beside me when a giant passed us, injecting my body guard with the mutation agent. He'd slip into a coma rapidly, so at the end of the block, we'd both be abducted. No, my security person couldn't be a human. Giant or dwarf? I ruled out giants since some of them had abducted Sam. I decided to ask Lara about dwarves in the morning.

The larger question remained. How could I alter the terrible future I'd seen? I couldn't go to the authorities with my dream vision. Only a handful of people in the galaxy would believe me. That's when Major Airla Baker came to mind. I'd forgotten all about her, the human-looking robot.

I remembered she'd given me a tiny electronic device which she said she could use to track me. Where had I put it? It'd been years. Thinking of her reminded me of Ted's unsolved murder. I rummaged through my clothes drawer for a half-hour to find it. I pressed the lone button, but saw and heard nothing. I put it back in the drawer and returned to the living room sofa to think.

My PI side kicked in. Did I have any threads to follow? Four dead giants and one captured giant. I'd left my laptop on my dresser, so I headed back to fetch it. Crap. Carrying it had become a problem once more. I mentally cursed the justice woman who had sentenced me to this torture again. Remembering the kids, I calmed down, thought for a moment, and found a way to pick it up and get it to the living room without dropping it. Once on the floor, I booted up and used my PI license to log into the Chicago Police Department's records. I opened a second holographic display window and logged into the city morgue records.

I needed names and preferably addresses. Who were these giants? Perhaps, I could locate where they worked or if they had a sponsor. According to Lara, the major corporations had begun sponsoring some of the new immigrants, paying them a monthly stipend. Heck, Galactic Entertainment was still my sponsor as a PI. Their funds paid my office rent, but no more.

The death records provided me with four names and

addresses, which with some footwork, I managed to copy to my computer. Again, I cursed what they'd done to me, forcing me back into agonizing slow motion to operate my computer. Okay, I'd gotten used to using my hands these past seven years. I reminded myself not to get so frustrated. Didn't help much, but thinking of my family looking up to me did. I had to be strong and face this.

The police records provided me with another name and address, but I got a huge surprise. They had released him! A lawyer came and argued he was merely a pilot and not responsible for the abductions. Case dismissed. It took all my will power not to scream as loud as I could. Crap. I didn't even have a hand to pound on the sofa. In high heels, I couldn't effectively stomp loudly on the floor. I fumed.

Then, I realized I'd gotten another clue: the lawyer. I added his name and address to my local file and signed out of the system. Time to think what my next move might be.

Our doorbell rang. "I've got it." I rose, careful not to step on my long hair that was draped partly over my laptop. At the door, I pressed the floor button to open it. A strange man stood before me. He had short black hair and light brown eyes. His height equaled mine, though my heels added six inches. He wore a business suit, but I could see he was well-armed. I spotted a gun hidden beneath his jacket, while an army-issue blaster rested in a holster around his waist.

"I'm Bishop Bentley."

Something about him seemed terribly familiar. The voice inflection, perhaps. The eyes?

"Do I know you? You seem familiar."

Considering all I'd been through, I used my telepathy to touch his mind. I had to know if he meant to harm us. Nothing. No mind. I felt my lips broadly grinning.

"Major?" I asked.

He smiled. "Damn, Molly. You never cease to amaze me. Now, I'm Bishop Bentley, security specialist. Got your signal. I heard what happened to Sam and how you and Bev prevented the kidnaping. When I learned what they did to you to thank you, I wondered how long it would be until I heard from you."

"Yes, someone believes they've taken me out of action. Frankly, I concur. My Glock is the only way I had of dealing with the overpowering strength of a giant. Now I can be abducted as easily as Sam was. Thank you for coming. I'd like to talk about a lot of things."

Bishop smiled, following me into the living room.

"So you can change your gender? Didn't know that."

"We are programmed to meet all types of needs. After your discovery of me, I had to alter my appearance and disappear. I've been successful as Mr. Bentley for the last seven years. So what's happening with you? I'd like to get your arms regrown, but I've not yet found a legal way to do that."

"Thanks. No, that's not why I called for you. Well, not entirely true." I told her about my vision of the future, what I believed was behind it, namely greed.

"Honestly, I'm scared to walk the streets, Bishop. I'm easy prey for any giant now. I don't know who to trust. Worse, some lawyer just got the man I captured, the pilot, out of jail and all charges dropped. I should have shot him."

"No. I know you, Molly. You did the right thing. He surrendered and followed your orders. You aren't a cold-blooded killer. By the way, I think I may have some clues regarding Ted's murder. I'll tell you about them later."

"True. What I need is protection. That is, someone to guard me as I move around. Mornings, I deliver therapy sessions at the Spiritual Recovery and Healing Center down in the Loop. Then, I go to my PI office and work out of there. I suppose I could turn down new cases and focus on trying to stop this disaster from happening, but who knows where I'll have to go around Chicago."

"Molly, consider me your new permanent body guard. Where you go, so go I. I'll have someone watch over Sam, too."

"Thank you. Sam should be easy. He walks the kids to school and from there goes to the UIC library stacks. Late afternoon, he walks to the school, picks up the kids, and brings them home. I'll have to adjust my schedule now.

Somehow, I'm going to have to cook supper for them. Hasn't been a problem until now." I shrugged my shoulders, wiggling my satin gown slightly.

"Okay. I'll also have someone monitoring Sam while he's in the stacks on the off-chance they might try to abduct him from there."

Just then, Sam wandered in. "Dear, tea? Oh, I'm sorry. I didn't know we had a guest."

"Sam, this is Bishop Bentley, my new personal security guard. He's going to accompany me everywhere I go. Plus, he's arranging for a security guard to watch over you and the kids when you're taking them to and from school. I can't shoot my Glock anymore, so this is the best I can do to protect us from other giants who want to abduct telepaths."

He breathed a deep sigh. "Whew. I feel better already. I wasn't going to say anything, but I am worried about walking the MTES with the kids. Damned thing has unsettled me."

Crap. I should have given him a therapy session to erase the kidnap trauma he endured. I vowed to do it later tonight, if possible.

"I was going to try to make you a cup of tea, but I can try to make some coffee, Mr. Bentley, if you'd prefer that," Sam said.

"No thanks. I'm fine," he said.

"I'll join you in the kitchen shortly, Sam. You put the kettle on for me."

After he left, Bishop said, "Okay. Let's get the times entered in my devices."

We made the arrangements, and Bishop left, promising to discuss events at length at my PI office tomorrow. So I joined Sam who finally had the tea kettle going. After a frustrating few minutes, we sat down to enjoy our tea. Okay, Sam wasn't frustrated, for he was used to all this, having done it for seven years. I was still struggling to adapt to my sudden loss.

"Okay, Sam. I want you to return to the first moment when you realized you were being abducted." An hour later,

Sam laughed about it.

"So that's why I've been on edge and worried. If mother hadn't said those words while I was lying there with a broken leg, I'd never been so worried about the kids and me today. Incredible the power words have."

"Only when they lay upon a foundation of pain and unconsciousness or on top of something you really shouldn't have done. Come on. It's late and it's taking me vastly longer to get ready for bed."

Chapter 4 Initial Clues

At one o'clock Monday morning, Bishop and I entered my PI office. As usual, I took time out to use my bug detection device. Times have taught me to be extra careful in my PI office. Damn it. What had taken me mere minutes to do before took nearly a half hour, but Bishop waited patiently for me to finish my sweep.

"Okay. No electronic bugs. It's safe to talk. If you'll set my computer on the floor for me, I'll bring up the names and addresses of the four dead giants, the pilot, and his lawyer. We'll start with them because I've no other clues to follow. If things get rough, I'll call in General Blythe. She'll bring in the First Infantry Division."

Bishop laughed appropriately. I had to admire the programming that had gone into her circuitry. For a moment, I wondered if Ted had written some of that coding. Maybe he had. Times like these, I wish he hadn't been murdered.

"I've an ulterior motive for being with you, Molly. I'm observing you so I can learn how to be a better detective."

"You mean you're able to learn new things? Things you weren't initially programmed to do?" This shocked me, but now that I thought about it, she or he must be able to learn.

"Absolutely. You'll find I'm a fast learner and that I've learned much during these last seven years. In particular, I've become competent at hyperspace navigation and piloting a light cruiser. So what's the next step with these names?"

"We check them out with corporation sponsorship. If they were human, they would be in the master database, since it's darn near impossible to survive without the monthly money from a sponsoring corporation. A PI has access to it. I'm bringing it up now. Sorry, I'm so darn slow, Bishop."

"That's quite all right. Take your time. I postulated you would need months to regain the agility you once had with your toes. Your saying has proved to be a good one. I've observed it's helped a great many people. What I can't grasp is why your leaders insist on having telepaths without arms. My computations suggest this is cruel and to be avoided. Yet, they've made it a law."

"Fear. That's the emotion many CEOs feel about us. You see, if a telepath was indistinguishable from any other person around them, how would they know if they were being spied upon, if their secrets were being uncovered, or if they needed to somehow shield themselves from a prying mind? In short, Bishop, we scare them, and yet they desperately need our help. Corporate espionage is big business. Then, there are valuable uses."

"Right. Like linguistics. So these CEOs are truly afraid of you telepaths? That's one detail I haven't been able to conclusively pin down. As Bentley, I've not had as much contact with CEOs as I had as Major Baker. They need you and yet they fear you? If I felt that way, I might blow a circuit."

I chuckled, guessing Bishop had made an attempt at humor. He smiled, so I figured I was right.

"So now they have become greedy?" he asked.

"That would explain much. What some will do for credits. The pilot giant explained that was their motivation when I arrested him. Look, the going rate for the services of a telepath is currently a million credits per year. That's a fortune for most people, a great inducement for normal people to get themselves mutated into one. Probably most figure to work for ten years and then retire with ten million credits in the bank. Of course, with some cures now available, it's more attractive to those who want to get rich quick."

"That computes well," he said. I'm running expected conversion numbers now. Just a moment. Ah, based on my observations of normal humans I've been among these past few years, I'd say that at least a million will undergo the transformation next year, approximately eighty-three thousand each month, scattered around the world. Many will be taking positions off-world. I've seen advertisements for telepaths to work on all the major planets of the Federation. What are the odds a telepath will be well-treated on these other worlds?"

"Probably not good. Look, as much as I hate the word, we're disabled. Handicapped in many ways. True, we have ways and means to do most things, but we're slow. Some actions we simply can't do, like firing my gun. A telepath would be hard pressed to defend themselves from any kind of trouble. About all we can do to defend is kick. That's what I mean by disabled."

"I've filed your opinion of not good. That correlates with my own computations. But how do we detect greed? I have been observing many people and trying to detect or sense their emotions. I believe I am able to detect fear in someone I meet, but I'm not positive. How do we sense greed? It is not an emotion."

"No, it's a state of mind, a way of thinking, an intense craving that can't be satiated. We spot greed by a person's actions—what they do. From what I've heard, telepaths are extremely rare in the entire galaxy. There's no question they're also incredibly beneficial to have in your employ—both good and bad points here. So according to Casper Hugo, our financial wizard, 'rare and beneficial equals valuable.' We've seen this with corporations paying a million per year to telepaths."

I saw Bishop paying close attention so I continued. "My hunch is that someone or someones watched this happening and realized if they had a telepath, they could sell him or her for a large amount of credits. All you have to do is abduct the telepath and sell to the highest bidder. Or look at it from the buyer's point of view. Why spend ten million credits to have the services of a telepath for ten years, when you can spend a million credits and own your own private telepath, especially if they are handicapped or disabled as we are—I mean we can't easily fight back.

"So my guess is that somewhere here on Earth, one or more have seen this as a huge money making operation and are gearing up to pull it off in a major way, probably soon."

Bishop said, "I follow your thinking. I hadn't quite gotten there on my own. So if your theory is correct, there is another side to the operation. They'll need transport ships to ferry the abducted telepaths, especially if there are large numbers of them to move. They'll need someplace to house them until they're sold. They'll need to advertise and to the right people who can afford to pay large sums of credits for the telepaths. My conclusion is they'll need a substantial off-world infrastructure to support this as a large scale operation. If they only abduct a few at a time, the off-world support would be hard to detect. However, handling a group of many thousands of abducted telepaths should make discovery of their base of operations fairly easy to find."

"I'll take your word for that, Bishop. If they take thousands of us, they'll have to feed, cloth, and house us, to say nothing of caring for our needs, especially if they don't provide the clever machines the Sixth Invaders invented and mass produced for us, like the hair and nail machine. I love that one. It gives great pedicures. That's something really hard for us to do—clip toenails. Anyway, I see your point. So how do we find their base on some other world?"

"Leave that to us," Bishop said. "I'll put Travis Jones on it. He's been traveling widely around the Federation, observing it and gaining intelligence for us."

"Thanks. Now all we have to do is find the Earth side of their operations," I said.

"Yesterday, you gave me a copy of the list of names and addresses of those giants. I checked. The addresses associated with the four dead giants are bogus. Two are derelict homes scheduled for demolition. Two are abandoned homes being maintained by Galactic Housing personnel. I believe your word for this is dead end."

"Thanks. That saves me some legwork. What about the pilot and lawyer?"

Considering how slow I now was, I let Bishop bring up the sat map of Chicago and enter the pilot's address.

That showed he was staying at a cheap hotel out by New O'Hare. Time to check on the pilot. I had a lot of questions I wanted to ask him. Bishop and I took the MTES out from the Loop. A perfect spring afternoon welcomed us, filling me with a bit of hope, though I walked very carefully.

"Still getting used to keeping my balance in these heels."

"I can't even imagine the difficulties you telepaths have. Still, such a peaceful day."

***

"Sorry lady, that guy isn't and has never been a guest here," the manager claimed. Bishop had shown him the pilot's image on his phone, hoping to jar his memory. "Only had one giant staying here for the last two weeks. And she was a she."

"Another dead end," Bishop said, as we headed back to the Parker Skyscraper.

"Figures. The lawyer did argue the pilot was a citizen of Liatos-D. That's what got the pilot released and not charged," I said.

Bishop displayed a sad expression on his face. I chuckled.

"You don't have to show me a sad face. Much PI work involves dead ends. We've still got the lawyer to check out. Probably should have started with him. Still, I hate loose ends; we had to check on the pilot. I'll make sure he departed Earth when we get back to my office."

"How? Checking New O'Hare records?"

"Exactly."

Late afternoon, I brought up the flight departure record proving the giant pilot and his deep space transport had lifted off for Liatos-D.

"Of course, this proves very little. He could just as easily land at say Buenos Aires or London. Still, I've gotten the expected result."

"Which is? I don't see it."

"That the pilot's new orders were to take off, lending credence to his not being a citizen of Earth. Next, let's search the other space ports on Earth and see if he landed

42

again. Tomorrow, we'll tackle the lawyer."

That search yielded nothing. Evidently, the pilot had fled Earth, at least for now.

Early Tuesday afternoon, I looked up the lawyer on the internet. Mr. Clyde Bromwell was a registered corporate lawyer and had worked for Galactic Expansion in New York City but had transferred to Chicago when NYC GPan CEO Mr. Truman Wyman became Earth's senator on the Council of the Senate, along with Mr. Asad Virishni of Mumbai. Each of the Sol Empire's "worlds" had two senators on the council, making the laws we followed. At least we have written laws now, even if terrible, unlike seven years ago when the corporations more or less said what the laws should be in their areas.

"So what is a high-power lawyer from NYC doing in Chicago working for Senator Wyman?" Bishop asked.

"Now you're getting the hang of the PI business. Ask questions. That's a good one. An even better question is why is Senator Wyman's lawyer interceding on behalf of that giant pilot?"

"So how do we find out?"

"Ask, of course. Time to pay the lawyer a visit. The Council of the Senate occupies the top ten floors of what used to be the Sol Empire-wide GPan skyscraper. The Admirals and Generals have their offices on ten floors below them. Our Chicago local GPan offices are on the bottom five floors. This notice says Wyman's office is on the hundredth floor, and Mr. Bromwell's on the fiftieth floor."

The skyscraper was down in the Loop, just minutes from the older Parker Skyscraper. Again, we enjoyed the warm spring afternoon's air, though there was a distinct lake odor in the air. The winds picked up some, blowing my long, raven hair behind me. That wasn't so bad, though coming back, the wind would make a mess of my hair. Ah well.

We walked into the reception lobby of his office where a Galactic Doll secretary sat behind a desk with a rather bored look on her face. When we walked in, she straightened up.

"We'd like a brief word with Mr. Clyde Bromwell, please," I said.

Her eyes stared at me, before glancing at Bishop.

"I'm sorry. Mr. Bromwell never sees telepaths." She pressed a button, and a giant security guard stepped out of a side door. He made no effort to hide his gun and blaster.

"How quaint," I said. "Mr. Bishop Bentley isn't a telepath. Perhaps I can wait here while Bishop has a few words with Mr. Bromwell."

She looked confused and reluctant. "Perhaps, if I step out of your office?"

The receptionist relaxed. "Please do. I'll buzz him then."

As I walked back out and stood next to the elevators, I saw the guard standing at the door watching me. But I also heard the receptionist until the door closed. "Mr. Bromwell, a Mr. Bishop Bentley would like a few moments of your..."

I know. I put Bishop on the firing line. If he really wanted to learn how to be a PI, he had to be able to think on his feet. But I should have told him the kind of questions I wanted asked. For what seemed an eternity, I wrestled with my having not thought of this aspect and prepared Bishop. What was he asking?

Ten nervous minutes passed according to the clock above the elevators. Finally, Bishop walked out, and the giant security guard stepped back inside. Together, we left the skyscraper. Only when we were back on the MTES, slowly moving north and east towards my office did Bishop talk.

"He said that the Liatos-D ambassador to the Sol Empire contacted Senator Wyman, asking for his assistance to free one of their citizens, a transport pilot. The senator asked his personal lawyer, Mr. Bromwell, to expedite the matter with the CPD. End of story. I asked him about his policy of not seeing telepaths. He claims a telepath could easily scan his mind and uncover privileged information about his clients. On the surface, he has a point. There is a legal aspect to lawyer-client relationships. Is that what you wanted to uncover? I presume if you could have been present, you could have used your telepath skills to uncover any and all things the man might be hiding."

"Well done, Bishop. You got the key questions answered. We have their cover story, which seems innocent enough. And no, even if he'd let me be there and ask questions, I wouldn't have probed his mind. That's akin to mental rape. I just won't do that not unless the situation is critical and lives depend on getting the information. Mind you, not every telepath feels the same way. I'm sure the corporate CEOs are making their telepaths probe competitors' minds for corporate secrets and such. I won't be a part of that. I hope Isabella and Bernardo also never do such unethical actions."

"Okay. I feel better that I didn't let you down. Now what do we do? It's another dead end. We're out of clues."

I chuckled, as the main doors to my office building opened for us. "Hardly, Bishop. A whole new avenue has appeared."

He attempted to show a shocked expression on his face. It was only partially convincing, but I smiled.

"How did the alien ambassador know about the pilot? Why did he contact one of Earth's two senators and not any of the other forty-six senators? Why Senator Wyman? Why did Senator Wyman choose to intercede on the alien pilot's behalf, *bypassing* our own local investigations by GD and also by the CPD and even New O'Hare's security team? Why make the pilot disappear less than twenty-four hours after I apprehended him? See, we have lots more questions to get answers to."

For once, Bishop had a human response. He ran both hands up across his face and back onto his head. "Oh my."

"Hey, that's a lot of sirens!" Suddenly, the sounds of many emergency sirens went off. Instantly, the Parker Skyscraper's EBS (Emergency Broadcast System) activated. The weather was picture perfect, so this wasn't a tornado alert or even a severe weather event, such as seventy mile per hour winds blowing off the lake.

"This is a Chicago-wide emergency alert. Please stay indoors until further notice. If you are outside, get inside the nearest building for your own safety. There is an ongoing terrorist attack in the Galactic Defense Skyscraper." The same message continued to repeat until I was able to use my nose to press the volume button on the wall.

"We need to get over there. Helen Hugo could be in trouble," I said.

"Probably can't get through the security if there's an ongoing attack. Maybe the GEnt EMACs are filming it. I'll turn on your comm center for you."

I didn't object. He moved ten times faster than I could. Soon, we watched as the camera zoomed in on the GD building and the people running out of the doors. Then, my stomach clenched. I spotted four men moving slowly towards the doors; they wore red bio containment suits, looking like prehistoric spacemen on a walk on the moon. I cursed.

"Maybe it's not widespread," Bishop said.

I know he was trying to minimize my upset, but analytically, he had a point. Mostly, the upper ninety five floors were currently empty. They once housed the Sol Empire-wide Galactic Defense corporation. Our local GD offices were on the lower five floors. Helen Hugo, the CEO, had her offices and support staff on the fifth floor. With so many people able to run out both the main front doors and the emergency-maintenance doors in the rear, the attack must be very localized. I saw no smoke and no broken windows on the sides of the building that I could see. Encouraging.

"Okay, come on. Time to see if we can find out anything. I see the CPD people are on the scene. I know many. We can pump them for info."

Bishop followed me out and onto the concrete sidewalk, my steel-tipped heels clicking loudly. At the corner, I carefully stepped onto the MTES, heading towards the heart of the Loop. In spite of the EBS warnings, a crowd had gathered across the street from GD. The MTES had been stopped and a number of emergency EMACs lined up outside the main doors. The "spacemen" had already gone inside.

"Hi Billy. Long time no see. How's it going?" I asked. Billy was a close friend of Detective Frank Wells, my fiancé and who had been assassinated shortly after discovering he, too, was a clone.

"Hey, Molly. Good to see you. Wow, a telepath no less. We miss seeing you around the precinct. Come by and say hi."

"I will, Billy. I've avoided it because I can't shoot my gun anymore."

"Aye, don't see how you could. Damn, Molly, you used to be a crack shot. Well, come by anyway. We miss your pretty smile."

"Okay. Say, what do you know about this attack? Anyone hurt? Another mutation attack? I saw the bio containment men heading in."

"Yeah, bio attack. Again. Fifth floor. Heard they got our local bosses. This time, security guards killed the terrorist. A giant. A goddamn giant. We never should have let them immigrate here. Must of had some beef with GD. Detectives are sorting that out now. Me, I'm not holding my breath. Just glad the perp is dead."

"Hey, I'm a good friend of CEO Helen Hugo. She and her family live next door to us. Any chance I can slip in and see if she's all right or if she's a victim? If she's hurt, I can help break the news to her family and pick up her kids from school."

"For you, Molly. Anything. Come on. I'll walk you over to the command center."

The CPD captain ran the emergency operation, though normally this was something GD personnel would have handled. "Oh, Molly. Wow. Telepath. Anyway, you look good. Haven't seen you in far too long."

"I'm a close friend of Helen Hugo, and they live next door to us. Is she hurt? If so, I can relay the news and get her children from school."

Muscles in his face slumped briefly. I had my

answer. "Yeah, she's in a coma along with a dozen of her closest associates. Guards shot and killed the terrorist, a giant. Got detectives scrambling to find out why the immigrant did this and if other attacks are planned." He paused to receive a message. "They are bringing them out now. Casper Hugo is also a victim, but he was already a telepath. Anyway, they'll be taken to the Med Center. It'll help us if you can get their children home and look after them for now."

"Will do, Captain. And I'll try to visit the precinct more often. It was so hard after Frank..."

"Yeah, hard on all of us. Tragic. Yes, put them in that EMAC."

He moved off directing the rescue personnel who carried the first of the victims out. I turned and rejoined Bishop. I told him the awful news, as we made our way northward on the MTES.

"Can you get my phone out for me while we're walking? I should call Sam. We'll meet him at the grade school."

Sam and I, along with Bishop, stood outside watching the many kids race out of the set of front doors, eager to get home to play while there was still light outside. Only a few more weeks before summer vacation. Then ours came out. Veronica and Nikita walked side by side, chatting as though they hadn't spoken in a year. Behind them, Fritz and Matt ambled along, talking about the three-wheeled bicycles.

"Fritz, Veronica, I've some bad news for you. There's been a terrorist attack at GD, a bio agent attack. Helen and Casper are both in comas. They've been taken to the Med Center. So you both will be spending the night at our place."

"Way cool," said Fritz. "Now I can ride a three-wheeler with you, Matt."

Kids. Not quite the reaction I feared.

"They aren't going to die or anything, are they?" asked Veronica.

"No, not at all."

"Whew. Okay, Nikita, you can help me with this

geography assignment. Why do we have to know all these cities and where they're located?"

Sam and I led the kids home, listening to their innocent, idle chatter. For a brief moment, all felt so right with the world, until we passed by the Hugo home. Then, it flooded back.

Sam and I struggled to make supper, while I sent Bishop off to see what else he could discover.

"Molly, I took your cooking for granted all these years. Doing it ourselves is a bitch," Sam said. We both sat on top of the counter, our feet leaning over the stove manipulating the spatula and stirring the pots.

"No kidding, dear. At least we're doing it. Remember, in the end, that's all that matters. Now if only I could figure out a way to draw and fire my gun."

Sam gave me a disbelieving look before he chuckled. "Teasing me, right?"

I grinned. "Yeah, there are some things we can't do. The main thing is to keep such things to an absolute minimum. You're on kid duty after supper. I best go to the Med Center and see how they're doing. Get some kind of prediction on when they'll recover."

Two hours later, I ignored Bishop's warning not to travel alone and walked to the Med Center. I found Casper and Helen in the same room. A nurse just finished hooking up Helen to a number of tubes.

"Hi. I'm their neighbor. I have their children at my house. How are they doing?"

"Oh, yes, I recognize you. You're that PI woman. Didn't know you were a telepath, too. Well, both will recover. They've identified it as the Armless Doll Telepath Agent. Dr. Hamid expects Casper, who already is a telepath Doll, to rouse in twenty-four to forty-eight hours. He'll have the ideal Galactic Doll form, just like you have. Helen will likely be in a coma for about eight days, along with twelve coworkers. She'll need all the support she can get when she wakens."

"Can you have someone notify me when they do so I can be here? Can I bring their children by to see them?"

"Of course, let me enter your phone number on their charts." She also reminded me of visiting hours, and I headed back home, sobered.

Sam just finished parking the four bicycles when I walked up our sidewalk. The kids were already inside cleaning up. I hastily told him what I'd learned.

When the four were ready for bed, I gathered them in the living room. "Veronica, Fritz, I've just returned from visiting your parents in the Med Center. They were attacked with the Armless Doll Telepath Agent. Your dad will awaken in a day, perhaps two. He will have a giant bosom and messed up legs and feet like I do."

Veronica merely giggled.

"Your mother will likely be out for seven or eight days. She'll need our support and help, since she'll look like us now. She's likely to be terrified and won't know how to do anything."

"We'll have to show her how, won't we? I'm glad Mom will be like us. Then, we'll be together, just like your family is," Veronica said.

"Yes, she's going to have a rough time learning. Remember, you were born this way. She's going to be terrified."

"We'll show her, won't we, Fritz."

He nodded. The kids had no real idea how terrified their mother was going to be. Yet, they were excited to spend the night. Veronica and Nikita shared one bed, while Fritz joined Matt.

I called up Celeste to tell her what had happened. "Yes, thirteen are going to need therapy sessions as soon as they wake up. Probably, I can handle Casper when he wakes, if he needs it." She promised to arrange needed sessions.

Early the next morning, I received word that Isabella's monthly call was coming through. Bishop escorted us to the GPan call center and handled the recording of our precious session for me.

"Incoming call from the Star Voyager for Molly Parkinson. Isabella Parkinson calling." A 3-d holographic image fluttered into existence. Once more we saw the holo image of our dark haired beauty.

"Hi Mom, Dad, Nikita, Matt. Oh my god! Mom, what happened to you? Over."

I explained what had happened, beginning with the giants kidnaping my family and my rescue of them, ending with the laws passed by our Circle of Senators. I avoided worrying her about the latest attacks and threats. No sense in worrying her.

"I think that's criminal of them, Mom. Anyway, according to the commander, we're still on for a May resupply from Earth. But I've got more news. I did it again. I cracked the Fourth Invader's language. Years ago, archaeologists on Mars uncovered six desiccated bodies. They must have looked like fifty-foot long, black praying mantises. As part of my thesis, I've been studying the documents found with their remains. I've just deciphered their pictographic language.

"They, too, were using implant machines on us, but they were also at war with the Fifth Invaders on the moon. I think each group managed to destroy the other. We still haven't a clue where either group came from—their home worlds. Owen verified the carbon dates. These Fourth Invaders died over a millennia ago. Isn't this just exciting? Over."

Nikita frowned. "Isabella, what about the Third, Second, and First Invaders? Are we going to get invaded again?"

I hadn't realized how much recent events worried our children. Funny how I'd never even asked about other previous invaders, merely content to call them the Sixth Invaders. I had asked Ambassador Commander L'Grina but she didn't know why others called them the Sixth Invaders.

Isabella said, "Nikita, the Third Invaders operated along the Nile River in Egypt over ten thousand years ago. About all we know about them is that they must have had pointed heads. We think they might have come from Gamma Orionis or from Sirius-C or maybe from stars in Orion's belt that are much more distant. The ancient

Egyptians only left us vague clues in their hieroglyphics. The other invader groups must have visited Earth in its distant prehistory, maybe the Stone Age. But don't worry. There's no invading groups around now besides the Sixth Invaders. The Federation of Planets says so. Over."

While Isabella and Nikita talked, I debated whether to tell Isabella more about current events, but I stuck with my decision not to worry Isabella needlessly.

Chapter 5 More Clues and a Guess

"Oh god, not again," Casper said.

I was there when he awoke late the next day, Wednesday. His breasts looked like mine, soccer balls, and his feet and legs were just as messed up. He nearly fell over trying to stand. Once he slipped into the tall heels, he stood up and complained.

"This is as bad as it was when I first got converted. Oh well, Molly, I got by then, so I can now. Just take some getting used to, right. Oh no! Helen. She's going to be devastated when she wakes up. Terrified. Shocked. Panicking. Molly, you've just got to help her."

"Casper, don't worry. I'll be here when she wakes. You're right. She's going to be terrified and freaked for sure."

"Well, I know what she'll be going through. Remember, I woke up like she's about to. The kids. Are they—"

"Fine. They've been staying with us. You're going to have to spend some credits and buy them some bicycles like ours. Best buy four so you can all ride together. It's a lot of fun. Oh, we'll order you new shirts and jackets when we get you home."

"Okay. Get me checked out of here."

At the nurse's station, Casper had to sign a number of papers. "What's this?" he said.

"Oh, by law, anyone receiving the Armless Doll Telepath Agent cannot receive any of the mutation cures for five years. That's to prevent people from undergoing this procedure and then two days later changing their minds."

"But I already was one."

"I know, Mr. Hugo, but this is the law passed by our new Council of the Senate. The initial date of the exposure to the agent has been entered into your medical records. When the five year waiting period is over, you'll be sent an official notice that you're eligible for whatever cures are appropriate. Until then, you'll have to get used to it. The same holds true for your wife. Helen will have to wait five years before she can have any of the mutation cures. That's the law now. We just have to follow it."

She cleared her throat, looked at me, and added, "If you don't follow these laws, they'll get you, like they did Mrs. Parkinson here. I looked up her chart. She can't get any cures for ten years, though I thought it would've been a lifetime ban."

I glared at the nurse. Casper fumed, but used his toes to sign, if only to get out of the Med Center. Then, Casper fired off a tirade of curses, some of which I'd never heard.

"Helen's going to be more than devastated. My god, she'll have to endure this for five years before she can get her arms back. I know she could care less about telepathy. I'm the one who does. It lets me be very close to the three of them. Molly, you've got to help her. I don't want her committing suicide or having someone kill her, like those thousands did. Please."

"Don't worry, Casper. I'll be there for her. Let's get you home, new clothes ordered, and then let's deal with this."

I made sure he ordered a good supply of new shirts, shoes, and jackets. After a lunch rich in proteins, I asked him to return to the first moment when he suspected something was wrong. An hour later, after plenty of moans and groans from the mutation pains of his unconscious body, he said, "I said 'Oh god—not again' just as I passed out." The ill effects vanished in a fit of laughter.

Then, we headed over to pick up our kids from school. Sam was already there waiting for us.

"Impressive look, Casper," Sam said. "Bet your kids will like your new appearance."

"Can you believe the laws won't let me get the usual two cures? What's happened to our world? Corporate greed. Molly, greed has climbed into the driver's seat."

"Wowie zowie, dad," said Veronica. "They're really big, like Molly's and my toy Galactic Doll Jeannie. Are they heavy?"

"Yes, but I hate having to wear these heels. Hard to walk and keep my balance, but Sam's always doing it, so I can too. Again. Damn laws won't let me get the cures for five years. Your mother's going to really need us."

She pressed her body into his. Then, Fritz did as well.

"Can we still go riding, dad? When can we get a three-wheeler like Matt's got?" Fritz said.

"Hey, tonight, kids. Tonight. Let's go home. We'll have to figure out how to make something to eat, since mom's not here. She's not going to be able to do that for us anymore."

"Molly and Sam do it together," Veronica said. "But I don't see how they can. Let's use that silly chef robot thing."

That was the entirety of the Hugo children's reaction to their father's altered appearance.

Thursday, with Bishop's help, I examined the surveillance footage of the attack. Already GD security and the CPD had reviewed it, but I wanted a fresh view. Honestly, not much happened. A giant walked into the main conference area where Helen worked, opened a valve releasing the agent as he walked through the area. I cringed when I saw Helen accosting the man before she coughed and slumped to the ground in a coma. Another giant security guard rushed in and shot the terrorist three times in his back, but the damage had been done.

"I didn't see any more clues. Did I miss anything?" Bishop asked.

"Several clues. First, from the size of the container, the area of effect has to be small, probably only this meeting area. Second, that means it was a targeted attack. Someone wanted to take out Helen and her immediate staff. That brings up the largest question of all. Why take out the top leaders of Galactic Defense in Chicago? To make it easier to carry out more abductions or mutation attacks."

"Goodness. You think—yes, now I compute your conclusion. GD is Chicago's main line of defense, not the police department. They only handle smaller crimes. Am I correct in making the assumption that any further mutation attacks or abductions will be here in Chicago?"

"Yes, Bishop. That's what I would conclude from this. One key factor will be how fast we can get Helen back as CEO organizing and running GD and its large security force. Now then, let's see if we can track this giant's movements."

"You'll use the MTES surveillance system?"

"Yeah. We've got his holographic image up. Let's go through the entrance videos and spot him entering GD. Then, we'll use outside cams to follow him backwards. If we're lucky, he'll lead us to others behind the plot."

Again, I discovered how slow I'd become or rather how much I'd come to depend on my hands these past seven years. An hour passed before we backtracked the giant in earnest. I chuckled, watching the giant walking backwards, along with all the people on the MTES. After watching twenty minutes of video, I realized the terrorist purposely took a meandering path to the skyscraper, knowing most would give up trying to follow him via video. Well, he didn't count on me. Helen was my friend. No way would I give up.

An hour later, he entered a building. I paused and check the City Directory. That building: scheduled for demolitions.

Bishop said, "Another dead end."

I chuckled. "No, we have to look further. We watch to see if he leaves or if someone else enters. Before we do that, I'll check if there are cams that include the rear of this derelict home. Ah ha. Yes. The thrift store's camera also catches the back door. Now we watch for something."

For an hour we watched nothing happening. That's not entirely true. Occasionally, someone would walk past the building. Just as I was about to give it up, someone left the building carrying nothing. Minutes earlier as we continued playing the recording backwards, the person entered carrying a backpack. The person wore a hoodie, so we couldn't see his face, but the person was male and a human, definitely not a giant or dwarf.

"That's the same backpack the terrorist carried,"

Bishop said.

"Good observation. Now we have two avenues to explore. Where did the giant come from and where did this human come from. It's getting late. Let's end for today. It takes me a long time to fix supper."

Friday afternoon, Bishop traced the human back, while I did the same with the giant. Hours later, I reached a dead end. The giant had arrived on a spaceship from Liatos-D. I could go no further with him.

Bishop had better luck. The man came from an abandoned warehouse carrying the backpack. A number of other men came and went during the previous day. Just as he was about to quit, the man in the hoodie left the building. Again, Bishop continued running the video in reverse.

"Molly, what do you make of this? Our hooded man came from the GPan skyscraper. Unfortunately, I've lost track of him there. Do we keep looking back from this point? We don't have a clear image of his face, so there's no way to identify him, especially if he changes clothes. He could be anyone who works in that building. The Council of the Senate, the Council of the Admirals and Generals, their extensive staff, and all of the Chicago Galactic Expansion people work out of that building. There's thousands to check."

I sighed. "Yes, for now, it's a dead end. We'll need to uncover more information. Let's call it a day. These people have been very good at hiding their trail."

Just then, I got a phone emergency message. I'd never gotten one before and was so startled by it going off in my dress pocket that I ended up dropping my phone while trying to retrieve it. Bishop retrieve it for me. Together, we watched the holographic image as it spoke.

"...has been attacked with a biological mutation agent. Your children are safe and have been taken to the Chicago Med Center. I repeat, your children are alive and safe. They are being treated at the Med Center."

"Come on. Phone: call Sam. Phone: cancel. Sorry Bishop. I'm flustered. We gave the school both our phone numbers in case of an emergency."

"Let's get going to the Med Center. I'll bring up the news on my phone while we walk," he said.

While I had to pay close attention to what I was doing to avoid a fall, I listened and glanced at the holo-video images being shown on Channel Nine GEnt news.

"Terrorists have attacked the Northbrook Grade School around two this afternoon. A passerby took this video of a low-flying EMAC. You can see it releasing some kind of gas, which doctors at the Med Center have confirmed is the aerosolized form of the Armless Doll Telepath Agent. Five teachers are in a mutation coma, along with one hundred-three students in grades one through five. All others at the school are under observation, but it's believed their exposure was insufficient to trigger the mutation process."

Chaos flooded the Med Center. Hundreds of parents crowded around the main registration window, shouting and yelling. Someone with a bull horn brought some order.

"Parents with kids in Grades 6 through 8, please go to the south wing, where you'll be reunited with your children. They are unharmed. Please be orderly."

Half the crowd rushed off. Lines formed. Sam found me and soon we stepped into a room designed to hold two people, but four were lying on bed. A nurse stepped in.

"Good. You're here. Nikita and Matt are doing fine. Since you're looking after the Hugo children, we put them in here, too. They're fine as well. Yes, they're in comas, but a light one. The doctor anticipates they'll be awake by tomorrow. Of course, they'll need tall heels, but nothing else."

"So the terrorists used the Armless Doll Telepath Agent?" Sam asked, as Casper arrived.

"Afraid so. Still, they're young and already telepaths. They shouldn't have any problems. Rather, it's going to be terrible for many of their classmates who were normal before today. And those five teachers. Such a tragedy." She shook her head.

"Ah, Mr. Hugo," she repeated what she'd told us.

After she promised to call us as soon as the kids awoke, we left.

When the shock wore off, I was furiously angry. If I could have shot my Glock, I'd have fired off several hundred rounds, disintegrating a target.

As we walked down the halls heading to the exit, we overheard one man yelling at a doctor. "What the hell do you mean she can't get any cures for five years? She's teaching second grade. She has twenty kids to teach every day. She can't be off work for five years."

"I'm sorry, Mr. Clayborne. That's the law passed by our Council of the Senate. Anyone undergoing the Armless Doll Telepath Agent must wait five years before they can receive any cures. That's the law."

The doctor saw me passing and called out. "Mr. Clayborne, Mrs. Parkinson here is in the same situation. As you can see, she's doing well."

"Hello. Is Ella Clayborne your wife?" I asked.

The red-faced man nodded, staring at my body.

"She's a great teacher. My Nikita and the Hugo's Veronica are in her class. Ella will really need your help and support when she awakens. I'll see she gets our therapy right away. Don't worry. With some practice in alternative ways of doing things, she'll be able to continue teaching. She's a wonderful teacher."

"Dalton Clayborne. Ella's my wife. The therapy thing isn't going to regrow her arms. I can't see why they can't just regrow them now. She was a Galactic Doll, just like all women are, and she had the two cures, too. This will just ruin her. I know it. God damn those senators!"

"No, therapy won't regrow arms, but it will help her recover her life and self-respect."

He didn't listen and stomped down the hall with each step threatening to crush a hole in the floor. Not really. He was just loud and angry. He wasn't alone. Hundreds of parents protested angrily that their children were doomed until they reached age eighteen. We could hear some of them yelling things similar to Mr. Clayborne as we left the Med Center.

"I'm glad I didn't have to tell these people their loved ones can't get any cures that would make their lives bearable," I said.

"Me either. Did you see all that anger in there?" Sam asked.

"Cut it with a knife. Seriously, they've a right to be upset. The Senate has passed some inhumane laws."

"You can say that again, only don't," he teased me, knowing I might just take him literally and repeat it just for fun.

"Well, our kids should be only lightly affected by this attack. They'll just be reaching puberty when the time barrier expires. They won't have to carry around these knockers."

"Still, I hate to see kids trying to get around in such tall heels. It's very tricky. I can't tell you how many times I've fallen down," Sam said.

"Same here. What was so freaky for me was trying to use my non-existent arms to break my falls. That's spooky."

"So are you going to investigate the terrorists who attacked the school? GD is in disorder, what with Helen and her staff still in comas. This is out of the CPD's league."

"You know I will, whether anyone else does or not. Those were our kids, damn it."

Bishop was waiting for me at our home. "Our kids'll be fine, but their classmates and teachers won't be. Honestly, you could cut through the anger at the Med Center. It was that acute. Anyway, we've got to track these terrorist down. Attacking a grade school. How low can they go?"

He said, "I made a copy of the videos of the attack posted on the internet. Several have gone viral already. I've captured the ID number of the EMAC and have traced it to GD. It was reported stolen last night. If we can find it, we can use its on board nav system to see where it's been. From the videos, someone modified the undercarriage by installing long tubular arms with jets to spray out the bio agent, much like farm robots do to spread fertilizers on fields. That must have taken some time to do."

"Excellent work."

"I've gotten copies of the Med Center's identifications of the agent used and have personally verified it was the usual Armless Doll Telepath Agent. Thus, there's no way to track where they acquired the agent. Any bio lab is capable of creating copies of the original agent. Dead end on the source of the agent."

Casper rang our doorbell and entered. "Mind if I sit here with you tonight? I don't want to be so alone."

"You're quite welcome. We've run out of clues at the moment anyway. Don't worry. We'll give therapy sessions to the kids tomorrow. Come on. We best order up some heels for them."

Saturday afternoon, Casper, Sam, and I rushed to the Med Center. Our kids were showing signs of rousing. The nurses and doctors probably had lots of practice in seeing the minute signs that someone was coming out of the mutation coma. We'd barely pushed up chairs to sit when they moaned. Eyelids fluttered.

"What happened?" Nikita said, wiggling to sit up. "What's wrong with my feet?"

I explained what had happened and that her teacher was also in a coma.

"Neato. Now I get to wear heels like you do, Mom. We'll look so grownup, won't we, Veronica."

Her friend giggled and nodded.

"We won't be able to run," Matt complained.

"Afraid not, Matt. Until you get used to them, you're going to have to walk carefully. Okay, let's get up and head home. You and Fritz can ride the bikes all you want today," I said, hoping to distract their attention. It worked.

By the time we reached home, all four had pale faces.

Nikita said, "Mom, Dad—I had no idea how hard it was for you to walk in these. Very tricky. Oh, hi, Aunt Celeste, Aunt Eve."

"Hi, kids. Therapy time," Celeste said.

"Say, can I learn how to do it?" Casper asked. "I think it's way past time that I learned how. I've got three who need it."

The afternoon passed rapidly, as Casper and Sam learned how to do it. Both men were very surprised at the severity and sharpness of the pains in the comatose victim's legs and feet as they mutated their shapes. Their feet rotated ninety-degrees downward around their heel bones, which generated the pain.

On Sunday, we heard a news report that the stolen GD EMAC had been found, ditched in a forest preserve and torched. Thus, Sunday provided no more clues.

As Tuesday approached, I had eleven emergency therapy sessions to schedule. I glanced at the names. I recognized some of them. They had been with Helen Hugo when she invited us to lunches. Like Helen, they had once been suppressed by their GD executive husbands, who'd committed numerous crimes that I uncovered while I acted as temporary head of GD. Instead of sending them off to our penal colony on Mercury, they'd begged me to turn their husbands into armless Dolls, just as I had followed Helen's request to punish Casper this way. At a later meeting, I saw how these women bounced back to vitality now that their husbands lacked the power they once held over them. Elaine, Betsy, Jane, Phillis, Sam, and Julie had followed in Helen's footsteps, taking over some key positions within our local GD after the loss of nearly all those in the skyscraper.

I made sure those six would get therapy sessions as soon as possible upon awakening, while I planned to handle Helen myself. As expected, Celeste made the arrangements for the sessions. Leslie got a selection of apparel delivered to them, while Deanna made sure Galactic Robotics delivered hair and nail machines, dressing machines, maid/cleaning robots, and the chef robots to the homes of each of the eleven. Leslie and Deanna also saw to similar deliveries to the families of the five teachers and the parents of the hundred and three student victims. I sighed. What a relief to have two more of the hair and dressing machines in our home. Less "my turn" hassles, especially in the mornings.

I made arrangements for the parents of these

children to bring them by the apartment complex where many hundreds of disabled children still resided. Celeste paired each newly disabled child with a veteran, forming up a buddy system. After giving them the needed therapy sessions, their buddy worked with them, showing how to do everything with their feet and toes. Celeste estimated by the start of the fall term, these young children would be able to handle going back to school.

Casper was with me when Helen awoke. Yes, she was shocked and terrified. She did get the opportunity to practice her screaming, but with Casper and my presence, she cooled down to a merely panic and terror stomach. The nurse got her dressed in a cherry red gown that fit snugly around her shoulders, Leslie's fancy design. I'll spare you her typical reactions while we walked to their home and just say her reaction wasn't any different from others.

Once home, Sam had a protein-rich meal ready for her. Casper helped feed her, and then I took her into a therapy session. Honestly, if you can't tolerate screaming, intense sobbing, wild emotional swings, you best not try running a therapy session. Yes, sometimes I wished I could wear earplugs. Helen had a shrill scream that came when she finally contacted the intense pain the mutation generated in her now gone arms. Today, my goal was to simply knock off the fright, the terror, the panic, and some of the underlying unconsciousness and pain trauma. In the following days, she experienced all manner of other side-effects, not limited to weird ghostly pains, strange emotions, feelings of no self-worth, to say nothing of helplessness and the occasional panic attacks.

As we ended for the day, I promised her I'd give her as many therapy sessions as she needed.

When we emerged from her bedroom, she walked carefully over to Casper.

"Honey, I'm so very sorry for the horrors I put you through seven years ago. I had no right to have you turned into an armless Doll. I had no idea how terrifying and horrible that was for you."

"Helen, dear. It's the other way around. By doing

that, you saved my life. I'd become a terrible person—a criminal. Hell, I had men abduct Molly and try to kill Ted. I was beyond out of control. Why you didn't have her send me to Mercury I'll never know. That was my wake-up call. You saved me from myself. So I should be thanking you. I've a way to do that now. They've taught me how to do the therapy sessions. Anytime you have any symptom or whatever, I'll work the magic on you. I promise."

He continued, "I've also hired us a live-in maid and cook. She's starting Monday next, so we're on our own for a few days. I've got a laptop loaded up with all the how-to videos. I promise I'll work with you all the time. It's not the end of the world. It's a new beginning for us and our family."

I never expected these changes in Casper. Right now, Helen was in a very fragile state. She needed his comfort, encouragement, and help.

"You show her the videos on how to eat. Come over to our place around five for dinner. Your kids have been more or less camping out with mine these past days. The school shut down early for the summer. I think that's wise of them. Hundreds of kids can use the summer to learn to adapt, just like you will. Also, the five teachers will need the time to learn, too. Honestly, Helen, we need you back running GD as soon as possible. We've so few clues to go on. Things are escalating."

"I don't know how I can possibly run GD—not like this." She sighed and fought back tearing eyes. "But then you did it for four months, didn't you?"

"Yes, I did. I won't say it was easy, because it was more like a nightmare, but I did it. Remember. Stop and think how. We can do most everything if we try."

"Speaking of that," Sam said, "I've found out I can become a spaceship navigator, and you can become a spaceship pilot. Arms aren't a requirement, only the skill and knowledge to perform the job is. So I signed us up for navigator and pilot classes starting in June."

"What? A pilot?" Helen said. Her eyes opened so wide I saw the whites clearly.

"Really? How interesting," I said. Then, I chuckled. "Me, a spaceship pilot. Okay, I'm game, Sam, but I bet it's going to be way too hard for me to do. I can visualize you as a navigator, though. Deanna once showed me how she flies her Airliner. It's really nothing but button pushing the nav coordinates."

"Lot more to it. I gotta know all sorts of star patterns in case we get lost or something. Still, I think it's a great change of pace. Something new for us to do."

Here we were trying to avoid a horrid future where giants mutated every human in Chicago and sold them off at auctions as slave telepaths and Sam wanted to learn some new things. That's why I so fell for this man.

Chapter 6 Perfect Planning

In his private office on the top floor of the GPan skyscraper, Senator Truman Wyman waited for his co-conspirators to arrive. Thus far, everything had gone as Morpheus promised.

First came the alpha test: could telepaths be abducted and taken off world. It had been a success until the meddling PI Molly Parkinson had gotten wind of the kidnaping. Truman rationalized it off as having been a mistake to abduct a telepath's spouse, though he hadn't known she was one. A few well-placed words to the Senior Investigator had taken her out of the game. Why kill her when she could be auctioned off along with all the others? That handling had produced the desired result. She hadn't interfered in the subsequent tests.

Next, the giant conducted the first of the beta tests. Several key questions had to be answered. Had they properly aerosolized the agent? What level of concentration was needed for uniform coverage? The target of this second test had been the command structure of the Chicago Galactic Defense. With the CEO and related personnel out of commission, GD wouldn't be an effective investigation or defense force for months, and by then, it no longer mattered.

That the delivery giant had been shot and killed was of no importance to Truman, but that the test answered the two questions was.

Then came the second of the beta tests, the one which would validate the entire concept or shoot the whole plan down. Morpheus' people stole a GD EMAC, not hard to do since GD was in chaos with its leaders in comas. In an abandoned warehouse, Morpheus' workers adapted the spraying system used on western farms to spray fertilizers and insecticides over vast fields to the underside of the EMAC, while canisters of the agent were filled and pressurized.

Again, the test would answer many questions. Would such a delivery system actually work, dropping sufficient bio agent to bring about the genetic mutation? Would enough be sucked in by the air recirculating systems to infect those inside buildings? This time the target was a school because there would be kids outside for recess and kids inside. A comparison of effectiveness could readily be made. It didn't matter much which school was used, so they chose the one closest to the abandoned warehouse.

As far as Truman was concerned, the test results weren't good. Yes, those outside were affected; they'd taken a direct hit. However, only a few classrooms inside the building had been effected. Much of the school escaped unscathed, or rather un-mutated. For this grand plan to succeed, one hundred percent of those inside buildings had to be effected and put into mutation comas.

Thus, Truman called for this meeting to discuss if the plan moved forward or if it had to be abandoned. For the hundredth time, he looked at the graph of future earnings on his investment in Morpheus' project. First year, seven figures; tenth year, nine figures. Even if only partially successful, he knew he'd struck gold—human gold.

Awful images of terror after the Sixth Invader attacks seven years ago when they mutated the corporate leaders in five of New York City's major corporations caused him to shudder again. Yes, at first he'd felt sorry for those powerful men, but that quickly changed. First, because of the management vacancies, he'd risen to become the new CEO of GPan, NYC. Second, these victims suddenly developed telepathy. He watched the stellar wages being offered by all corporations for these telepaths. That they appeared to him to be utterly helpless didn't matter to the buyers. It seemed grossly unfair to him; he, who had followed all the rules, who had worked so diligently up the corporate ladder, who had never received the wages being offered to these mutants—he felt betrayed.

Yet, that hadn't stopped him from rising. Soon, the corporate world turned upside down over the shocking discovery that the Sol Empire was only one of many advanced empires scattered across the galaxy. Earth had to adapt. Truman did so, jumping at the opportunity to become one of Earth's two senators to the Sol Empire's Council of the Senate, the new body formed to write the laws for all citizens of the empire, including the new immigrants, the dwarves and giants.

He, Truman Wyman, had been instrumental in getting the new telepath laws passed. These freaks who commanded such impossible salaries had to have limitations on them. In his mind, he saw an average Joe walking into a Med Center, being mutated into a helpless telepath, going to work for a corporation, making a million credits in one year, and then getting all the cures and going off to enjoy the wealth. Initially, his proposal called for a total cure ban of ten years, but he'd had to compromise to get it passed and be satisfied with a five year ban. He'd campaigned hard to get it passed, because many wanted to append exception clauses. At least his proposal that children must wait until they turned eighteen before they could have any cures had passed.

Now mere days from becoming fabulously wealthy from these same telepaths, he snickered. Besides, this plan would make them widely available throughout the galaxy. Morpheus claimed that guaranteed prices would remain high, since no one market or world would become saturated with telepaths. The expected auction price: a half million per telepath. His computer displayed that number multiplied by three million. He didn't bother to attempt to work out his own share of that result. He'd be off to the new world, Merlin-C, a combination of Tahiti and Las Vegas, a world for the wealthy only. He even had his ticket on a passenger transport scheduled for departure on Halloween, just five more months. That he would leave his wife and kids behind didn't matter. In fact, they'd be mutated and sold along with all humans in Chicago, except himself, that is.

Morpheus had promised to build him a safety room and had followed through. In back of his desk, a false wall hid the door to the tiny safe room. Here, he'd ride out the aerosol attack on Chicago when it came. Of course, now whether that could happen was in doubt. Hence the meeting. He glanced at the wall clock. Ten o'clock. He grabbed his briefcase and computer and marched into his conference room. Morpheus was already there, using a handheld electronic bug detection device, guaranteeing the room wasn't bugged.

Soon, others arrived and took their seats. Senator Wyman watched as five humans slipped their computers out of their cases. Morpheus already had his out.

"Have you analyzed the results from the second beta test?" Morpheus asked.

"Yes, based on concentrations measured after the victims were removed tells me how the projected distribution compares with actual distribution. Frankly, I'm encouraged by the results," one man said.

Murmurs of disbelief and surprise interrupted him. "Look at these graphs." He enlarged his holo projection to be six feet across. "The red is the actual distribution as measured. The blue is our theoretically calculated result based on the time delay before measuring. As you can clearly see, we are much closer than we first believed when the initial reports came in. We were only off by about five percent."

Another said, "Are you saying if we'd used five percent more the agent, the whole school would have been affected?"

"Precisely."

Many sighs echoed around the room.

"Then, gentlemen, we're still on track," Senator Wyman said.

"Precisely." The giant said. "The beta test wasn't a failure as we thought. I've always said fine tuning adjustments must be made. If we're all in agreement, it's time to launch Phase One of our plan. The manufacturing of vast quantities of the agent and the construction of the vehicles to deliver it will commence when you give your official okay and, of course, transfer the funds."

Senator Wyman said, "Are we all in agreement to

move forward onto the first phase of the program?" Five heads nodded. "Good. Let us upload the funds to Morpheus now. Morpheus, monitor your account, please. We need verification the funds have arrived."

He nodded. Fingers typed on the virtual keyboards. When the giant nodded again, the six turned off their computers. Silently, each rose and departed, leaving Truman and Morpheus alone in the room.

"Time scale?"

"It's not changed," Morpheus said. "I believe all necessary changes can be made without compromising our time scale. I'll notify you if that alters."

"Excellent. Good day then."

***

"But it's not a good day," screamed Dalton Clayborne. "Ella's coming home a hopeless cripple. I've had to hire a live-in personal assistant for her and to cook our family's meals. The kids are just sick over this."

It didn't matter that the kids were married and living on their own. Dalton arrived at the Med Center on a sunny May day to bring his wife home, but he continued arguing with the doctors.

"Dalton, she won't be a helpless cripple," I said.

I'd promised Nikita and Veronica I'd run the therapy on their teacher, Ella, and help her adapt as much as possible. I sensed the anger still boiling in Dalton, but right now Ella needed me and all the help she could get.

As expected, she'd awakened from her coma with the usual extreme shock and total terror, screaming loudly before breaking down into a sobbing puddle. That Dalton had witnessed this hadn't helped. While the nurse got her dressed to go home with us, we waited outside her room. Dalton argued and yelled, but signed the exit papers. He took the mutilation of his wife very hard.

In hindsight, I should have arranged for someone to come give him therapy sessions or even asked what his job was, but I didn't, choosing to focus my help on the terrified Ella. Her new ID card showed her real age to be forty, but gave her biological age as twenty-one. Thus, rejuvenation gave her another beneficial side-effect, if she could just get by until she could get the cures.

Since she was Nikita's teacher, I spent as much time with her as possible. For the next week, I spent mornings helping Helen and afternoons working with Ella. When the inevitable back slides or emotional upsets occurred, I ran another therapy session on them, tracing each back until an erasure occurred. Nearly always, the true source of the emotions lay in a previous lifetime trauma. The results yielded a stabler person, better able to face life and learn alternative ways.

By the following Tuesday, both no longer needed emergency sessions, but spent their time practicing necessary skills and learning new ways to accomplish what they'd needed to do. Besides, I was anxious to get back to the investigation and to find a way to alter the future racing towards us.

***

Dalton Clayborne worked in a genetics lab as a technician. Thus, he knew about the many various biological agents and cures. While Ella remained in her coma, he set about obtaining revenge for what he considered inhumane laws passed by this new Council of the Senate. He used his lab access to acquire the samples he needed. Based on the Sixth Invader's internet posting on how to construct airborne mutation bombs used against corporations, he made his own version. For several days, he worked on a delivery system. If he just walked into their chambers and released the bomb, then he, too, would be affected.

He worked late, not returning home until the wee hours of the morning, because he couldn't bear to see Ella's plight. A hundred times, he vowed to make them pay for their inhumane laws. Making the senators pay occupied his waking thoughts, so much so that he began to make mistakes while at work. Little things, like cracking beakers or overflowing a test tube. At last, he pounded his head against the lab's wall. "There's no other way. There just isn't. Maybe they'll just kill me."

On the Tuesday that I wrapped up Ella's daily

therapy sessions, Dalton acted. With his pressurized cylinders attached to his chest and hidden by a jacket, he walked into the GPan skyscraper, obtaining a visitor's pass to watch the current Council of the Senate session. He walked into the huge room on the ninetieth floor, showing his pass to the guard on duty. Dalton took a seat at the back in the visitor's gallery. Before him, he watched as the forty-eight senators filed in for the morning's session. The guard stepped back outside to watch the door, leaving Dalton as the lone visitor.

"This session of the Council of the Senate is now in session," Senator Wyman said, banging his gavel sharply on the large round table. Many overhead LED lights provided excellent illumination, though the cold white walls and stainless steel table and chairs made the chamber feel like a medical center.

Just as he was about to bring up the first topic, Dalton stood up and pulled the wires attached to a nozzle on each of the cylinders. The aerosolized agent shot out of the pressurized cylinders. He yelled, "This is for your inhumanity to telepaths—not allowing mutated people to get the known cures at once. Now you get to experience..."

His voice trailed off as he slumped to the floor slipping into a mutation coma. The senators gasped, stood up, and attempted to flee the room, but none made it to the door. Later when the guard smelled something, he looked in and saw everyone lying on the floor. Wisely, he sounded the alarm and fled. Later officials concluded the air ventilation system rapidly diluted the airborne agent so no one beyond this chamber was effected.

Bishop called me as I walked home and told me to catch the news. He joined me an hour later.

He said, "I'm afraid this time the terrorist is known. Dalton Clayborne. He wanted the senators to experience what Ella and others are having to endure because of their inhumane laws on waiting years for the cures. I checked into the Senate rules. When the senators revive, they, too, must wait years before they can have any of the known cures. They can't just suddenly make a new law. I'm afraid such a change will require the Sol Empire worlds to elect two new senators, who can then bring up such a proposed change to the laws. That's not going to happen for many months, if they ever decide to alter those laws. So Dalton has his wish. The question now is what will the Senior Judge do to him. It's my calculation Dalton expected to be killed or perhaps sent to the penal colony on Mercury."

"I'll break the news to Ella. Right now, her daughter is staying with her. I'll go do that and then return. We need to make progress. This is getting out of hand."

Bishop nodded.

Ella took the news hard. So I gave her another emergency session, erasing this new shock. Hours later, near suppertime, I rejoined Bishop. Thankfully, Sam had ordered synthetic pizza for us. While we could afford real pizza, such was hard to find.

That handled, Bishop, Helen, and I sat down to discuss what to do next. We had so few clues.

"Should we offer therapy sessions to the senators?" Helen asked.

"Hell no." I barked before I realized I was being very biased. "Look, they're the ones who insisted on these inhumane laws. Let them stew in their own brew for now. Maybe we'll give them sessions later. Right now, if we don't do something, that horrible future is coming to us all. Whoever is behind this, they're doing a perfect job of hiding themselves. They must have put considerable thought behind each of these attacks."

"Probably didn't count on my guard getting the giant in his back as he fled," Helen said. "I feel so helpless now. Damn it. I can't help it. It feels so weird to be like this."

"In time, you'll get somewhat used to it," I said. "But this attack on the senators wasn't part of their plan. Dalton was angry because they passed laws that are forcing his wife to be disabled for years even though cures are available."

Just then, Helen's phone rang. Thankfully, Bishop retrieved it for her, because as slow as she was, the call would have gone to voice mail before she even touched the phone in her pocket. He pressed the speaker phone button and placed it on the floor by her shoes. She took this long to get them off so she could retrieve her phone.

"Ah, Helen. I hate to bother you, considering, but something's just happened that GD needs to be involved in." A Med Center security guard called.

"Go on," Helen said.

"Someone's tried to assassinate one of the comatose senators. Truman Wyman."

"Mutating him isn't enough? Details, please," Helen said.

"A giant entered his room, knocked a nurse's aid unconscious, and put a 9mm shot into his chest. That brought many rushing to the room, so the giant fled. We couldn't get a direct shot at him, and he's escaped. The doctors rushed in, saw he was still alive, though dying, I'm told. They followed the new protocol and injected the Armless Doll Telepath Agent into his leg. I'm told they got to him in time. After they did emergency surgery, his body is regenerating the hole in his heart. They'll know more in a few days. CPD has detectives on the scene, but as you know, this is a GD matter, since it was a senator who was shot."

"Okay, I'll send someone over shortly. Thanks for calling me. Goodbye. My god, has our city gone crazy?"

"Why shoot this senator?" I asked. "Is it a coincidence that a giant is the perp?"

Bishop said, "It could be a coincidence."

"My gut tells me it isn't. Some giant definitely wanted Senator Wyman dead. Dalton only wanted him handicapped like Ella is. Why does someone want him dead? Helen, it might be a good idea to have someone check his residence and office. I've a hunch they'll find them ransacked."

Helen placed the calls, then asked, "Why do you think they'll be ransacked?"

"Because it's not a coincidence. Dalton did something wholly unexpected, something that has effectively eliminated our entire Council of the Senate, which won't be reconstituted for many months. Senator Wyman is going to wake up and discover he's now an armless Doll telepath. Say for a moment he knows something about this plot to turn us all into slave telepaths. When he wakens utterly terrified, he's likely to tell everyone about it, implicating any others involved in the plot. Thus, killing Senator Wyman shuts him up. What the giant didn't count on is the new law that says to inject that mutation agent into anyone whose life is endangered in an effort to save them. You know, the darn red pocket syringes we're supposed to carry with us."

"Wait a minute," Helen said. "You're saying that Earth's Senator Wyman is somehow involved in this alien plot to mutate, abduct, and sell Earth's telepaths?"

"That would explain what's happened. Look, he's only been in a coma twenty-four hours before he's been shot. If they find out he's still alive, they'll likely try again."

"Oh hell. I best put a twenty-four hour guard on him. The other senators too. Damn, all this when I can barely function. I feel so helpless, Molly. I don't think I can do my job anymore."

Bishop helped her place the calls. I relaxed when I heard fifty security men would be guarding the senators. We agreed to meet in the morning.

Day two of the senators' eight day comas brought us more curious news. GD men followed Helen's orders and checked Senator Wyman's home and then his office in the GPan skyscraper. At home, his wife had been murdered and the place ransacked. His office had also been thoroughly searched. Considering the severity of the situation, Helen asked me if I would directly assist her people in solving this case. Even if she wasn't a good friend, I would've helped out.

All day, Helen's people, Bishop, and I reviewed surveillance videos. Because Helen had made this case top priority, for once, we had enough people working the video angle. Some reviewed all footage from inside and around the Med Center. They spotted the giant, followed his path into the Med Center from a forest preserve, and then back. Double unfortunately, he wore a hoodie and never presented his face to any of the various cameras, and there was no surveillance inside the preserve. While the GD people gave up on this angle, I didn't. It just meant we had to be more clever than he was.

Others reviewed footage of the senator's home, verifying a giant wearing a hoodie entered and left around the medical examiner's stated time of death of Mrs. Wyman. Once more, they followed him coming from an abandoned warehouse and returning there, before they too gave this up as a dead end.

Likewise with his GPan office, except this time, we caught a break. The break-in occurred around one this morning. A GPan security guard let the giant in, but the giant shot him on his way out. The sound of the shot being fired triggered the sensitive sensors which sounded the alarm at both GD and CPD headquarters. Police and guards found Jerry bleeding out on the floor by the main entrance doors. Once again, the new policy advocated by GMed saved Jerry's life. While a policeman kept pressure on the bullet wound, the emergency technicians injected him with the bio agent from the usual red pouch. After rushing him to the Med Center, doctors performed surgery and allowed the rejuvenation coma to handle the rest. No one considered that Jerry might hate what they did to save his life because now he'd be out of his job and monthly stipend.

I had Helen put a constant guard on Jerry's room, as well. The CPD kept patrolmen on the alert for any giants going into the Med Center. Now, we had two people to question when they came out of their comas and got over their initial terror.

That morning, GPan security personnel checked over the night's records of people being let in after hours. Unfortunately, the giant had erased that evening's records. I suspected if Ted were still alive, he would have found a way to get them back. Such was beyond my knowledge. I'd have to wait and question Jerry some eight days from now, though with luck I could talk to the senator in seven days.

I didn't want to wait for days. Plus, my eyes were bloodshot from watching so much video, so I decided to look into Senator Truman Wyman's background. He'd been an underling with GPan NYC for many years. With the massive mutation attack, he'd stepped up to help reconstitute the corporation that lost most of its top personnel. Then, six years ago, he ran a massive campaign to get himself elected as one of Earth's two senators. According to news reports, Senator Wyman often influenced many other senators. All I uncovered during the day's work was that he was a go-getter, a very driven man.

The next day, I looked the senator's financial side. Late afternoon and about to give it up, I spotted something. A month ago, he'd deposited a hundred thousand credits in cash. Immediately, he used that sum to pay for a single, one-way ticket on Uni-transport to Merlin-C. Huh?

Off I went a Googling, using a marvelous piece of technology invented over two hundred years ago. I said to my computer, "What or where is Merlin-C?" I waited impatiently for the computer to tell me the answer. What? The Earth internet had no reference to it. How strange. So when Lara dropped by for lunch, I asked her if she knew anything about this world.

"Merlin-C? Sure, it's the wealthiest resort world in the Federation. Kind of like your Tahiti islands and Las Vegas rolled into one paradise. I've heard it takes vast wealth to get permission to visit that world. Where did you ever hear of it?"

"Senator Truman Wyman bought a one-way ticket to that world. His flight leaves October 31. Fascinating. I think I smell something rotten."

"Do you suppose that's the date planned for the destruction of Chicago that you saw in your vision?" Lara's eyes widened, brows rose.

"If so, that gives us time. Like five months. But maybe he was planning to duck out later, after it was done. I don't know whether to relax or not. We really need to talk to Senator Wyman."

"If he was involved in this, do you think he'll actually talk about it? Incriminate himself?"

"Don't know, Lara, but I aim to find out."

I continued browsing through financial records. Late

afternoon, I spotted another unusual expense: ten thousand credits to Baker Vaults. The juxtaposition of a bread maker with a burial vault so attracted my attention. Again, I barked out the command to identify Baker Vaults, only to discover that was a person's last name and that they made air tight chambers, usually called safe rooms. At first, I chuckled over my complete mis-duplication of the business.

Then, I looked into what was meant by the safe room. "Shit! That's how he was going to avoid being mutated himself. Wow. Wonder where this room is at?"

The next day, Helen sent a security force to check Senator Wyman's home and office for anything incriminating and to find this strange ticket. She called, telling me they found nothing. So I asked her if I could join the search.

An hour later, Bishop and I walked into the thoroughly ransacked office on the hundredth floor of the GPan Skyscraper. Stuff lay strewn about the floor and over the desk and tables.

"Not sure what you hope to find that we didn't," the leader of the security squad said.

Bishop said, "Looks as though you've done an excellent search. Wish it had turned up something. We need clues."

"Yeah, well, terrorists are striking everywhere these days. Nothing's safe."

At first, I felt another pang of loss. I had no arms to do help me do a proper search. A tear formed in my right eye, but I looked away and rubbed it on my shoulder, while pretending to look at something on the floor. I took a deep breath, slowly exhaling. My "cool head" attitude kicked in, and I began closely observing the suite of rooms.

He had an office with a large table—sterile white and steel. A smaller private room adjoined with a bathroom and small refreshments area attached. Using a toe, I opened the tiny refrigerator. Snackables. Made sense. A coffee maker and teapot sat on a small single burner stove. I rather wished I had this setup in my PI office. Ah well.

I walked back to the main meeting room where the

others now sat around on chairs waiting on me so they could head back to GD. I just got to the doorway when something struck me as slightly off. I turned around and paced the distance to the back wall of the office. Then, I returned to the meeting room and paced off the same distance.

"Hey, you ready to go now?" someone asked.

"How interesting. His office back wall is six feet short. Come on, fellows. I need your hands."

I led them into his office. His desk was perpendicular to the glass walls and a fabulous view of Chicago. But the wall behind the desk was six feet short of the suite's outer wall.

"Okay fellows. There," I nodded with my head, "that wall is this way about six feet. More than enough for a safe room. See if you can find a way in."

The three men moved past me and began tapping the wall and moving picture frames aside. Bishop came up behind me.

"I would have missed this detail. I've filed it away for the future. You're teaching me a whole lot about how to be a PI," he said softly.

I smiled and nodded.

"Here, this switch," one man said.

Silently part of the wall swung out, revealing a door. He opened it. As he did so, LED lights turned on, illuminating a small room, with cot, portable toilet, and some food and water bottles. On one wall held a control panel with an oxygen dispenser. Two additional cylinders of oxygen rested in a corner. A very tiny desk sat at the far end of the long, narrow room. A computer rested on top, along with a packet of ID papers and a fancy ticket written in a strange alphabet, if that's what one would call the squiggles. That had to be the ticket to Merlin-C.

"You fellows take that packet to GD and see what you can find out from them. I'll confiscate the computer and see if it holds any clues."

"Call Helen Hugo," their leader said to his phone. He told her what we found and asked if they should allow me to take the computer. Helen hesitated a second before agreeing to let me have it.

Over the speaker phone, she added, "Molly, return it to GD when you're done with it. I trust your discretion if there is anything classified on it."

"Will do. And thanks, Helen."

An hour later at my downtown office, Bishop and I attempted to fire up the senator's computer.

"Damn. It's got a biometric lock. No way to turn it on without his DNA," I pointed out the obvious.

"Well, let' go get it," Bishop said. "We'll pay a visit to the Med Center and get his body to activate it for us."

I chuckled. "You're getting the hang of this PI business. Stick it in my carrying sack—oh heck. Just carry it, please."

At the Med Center, Truman Wyman lay on the narrow hospital bed, tubes going in and out of him, while his body mutated. All ready his breasts had grown quite large for a normal woman, and his arms looked withered and shrunken in overall length. From previous therapy sessions, I knew this was the part of the mutation process that created excruciating pain that lay completely buried underneath the unconsciousness.

Bishop handled the tricky part for me, first swiping his leather-like index finger on the computer, followed by a retinal scan, which he did by forcing an eye open and aligning it with the computer sensor. Perfect. The laptop began its boot process. Hastily, Bishop stuffed it back into the bag, and we headed back to my office.

Two excited people—okay, so Bishop wasn't a person—studied the main directory, looking for anything that might help us find out if he was involved with the terrorists. We watched a promotion video for Merlin-C, but to understand what was being said, we needed a translator box. Still, the images left no doubt that only incredibly wealthy people could afford to visit this world.

After spending much of the afternoon searching through the files, we had only one directory that was closed off, requiring an encryption key to open. After trying a few things, I had no choice but to return the computer to GD and see if Helen's technicians could crack it. Ted could have cracked it for me, but he was dead, and I'd moved on. Helen promised to call me if they found anything useful.

"Oh yes, that was the ticket on the deep space transport that you found. He also had his bank account records with him and most peculiarly, a new account on Merlin-C, which his records show only contains ten thousand credits. I checked with several ambassadors who told me this was the absolute minimum amount to open a new account, but it only reserves the account for six months. Evidence is mounting that Senator Truman Wyman is involved in this horrific plot, but we've no idea why he would become a traitor to his own people, his own race."

"Greed, I suspect. Maybe the encrypted folder will contain some documents that we can use to stop this before it escalates."

I spent another two fruitless days uncovering nothing new. While I had some outside hope Helen's people would find something useful on Wyman's laptop, I couldn't sit back and do nothing. Each day that passed meant one less day before that awful disaster struck, wiping out Chicago, turning millions of people into human telepath slave Dolls sold at auction to god knows where. Perhaps in another day we might learn something from Senator Wyman when he came out of his coma, but I wasn't about to sit idly by and wait. I hated waiting. There had to be an angle I hadn't yet explored.

I leaned back in my office chair, while Bishop kindly made me a cup of Earl Grey. As he brought my teacup, he said, "I wonder if other humans are involved or only giants."

"Hum, good point. If other humans are involved like Wyman, then it would be reasonable to expect they, too, would have purchased tickets to this Merlin-C world."

"And to have built a safe house. The GD report states that once Wyman's safe room door was shut, it was totally insulated from the outside world. They estimated he could have stayed in there for three days before the oxygen was used up."

"You're a genius, Bishop. That's one clue we haven't looked at. Other safe rooms. Has Baker Vaults built similar safe rooms, say within the same time period as Wyman's was made?"

"How do we find out? Ask the company?"

I bit my lip. "If I showed up and asked, they aren't likely to divulge those records. After all, then it wouldn't be a such a safe house any longer. Those things are supposed to be a secret hideout. We're going to need more force. Phone: Call Helen Hugo."

Later, Bishop and I walked into Baker Vaults on Oakton in Skokie, accompanied by a squad of GD security guards in their green uniforms—very official looking. With only a minor protest, the owner turned over his digital records, but I did promise to delete my copy of them once we finished our study of them.

By suppertime, Bishop and I had made a list of ten safe rooms built within the time range we guessed at. Next step, examine each, though the how eluded me at the moment.

Sam said, "Why don't we do like the Hugo's are doing? Hire a live in cook and maid. Save us tons of time and frustrations."

"Yeah, it would. But do we really want to give up that part of our independence?" Sam, Nikita, and Matt nodded. "Oh great." I rolled my eyes and tossed back my head, before chuckling. "I'll see about it."

Three smiling bodies pressed into mine.

Chapter 7 Conspiracy

Helen called the next morning to let me know what they found on Wyman's computer. He was involved in the plot, but so were five other people and a giant who went by the name Morpheus. The five only had aliases, Larry, Moe, Curly, Doc, and Mata Hari.

"Yeah, those are the names of some very ancient comedians and spies. No help in identifying them. Perhaps Wyman will be able to tell us the conspirators' real names. I've got my giants looking into this mysterious Morpheus. Are you going to be at the Med Center when Wyman wakes?"

"Won't miss it for a moment. Maybe we'll get the clues we need to put an end to this threat. How are you holding up?"

"Molly, I won't pretend. It's horrible. I wouldn't wish this on my enemies, though I did do that to Casper. But like you keep telling me, we have to try or go crazy. I'll call you when it's time. I'm also curious what the guard will have to say when he wakes up tomorrow. Who shot him? Bet it was this mysterious Morpheus fellow."

"Maybe the giant has henchmen. Okay. Catch ya later."

I was about to head to my office when Bishop dropped by the house.

"Turn on the Channel Nine GEnt News," he said. Considering how slow I was and the urgency, he did it for me, and I slipped onto a sofa to watch.

"...dawn hours, disaster struck a several block area of downtown Tokyo, a residential neighborhood densely packed with apartment complexes. Authorities estimate over a thousand men, women, and children have been affected in this terrorist attack."

I could see emergency crews wearing the familiar bio containment suits carrying bodies out of apartments, while rescue EMACs shone their lights onto the buildings. It was still dark there.

"From the first arrivals at the hospital, doctors have determined the terrorists used the Armless Doll Telepath Agent—first used as a weapon in Chicago. TV Asahi News captured these images from various lucky passers by. Authorities describe it as a modified EMAC with spray nozzles on long booms. Eye witnesses report the vehicle made ten overlapping passes over these blocks and that they could see some vapors coming from the booms. The first to be rescued and taken to the hospitals were those unfortunate people caught on the streets and MTES."

The local Channel Nine reporter appeared. "We now take you to Philadelphia, where a similar bio agent attack occurred late last night. I must warn viewers the images you are about to see are very graphic and disturbing."

Videos shot by handheld phones rolled by on the screen. Again, I saw an EMAC with booms spraying something down on the buildings and people below. Some videoed others who were close and also videoing the event only to drop their phones as they slipped into their own mutation comas. It was quite disturbing.

"Initial estimates suggest there could be as many as fifteen hundred victims in these apartment complexes. In the background, emergency personnel in bio suits are going door to door, bringing victims to the nearest available medical facility. All ready, local hospitals are overflowing and are sending many to the local Med Centers around Philadelphia and neighboring cities. As yet, no one has claimed responsibility for this attack or the one in Tokyo. Based on the visual evidence, the vehicle used to dispense the bio agent may have been the same one in both cases."

Bishop turned the volume down. "That summarizes it. I have to visit both sites and gather information. Will you be all right here for a few days? If not, perhaps Helen could assign you some bodyguards."

"I'll be fine. Go see if more clues can be found. Two thousand five hundred more victims. It's escalating and not going away, so it's likely Wyman wasn't the only one behind this."

Senator Truman Wyman woke from his coma around two that afternoon, surrounded by more authorities than had ever gathered around anyone in the Chicago Med Center. Yes, Helen and I were there, along with her security guards, two CPD detectives, the Senior Investigator, a telepath, and also the Senior Judge with security men. And of course, the usual medical staff.

His terror screams shocked everyone, save the medical personnel, Helen, and me. Eventually, Truman ceased yelling and dropped down tone into grief. Finally, everyone could overhear the doctor.

"Senator Wyman, yes, you've been exposed to the Armless Doll Telepath Agent, along with all the other senators. They were released yesterday when, like you, they came out of their mutation comas. Senator Vrishni returned to Mumbai, while the off-world senators have been placed in assisted living homes for the time being. Per the usual laws, you'll be given a set of the Sixth Invader helping machines, such as the hair and nail machine. Per Council of the Senate laws, you cannot have any known cures for the next five years."

Wailing, he cried, "Kill me. Please, kill me. I can't live like this."

The doctor ignored him. "The terrorist who did this to you was Dalton Clayborne. He was angry you senators passed those laws. The terrorist attack on the grade school mutated his wife, a second grade teacher. Revenge was the reason he gave. He has a lifetime ban on any cures."

"I don't care about anything. I gotta get to my home and office."

"Further, you should know that a giant broke into your office and home, killing your wife, before ransacking both."

"Oh no, no, no. I gotta get to my office. Oh god, kill me."

"Also, while you were here in your coma, a giant came in and shot you in your heart. You would have died, but we applied the new Senate protocol, injecting you with that same agent. Surgery removed the slug and closed the artery hole. The rejuvenation process handled the rest. That's why you are awakening later than the others."

"No, no, no." He sobbed uncontrollably, while the doctor allowed the nurses to dress him in his new gown. His hair had grown several feet, and he looked like a perfect Doll, though lacking arms. Once they had him dressed and sitting on the bed, they left the room and our group swarmed around him.

The Senior Investigator spoke first. "Senator Truman Wyman, we have found evidence of your involvement in a plot to wipe out millions of people in Chicago by subjecting them to the same mutation agent as you have been. Next, they were to be abducted and sold at auctions off-world as telepath slaves. Molly Parkinson discovered your safe room. We've recovered your ticket to Merlin-C, your bank account there, and ID papers. Molly managed to unlock your laptop, and GD's technician have broken the encryption on your secret folder. We've studied all those documents."

As the investigator spoke, I noticed the telepath focused on Wyman, probably observing his thoughts for their accuracy. His incessant sobbing slowly subsided, while his complexion grew increasingly paler. At this point, all color had drained from his face.

He mumbled, "So kill me."

"Senator Wyman, tell us who else is involved in this despicable plot. Who are Moe, Larry, Curly, Doc, and Mata Hari? Where can we find this giant called Morpheus? Tell us about this plot, and we'll recommend your termination to the Senior Judge."

"I don't know their names. For security. Used aliases. Gonna get trillions of credits and move to Merlin-C and be treated like I should be, a god. Damn that Dalton fellow. He ruined my life, my plans. So kill me like you promised."

"I said I'd recommend termination. It's up to the Senior Judge what happens to you. Now then, we need more from you, much more. When was this going to happen? How do you make contact with these co-

conspirators?"

"I'm not saying another word until I get a guarantee that you'll terminate me when we're finished here. I can't live like this. No one can."

Helen and I roared.

"You fool, if you thought that," I said, "then why make it illegal for us to get the cures and have to wait five years for them?"

His head slowly turned to look at me. Already, he'd slipped from grief down to apathy, giving up on life, not a good sign at all.

The Senior Judge spoke up. "Sorry Senior Investigator. I've already heard enough to pronounce his sentence. He and his fellow senators made the laws that are adversely affecting so many terrorist victims. Termination is simply letting him off the hook, so to speak. The easy way out. No, he will not be terminated. Rather, he will be forced to live a full lifetime as an armless telepath. Any monetary compensation he receives for work as a telepath will be divided up among all terrorist victims. Further, someone will always be with him, ready to inject the red bag's syringe containing a dose of the Armless Doll Telepath Agent. Thus, any attempt on his part to commit suicide will not be permitted. In fact, should he attempt to terminate himself, when he finally reaches a biological age of sixty, he will be injected with the agent again, so he can live out a second such lifetime. I will see his medical records are so updated."

"You—you can't do that," Wyman mumbled futilely, but was too apathetic to even make much of a protest over it.

Bang. Bang. Gunfire erupted. Several guards dropped, as a giant shoved his way past them and into the doorway, knocking me off my feet and out of the way. Bang.

Three more popping sounds echoed in my ears, as chaos broke out. Oh how I longed to be able to use my trusty Glock. My shoulder hurt where it struck the floor. Someone helped me up. The haze cleared. Medical staff dashed in.

The giant's body lay dead on the floor, ignored by the

medical people, who stepped over him, rushing to aid Wyman, who'd been shot again. I saw someone injecting him with a syringe from a red bag. Helen look ghastly pale. I turned to look at the commotion outside the door. Medical personnel worked on two guards who'd been shot, while the remaining guards rushed to form a defensive perimeter, though I doubted there would be any more action.

"Missed the artery. He'll survive," the doctor called out to us. I sensed relief among everyone present. Wyman wasn't getting off the hook so easily.

The Senior Investigator said, "Okay. Sentence pronounced. However, we're going to take Wyman to an undisclosed location as soon as he's able to be moved. There, we'll continue to attempt to get more information out of him. We'll keep him alive. Acceptable to everyone?"

Helen, the CPD, and the judge agreed. Quietly, we left the Med Center. Anger surged in me. We'd not learned much at all, and again I felt the sharp loss of not being able to fire my gun to defend myself. Okay, I could use a therapy session. Grrr.

I headed home, hoping Bishop had better luck than we did. There was always tomorrow when the GPan guard came out of his coma and could tell us who he let in and who shot him. Had to be this elusive Morpheus, so that wasn't likely much help.

"This is shit," I said to the stove, while trying to make a cup of tea and think. If only I still had my hands. I imagined going to the range and firing off several clips and calming down.

When I finally got to sip tea, some twenty minutes later, I knew I had to get a better handle on this conspiracy. Senator Wyman definitely was planning to become fabulously wealthy by making and selling human telepaths by the millions. Clearly, he planned to leave Earth on October 31. That could only mean by then millions would have already been turned into armless Doll telepaths, taken off-world, and sold at auction with his share in his new account. From what I'd seen of this Merlin-C world, he wouldn't be allowed to land without having a huge amount in his account. Thus, discounting the unknown days the trip would take, all this had to have been done by that date. Working back, allow, say two or three weeks for telepathic skills to appear in a new person, allow another week for travel from Earth to their staging area and then on to the delivery world and person, and allow another week for comas though it might be included in the travel time, then the first major attack could come as late as the middle of September.

Of course, it could come sooner, but I suspected it might not, since the GD techs suggested Wyman could only have stayed cooped up in his safe room for maybe three days. He couldn't afford to emerge to a city filled with comatose humans and the likely ensuing chaos. Wyman would stick out. I glanced at the calendar on my laptop. June came, so we had at the very most three and a half months to stop this from happening.

"Ah, here you are, dear. Guess what. Our lessons begin tonight," Sam said. He'd come home a little early.

"What lessons?"

"My space navigation lessons and your piloting lessons."

"But I didn't sign up for that."

"I know. I signed you up. Look, learning how to do new things keeps our brains healthy and minds occupied. Less stress."

"But my mind is occupied with how to stop this awful future from happening. Only got a few months at most. Plus, there's what to do with those thousands who are going to wake up in a few days to their worst nightmares. I can't go to Philadelphia and certainly not Tokyo to give them therapy sessions or even help train them in all these alternate ways."

"Right. So we go do something completely different. Pilot and navigation school."

Sam seemed so pleased that I didn't want to disappoint him. I figured they'd take one look at me and tell me to get real, that there are some things I just couldn't do.

Going out to New O'Hare Spaceport for a class was

something completely new to me. Sam's enthusiasm became contagious, but I hoped they'd let us down gently.

The roars were loud, as we rode a branch of the MTES up to the main terminal building, a sprawling octopus of a building, its many arms stretching out to various sections of the port. We entered through the automatic doors. Instant silence. How wonderful; the interior was heavily sound proofed.

"Welcome to New O'Hare Spaceport. How can I direct you? Speak clearly," the computerized voice greeted us. It came from a kiosk just inside the doors.

"Where are the navigation and pilot classes?" Sam said, grinning broadly.

We followed the directions and soon saw signs with arrows. Entering a small room, a young Galactic Doll greeted us. She sat behind a desk with a computer, its holographic display facing her. "Welcome to Flight School. Are you registered?" Sam nodded. "Names please?" He answered.

"Sam Parkinson-Kross, your class starts in ten minutes, through the door to your left. Molly Parkinson, your class starts in ten minutes, through the door on your right. I see Sam has already paid for your courses, so you both are all set. Go on in and join your fellow classmates. Each evening when you come, you can just go right on in. You don't have to check in with me each time."

"Have fun, dear," Sam said. He proudly walked up to his door, which automatically opened.

I took a deep breath and headed through the door on the right. I entered a square room with a huge monitor on one wall. Facing it, a dozen chairs beckoned. Two young men sat in the front row, but they stared at me. I didn't need telepathy to pick up their thoughts. What's that freak think she's doing?

I took a seat in the second row just as a side door opened. A brown-skinned Galactic Doll wearing a purple uniform entered—the colors worn by Galactic Expansion personnel.

"Hello. I'm your instructor for this ten-week course.

Mrs. Chandra Sakra. You may call me Chandra. It's my job to train you to pilot shuttle craft, deep space transports, and even a freighter. If you pass this course and if desired, you can move on to learning to pilot a delta wing fighter or a cruiser. However, those will be beyond the capability of Mrs. Parkinson. I'm afraid arms and hands are required to pilot those."

I figured I'd be kicked out, but she thought I would be able to pilot the smaller, non-combat spacecraft. Maybe this wasn't such a far-fetched idea. However, the two men turned to give me a strange look.

"Hey, she didn't say I couldn't learn to pilot transports, fellows," I said.

"She's right. You don't need hands for that, but you do need many mental skills and lots of practice. You've probably heard our ships are computerized and fly themselves. In essence, that's true. On a routine flight with a proper navigator to set the coordinates, anyone could fly it. However, the unexpected happens. And that's where your skills at piloting spell the difference between a crash and survival.

"Today, we'll watch video instructions that cover all the basic steps. Starting tomorrow evening, we'll focus on each step, covering what to do in all circumstances. At the end of the week, you'll take an examination over this material. If you fail, you can retake the week or drop out. Personally, statistics favor your dropping out. Questions? None, good. Let's get started. First, introduce yourself to your classmates. We'll use first names here."

We did so and watched the video presentation which lasted nearly an hour. It gave us an overall view of what being a pilot on a transport involved. Much was going down checklists, verifying all was in order before taking off. When we ended, Chandra asked me to stay a moment.

"I recognized you from your GEnt newscasts from years back when you investigated the corruption within the GD corporation. You haven't aged a day."

"That's me. I was mutated again, so I look twenty-one once more. Is there really hope for me to be able to pilot a transport? Really? I thought my husband was dreaming when he signed me up."

Chandra smiled, before becoming serious. "Yes, it's possible for a handicapped person to be able to pilot a transport. It's not going to be easy, mind you. I've had three others over the years make the attempt, but each finally gave up. One actually made it to the final test, before he failed trying to handle the emergency situation. Will I see you tomorrow night?"

"Sure thing. I'll certainly do my best."

I left and waited for Sam to come out. When I saw him, I knew this had been a right move for him. His face radiated happiness. His skin shone, and his eyes had that sparkle in them that I so fell in love with.

"I take it you had a great time."

"You bet I did," Sam said. "How about you?"

"My instructor said it was theoretically possible for me to be a pilot, but three like me have tried and failed. Odds not so good. Still it was intensely interesting. Thanks for signing us up."

Sam puffed up even more. We both had a bit of a spring in our step as we walked home.

Lara watched the kids for us. So when we entered, Nikita, Matt, and Lara were there to greet us.

"How'd it go Mom? Are they going to let you be a pilot?" Nikita asked.

"Dad, a navigator?" Matt asked.

Lara smiled and said, "I'll make some hot chocolate." We both knew what she meant—something to calm down the excited children before bed.

Chapter 8 News

"Turn on your comm center. The Padella doctors are about to make history in genetics," Eve said.

She'd called me just after we finished breakfast and before I left for work with Bishop. I did as she asked, when Lara joined us.

"Big news today," Lara said. "Eve and I have some too, but we'll share ours later on. It's those Padella doctors, Nelson and Janet. Genetic breakthroughs."

We sat down on the couch to watch. At nine o'clock, the program began.

"We're here with Drs. Janet and Nelson Padella, who have announced a series of genetic mutation breakthroughs. Their recent research has led to several great discoveries." He talked on before turning it over to the CEO of Galactic Medicine here in Chicago.

"Yes, today, you can walk into any Med Center and request your own personal genetic mutations. You can pick your hair color. Blonde, brunette, redhead, a dozen shades. You can change the color of your eyes. You can pick the color of your skin to some degree from the light brown of those on the sub-continent to the pale yellow of Asians. Dark skins can be lightened, but not entirely, just as light skin colors can be darkened. Those with skin diseases and slight deformities can be wholly cured. Even poor eyesight can now be genetically corrected, along with cavity-prone teeth. Men, you can eliminate the need to shave.

"The Padella doctors have achieved a list of genetic breakthroughs, all now available through your local Med Center. All are inexpensive and affordable by most people. Unfortunately, none of these apply to giants and dwarves as yet, though they may well be in the near future.

"Telepaths, these modifications are available to you. None fit the definition of cures as prescribed by law. So take advantage of these breakthroughs. Have the natural color of hair and eyes you've always wanted."

The reporter discussed these changes with the two doctors, but Lara turned the volume down.

"How silly," she said. "These are merely cosmetic changes to your bodies. Eve and I have perfected our initial cure to shrink mammoth breasts down to merely large ones with no side-effects. However—"

"There's always a but." I interrupted her with a wry grin.

"Yes, we finally got permission to field test it. The problem is that seven years ago nearly all women on Earth were implanted by the Sixth Invaders to both desire and crave these whopper bosoms. Our field tests did reduce bosoms properly, but the women couldn't handle that. Constant low grade headaches, irritability, and other symptoms occurred and didn't diminish with time. Thus, each had to be re-mutated with their original Galactic Doll mutation, restoring their bosoms. So while our cure physically works, it brings about untenable mental stress, unless the implant is erased via therapy."

"Wow. I'd so hoped you'd be able to get rid of soccer ball breasts," I said.

"We did. However, it isn't all bad news. Breast reduction is also more or less a cosmetic effect. As you have pointed out, the real damage is the dominant inheritance of these mutations. Children, male or female, born to a Galactic Doll ends up a Doll too, regardless of the child's true gender. Within a couple generations, all males on Earth will be Dolls themselves. Eve and I've made another breakthrough. But I should explain further.

"We first checked with Galactic Medicine. We could provide a worldwide cure that would change everyone back to their original DNA as given in your worldwide database, with some special handling for those who's original DNA isn't in it. That was vetoed by GMed. Why? People demanded to look the way they do, thanks to those same implants. We couldn't just restore everyone.

"So we dug deeper and have solved it another way. We've invented a genetic mutation that does nothing to the host's body; it only affects the reproduction cycle. When fertilization occurs, our mutation kicks in, removing the dominant Galactic Doll changes to both genders. In short, children of Dolls would be normal humans again. However, we've not yet been able to do that to those exposed to the telepath strain, whose mutations are incredibly dominant."

"Wow! Best news in a long time. Now, children can make their own decisions about their bodies. I suspect some girls will want to look like their mothers, but few men, if any, will. Great job, Lara. I'll call Eve and thank her later."

"Yes, we've already gotten permission from GMed to begin implementation. They calculate six months to a year to cover the entire Earth. Once that's done, the safety of future generations is ensured, except for children of you armless Dolls. We're hopeful of one day handling that, too, Molly."

"Great news, Lara. I hope we're still here in six months."

"Downer, Molly. Think positively."

"Grr. Okay."

My phone rang. I slipped off my right shoe, pulled my phone out from my dress pocket, and answered Helen's call.

"Molly, watching the news?" I said so. "Good. Keep on watching. Dimitri Leonovich, CEO GPan, Moscow, is going to make huge announcement. About me. I won't spoil it, but Molly, call me back when you hear it. I don't know if I can do it. Bye."

"Well, that was cryptic. Keep on watching."

We did, and Bishop dropped by, back from his trip to Tokyo and Philadelphia.

Dimitri, another Ted, Felix, and Frank Wells clone, appeared amid a wall of microphones and cameras.

"Earthlings, citizens of the Sol Empire, I'm Dimitri Leonovich, CEO of Earth's Galactic Expansion corporation. With the disastrous loss of our fledgling Council of the Senate, I've been in touch with representatives of our two dozen worlds, moons, asteroids, and stations. All are very leery of sending more of their people to Earth, fearing another mutation attack. I've gone over the legal aspects with many lawyers. I'm afraid the laws passed by the Council are in force and binding on us and on future senators.

"Next, the top leadership positions of our empire must be filled and functioning, to say nothing of protecting the empire. I've thought long and hard about this and have decided on the first step that must be taken to guarantee every member's safety. We must have our original setup back, in which the Sol Empire-wide Galactic Defense corporation handles just that. My wife, Natalie, is the CEO of GD Earth. In lieu of all the terrorist attacks happening around Earth, her attention is focused totally upon preventing more such assaults.

"So I've decided to reactivate the GD Sol Empire-wide corporation that used to be in Chicago GD's skyscraper. We will once again have a GD that is focused on defending our entire empire. I've assigned our First Infantry Division under the leadership of General Beverly Blossom Blythe to once more help defend our entire empire. Of course, we need to man up this corporation. I've chosen two most capable individuals. CEO Helen Hugo of Chicago GD has done an admirable job in the Chicago area. I've promoted her to be the CEO of our new empire-wide Galactic Defense corporation, stationed in the upper floors of that skyscraper.

"Further, I've appointed her husband, Casper Hugo, to be the empire-wide Chief Finance Officer, the post he used to hold nine years ago. As many may recall, Casper arranged financing for many of our newest cruisers and battleships. Now, more than ever, we need solid financing to enlarge our fleet so we're not dependent upon other empires for our defense. Both Helen and Casper are telepaths, so this gives them both a keen edge in their positions. Within a few days, look for hiring announcements for many positions within GD, as CEO Hugo mans up her vitally important corporation.

"Now then, what about the Council of the Senate, the Senior Investigator, and the Senior Judge? We're retaining the Senior Investigator and Judge with their subordinates. Those two departments will continue their normal operations. Everyone is satisfied with the quality of their work, but the Senate is another matter. As of today, I am not hopeful I'll be able to convince the other members to elect and send new senators. So for now, the Senate no longer exists.

"Yet, we need top empire leadership. To that end, I have been holding discussions with all member worlds concerning bringing back the empire-wide Galactic Expansion corporation, which used to run our empire. They have agreed, but insist that all senate-passed laws must remain, and the new corporation must be answerable to all the other member worlds, as well as pass new laws for the benefit of the entire empire. Look for future announcements regarding the Council of the Senate and the possible empire-wide GPan. Thank you."

"Wow. That's a shocker. No wonder Helen sounded so nervous. Phone: call Helen Hugo."

"We need to protect other worlds from this telepath mutation," Bishop said.

My call went to voice message, so I left her a note to call me when she was free—that and congratulations.

I said, "Yes, I've been wondering what the other worlds would do. First, they blocked immigration of any Galactic Doll or variation thereof. What will they do when they learn giants are mutating humans, abducting them, and selling them at auction? Guess Helen gets to deal with that issue."

"Right. Now then, Molly, I've some disturbing news from both Tokyo and Philadelphia. Based on known head counts of the people who lived in the infected areas, each city is short one hundred people, men and women."

"Huh? Short?"

"Yes. They went door to door recovering the unconscious people and taking them to Med Centers and hospitals. Once that task was done, they tallied up how many people had been living there. The two numbers differed by one hundred. Weird, but precisely one hundred.

No children missing, only adults. If they were married, both were not found. It's as if someone intentionally took one hundred of these comatose people away."

"Crap! That's what we'd expect they'd be doing—abducting those they're mutating. Anyone spot anyone taking the people away? Clues?"

"None. I'm afraid officials in both cities were dealing with a very chaotic scene. The discovery of the missing people didn't occur until the sixth day into the mutation comas. By then, it was long after the fact. This information is being withheld from the news for now." Bishop finished.

"Okay, then. Is there anyway to see if there were transport ships that arrived and departed around those days when the people went missing? Probably during the night hours right after the attack and before anyone knew what was happening."

"I can check on that. Generally, commercial transports from other Federation worlds carry one hundred passengers, while ours carry only twenty-five."

"Do that. I'm going to research these other ten people who purchased a safe room from Baker Vaults. Let's meet back here late this afternoon."

As he left, Helen returned my call.

"Honestly, I'm frightened. I just don't know if I can do this, Molly. It's so hard."

"Sit tight. I'm on my way over."

I knew I had to give her a therapy session.

Shortly, I sat across from her. Her relief shone on her face. "It's so crazy. I mean normally, I can sit here and do my work. Most everything I need is voice-activated. But then I have to go down to the lunch room, where I feel so helpless. Everyone stares at me. I can't carry anything. It's so frustrating to want to point to something or to hand a folder to them, and I can't. I'm barely able to run our local GD. Now he wants me to protect the whole empire?"

"I understand, Helen. Close your eyes. Let's return to when you first felt so frustrated."

She did. Off we went, re-experiencing her yesterday. After a couple passes through it, I asked for something earlier. She ran through dozens of similar experiences since she awoke from the mutation attack. Pushed even earlier, she ran through her first day as our local GD CEO nearly seven years ago. Her symptoms didn't vanish, but grew more acute, so I asked for something even earlier.

She floundered about before spotting something blackish. I had her go to its beginning and run through it. After several passes, more of what happened became visible.

"This happened so very long ago. I'm with my husband. Right. We're in the air. Flying. I see a wing off to my right. He's got a thing like a wheel in front of him. He uses it to steer and fly this machine. There's a loud motor in front and lots and lots of dials and switches. We're way up high. Oh no! He clutches his chest. He's having a heart attack. Oh god. What do I do? I can't fly this thing. He's unconscious. What do I do? I can't do this. They're looking at me. Friends. We brought along four friends. They yell and stare at me. Do something. I can't do this. I don't know how. Everyone's staring at me. Oh god. The ground is coming up fast. What do I do? Pain. A wall of pain. Now I'm up high again. Looking down. Smoking wreckage. I just knew I didn't know what to do, and they were all staring at me."

Suddenly, Helen opened her eyes and started laughing. "I didn't know what to do. Hey, I really didn't know how to fly that machine. Everyone staring didn't help either." She laughed heartily. I ended the session.

"Well, that's dumb. I know how to run our local GD, so it's just a matter of expanding that to our neighboring worlds. I can do this, Molly. Still, it's frustrating at times. I so hate people staring at me. Makes me feel self-conscious."

"Well, we do have to do things differently than most people. What's important is that we do them."

She pressed her body into mine—a hug. I left for my office. Now I had to check out the ten people who'd ordered the safe rooms. I began by seeing what the internet had on them. Within minutes, one aspect became very clear. None of these people had top positions in any of the major corporations, but all had a net worth in the billions of credits, with a couple at a hundred billion. Several lived several hundred miles away. So I decided to scratch those off the list, leaving me with seven names.

I needed to visit each of them, so I made a list of addresses. To be efficient, I brought up the online map of the greater Chicago area and put a pin on each location. Then, I rewrote the list in the order I'd visit them while taking the shortest total route.

When Bishop came, together, we began a lengthy walk around the far north of Chicago where the wealthiest lived in wooded mansion estates that covered city blocks triple the size of those in the Loop. We walked up to Kay Walton's mansion. A steel fence twelve feet tall topped with barbed wire surrounded the giant estate. Two heavily armed dwarves stood guard at the main gatehouse.

"We'd like to talk with Kay Walton, please," I said.

"Look into the vid-cam," he said, before buzzing the house.

Over a speaker, I heard her. "Make sure the man isn't armed. Then, send them in."

When we met Kay, I had no idea of her true age. She, too, had been rejuvenated by the Galactic Doll mutation and had had none of the cures, so she and I looked very similar.

"Oh that thing," she said after I asked about the safe room. "I got it for safety's sake. What with all the strange happenings around Chicago and these aliens, I don't know who to trust, except these dwarves, who convinced me to have it installed in case bad men get past them and run up to the house. I can duck into the safe room."

While she was pleasant and intelligent, she definitely wasn't involved with the giants, since she detested them, claiming they shouldn't be so big and intimidating. She suggested we send them back to their world. Yes, she was a bit biased.

"He (or She) doesn't see telepaths." That became the sole comment delivered by giant guards at the next five stops. This refusal to even see us made me even more suspicious of these four men and one woman.

The last man was elderly and pleased to chat with us. His security guards recommended he install the safe room because of the wildly unpredictable events that had been happening around Chicago and the world. I sensed he wasn't hiding anything.

As Bishop and I returned to my place, I said, "Well, those five warrant further study as potential co-conspirators. While they are wealthy by Sol Empire standards, from what we've seen, their wealth won't get them a landing permit on this Merlin-C world. The question is what can we do about them, since they are so wealthy."

Neither of us had an answer. Worse, days passed without yielding anything helpful. As June ended, we were no closer to identifying them or stopping the inevitable.

On the other hand, our night classes in navigation and piloting continued to offer new challenges, stimulating our minds, even if we didn't pass the course. My first real obstacle appeared the second week. How to fasten my own four-point safety belt. An X design of straps held one's torso securely to the seat no matter what orientation the ship had, even upside down. It left ones arms and legs free to work the controls—feet in my case. Again, I had to stop and spend some time experimenting with the how. Chandra patiently allowed me ample experimentation time, while the two men snickered at me and moved on with their course work, leaving me behind. I stuck with it, though, determined not to let an X harness defeat me. I finally succeeded by first fastening it shut, but with the straps loose. Then, I stepped up onto the seat and slipped my legs and body down through the X straps. Finally, I pulled the belts as tight as they were supposed to be, checked by Chandra.

Having worked it out, I spent one whole evening practicing that action, until I could get into my pilot's seat rapidly. On the Friday night test of the week's learned skills, I was only slightly slower than my two classmates.

The third week consisted of pre-flight fuel checks,

looking at various dials and gauges. However, I didn't get the chance to get overconfident. The checklist had a triple check on the fuel levels.

Chandra explained, "The gauge in your cockpit is accurate ninety percent of the time. However, pre-flight checks demand you go down to engineering and check the fuel level dial there as a double check. Checking on both handles ninety-nine percent of all situations, but you don't want to drop into hyperspace and run out of fuel. That's a death sentence. So always triple check the fuel levels. Don't believe or put your full trust in these dials and gauges. Rather, go check the level in the tanks yourself. At the rear, climb down the ladder beside the tank or tanks and look thorough the transparent view slit. You can see the level of fuel. It has a yellow dye added to make its level in the tanks very visible in the dim lights. Always triple check. Your life and the lives of your passengers may depend on it."

"Do these gauges and dials break?" one man asked.

"Not so much as break, but electromagnetic effects can temporarily adversely alter their accuracy. Some planets, asteroids, and moons might have an overly strong magnetic field close to where you landed. Usually, the dials read full when the tanks aren't, a recipe for disaster."

The men had no problem descending and ascending the vertical metal ladders. But I sure did. When I first saw them that Monday night, I thought here's where I flunk out. No way could I scamper down and up those ladders as the men rapidly did, before moving on to the next step. Me, I just stared down into the gloom beside the tank.

The ladder was only eight feet tall, but to me it looked like a mile. Fortunately, I'd followed Chandra's advice and wore a blouse and pants to class. I'd never have made it wearing one of my satin gowns. I hooked my chin over the top rung for support and carefully put one heel onto a rung. When it was secure, I let go and swung the other leg over to the ladder and onto the rung. Very carefully, I managed to step down rung by rung, all the time pressing myself into the ladder. The scariest part was releasing my chin hold on one rung while going down or up to the next one.

I eventually made it down and up, but once more, I decided to practice this many times, until I felt somewhat comfortable doing it. That I had to wear these tall heels didn't help. Still, by the end of that week, I passed the test, which is what mattered to me.

In contrast, Sam had a more difficult task, one which I could never do. In space, a ship can move in three directions, three hundred sixty degrees in each or in any combination. Thus, the navigation window onto the stars around the ship can be positioned in all kinds of orientations to the star field outside the ship. The navigator must be able to look at the stars and determine the ship's orientation in three dimensions rapidly, along with its location within our part of the galaxy's spiral arm. Heck, I got nauseated just imagining his task. Sam's photographic memory really helped him master this. For him, it was just a matter of moving the mental image of the star field about until it aligned with what he saw out the view port. Okay, it wasn't a real view port. Chandra projected the appropriate images on a screen they saw through the view port. Sam excelled at this.

Thus, as June moved into July, Sam and I continued to do well in our night courses. We both failed to notice that Isabella and Bernardo missed their late June calls home.

Chapter 9 Taking Action

During the night of July 10, the terrorists struck again, this time in Mumbai in a densely packed residential area. Initial tallies suggested over two thousand people dropped into comas. Upon hearing of the attack, Helen Hugo requested Admiral Rossi to dispatch part of his fleet to that area and watch for arrival and departure of deep space transports. He had orders to blast them out of the skies. She also ordered an accurate discrepancy count, wanting to know how many people may have been abducted this time.

By the third day, she received the count of two hundred missing men and women. A team of giants had been spotted carrying off comatose victims. Admiral Rossi spotted one alien transport trying to leave Earth orbit and had his cruisers challenge it. The unidentified ship refused to be bordered and attempted to accelerate and drop into hyperspace, but the blasters and cannons of the cruisers disintegrated the ship before it could do so.

During the next few days, parts of bodies were recovered as they cleaned up the debris field. ME's estimates suggested there might have been one hundred humans killed along with six giants.

Helen Hug had enough. On July 15, she acted, broadcasting via GEnt to the two dozen worlds of the Sol Empire. We watched it live.

"Greetings fellow members of the Sol Empire. I'm Helen Hugo, the CEO of Galactic Defense for the empire. I'm speaking to you today about a terrible terrorist plot currently against humans on Earth, but by extension, soon to every human in our empire. Some facts are proven; some, we have good reason to believe are true; others, we are only able to speculate about at this time.

"Certain human individuals, we believe total six, and one giant who goes by the name of Morpheus have created the most diabolical and inhumane plot I've ever heard of. It goes like this. Using stolen EMACs and with spray booms

104

attacked, giants working for this Morpheus spray a large section of an Earth city with the Armless Doll Telepath Agent, turning thousands of unsuspecting men, women, and children into handicapped telepaths. While these victims are in their mutation comas, giants sweep down and gather them up, whisking them off in deep space transports. This has happened numerous times in the past few months, the last one being in Mombai. In that one, the giants in their transport were stopped by our cruisers and destroyed. Recovery crews retrieved the bodies of the hundred victims being stolen.

"What happens next is likely true, only we haven't yet been able to prove it. The comatose victims are taken to an off-world site and kept alive until their telepathic skills develop. Then, they are sold into telepath slavery at an auction to the highest bidders from across the galaxy. Estimates are that each sells for about a half million credits.

"One of these terrorists was our own Senator Truman Wyman. From his computer and documents, we've learned of this plan, which initially intended to mutate all humans in Chicago, or about three million of us. His share of that profit is unbelievable and was to be deposited into his new account on the Merlin-C world, which caters to the ultra-wealthy of the entire galaxy.

"Why are they doing this? Greed. They see the making and selling of telepaths as a giant money maker, since telepaths are extremely rare throughout the galaxy. Only a handful are known to exist, beyond those recently made on Earth. Greed appears to be the motive for the other five Earth men and woman who are part of this plot. As of this point in time, we have the suspects under surveillance.

"On the screen is the best surveillance image of the giant known as Morpheus. If you know this individual or have any information concerning his whereabouts, contact your local GD office. He and his henchmen are considered armed and utterly ruthless, killing without conscience.

"I'm alerting everyone in the Sol Empire today for another reason. Thus far, this plot, this manufacturing of armless telepaths, kidnaping them, and selling them at auction is confined to the Earth. I'm convinced it won't remain a purely Earth problem for much longer. Unfortunately, that terrible mutation agent is widely available and has been duplicated many times at many labs. It isn't *if* someone will bring that Armless Doll Telepath Agent to your world, your moon, your base, but rather *when* will it be brought there. I assure you Earth doesn't have a monopoly on greed.

"Once that agent is on your world, you can expect others to victimize your people, kidnap them while they're helpless, and sell them off-world for a heady profit. No human anywhere in the galaxy is safe from these greedy people. If you're human, you can be injected with the agent or breathe in its gaseous form and wake up to find yourself like I am today, only you may find yourself on some other world working for your slave master.

"Because of the seriousness of this, I sent word of this to our Federation Senior Ambassadors on Bela Prime, asking them to alert other leaders. Further, I've asked them to pass severe laws banning this practice and to have their scientists test to see if this agent will mutate their people. We need to know which worlds in the galaxy whose people could be adversely affected by this mutation agent. They need to take safeguards.

"Speaking of safeguards, that is precisely why all other Sol Empire worlds have banned the immigration of people from Earth. Most of us have already had our genetic makeup altered, the Galactic Doll phenomenon. Children born to parents, at least one of which is a Doll, inherit the Doll genes, irrespective of the child's gender. While some believe we women look good as a Doll, male Dolls are highly frowned upon throughout the empire. Further, all children who have at least one telepath Doll parent will themselves be a telepath Doll; this gene is highly dominant.

"Thus, I hope your world also implements an immigration ban on us telepath Dolls. Currently, our geneticists are working to find cures for the Sixth Invader mutations, but until they do, we have to deal with the consequences of them. Today, greed has replaced fear here on Earth. We must all do our parts to prevent greed from invading your world. Thank you. I'll take a few questions now."

"CEO Hugo, these other five wealthy people—can you tell us their names?"

"I can tell you, but I certainly won't. It would be wrong of me to reveal their names until I have proof of their involvement. At this point, we have very strong evidence but it isn't enough to warrant prosecution. The moment that we do, I'll release their names."

"Are they here in Chicago?"

"I can tell you that much. Yes, they are."

"Will there be a ban on telepaths traveling around the Sol Empire?"

"I hope not. Telepaths have a very powerful gift which we prefer to share with everyone. Yes, it's difficult for a person to withhold a lie from us."

"Some are suggesting your handicap prevents you from doing a good job as CEO. How do you answer them in light of the recent Mombai terrorist attack?"

"My skills are in organization and leadership. I am not and never have been a field agent. Yes, I'm handicapped at the moment. I won't hide the fact that at times I get very frustrated with it. But it doesn't affect my position. As far as Mombai is concerned, first, we have no idea where these terrorists will strike next. Second, now that we know their objectives, we have taken actions, as witnessed by stopping one of their transports from getting away with a hundred people and selling them at auction as slave telepaths. Granted, I wish the telepaths hadn't lost their lives, but the alternative of being on a strange world as a nearly helpless slave telepath is too horrible to even consider. It is my hope that we can react far faster the next time the terrorists strike."

"What did Senator Wyman actually do? Why wasn't he terminated or sent to the penal colony?"

"As far as we know, he helped setup and organize the project, handling Earth-side aspects, while this Morpheus giant handled the off-world aspects. He had a ticket to this Merlin-C world, scheduled departure on Halloween, which is when we believe they planned to wipe out Chicago. These other attacks, they're preparatory tests, as they get ready for the main event, which we have estimated was initially scheduled for the middle of September or so. They needed time to abduct the millions of us, take us to their off-world staging area, wait until telepathy developed, and then sell us at a galaxy-wide auction. We estimated that might take six weeks.

"Senator Wyman planned to leave for this rich-man's world when substantial funds from the telepath sales had been deposited into his account. The authorities on Merlin-C won't let anyone land and visit unless they have a hundred billion credits in their account.

"As to his punishment, that's in the hands of the Senior Judge, who ruled termination was too easy a punishment. Senator Wyman will have to live as a telepath for at least another fifty years without ever being allowed any cures. Any money he may earn will be donated to his many victims. In case you weren't aware, a number of cities besides Chicago have experienced similar attacks with this terrible bio agent. Earlier this year, GPan and GD were both struck by Sixth Invader attacks. Thousands of the victims begged to be terminated rather than to live as an armless Doll. Personally, I agree with the Senior Judge. Make him suffer what we're all suffering."

"Is it true many giants are involved? And that some have been terminated?"

"Yes to both. By now, everyone knows giants make excellent security guards."

"Some are calling for us to deport all giants. Why don't we do that?"

"There are bad apples in every group of people. Just look at Senator Wyman. I'm not about to condemn all giants for the actions of a few. Besides, we believe many of these giants who were involved and have been killed were not immigrants, but citizens of Liatos-D. Look, Earth has already endured one attempted genocide, the Islamic

Muslims over two hundred years ago. I hope we've become more civilized since then."

"Why are you telling this to the entire empire today?"

"By being alert to the plot and how it works, when it happens on your world, your authorities will know what to expect and how to respond. Look, as we get closer to shutting these terrorists down here on Earth, I predict they'll head to your worlds to attack, mutate, steal, and sell your people as telepaths."

"What's their motivation for doing this?"

"I told you. Greed. Some people can never have enough money. Considering the going rate for a telepath is around a half million credits, make and sell ten and you are set for life, at least here on Earth. It's a quick way to make mega-credits. I believe greed is the underlying motivator. I'm afraid Earth doesn't own that attitude. Greed, the intense and selfish desire for wealth or power, is universal. Just ask the ambassadors."

"How do you know this giant named Morpheus is involved?"

"He has been recorded on surveillance videos. His name was found on incriminating documents of Senator Wyman. He definitely is the go-between person, working with those six humans here on Earth and the unknown persons off-world. He and his men think nothing of murdering anyone in their way. He shot and nearly killed a GPan security guard who let him into GPan. Morpheus covered his trail, but by a lucky chance, by injecting the guard with the red pouch syringe, which contains the Armless Doll Telepath Agent, doctors were able to save is life. He identified Morpheus.

"Look, these people have no sense of humanity, no sense of what's right or ethical. Mass mutation, abduction of victims, and selling them as slave telepaths means nothing to these people beyond a lot of money. So if you have any knowledge of this Morpheus, call your local GD. Don't try to deal with him on your own. He'll kill you or worse, mutate and sell you."

"What roles are these five other people in Chicago playing? How do they expect to be missed if the whole city gets attacked? In Mumbai, the aerosolized agent mutated whole city blocks of people. You're talking like they'll gas all Chicago, like the Sixth Invaders threatened."

"At this time, we don't know their precise roles. It would be wrong of me to speculate. Senator Wyman planned for the gas attack of Chicago by installing a safe room that has no outside connection and with its own oxygen supply—enough to last him three days."

"Are you going to provide safe shelters around Chicago?"

"A safe room setup cost around ten thousand credits and holds only a couple people. More importantly, all recent attacks occurred at night when most people sleep. That way, the giants can use the cover of darkness to hide their actions of carting comatose people away. So even if we had shelters that would work, making effective use of them is highly unlikely, unless like Senator Wyman, you knew in advance when the attack was coming."

"Do you have any advice for other worlds in our empire?"

"Yes. Expect this mess to come to your world at some point in time, likely after we make it too hot for them to continue operating on Earth. Be alert for area mutation attacks. At the first sign of a mutation attack, be alert for giants abducting comatose victims; scan the skies for alien transports to take away the abducted victims. Oh, yes, and shoot to terminate them. One other detail. Our geneticists have proven this terrible bio agent has no effects on giants or dwarves. So make use of those you can, especially right after such an attack, since they're immune.

"Okay, that's enough questions for this briefing. I'll let you know when I will hold another. Thank you. Be vigilant."

I turned off the comm center. "Well, that ought to make it more difficult for these terrorists to wipe us out, since everyone now knows about it."

***

"Did you see Hugo's special report? The rabbit is out of the hat. Damn. Damn. Damn." The man known as Moe met with Larry and Curly in Moe's private estate later that same day. "Unless Morpheus has some grand plan, our dreams of amassing a vast wealth have just vanished."

Curly said, "I'm inclined to agree with Moe. Even though Morpheus and his beta phase two worked perfectly, a thousand or two is a far cry from three million. Besides, getting them transported off-world has become problematical. They blew up one of the two transports, killing a hundred victims and the giants. It's beyond me how Morpheus hopes to park thirty thousand transports above Earth without Admiral Rossi detecting them and blasting them to scrap metal."

"But perhaps," Larry said, "this could be successfully done on a smaller scale. Hell, even marketing ten thousand of them would gross ten billion credits, more than enough for us to turn a profit on this venture."

Moe typed a few strokes on his virtual keyboard. "Look, we've each put up a half billion credits for this venture. We're promised ten percent of the gross sales each. We'll have to market five thousand telepaths just to break even. What have we gotten thus far? Morpheus had marketed just under four hundred from the basic test phases. We've received barely forty million credits return on our investment of five hundred million credits. Not good at all, but then we haven't reached the actual date of the mass mutations."

"I'm still concerned," Curly said, "we aren't going to recoup our initial investment. Worse, according to CEO Hugo, we could well be under GD's scrutiny. Lord knows what those idiots will do if they knew about us. This whole plan could be our undoing."

"Yes," Moe said, "but we have our safe rooms setup."

"Hugo had a point today," said Curly. "How the hell do we know Morpheus will tell us when his people launch the big attack on Chicago? He might not tell us, and we'll be doomed, too."

"But don't we have that covered with the databases

we've amassed on him and his giant associates?" asked Moe. "When the big attack comes, if we aren't around to send our failsafe machines the right codes, it'll send the complete files on Morpheus to GD."

Larry grimaced. "What the fuck good is that going to do us? We'll be just another bunch of helpless telepaths, sold off to the highest bidder. Hell, we won't even have time to put a bullet into our brains. One good whiff of that stuff and you end up in a coma in seconds."

"Well, what can we do?" asked Curly. "As wrong as this whole thing has gone, I wouldn't give much on our chances of not being mutated. Plus, I'm sure Hugo is on to us. One of her cronies, that Molly Parkinson, came poking her nose around here. Don't forget, she's the one who played CEO when Hardy shot himself. Now she's a damned telepath, too. How far can a telepath be from a target and still read their minds? Anyone know?"

"Hey, she came by my place, too. Didn't let her beyond the security gate," Moe said. "Look, it's only mid-July. The big attack isn't supposed to come until September 15. We've got time, unless you think all this scrutiny's going to force Morpheus to move up the timetable."

"Hell, he certainly could do that," Larry said. "I wish there wasn't a total ban on immigration from Earth. At least, we haven't been mutated. Knock on wood. Still, I've a mind to take a trip to Brussels, Tau Ceti, and check on my estate there. Might be a good time for you two to take similar trips. After all, we're key businessmen."

"Speaking of business," Moe said, "Casper Hugo is back to being GD's CFO and has been looking for donations to build more cruisers and such. I've not taken his phone calls, since he's one of them freaky telepaths, but he's been emailing me and texting me about making a donation. Perhaps, we should make a sizeable donation. Help convince GD we aren't working with Morpheus."

"You think Casper would believe us?" asked Curly.

"Hell, if a telepath gets near us, we're doomed. There's just too damned many here in Chicago," Moe said. "I think Larry's right. Time to check on our holdings on other worlds, like say for the next six months. Probably won't hurt to donate some big funds to Casper, if only to get him off looking at us. We should let Doc and Mata Hari know we're splitting, don't you think?"

"And leave quickly before Morpheus finds out we've split," Curly said.

***

"Great news. I've got the funds to build another light cruiser for the Sol Empire's fleet. My guys came through after all," Casper said.

"Superb. You're the best CFO GD's ever had," Helen said. "We should celebrate. Who came through this time? Do I know our benefactors?"

Casper rattled off their names. "Say, aren't those the men you have under surveillance?"

"Yes, the very ones we suspect are Senator Wyman's accomplices. So they are donating millions for us to build a new cruiser? Why? If they are part of this conspiracy, why would they give us money?"

"Now it makes more sense."

"What does?" she asked.

"Why I never could get them directly on their phones. If they are involved, I might have sensed it. So they avoided me, forcing me to text and email for their donations. Still, I'm thankful for their funds. We need a larger fleet and fast."

"What's this email?" Helen said. "They want me on this year's Miss Galactic Doll 2360 show to be recorded August 15th. Huh?"

"Oh crap. I just got an invite, too. What's wrong with them?"

"It says they want to use me to encourage other young women to achieve greatness. Well, I guess you can say being CEO of GD could count that way."

"Okay, but why me? I'm not a miss."

Helen grinned. "Could have fooled me, dear."

Casper flushed and bumped his hip into hers. "Good one. Are they trying to embarrass me or you, perhaps?"

"I'll call them up, Casper, and see if this is on the

level. Hold on—my phone." She used her nose to activate her phone resting on her desk. "Molly. Hi. What's up? Anything wrong?"

"No, I'm fine. It's just I've gotten the weirdest email ever. They want me on the Miss Galactic Doll 2360 show, something about using me to encourage other young women. I'm supposed to be a role model. They should've asked Leslie. She's into this looking beautiful stuff, not me. I've never paid much attention to my appearance. I'm hardly a role model. Weirder yet, they want Sam on the show, too."

Helen laughed. "Casper and I have just been invited as well. I'm going to call them up and see if this is on the level. If it is, I suppose you and I do make good role models for young women just starting out. We're proof women can make a difference in our world. But I'm hardly Miss Galactic Doll material."

I chuckled. "Helen, you've always looked glamorous."

***

The last week of my pilot training proved the hardest for me. Each of us was allowed as much time as we wished reviewing the material before we took the final theory exam and the practical test. The theory test went well, but I did have to mark the answers more rapidly than I would have liked. My foot got a work out. I took the test on Tuesday night, leaving three nights for the practical test, which Chandra had warned me would be challenging. I hadn't forgotten what she'd told me that first night—that an armless person made it all the way to the practical test which she failed to pass. That had me worried.

Wednesday night turned horrible, and I was about ready to give it up. I began standing in the passenger area of the simulator machine. The test began with a major engine failure that caused the ship to pitch, yaw, and roll simultaneously. I got tossed about like a rag doll. My job was to get to the pilot's seat, strap myself in, get the ship under control again, and then locate what system failed, recommending a solution or solutions to the captain.

By the end of class Wednesday, I had only managed to get to the pilot's seat. Dismal.

"Chandra, if I'm the pilot and if I leave my seat for some reason, I won't leave the X seat belt undone like the men do. I'd leave it buckled and loose so I can slip back into it."

She rubbed her chin a moment. "I see your point. The test assumes you have been piloting the ship and have gone back to deal with a passenger. So what you're saying is a reasonable assumption. Okay, tomorrow night, I'll see it's fastened but loose."

The next night went better, but I still failed. Friday night, I was determined not to flunk the test. I wore some old jeans and sleeveless blouse, as close as I could come to the uniforms I'd seen others in the space fleet wearing while shipboard. I had Lara tie my hair up in a tight bun, too.

As always, when the test began, the wild motions in three directions knocked me onto the floor, but I did my butt scoot across the floor and into the cockpit. Butt scooting in my heels proved harder than expected—on the heels, that is. When I reached the seat, I slipped them off and tried to get up and onto the top of the seat where I could slip down between the X belts. The wild motions made that nearly impossible for me to do. The men had grabbed onto things to stabilize themselves and pull their bodies into the seat. I had to find another way.

From the first night, I knew what had caused the problem and how to fix it. If only I could have been sitting strapped into my seat, why, I'd have corrected the problem in a minute, maybe two.

Bouncing around the cockpit, I realized there was another way. I timed my rolling motion such that my toes could hit the bank of switches. Pass one, missed, but on the second pass, my right big toe flipped one switch, allowing the computer to correct the out of control yawing. On the next roll, I flipped the next one, and the computer responded by remedying the roll. With only the ship pitching, I was able to compensate. I hopped onto the seat, slipped down between the X straps, and used a toe to flip the final switch. The ship or simulator rather resumed a normal stable flight. Then, I pretended to call the captain, telling him I had control and to have an engineer check on the aft stabilizer jets.

Her face cracking with a huge smile, Chandra entered and pressed stop. "Wow, Molly. You did it! You passed. Congratulations. You're now licensed to pilot any transport or even a freighter. Well done."

Sam passed as well, and we floated home. Seriously, we stopped at a bar and had a couple ales to celebrate. The next night, Bev dropped by with two six-packs to help us celebrate, too. Of course, neither of us knew what we planned to do with our pilot's and navigator's licenses. That wasn't the point. We'd done something new, challenging, and exciting. I wondered if I should mention this on the Miss Galactic Doll show.

With all the mutation attacks and the excitement over passing our classes, Sam and I failed to notice Isabella and Bernardo didn't call us this month. They'd missed their monthly calls twice in a row, something that hadn't happened in seven years.

Chapter 10 The Miss Galactic Doll 2360 Taping

Helen, Casper, Sam, and I flew to LA for the taping of the show on a GD Airliner. Bishop followed along, staying in the background while posing as a security person. A fancy GEnt EMAC, with leather seats and a built-in bar, met us at the LAX Spaceport and took us to the studio, which also had guest overnight rooms and a cafeteria. We were told the show took three days to tape and ushered to our rooms. Sam and I believed we must be in some kind of penthouse suite for the rich and famous. I couldn't tell if the bath fixtures were real gold or brass.

Would they have the necessary machines that the Sixth Invaders developed and on which we depended to maintain our independence? That worried us the most. Upon entering the room, we spotted them and relaxed at last.

At nine o'clock on the first day over a late breakfast in the dining hall, we met our host, other guests, and the twenty-four candidates for this year's Miss Galactic Doll.

"Hello everyone. I'm your Master of Ceremonies and Miss Galactic Doll 2300, Jill Koch. Yes, I won this very title at the turn of the century."

She was a tall brunette, hair falling in waves to her waist. Her hazel eyes seemed to captivate one's gaze. I could see why she'd won the title, but that meant she must really be in her seventies or eighties. She'd used the Doll rejuvenation.

"This is my thirtieth year running the biggest beauty pageant in the Sol Empire. This time, we have a number of distinguished guests with us. Doll Helen Hugo, CEO of Galactic Dynamics for the Sol Empire, and her husband and fellow Doll, Casper Hugo, her CFO. Please stand up you two so everyone can see you."

They did and received polite applause. "Also with us

are Dolls Molly Parkinson and Sam Parkinson-Kross. You may remember Molly was temporary CEO of GD some years back. These four will be guests highlighting just how high a Galactic Doll can rise, how effective we can be. Also, last year's Miss Galactic Doll, Miss Fleur Girard of Ceres, is with us. Stand up, please."

Again, polite applause for the hazel-eyed brunette with a round face, unlike the elliptical shape of Jill's face. She definitely was a beauty. I sensed Sam and Casper's arousals.

Jill introduced the two dozen candidates, one from each of the Sol Empire worlds. "Finally, the most important woman in the room. Miss Rae Miller of LA. She is in charge of everyone's makeup and dress. Rae will personally prepare each of you for the cameras. Yes, she'll also be the busiest person here, short of the cameramen. Here's our shooting schedule. Once breakfast is done, you'll change into your bathing suits for the pool side shoot. Tomorrow, you'll don your evening gowns for the formal ball shoot. On the third and final shoot, I've a big surprise for our billions of viewers. Fetish night and one of you ladies will be crowned Miss Galactic Doll 2360.

"Before we begin, each of you must sign a non-disclosure form. You must agree not to divulge this year's winner before the show airs on August 20. Rae will pass around the forms now. Eat up. It'll be a long time before you can eat again."

Later, Sam said, "I've never worn a bikini before. This is really weird for me. We're almost naked. Our boobs aren't even covered."

"I think that's the point, dear, but I've never worn one before either. Make the best of it, I guess."

We joined Helen and Casper, who also felt ill at ease wearing next to nothing.

"Well," Helen said, "it does show off our incredible curves I suppose. Still, I'd never go swimming in something this flimsy. But then, I'd never even attempt it now—without arms that is. I'm sure I'd drown."

Rae came around and first put our hair up in various

high fashion styles, similar to the ones that I'd seen on Helen and her friends when we met at Barnaby's to dine. She affixed sparkling tiaras to each of us. Casper suggested each must be worth a hundred thousand credits, for they contained many small diamonds.

Then, she made another round applying light makeup, explaining it was needed for the cameras. "Without it, you'll look like pale, sickly ghosts."

We strutted in following the two dozen candidates. The "pool" turned out to be a virtual reality imitation of a swanky pool. In the background we heard Jill barking out orders to her camera crew. "Zoom in on Ilse. Back out on Lenka." Occasionally, she told us as a group what to do, such as: "Parade around the pool, please." So we walked like penguins around the spot on the floor which looked like a ritzy pool. How fake.

Jill was right. Supper came far too late for my starving stomach. Around seven, we sat down to dine. The food was superb, but with scanty portions. I guessed everyone watched their weight, at least while taping the show. Earth's candidate sat by us.

"Hi. I'm Lenka Zelenka from Prague. I've never met any Doll telepath before. Is it true you can read our minds?"

"Hi, Lenka. I'm Molly Parkinson. Yes, we can, but we don't do that unless the person gives us their permission. Otherwise, it's like mental rape. So what are your plans once this pageant is over?"

She had wavy, waist-length blonde hair and the most gorgeous blue eyes. From what she said next, I guessed Lenka must be twenty-two or so.

"I've just graduated from university. Astronomy degree. One day, I want to fly among stars. I'm enrolling in space navigation course when we're done, that is, if I'm not crowned Miss Galactic Doll 2360."

"Hey, it's a great course. I just finished my navigation course a couple days ago," Sam said. The conversation shifted onto that topic. While I knew nothing about it, clearly she and Sam were excited about it.

The next day was more normal—if anything about

this pageant was normal. Each of us wore identical white evening gowns—satin and billowing out several feet at our knees. Rae again dressed us, while I presumed the candidates could do that themselves. This time, though, I was surprised. She fastened a garter belt around my waist and then slipped silky nylon hose on each leg, fastening them securely to the belt.

"But we need the use of our feet and toes," I said.

"Until I undress you tonight, I or one of the other assistants will be your hands for you," Rae said. Her tone suggested she'd done this many times before. That got me wondering.

After a bra and slip, neither of which I normally wore, she zipped me up in the off-white, satin formal gown. I slipped into matching heels, but these had ankle straps. Again, once she fastened them, I really couldn't use my feet as hands any longer. I felt incredibly constrained and ill at ease. Soon, I knew Helen, Casper, and Sam also were uncomfortable in this outfit. Rae later came by and did up our hair, fastening the tiaras on our heads, ending with the light makeup.

This time, the stage appeared to be an elegant ballroom with marble inlaid floors and a dozen golden chandeliers overhead. Waltz music in the background added to the atmosphere. For a time, we guests mingled among the identically dressed contestants.

Then, the MC conducted the interviews, beginning with us guests.

"Tonight, we're showcasing four extraordinary Galactic Dolls, showing all young women that you can achieve greatness. With us is Mrs. Helen Hugo, the CEO of the Sol Empire Galactic Defense corporation, leading the fight against the alien terrorists. Her leadership example demonstrates just how far an armless Doll telepath can rise. Let's give her a big hand."

An applause machine obliged, but Helen didn't get a chance to say anything.

"And here is her husband and male Doll, Casper Hugo, her Chief Finance Officer, who I've just heard has managed to get enough donors to pay for another desperately needed light cruiser for the Sol Empire. Casper, would you mind telling our viewing audience what it's like being a male armless Galactic Doll telepath? Is this something more males should consider as a career path?"

I cringed. I knew he didn't want the focus of attention, let alone talk about such things.

"Jill, I've seen thousands of men waking from their comas to find their bodies altered like mine is. Most of them found a way to commit suicide or begged to be terminated and were. I was a successful CFO, so it's easy for me to continue doing what I was trained for. As for what it's like. I continue to be a male Doll for the sake of our children. Every day, I provide encouragement and try to be a good role model for them as they grow up. That's what fathers should do for their sons and daughters, especially if they were born like Helen and I are now, because the laws won't let us give our kids the many mutation cures that are available. So I must step up and show them they can survive and do well."

"I'd say you have done just that. Let's give him a big hand."

Again the applause machine provided it. Then, Jill began with me.

"So, Molly, you are a private investigator among your many talents." I nodded. "I've just heard that you've passed your transport pilot's course and are licensed to pilot everything up to a freighter."

"Yes. True." I wasn't about to talk more than I had to.

"So why? Are you planning to join the fleet as a pilot?"

"Who knows. I've just added another ability to my skill set. Have you added any new ones lately?"

"Let's give her a big round. Ladies, the sky is your limits on what you can achieve."

Sam said even less. Then, we got a break. Jill began the contestant interviews. She began with Lenka.

"I'm twenty-two from Prague, Earth, and have just

graduated university with degree in astronomy. One day, I want fly among stars."

Jill then asked her a prepared question. "What's the most important aspect we Galactic Dolls must have?"

I expected to hear beauty, poise, elegance, something along such lines.

Lenka said, "To study much, work hard, and never give up. We can do it, only if we try."

Hey, I really liked her answer and began to pay more attention to her. Kindred spirit?

She introduced Ilse Ziegler from Brussels, Tau Ceti, a twenty-one year old with dark brown hair and brown eyes. She was in her last year studying astro-biology. She was asked the same question.

"The most important thing is to do something valuable with your life. On Brussels, we faced the Sixth Invaders and their robot army, though we didn't know they were robots then. I watched men's bodies being mutilated by these aliens. I made myself a promise that when I grew up, I'd study alien life forms so I could help defeat them in the future."

Again, I was pleasantly surprised. Perhaps these beauty pageants didn't just attract those only interested in looking beautiful. Maybe I'd been biased all my life.

Then, Jill introduced Mila Nevsky from Pylon, Epsilon Eridani, a twenty-one year old black haired beauty. Her answer again changed my budding opinion.

"We Dolls should look beautiful, bringing a touch of beauty to the world and people around us. Looking pretty, feeling pretty, being pretty makes those around you happier."

Ah, well, back to reality. I continued to pay close attention to Lenka and Ilse, though. Slowly, the afternoon passed. But I was very annoyed to have to have someone assist me with bathroom trips. I sensed the others were, too. Late in the day, Bishop check in with me.

"All okay so far?" he said.

"Yes. Annoying, but okay. I think this is nothing more than a beauty pageant."

"But Jill Koch refused to see us when we dropped by her estate in Chicago. Have you tried to read her mind?"

"No. She's entirely focused on running this pageant. If I touch her mind, that's all I'm going to pick up—show stuff. I'd have to dig deeper into her mind, and that would alert her to what I'm doing. Besides, I would never do that unless they gave me their permission or if it was a matter of life and death."

"Are you sure you haven't been programmed with our laws?" Bishop teased. "I'll continue to monitor the perimeter."

Day three dawned. As I rose, I wondered what she meant by fetish day. Anyway, we only had one more day of this to endure. As usual, over breakfast, Jill outlined how the day would go.

"First, you'll get dressed in your new fetish outfits. Yes, they'll be more difficult to manage, but this is what the audience requested last year in the after-show survey. Our audience is younger these days. Expect dressing to take Rae a bit longer today. You'll then do the promenade walk into the fetish club, complete with strobe lights and dance music. After dancing for ten minutes, you'll then walk out of the club into the foggy London street, circa 1850. It's at this point that I'll announce who is Miss Galactic Doll for 2360. She'll then continue to walk down the long boardwalk. It'll look as though throngs of clapping people are sitting on either side of the walkway. Once she's returned to the rest of the group, you'll all bunch together for a final group shot. Then, you can return to your rooms and be home by morning. On behalf of Galactic Entertainment, I want to thank you for participating in this the two hundred sixtieth Galactic Doll pageant."

We returned to our quarters. Rae posted a note on our doors to strip, so we did, waiting patiently for her to drop by. She arrived noticeably later than usual, pushing a cart filled with fetish garments: latex and rubber.

"Molly, I've checked. Isn't Leslie your sister?" I nodded. "Well, she and her husband Felix are into the fetish scene in Chicago. She would enjoy these outfits, but I should warn you. Both of you probably won't. Still, the show must go on. It'll be over in a few more hours. Again, I'll be your hands."

Rae wrapped a black and red stripped, heavily metal-boned corset around my waist. She tightened it part way, until I complained. Then, she slipped, pulled, and tugged a pair of tight plastic-like stockings up my legs, fastening them to four garters on each side. She had me sit there, trying to breathe, while she got Sam this far along, and then Helen and Casper. Only then did she return to me.

"Gotta tighten it fully now."

"What? I can't breathe as it is."

She laughed and tightened it all the way. Shallow breaths, I told myself. I couldn't even gasp now. Then, she slipped a black latex gown on me. It fit so tightly I thought she wouldn't be able to zip it up. Somehow she managed. While sitting, she laced on Oxford style black patent heels whose soles were bright red. She had me stand up and promptly attached the red-black striped outer corset. Now I couldn't breathe or bend much. Worse, this was a hobble dress or skirt that had no ease at all down to my knees. The gown flared out just above my ankles. I was just able to put one heel in front of the other, barely able to walk.

While I groaned in my misery, Rae finished doing the others, before returning and brushing out our hair. This time, Jill wanted our long hair to fall down our backs instead of having it up in high fashions.

"Molly, while I'm finishing up on the others, why don't you start walking to the stage. It'll take you much longer this time. Tiny, tiny steps."

I wanted to curse, to protest, even to scream, but I dare not. If I screamed, I'd faint. Besides, keeping my balance took my attention. If I fell over, I couldn't get back up without help. Well, I knew Leslie and Felix loved to dress up. I recalled my first meeting with Leslie outside the Lariat Club when that man shot at her. I smiled in spite of my misery. Well, I knew I wasn't alone. Sam, Helen, and Casper were shuffling along behind me, each just as miserable as I was.

Near the stage, Lenka and Ilse merged with us.

Lenka said, "We barely walk in this. Hard breathe."

"Ya, not much fun," Ilse added.

Eventually, the stage morphed into a dance studio with revolving strobe lights that reflected off our gowns. Jill halted the action briefly while assistants came by and rubbed a light oil over our outfits. When action resumed, our gowns reflected the light, bouncing light beams off each other. Okay, I had to admit it made a spectacular scene for the viewers at home. Leslie and Felix were going to love to watch us. Perhaps, when I was home sitting with them and watching us on the comm set, I'd feel better about this.

After wiggling, which passed as dancing, for about an hour while Jill ordered cameras to zoom in here and there, Jill signaled the finale set. While we stood still, gasping for breath, the stage morphed into a London street circa 1850. Fog clouds rolled in. Jill called out, "Action. Walk down the street. Don't forget to smile."

We four brought up the rear, giving us more time to recover from the dance wiggles. Something wasn't right. As I looked into the fog ahead, one by one, I saw the women slumping to the ground.

"Hey, Jill, som—" I said, but I felt weak and sleepy, so sleepy. Something was wrong, but my mind reacted so slowly. I didn't know it had hit the ground and was unconscious.

Chapter 11 Got You

I can't be being mutated again. There's nothing to mutate. So why am I unconscious. I'm not unconscious. I'm thinking. Body's knocked out. Is it dead? No, it's breathing. What's going on? What's happened? Focus, Molly, focus. We're in a real pickle. Wait, if I'm alert and thinking, I wonder if I can see and hear, too.

Whoa. Vision turned on. Seeing in a three hundred sixty degree sphere—all around me at the same instant shocked me. I finally sort of ignored everything above me by the ceiling. While not as clear as sight via my eyes, I could view what was around my unconscious body down there. I could do this because of all the therapy I'd had. I heard sounds, too, but they seemed very distant, until I realized that was because I wasn't in my body's head, but above it.

There was the stage floor, but giants moved about, laying the twenty-four contestants out in a long line. I also saw Jill's body lying there, along with Rae's and the camera crew, cook, and other helpers. I saw one giant moving down the line of women injecting them with something, refilling the syringe from a bottle. I couldn't make out the writing on the bottle, too fuzzy. He injected the contestants and then Jill.

"Yes, Morpheus said make damn sure you inject Jill Koch," another giant said.

Curiously, they didn't bother with us four. Nor did they inject Rae or the rest of the crew. I tried to work out why not, but gave up. No data.

Where was Bishop? Then, I spotted him at the very end of the line. Wait. He was moving. Ever so slowly, his body inched way towards the darkened end of the stage. Then he was gone. I counted three giants, but none of them noticed Bishop's disappearance. I wished I had a way to communicate with him, but he had no mind for me to contact, presuming I could still use my telepathy.

Two giants wheeled in an electronic device. Instantly, I recognized it. A Sixth Invaders' implant machine. We were screwed for sure. Wait, why would they want that thing? They pointed it at our line of heads. Now I saw why they lined us up as they had. They could implant everyone at one time. Shit.

The giants put on sound dampening earphones. Then stepped back and turned it on. A recording began playing on a repeat loop while we were flooded with the most aesthetic white energy, so pure, so utterly beautiful.

"I am beautiful. I am happy. The show must go on. I must finished this show."

The recording continued to repeat countless times. Soon, though, I was utterly bored with the words, focusing on just how wonderfully beautiful this white energy truly was. Then, the light faded. No, no, no, don't turn it off, I begged. When it was gone, I felt as though someone had ripped something precious from me. Then, I saw the giants aligning the device towards the heads of Rae and the other assistants.

This time, the words being repeated were shorter. "The show must go on. I must finished this show."

I doped off for a while, thinking about all this. Of course, I was beautiful. And I certainly was happy. Why wouldn't the show continue? Everyone wanted to know who would be Miss Galactic Doll 2360. We had to finish it. Besides, Jill said the next step was to reveal who won the pageant, for her to take her promenade walk, and the group photo. There wouldn't be a show if we stopped now. What a silly implant. Wholly unneeded. These giants must really be dumb.

What are they doing now? As I watched, they undid the bottom of the contestants' gowns and inserted tubes. Finally, I figured they were providing nourishment and removing bodily fluids. Why? I didn't appreciate the rough hands rolling me around while doing it to me. I doped off again.

Later, I became more aware and noticed whatever they were putting into me and my friends was different from what was being given to Jill and the contestants. Now I had something else to puzzle over. I think my thinking had become slightly off, slightly goofy. Pondering the meaning of this, I doped off again.

Aware once more, I noticed subtle changes in Jill and the others. Their arms—something was happening to their arms. They looked all skinny and crinkly. Hum. Then, I knew. Mutation comas. The giant injected them with the Armless Doll Telepath Agent. We four were already mutated, so that meant they were just keeping us in a drugged sleep. But why not mutate Rae and the rest of the crew? My muddled thinking finally concluded they were needed to finish filming the show. Duh. Feeling proud I'd deduced all this, I promptly drifted into sleep once more.

The next time I awoke, days must have passed because Jill's arms weren't there. They'd been absorbed by her body and excreted through the tubes. I could see no other changes in their bodies. All had been Galactic Dolls to begin with. This time, I didn't fall back asleep, but slowly continued to be more aware, concluding I was coming out of the drugged stupor. Maybe they were about to come out of their comas as well.

Pop. Pop. I heard a distant noise. What was it? Duh, a gunshot. Someone was shooting. My thinking still wasn't to clear. Then, I heard another pair of popping sounds. Then, another pair, these closer to me. I looked in that direction and saw a giant lying on the stage, Bishop, gun in hand, stood over him. I watched as Bishop picked up the giant's hand and dragged him off stage. He must be very strong to do that, my muddled thinking thought. Later, I realized that was the case, for he'd moved these eight-foot men into a back storage room.

An awful smell caused my head to jerk away from it. I was back inside my head looking out my eyes, seeing clearly again. That was a relief. Bishop stood over me, a smelly rag in hand.

"Ah, you're awake. The giants who did this are dead. GD has sent a large security force, but per the recordings played into the implant machine, I believe it's best if the show continues."

"Oh, of course, the show must go on. I must finished this show. Oh, they've been mutated."

Now that was the silliest thing I've said in a long while. Chalk it up to just waking from being drugged unconscious for eight days. Bishop helped me sit up, which I barely could in this restrictively tight outfit. I watched as he revived Helen, Sam, and Casper. Then, he revived Rae and the camera crew.

"Oh my god," Rae said. "But the show must go on. I'll need to touch up their makeup. Guys, get the stage ready for the last scene. London 1850."

Slowly the others woke from their comas. Rae and Bishop helped each into a sitting position, for everyone was too groggy to stand in these fetish outfits. Normally, I would have expected shrill screams of shock and terror from the twenty-five new victims. Yes, each cried out in shock, but only briefly before reciting, "I am beautiful. I am happy. The show must go on. I must finished this show."

Repeatedly, we heard these words being spoken by the twenty-five women. Finally, I recovered fully and made a key decision.

"Bishop, get everyone on their feet. Tell them the show must go on." While he and Rae did as I asked, I spoke to Jill.

"Jill, you know the show must go on. We have to finish the show. We're getting up now. What do we have to do to finish the show? Help us finish the show."

I kept punching in the implanted behavior, hoping it would override the shock and waves of terror beginning to form on her and on the contestants, particularly now that they were upright, fighting to keep their balance.

For once, an implant actually helped us, though I knew it would make subsequent therapy sessions drastically more difficult for these people. Jill's body shook uncontrollably, but she kept saying, "I am beautiful. I am happy. The show must go on. I must finished this show."

Having run this program for so many years had to have helped, for she barked orders, as though running on an automatic script. The camera crew jumped to obey, also muttering the show must go on. Rae and two assistants dashed down the line of contestants, making adjustments, zipping up the gowns, and so on. When she finished with us, the fog machine began pumping out fog. The final stage checked out. Jill called for action.

As each contestant began walking as Jill instructed, albeit minuscule steps, she continued to whisper the implanted words. Lenka stood in front of me, the last in line. Her body continued to shake nervously, while she whispered the four sentences repeatedly, as though they would make everything all right. Of course, it didn't; it only masked the entire trauma, both physical and emotional, which had often caused victims to find ways to die. I just hoped this scene was a short one.

Music played and we shuffled along barely six inches a step, if that. Even though I wasn't touching their minds, fear and terror radiated from the twenty-four women and Jill. Helen, Casper, and Sam mumbled the show must go on, but their faces showed their annoyance with the fetish look. I suppose mine did too.

Her voice shaking slightly, Jill continued to direct this penguin-like walk. When the music climaxed, she signaled us to halt in a line. Jill insisted Helen and Casper continue walking to the other end of the line of women.

"Now comes the time everyone's been waiting for. Who's going to be the Miss Galactic Doll for 2360? First runner up is Miss Ilse Ziegler of Brussels, Tau Ceti."

A big round of applause from the machine thundered in our ears, while Rae rushed up and put a banner over her and replaced the tiara with a small crown.

"Now for the big moment. This year's Miss Galactic Doll is Mila Nevsky of Pylon, Epsilon Eridani."

While the applause machine added it's illusion to the mix, Rae hastily put a large banner around Mila and a large crown on her head, replacing the sparking tiara. I felt sympathy for her. Her body nervously shaking from the suppressed terror, Mila continued to whisper the sentences as she made her walk down the victory promenade, accompanied by rousing music.

"Cut. That's a wrap," Jill said on automatic.

When minds registered the show had finished, panic ensued as the implant broke down. Grief, fear, terror, shocking loss— these struck with hurricane-like force. Shrieks and wails predominated. Rae and the crew had no idea what to do, but Bishop did.

He ordered, "Quick. Get them to their dressing rooms and out of these fetish clothes."

Rae responded by leading Sam. I followed him, hoping the others would follow. They didn't. The twenty-five no longer could control their bodies well enough to maneuver in these outfits. Many fell to the stage and thrashed about. Many now gasped for air, exhausted from their screaming. Some fainted. Bishop picked up Lenka and carried her to her room. Rae and the crew emulated him, carrying another four to their rooms.

Soon Sam and I were naked and felt far more comfortable, sending Rae on to help the next ones to undress. We stacked our original clothes onto the dressing machine. I went first. Dressed and relaxed, I went next door to check on Helen, who all ready had called GD back in Chicago and also GD LA.

"We'll have help here shortly. I do look good don't I?" Helen shook her head.

"Implant, Helen. I'll get it run out of you and Casper as soon as possible. It should be pretty benign now."

"Okay, but let's get this show on the road. Now why did I say that? Jill Koch was under our surveillance as one of the terrorists. I think we can rule her out, unless this Morpheus double crossed her."

"Glad I brought Bishop along. He terminated the giants before they could abduct us. Close call," I said. "You're right. We need to get this show going. Darn it. That's what I'm compelled to say. But we should give everyone therapy sessions quickly."

"It's going to be grim. They can't return to their home worlds now. That's the law. Keep this genetic mutation from spreading beyond Earth," she said.

"Let's take them to our mansion. We've got extra rooms between us. I'll have Celeste get session givers lined up when we get back."

Her phone rang. "Okay, the Airliner is ready. All we have to do is get these women to LAX. Considering the shape they're in, can they walk on their own?"

"Do we have enough people with arms to steady them?" I asked.

"I'll make it happen. The show must go on," Helen said. Casper nodded his agreement.

With minutes, strong arms steadied the terrified women, as they walked the short distance out of the studio and up the EMAC ramp. There LA GD security men assisted us, even though I kept saying I didn't need the assistance. Rae stayed behind to prepare the final video, which GEnt planned to show in two days.

A doctor with a staff of six waited for us at LAX Spaceport. He examined the twenty-five women and found their health good. But he gave each a sedative so they'd sleep during the trip back to Chicago; he'd seen many coming out of these mutation comas earlier this year.

During the flight, I called Celeste, who promised to have enough therapy givers available when we returned. Then, I gave Sam a therapy session to erase the implant the giants had given him and the effects of the drug. Since that went without difficulty, I did the same to Helen and then Casper. All three laughed when the incident erased. Each saw what the effects of that implant had been, not only on their own reactions, but more importantly on the other women. An interesting side-effect happened. The effects my own trauma pretty much vanished, though later Celeste ran me though it as a precaution. I discovered handling other people's traumas gave me power over my own situation. How interesting.

Since Chicago was still an hour away, I chatted with Bishop. "So I take it none of those giants was the elusive Morpheus."

"Right. ID cards declared them citizens of Liatos-D. I suspect Morpheus is also an alien and not an immigrant.

Helen's people did detect an unidentified transport ship descending towards LAX Spaceport, but it dropped into hyperspace when the control tower challenged it. I conclude my interrupted their plans. Might have been interesting if they'd identified themselves."

"Excellent work. You kept us from being abducted and sold. Thanks. I owe you."

"We all owe you, Bishop," Helen said. Sam and Casper echoed her words.

***

When we landed at New O'Hare, Celeste met us, along with a dozen others. We took Lenka, Ilse, Jill, and ten others to our estate, while Helen and Casper took the rest to their mansion.

"Thanks for putting them to bed, sis. We really needed your arms tonight," I said.

"It's going to be rough on everyone for at least a week. Isn't Jill the woman you suspected of being a terrorist?" she said.

"Yes, so I plan on running her therapy sessions. We have to stop Morpheus and his giants. We also befriended Lenka and Isle. I see great potential in both them."

"Okay. We'll be here early to help get them dressed and fed. Expect therapy to be rough, what with all the suppression of their emotions along with the implanted words."

Chaos reigned the next morning as we handled their basic needs. It didn't help that their emotions turned on full when they awoke. Grief, fear, terror, helplessness, and enforced manic behavior mixed a potent cocktail. Nikita and Matt calmed the women with their charm and youth. Once they'd eaten well, the therapy sessions began.

I handled Jill Koch. Surprising me, Nikita wanted to help Lenka, while Matt chose to work with Ilse. Some of Celeste's associates dealt with the other eight women.

Days passed as I ran Jill through the awful trauma. Each day, we recovered more details. The implanted words blew off first. Then, she pierced the veil of unconsciousness, shrieking when she contacted the excruciating pain of her

133

arms being dissolved, reabsorbed by her body. I knew this wasn't the basic trauma. She had already had the Galactic Doll mutation, probably years ago.

Thus, when no further details appeared, I asked for a similar trauma that happened earlier and ran smack into that one. As I expected, that one erased fairly rapidly. With the pain and emotional loss gone, she became alert to the present time and laughed.

"That wasn't supposed to happen. I've been tricked. Morpheus was out to get me. He ordered me to invite the four of you and arranged that last scene of the London fog. I had no idea he planned to mutate all of us. My god, Molly, if Bishop hadn't stopped them, we'd have been taken to some world and sold a slave telepaths."

I grinned, proof I'd been right about her all along. "Okay, you best tell me all you know about Morpheus and what your plans were and are now. Honestly, you'll fare much better if you don't withhold anything."

"I feel so relieved and frightened at the same time. I can see now how foolish I've been. It began when Senator Wyman paid me a visit. He knew I was keenly interested in supporting genetic research into finding cures for these Sixth Invader mutations. He convinced me that billions of credits would speed up research ten-fold. 'There's another way we can pull in the kind of funds such research costs.' I believed him, especially since almost no cures were available back then.

"He had this business associate who had a way for us to make hundreds of billions of credits in a year, all of which I could donate to Earth's geneticists to help finance their research and development. It sounded ideal back then. Only later when I learned how he planned to make this money did I try to back out. He threatened to expose me, forcing me to go along with the plan. I figured the loss of a few thousand people balanced the cures for three billion of us.

"Now I'm one. I'm terrified. How can we even live like this? I know you'll have to turn me over to the Senior Judge. Oh how I hope she'll have me terminated and confiscate my fortune. With luck, she'll donate it all to genetic research."

"I doubt she'll terminate you. Your next step is to watch hours and hours of how-to videos, the very ones the Sixth Invaders collected up for our men to watch, had their mutation actually worked seven years ago. One more thing, this Morpheus giant. How do we contact him? How does he contact you? Who are the four other men involved in the plot?"

"Oh, you mean Moe, Larry, Curly, and Doc. I don't know their real names. I have suspicions, but I've never met them socially. We get secure emails telling us about meetings—where and when. Morpheus always contacts us. We have no way to contact him, except by return email. I've his address on my computer, only now I can't even operate it. Maybe you can have Lara drop by my place and get it for you."

How did she know my dwarf's name? I hadn't introduce them because Lara worked in the background, cooking and running my household while I worked on these therapy sessions. Jill had volunteered an awful lot of information, incriminating information, but I felt confident I'd erased the trauma arising from the mutations. I sighed and placed the call to the Senior Judge, who insisted I bring her in to her court in the GPan building.

"This is so scary," Jill said. Mid-afternoon, I took her on the MTES down to the Loop for her appointment with the judge. This being her first time outside since the mutation, I sensed her feelings of helplessness, her fears. Yes, those could be addressed by many more therapy sessions, but I didn't want to do that. She'd been behind doing this to thousands.

"It's not fun, but you can do it. Just don't fall down. I've no way to help you back up." Okay, I admit that wasn't a nice thing to say to her—to anyone who had just had their world turned on end—but she was one of the six who set up this disastrous plan to make and sell us.

Before the Senior Judge, Jill repeated her story. Almost word for word. That bothered me. A person in therapy never recited the incident the same way unless they weren't actually in the incident. "Oh, I fell down and broke my arm. That's all. Nothing happened." When someone tells me that, I know they aren't in the incident, because breaking an arm *is* painful.

"Miss Jill Koch, that's an admission of your guilt in this affair. I order you to take security men to your home and give them this laptop so GD can track this Morpheus giant. I'm not going to terminate you, for that would be letting you off far too easy. You are hereby sentenced to this lifetime as an armless Doll. You cannot have any of the cures until your body reaches the biological age of sixty-five. Any attempt to terminate yourself will result in your being injected with this bio agent again, rejuvenating your body back to around twenty-five. Further, any funds you have or will acquire from this venture will be given back to all the many victims of these attacks. In addition, since you are already wealthy and since you inherited much of that wealth, only half must be immediately donated to these many victims. The rest goes to finding genetic cures. Guards, accompany Jill Koch to her home and return with that laptop. Case is closed."

A guard in a GPan purple uniform marched her out, while I returned home alone. Something wasn't right, but I wasn't sure what. Once home, the plight of the other dozen women swept up all my attention for subsequent days. I took over Lenka's therapy sessions. I'd grown fond of this young blonde with the most gorgeous blue eyes. Maybe because she'd just graduated with an astronomy degree or that she want to fly among stars. Sam couldn't stop talking about the space navigation course he'd completed, the one she wanted to take.

I learned she'd tried out for the Miss Galactic Doll pageant because of the prize money. Sadly, her parents worked for Galactic Housing in Prague, maintaining old buildings, meaning they were low IQ people. They'd jumped at the chance to work for double wages on Felt-D. Home wasn't the same after her folks left, and she needed the prize money to tide her over until she found sponsorship and a job. She hadn't won, and her prospects for a job had vanished with her arms or so she believed. I just couldn't send her back to Prague alone, broke, and more or less helpless. I invited her to stay with us and take the navigation course, once she learned to effectively use her toes and feet.

Helen became an activist for the other contestants. Ilse did receive the second place prize money, ten thousand credits, and advanced degree offers, dependent upon her actually being able to work in her field of astro-biology. So we took her under our wings, too. Mila had her crown and first prize of twenty-five thousand credits, and GEnt promised she would have a normal, full reign as Miss Galactic Doll 2360, but she had to be able to sign autographs.

Unfortunately, laws pushed through by other members of the Sol Empire dictated these women couldn't return to their home worlds. I understood why. These mutations were dominant over normal human genes, so if they returned to their worlds and had children, they'd only spread the mutation there. These women felt a double whammy, wanting to go home but unable and not wanting to spread the awful mutation to their world.

GEnt came to their rescue by offering them employment as fashion models with the proviso they had to learn to be somewhat independent before they could begin work. They were also free to accept any corporation's offer of a telepath's job. That they had a monthly stipend coming in truly helped these women, removing one fear. As the early days of September came and went, one by one, these women resettled around Chicago.

Sam helped Ilse move into one of the older condos that we'd lived in and got her enrolled in her last year of college. She only had one more year to go to finish her astro-biology degree. And Sam promised to help her whenever she needed help. Because there were so many others like her staying in these condos, she found instant companionship.

By September 15, only Lenka remained living with

us. Our children were back in school. Sam returned to his job at the UIC library, leaving me to work with Lenka, helping her practice life skills so that she had a chance of passing the navigator course.

Chapter 12 Boom

I checked with Helen to find out if they had gotten any clues to the mysterious Morpheus from Jill's laptop. Unfortunately, they hadn't, but her technicians continued to work on it. For a moment, I felt the loss of Ted, my first husband. He would have cracked her laptop long before now or so I believed.

"Why you walking in circles?" asked Lenka.

"Am I? Oh, just worried." I sat down. "It's mid-September. That's kind of when I estimated the terrible attack would come."

"What attack? Haven't you stopped the terrorists?"

"We got Senator Wyman. His plan was to flee Earth on October 31. The other men we suspect might have been involved are now off-world. Anyway, working back under the premise that the world he wanted to migrate to, this Merlin-C, required he had hundreds of billions of credits in an account with them, that some of the victims would have had to have been sold and his share of the funds deposited into his account. Working back all those details suggests their main attack would happen about now."

Lenka giggled. "Well, guess we won't have to worry about being mutated. We already are."

"Yes, but if half Chicago goes into a coma, how are we going to stop giants from barging in here and carrying us off? When I had arms, I used my gun to kill the giants who tried to abduct Sam. Now all I can do is kick them. Hardly effective. No, if that attack comes, we could be screwed."

I wanted her to grasp the severity of the threat. She sobered up.

Bishop dropped by. "Molly, I've been monitoring the spaceports around the world like you suggested. An anomaly has appeared."

"Oh?" I looked at him curiously. Was doom upon us after all?

"During the past week, twenty-five transport ships from Liatos-D have landed at New O'Hare. Some have unloaded cargo. Mostly non-perishable foods and native apparel. Reasonable imports for the immigrant giants. Still, we've never had this many transports in one place at one time. Anomaly, right?"

"More like a harbinger," I said. "Phone: call Helen."

"I've alerted her, per your request."

"Phone: cancel call. Good thinking. I hope she contacts Admiral Rossi. This could be the big one, Bishop. God, I hope not."

"Don't worry. I won't let anyone abduct you."

"Times like these I feel so darn useless. Being handicapped sucks when there's a crisis."

Lenka chuckled nervously. "Doesn't it suck all the time? It does with me."

***

At New O'Hare, a deep space transport parked in Bay 206. Captain Thanos looked at his watch, then his crew.

"Okay boys. It's almost time. You've got the boss's orders. She doesn't want any foul ups this time. Stay alert. Shoot to kill. Remember, bring back twenty-five hundred. If you don't, she'll have your hide."

His fellow captains nodded and headed off to man their ships. *She sure as hell won't get their hides. Not now. In fact, she's going to be part of the twenty-five hundred. Why split the profits, eh? Thanos, you're a genius.*

"Kratos, you got everything ready to go? No frack ups allowed. Not this trip. We're going to be fabulously wealthy."

"All set. Don't worry. We've got everything covered. Diversion strike is set for three this afternoon. Main one is at midnight, and Squad Six will fetch her here as she desired. We got this, captain."

"Yeah, well, I'll rest easier when we're on our way. Remember, don't knock her out unless you have too. We have to let her think she's still our boss for a bit longer."

***

"Molly, it's happened again. Terrorist have just struck the

140

GPan skyscraper. I tried my best to get people temporarily moved out of there, but some refused to budge. All of the Investigation and Justice Department personnel are there, along with some obstinate GPan personnel. I've got emergency personnel in bio containment suits going through the building floor by floor, along with well armed GD giant guards. One of my giants managed to turn off the flow of the aerosolized agent in the air filtration system, but that was too late. Many are in comas now."

"How did it happen?"

"Three giants got visitor passes to view the many Sol Empire displays on the main floor. Somehow they got into the basement and sabotaged the air filtration system, infecting all hundred stories. Thank heavens the building is only partially occupied. What bothers me is that these giants left behind a valid ID card that allowed them janitorial access to the basement. I've got people trying to trace that ID card back to its owner. It's a generic pass, unfortunately."

"Okay. Stay alert. Let me know how many victims we have this time. Any signs the giants are going to kidnap the victims?"

"Nothing yet. Seems to be just another terrorist attack."

Why didn't I agree with her assessment? Probably because it was mid-September. "Phone: call Celeste. Hi. Have you heard the news? The GPan skyscraper has been attacked with the mutation agent."

"Not again. Okay, let me know the number of victims. We'll try to line up enough therapy givers, if there aren't too many victims. I'll coordinate with Leslie and also Galactic Robotics. They'll need clothing and the many machines, if they don't already have them. Keep me posted. Yes, it's just now coming on Channel Nine news. Bye."

Lenka sighed. "Molly, I feel so useless. Can I possibly learn how to do this therapy thing of yours? I can't do much else to help."

"Sure. It's not hard. Maybe there won't be thousands of victims this time. So where are the giants? Why aren't they trying to abduct them? I don't get it. They aren't following their usual pattern. Why attack if they aren't going to try to abduct the victims? Something is off, Lenka. Really off."

Bishop said, "I've sent word to others I have watching New O'Hare. Let me check with them."

I watched as he pretended to send and receive text messages. I knew he had electronic means of communicating with the other human-looking robots. Though he never said, I suspected he had one watching the many giants and their transports at the spaceport.

"No activity there at all," he reported. "I would have expected something from them. Ah, look. Channel Nine is showing some of the victims being recovered from the building. This definitely doesn't fit their pattern. I'm confused."

All afternoon, we watched the news. Emergency crews continued to enter the building, only to exit much later carrying another comatose victim, taking them off to one of the Med Centers or hospitals. With so many victims, the emergency crews spread them out, avoiding overloading any one facility. They were still removing people when I went to bed around ten.

"Molly. Molly, wake up!" Bishop said. He rocked my body slightly, as though unsure how to wake a person.

"It's happening. Big attack. North Chicago. The wealthiest homes. Twenty block wide path."

"Shit! Help me dress."

***

Captain Thanos watched the specially rigged EMACs lift off, heading for North Chicago. Centuries ago the suburb of Glenview had been transformed into hundreds of very exclusive estates, home to many of Chicago's wealthiest people. The smallest of these occupied a city block, while some took up four such blocks. He and the boss lady had discussed at length where to launch their first major strike. She'd warned him about the low IQ people.

"Look, no one's going to buy a stupid moron, even it they have telepathic skills. So we go where those people

142

aren't. The ritzy estates of North Chicago," she told him.

Together, they picked out this twenty-block wide swatch some four miles long. She computed the total number of people in the area and ordered Thanos to bring twenty-five transports, staggering their arrivals to avoid drawing suspicions.

As he watched the EMAC lift off, he redid the calculation in his head. He was good with figures. Twenty-five hundred times one million credits each yielded two and a half trillion credits. She, of course, expected to receive half of this, but Thanos had other plans. He grinned, waiting an hour before sending off the squad to pick her up. He muttered. "Play along a few more hours, Thanos." Then, he laughed.

The EMAC's boom covered one block, so twenty passes would have been required, far too long. Thus, the giants stole five EMACs, modified them in an abandoned warehouse, and had flown them here minutes ago where they filled them up with the mutation agent. Each had to make four passes. Using the GPS nav system, each flew one four mile long path before turning around and flying a slightly overlapping route. Each flew down and back twice before returning to New O'Hare, where the giants quickly removed the booms, readying them to transport the victims.

When Thanos heard the EMACs had begun their first pass, he ordered Squad Six to fetch their boss from her home. He watched the action on a small streaming video monitor. His men reached the gates and guard house, where they knocked out the giant on duty. Despite the boss's orders to kill the guard, Thanos refused to kill his own kind. She was just a human. Shortly, he watched them carrying her out of the mansion. One rested her body over his shoulder as they jogged to the waiting EMAC.

"Put me down," she said. The giant carried her down to the tarmac before setting her down.

She breathed deeply. "Captain Thanos, are we on schedule? Problems? Following my plan to the letter?"

"Yes, boss. They're finishing up the second pass now.

Be back here shortly. Going just as you ordered."

"Good. Ah, here they come. How long to remove the booms and get them ready to go back and grab the merchandise?"

"Ten minutes. Relax. Nothing is going to go wrong this time. I don't see why you had to get yourself mutated."

"They were getting too close to me. I was under constant surveillance. All because that foolish Senator Wyman got himself caught and the other men panicked and fled the Earth. Well, Thanos, you and I are going to be fabulously wealthy very, very soon. You figured out what to do with your trillion credits?" she said.

"Not yet. Don't count your credits until they're in your account. That's my motto. How are you going to spend it? You're darn near helpless now."

"Not a problem. I hired a personal live-in assistant, who'll find herself like me when she comes out of her coma. Once I'm off-world, I'll buy the arm regrow cure. I'll be back to normal in no time. Although I do have to admit I had no idea of the pain we go through while we're in comas. Guess that's why we're in comas while mutating. Captain Thanos, two and a half trillion credits here we come. Say, are the implant machines on each of your ships programmed and ready to go? My implant idea worked beautifully at the Galactic Doll pageant. It kept their shock and terror at bay. We want them to always obey their new owners and not cause trouble. Lordy, I don't want to give refunds."

"No refunds. Yeah, your recording has been copied and installed in each implant machine. All has been taken care of just like you ordered. Relax. They're off."

He smiled as the EMACs headed out to begin bringing back the victims to the transports.

***

Dressed, I called Helen. "Do you—"

"Yes, we're on it," Helen said. "Can't talk now. Time is critical. Comm channel 42. Later."

"She knows about it, Bishop. Tune on Comm channel 42 for me, please. Never heard of that one."

"It's a military-only line. She's authorized you.

Interesting. Isn't that Admiral Rossi's voice?"

"Yeah, think so."

"We're on it. All cruisers and my battleship will be above them in ten. Contacted New O'Hare control tower. They're quietly moving their personnel off to the southern tarmac refueling station. General Blythe, how soon will your forces be in position?"

I heard Bev's voice replying and cheered. "ETA fifteen. Don't want to spook 'em. Are you sure we have to take prisoners?"

"Shoot to disable, not kill. I want to question them, General Blythe."

"Aye, sir. Relaying that now." She sounded terribly disappointed.

I heard Helen's voice. "My people are calculating an estimate on victims based on the area of the attack. They hit the wealthiest Chicagoans this time. So we get a break. Had they hit the main residential blocks, we'd have tens of thousands of victims. The estimates range between two and three thousand people. I'll start lining up medical facilities for them. If it had been twenty thousand, we simply couldn't handle them."

Silence reigned for a few minutes. That's when I realized I was listening in to real time conversations. The events happened as I heard them.

Bishop gave me a funny look, one I couldn't decipher. "Molly, my spy just recorded a conversation out at New O'Hare. I think you should hear this and then decide what to do."

He took my phone, dialed a number. "Bishop here. Go ahead and replay what you've recorded."

"This dish microphone worked well, Bishop. I'm a mile from them. Here goes."

"Captain Thanos, are we on schedule? Problems? Following my plan to the letter?"

"My god! That's Jill Koch's voice," I said.

"Yes, boss. They're finishing up the second pass now. Be back here shortly. Going just as you ordered."

I listened to their short conversation, including how

she'd played us all with the fake attack on the pageant.

"Get a copy of that to Helen Hugo, CEO of GD."

The voice acknowledged my request.

"Bishop, looks like Jill took me for a ride. I should have—well, I don't know what I should've done."

"Hey, she played everyone. So this Morpheus doesn't even exist. Incredible. She's had us chasing a fictitious giant for months."

"I feel like such a fool. I missed the signs. They were right there when I finished up her therapy session."

"This PI business is very challenging. Not logical. Hard to calculate. To compute."

I sighed. "True, Bishop. Some is mundane legwork, but without intuition—oh! I see what you mean. Sorry. Still, you've saved me and many thousands too. Don't be hard on yourself."

"I won't if you won't."

I smiled. The perfect thing to say. I admired his programming.

***

Admiral Rossi stared down at the 3-d display on the battle board in his Comm and Control Center in his battleship. Highlighted in red were the group of transports parked in the long-term area on the northern edge of New O'Hare Spaceport. Small green delta shapes represented his cruisers, light and heavy, in high, stationary orbits. His combat officers issued orders to the commanders of the cruisers, coordinating the expected attack.

Someone brought him a hot coffee, and he rubbed his face, getting the grit out of his eyes. He glanced at the clock. 01:30 a.m. Helen Hugo had warned him to be prepared for an emergency attack that could come anytime from mid-September on. Admiral Rossi thought that might be happening when GPan was attacked in the afternoon, but nothing had come of it. So he'd gone to bed, annoyed that yet another terrorist attack had occurred on his watch.

Then Helen's frantic call came a half-hour ago. That he'd gotten most of the empire's cruisers here and on target in so short a time pleased him. Efficiency. He'd drilled that into all his commanders. This time, he told himself, we're going to put an end to these terrorists. One by one, his officers reported their cruiser commander had calculated a firing solution to their enemy transport parked on the tarmac miles below.

His second in command looked up from the display. "Admiral, all twenty-five transports are targeted. Firing solutions are locked and ready for your order."

"Excellent. Have everyone standby but don't lose their firing lock." He picked up a special phone. "General Blythe, we have firing locks on all transports. If they fire up their engines, we'll blow them up. Awaiting your orders."

"All right. Time to kick giant ass. They're using five stolen EMACs to transport unconscious victims from North Chicago here. We're going to take them down when all five EMACs are here. Don't want to lose one. Stand by."

"Regimental commanders, check in," she ordered. "Goddamn darkness. Can't see a thing on these screens."

Lieutenant Gail, her aide and mate, said, "Night vision will be activated soon. Patience."

"Can't believe we're gonna get them this time. Way too many victims. Wow. Now that's a whole lot better. The IR overhead drone's image is on screen now."

"General, all five EMACs have landed," an aide said.

"Now. All squads: move in and attack. Remember, shoot to maim, not kill unless you have to. The human traitor Jill Koch is to be captured alive. Admiral Rossi, it's a go here. All right!" Bev saw gun muzzle flashes and stopped looking at the screens and gazed longingly out onto the dimly illuminated expansive tarmac. "I hate being stuck back here, Gail. I really miss rushing into battle leading my company. This general thing sucks."

I grinned as I watched this unfold on this special comm channel.

Lieutenant Gail chuckled. "Yeah, but you aren't likely to be killed either. And I like that and so does Sasha."

Bev grunted, but continued to watch, frustrated she couldn't do more, even though she had her gun drawn and cocked. Fat chance the giants would storm her command center in the forest preserve north of the spaceport.

***

Captain Thanos watched the first five EMACs landing close to their designated transports. Giants stepped down the bay ramps, carrying comatose victims tossed over their shoulders.

Standing beside him, Jill smiled and continued to try to maintain her balance, which she found more difficult than she'd expected. This whole mutation experience had taken its toll on her, far worse than she'd expected or even allowed for in her planning. Weeks ago when she finalized the plans for this attack with Captain Thanos, she knew she had to do something to throw suspicion off herself. Her spies inside GD alerted her to Helen's belief that she was involved in the conspiracy, thanks to Molly Parkinson's investigations.

Thus, she'd devised the Miss Galactic Doll pageant attack, making sure both Helen and Molly were present. That she would get mutated herself should throw suspicion off her; she'd be a victim. However, her original plan called for the giants to abduct Helen and Molly along with most of the contestants. Just how her giants had missed Bishop eluded her. Still, she found it impossible not to play the victim. Life had become a living nightmare—Molly and her how-to videos notwithstanding. Still, Jill knew she'd soon be back to normal. One of her contacts in GMed had already given her several syringes with the known cures.

As soon as she lifted off, she planned to have Captain Thanos inject her with the arm regrow cure. Once that mutation completed, she would decide whether to reduce her impressive bosom. She always wore tall heels anyway. Soon, she thought I'll be inside and can sit down. I can't show him weakness.

"The spaceport is surrounded by the First Infantry Divison. Surrender and you'll not be shot."

Someone yelled these orders over a megaphone amplifier. It was so loud Jill wished she could cover her ears to dampen it out like Captain Thanos did.

Hundreds of giants frantically looked in all

148

directions before bolting towards their transports. Any control Captain Thanos had vanished. He, too, turned and dashed towards his ship, some twenty feet from where Jill stood.

As Jill tried to grasp what was happening, massive gunfire erupted around her. Tracer shots arced. Hundreds of muzzle flashes looked like flashing Christmas lights. She saw Captain Thanos fall down just as he reached the ramp. Bleeding from a leg wound, he continued crawling up the ramp.

Jill wanted to join him, her ride to safety, because the giants had already stowed her backpack with the precious cures in it inside his transport. In her heels, she couldn't run. Terrified of losing her balance, she walked very slowly, constantly flailing her non-existent arms to help.

"No!" she screamed. She watched helplessly as the bay door slowly closed. Even if she could reach the ship, she couldn't get in. Captain Thanos must have reached the cockpit, for she heard the engines firing up. Her heart sank. How had this perfect plan gone so wrong?

Boom! A laser cannon blast arced down from somewhere far overhead, disintegrating part of the ship's rear engine. The concussion shock from a secondary blast knocked her off her feet. Her head struck the tarmac. Her world went black.

***

"Fire at will," General Blythe said. After the captain yelled the surrender order, she saw the giants trying to flee. Hundreds of soldiers opened fire. Her squads directed their fire to specific transport groups. Bev punched her fists into the air. "Go get 'em!"

Then, she remembered Admiral Rossi and notified him.

He laughed. "We're seeing the fireworks up here."

As Bev and Gail watched from their secure position, both saw the laser beams arcing down, followed by loud explosions.

"Blast 'em to oblivion!" Bev said.

"I think this time we're gonna win," Gail said.

"Oh, nearly forgot. Phone: call Helen. Hi, we're attacking them, blowing up transports and all. They aren't going to be going back to grab victims. So you can get your rescue people in there now. Full report shortly. We got 'em good this time. They can't get away. Wow. There goes another ship up in smoke. You did good, really good."

"Okay, sending in the emergency crews with their bio containment suits and a small army of dwarves who are immune. Remember, we want Jill taken alive. Keep me posted."

Gail and Bev continued to watch the fireworks, but soon stillness fell. The night took over once more.

"Okay, general. Time to join our troops," Lieutenant Gail said. She and Bev, along with ten HQ staff took an EMAC over the short distance to the spaceport. As they walked down the bay ramp, squads had already begun setting up strong field lights. Giants, mostly wounded, lay scattered about the tarmac, and six transports were smoking, their main engines destroyed. Already division medics could be seen carrying comatose victims out of the stolen and now damaged EMACs, depositing them in divisional vehicles.

A captain said, "General Blythe, we found a hundred twenty-five victims in the EMACs. Where do we take them?"

"Call Helen Hugo. She's controlling that part of this operation. Found our traitor, Jill Koch?"

"Yes, medic is tending her now. Slight concussion. The engine explosion knocked her down."

"Make sure she's arrested. Keep her under guard at all times."

"What do we do about the wounded giants? There's hundreds of them."

"I'd just as soon terminate them, but patch them up for now. Get me an accurate count. It'll be Helen's call. But if they try anything, terminate them. Spread the word. Damn aliens."

Her soldiers brought order to the chaos. Several

carried Jill Koch up to her and stood her before General Bev. The woman had a bandage on her forehead.

"Gotcha traitor," Bev said. "You'll never mutate another person ever again."

"Terminate me. Please. I beg you. Just terminate me."

"Fat chance. In fact, Helen ordered me to bring along a red bag and inject you with the mutation agent if you got seriously injured. No, you're screwed big time, bitch."

"I can't live like this. Just kill me."

"No way."

"But think of the thousands of innocent people I've turned into armless Dolls, ruining their lives."

"You'll get yours."

"Think about those we've already abducted and sold off-world."

General Bev drew her Glock, pointed it at Jill. Gail gasped. At the last instant, she popped the clip and ejected the round.

"I'd love to terminate you, traitorous bitch, but they have other ideas for you. Can't let you off so damned easy. Haven't you figured this out from therapy sessions? I kill you now and you go pick up the next baby body around here. You'll be back in the game right away. No way am I giving you that easy way out. You've ruined so damned many lives. You need to experience what you've caused, if you ask me. But then, I'm not the Senior Judge. 'Course, she's in a coma now. Guess you'll have to wait a while to find out your punishment."

Gail said, "I hope they take away all your money and give it to those you've harmed. Let you then make a living like the rest of us. Oh, guess you'll find that a bit difficult to do. No one will hire you as a telepath, that's for sure. Maybe you can wipe windows or something. Hell, not even sure how you could do that."

Bev said, "Phone: call Helen. Hi. Got the traitor here. She wanted me to kill her. Ha. So where do we deposit her? Wrapping up here. Lot of wounded alien giants, though.

Can't we just terminate them?"

"Well done, general. Have someone bring her to GD. I guess there never was a Morpheus. I'd just as soon have them terminated, too, but I've got a call in to their ambassador. Will get back to you when I know what we're to do with them. Kill them if they try anything at all. Bye."

"I'll take her to GD, Bev," Gail said. "Will you be okay without me for a bit?"

"Sure. We've made Chicago safe for Sasha tonight."

"Okay, traitor. Move it. That way," Gail pointed to their EMAC.

"It's hard for me to walk that far," Jill said.

Her body shook slightly. Bev noticed that and smirked.

Having gotten a field report on the number of mutation victims found in North Chicago, Bev muttered. "Twenty-five hundred more lives ruined. Damn. I wish we could have known when and where they were striking so we could've stopped them sooner. Still, Helen called this one right. Caught the bastards in the act. Maybe this'll put an end to these terrorist attacks."

Chapter 13 Reactions

At first light, Channel Nine News covered the aftermath of the attack, showing panoramas of the transports on the tarmac, some damaged. GEnt reporters interviewed both General Blythe and Admiral Rossi, but Bev gave more interesting commentary. Finally, Helen took to the air.

"Hello. I'm Helen Hugo, CEO of GD Sol Empire. As you've been hearing, last night the terrorists we've been battling for months attacked a twenty block wide-four mile long section of North Chicago, home of the wealthiest estates. Molly Parkinson and I have been keeping close watch on the suspected ringleaders, five of whom have fled Earth's jurisdiction. We're in the process of tracking them down and filing extradition papers to bring them to justice.

"Last night's attack had long been anticipated. But we didn't know when or where it would occur, so we've had our forces in readiness for many days. Admiral Rossi had our space fleet on high alert, ready to respond within minutes of the attack. General Blythe had the First Infantry Division mobilized and ready to deploy. All we could do was monitor and wait until they attacked. Our first clue that it would soon happen came when twenty-five transport ships from Liatos-D arrived during the last ten days. I directed the control tower to park them at a far end of New O'Hare, in case we had to attack them.

"As you know, GPan was attacked early yesterday. We now know that was a distraction to get our attention focused in the wrong place. I'm happy to report we didn't fall for it. In the middle of the night, we got word five EMACs flew over North Chicago releasing a gas. I sent in dwarven security guards who reported this was a major attack. We now know two thousand five hundred six men, women, and children are in comas. Yes, they used the usual Armless Doll Telepath Agent on them. At this point, we're still working on contacting next of kin and have them spread out among area hospitals and Med Centers.

"One of our spies recorded Mata Hari talking with her giant representative. I'll play it for you shortly. When they began to transport the victims to the spaceport to abduct them, take them off-world, and sell them as slave telepaths, I ordered the strike. General Blythe insisted on a combined arms approach which worked well. Her force engaged the giants, shooting to wound them, not to kill them. A few made it into their transports and attempted to take off. Admiral Rossi and his overhead fleet of cruisers shot out the engines of six transports attempting to take off.

"We've arrested two hundred sixteen alien giants from Liatos-D and await word from their ambassador on their disposition. Mata Hari has been captured. She is Jill Koch. Yes, the extremely wealthy woman who has been running the Galactic Doll pageant for years. Here is part of what she said to her giant conspirator, a Captain Thanos. It's their voices you'll hear."

Helen played back the relevant section of the recording, which proved her guilt beyond any doubt.

Helen continued. "Since the attack on GPan yesterday has put our Senior Judge in a mutation coma, along with her entire staff, Jill Koch's punishment decree will be delayed. She remains in my custody until such time as the judge is able to make her ruling. In summary, I believe we've put an end to these terrorist attacks by this group. This is not to imply others won't try similar things in the future, but for now, this awful threat is over. Thank you."

With Sam off at the library and the kids at school, I decided to visit Helen and perhaps have a chat with Jill. Celeste insisted on coming with me.

Helen said, "What a busy morning. I can't thank you enough, Molly. I think we've ended that vision of yours, don't you think?"

We sat on plush chairs in her office on the hundredth floor of the GD skyscraper, CEO Hardy's old office and the very one I used as temporary CEO some seven years ago.

"I think so. I wanted to talk with Jill. Just to make

154

damn sure. This time, they did a job on GPan and our investigation and justice department personnel, right?"

"Yes. On the bright side, I had convinced the local GPan people to avoid the building, so those men and women weren't affected. They ducked a bullet, unlike those that we need right now. I'm holding Jill until the Senior Judge can rule on her disposition. I'm waiting to hear back on the giants. A number of our immigrant giants want me to terminate them."

She sighed and continued. "Celeste, what are we going to do with all these new victims? How can we deliver therapy sessions to almost three thousand?"

"We can't," she said. "I talked with Leslie this morning. She's working to provide several sets of apparel and shoes for each victims, and she's coordinating with Galactic Robotics to have a complete set of the machines and robots delivered to every victim's home. Leslie's also asking them to provide laptops loaded with all those how-to videos. I'm pretty sure they'll do it, since most of these victims are very wealthy."

"They'll have to rely on the videos," I said. "Later on, we might be able to work on a few at a time, but it'll take years to get them all handled. We could try to pull the kids out of school and have them run sessions on the adults, but..."

"These particular adults aren't going to accept a child giving them therapy," Helen finished my sentence. I nodded. "Okay. I'll let the hospitals and Med Centers know. I'm also suggesting they hire personal assistants for the near future. I'm drafting an ad today. With luck, we'll have a pool of assistants ready to be hired. I know the wealthy. That's the first thing they'll want—not to learn from the videos, but have someone wait on them. We'll see how it goes. After all, it took Casper half a year to knuckle down and learn from the videos."

The next day, Helen paid me another visit. "I've got some news for you. The acting Senior Judge has ruled on Jill Koch. She's sentenced to live out two full lifetimes as she is. No cures ever. When she reaches sixty-five, she's to be injected a second time. Her fancy estate is being sold and then her vast wealth will be divided equally among the recent victims, in some cases posthumously to nearest relatives. She's going to be forced to earn her living as a janitor, but always watched over by a security guard."

"Wow. Well, maybe her greed will be cured," I said.

Helen smiled. "Next, as expected, the two hundred sixteen alien giants from Liatos-D have been released to their ambassador, who put them on a pair of transports."

"Damn. They should have been punished somehow. I can't believe they're getting off without even a slap on the wrist. So much for justice."

Helen's smile broadened. "I let Admiral Rossi know about it. I just heard there was some kind of accident after takeoff. Both transports blew up. Total loss of life on the ships."

My eyes connected with hers. I understood. "Yes," she said, "justice comes in strange ways. I think giants on Liatos-D might not try such a plot again. There's been another development. As you know, when victims awake from their comas, many beg to be terminated. Seven years ago, Dimitri obeyed their wishes, but shooting them in their heads was messy and not humane. Galactic Medicine in Mumbai has found another way. They were approached by Able Cremation Services, a small company that operates out of Toronto. They have agreed to humanely terminate the victims, transport their bodies to their facilities in Toronto, and cremate them—all at no cost to anyone. They claim this is their civic duty to help. Apparently, they make enough from regular operations to cover this extra operation."

"Interesting. I agree. Shooting the victims in their heads as Dimitri and his men did was disgusting and awful. As long as it's done humanely, that has to be better for everyone. Still, I wish the victims would at least try to adapt."

Helen commented. "I know most people believe they are their bodies and that they only live once. But do you suppose somehow in the backs of their minds they know that once this body dies, they're going to quickly pick up a new baby body and start over? Kind of like a hidden instinct or something? With a clean slate. That process is very clear to me now, thanks to the therapy sessions."

"Could be, Helen. Each person has their own reasons for living. I expect some victims are ready to start over rather than adapt and carry on."

She laughed. "Well, Hugo and I have a vice-grip cling to life. We're not about to give up and succumb, quite the opposite of Jill Koch, who desperately wants to be terminated since she can't have any of the mutation cures."

"I'm very glad you both are. Say, any word on how many in Mumbai, Tokyo, and Philadelphia chose termination? Or is it too soon to know?"

"The Senators, Senior Investigator, and Senior Judge are not going to be allowed to request termination. Their new laws have backfired. Popular opinion has demanded they live as they are. I can't blame people for insisting those who passed these inhumane laws live with them. As far as the others go, check with GMed. I don't have their figures yet."

***

Edgar Gascon, owner of Able Cremation Services, looked over his sprawling factory floor. Ten cremation furnaces lined the back wall, all converted blast furnaces. Ten years ago, he'd trusted his instincts. Thus far, his French-Canadian heritage had not let him down. Single handedly, he'd converted the small, abandoned steel factory into the largest crematorium in Toronto.

"People die. That you can count on," he'd told his sponsor, a VP in Galactic Medicine, Toronto. "We both know burying people in caskets is too costly, and loved ones don't want their newly departed to be tossed into a hole in the ground. Cremation is cheap, effective, and acceptable. Has been for many scores of years. Rather than continuing to have each corporation maintain their own crematoriums, I propose to handle all body disposals for every corporation."

He got the contract. That was ten years ago. Today,

he handled thousands of cremations, usually within a radius of a hundred miles from Toronto, though he continually expanded his coverage. At fifty credits per body burned, he pocketed a tidy profit.

Seven years ago, Edgar watched the Chicago news coverage of the deaths of those who awoke from their mutation comas demanding to be terminated. An idea formed, but the mutation attacks ended before he could deliver his proposal to GMed Chicago. When the terrorist attacks began again, he polished up his document and sent it off to GMed Chicago and GMed Moscow. For fifty credits per person, his company would pick up the person to be terminated, see that they were humanely killed, and cremated, their ashes fertilizing the land for future generations.

When the Tokyo attack came, GMed Moscow called. "Mr. Gascon, we've reviewed your proposal. We can offer Able Cremation Services a contract to handle this awful situation in Tokyo. Hundreds wish to be terminated. Years ago, this was done by shooting them in their heads."

"Yes, I saw that on the news. Painful, no doubt. As you have read, my proposal uses the latest anesthesia drugs to render them unconscious before we use termination drugs. Painless. Very humane. They won't feel anything, especially after what they've gone through."

"We agree. Can you handle these victims at a paltry fifty credits per person?"

"Absolutely."

"Okay then. I'll email the contract now. Once you sign and send it back to me, I'll set up a location for you to use. We need you in Tokyo as soon as possible."

When Edgar finished up in Tokyo, he'd transported five hundred unconscious men and women to his facilities in Toronto, picking up a fast twenty-five thousand credits. However, he had to pay his "doctor" and his transport staff, all were low-IQ personnel working to make a few extra credits for their families.

On site in Tokyo, "Doc" injected each person with a very strong sedative, while his assistant carefully logged the person's name and ID number. Meticulous records were required. "Doc" upped the dosages until the terrified, screaming victims became completely docile and could be moved. Several giants then carried the victims to the waiting Able Cremation Services Airliner for the long journey back to Toronto. Meanwhile, Edgar worked on the next phase: humane termination and cremation.

That's when his fortunes changed dramatically. A giant wearing an expensive business suit walked into his warehouse.

"Ah, Mr. Gascon, I presume. My name is Thebes, and I have a proposition for you." A translator box attached to his belt spoke the words. Edgar found the sounds from the giant's mouth unintelligible.

"Kind'a busy at the moment. All these terrorist victims."

"It concerns them. As I understand your contract with GMed, you are bringing them back here."

"Yes, we're sedating them as we speak. My crews are bringing them here. I'm just now getting the drugs that'll terminate them in a humane way before I cremate their bodies and use their ashes as fertilizer."

"Ah. So you don't actually terminate them until they are in this facility?"

"Right. I plan to use a few bodies as cadavers for the various medical schools. There's always a need for training new doctors. Why?"

"Will each body have identification papers?"

"You must be an alien. We don't have papers, just ID cards. Yes, I'm obligated to maintain accurate records of the deceased. My personnel will have a toe tag attached to each when they arrive here. Why?"

"I represent a research consortium that wishes to purchase some of these bodies scheduled for termination before they're actually terminated. You may keep them on your records as terminated and cremated. I'm authorized to offer you two hundred credits per each alive but mutated body that's scheduled for termination at this facility. No questions asked. Consolidated Research would like to purchase both male and female adult samples, up to a maximum of twenty at a time."

"Two hundred per body? Do they have to be mutated bodies?"

"Yes. Preferably those that underwent what your world calls the armless Doll mutation. Consolidated Research will pay two hundred for each such alive body, though they will appear to have been cremated per your records."

"I never turned down a money-making opportunity. Their bodies are for research purposes?"

"Yes, research."

"Hum. Trouble is you never know when another batch will come. Hasn't been any terrorist attacks for seven years. Now suddenly Tokyo is attacked. Over a thousand victims, I'm told. Looks like my crew is picking up about five hundred bodies to be terminated."

"I see. Very sporadic. Okay, what about taking fifty alive bodies out of this large batch? That would make it an even ten thousand credits."

"Research you say?"

"Yes, biological research. Perhaps the next breakthrough will cure dementia."

"Okay. Consolidated Research has a deal. I'll hold fifty aside for you. My Airliner is scheduled to arrive late tomorrow night."

"I'll be here with a medical crew and the credits. Here's my business card with my email address."

"Right. Just remember, this is off the books. I'll have to record their bodies have been cremated."

"Of course. Until tomorrow night, Mr. Gascon."

The giant turned sharply and strode out of the warehouse.

An hour later, a non-descript man entered, looking for Edgar. He had one of those invisible faces and personality—a man who could vanish in a crowd.

"Hello. I'm here about the medical doctor's position."

"Ah, yes. We're getting many of these mutation

victims who desire to be terminated. I'm required to have a medical doctor administer the humane drugs."

"I'm Dr. Jim Smith. I heard about this from GMed, Toronto. I'd like to volunteer my services to you at no cost. It's my humble way of helping these poor victims." He rattled off the drug Edgar proposed to use and the proper dosage based on body weight.

"I don't have to pay you for your services?"

"No. It's the least I can do for these poor victims."

"Wonderful. You're hired. The drug shipment just arrived. Get the facility setup to handle about five hundred victims arriving tomorrow night. There could be more. I heard Philadelphia was also attacked."

The working area of each furnace was shielded from the others. When anyone worked at furnace Number Ten next to the side loading docks, no one could see the action, except from Edgar's second story office, which he only used for logging records. While the two men set to work arranging examination tables in the center of the warehouse, an EMAC arrived with three deceased men from Toronto General. Dr. Smith joined Edgar's three workers and watched the procedure.

Each body's toe tag was removed and entered into the termination records via a code scanner. Strong arms slid the cardboard boxes with the deceased down roller ramps that fanned out, servicing all ten furnaces. It stopped at one of the furnace doors. Once slid inside and its door latched, the worker pressed the red Cremate button. Roaring flames danced inside the small viewing window.

One worker said, "It'll shut off automatically when the cremation is done. Sometimes we have to collect the ashes, but usually we don't."

Dr. Smith asked, "So record keeping is done by scanning the toe tag?"

"Yes, fully automated. If you wish, you can bring up the deceased's information on the small monitor there, after you scan the tag. Usually we don't bother. The dead is dead."

"Okay, fellows. Take the rest of the day off.

Tomorrow night, we have five hundred to cremate. We'll be at it all night. Overtime pay, of course."

Edgar's last statement changed frowns into smiles.

His EMAC crews met the Airliner as it touched down around midnight. Each vehicle carried twenty bodies laid in long, narrow cardboard boxes. Heavily sedated, the victims made no sound, just an occasional moan. The Airliner carried two hundred fifty victims. Thus, his three EMACs made four trips to the spaceport. Hours later, the Airliner headed back to Tokyo for the rest of the victims.

When the first EMAC unloaded their bodies, Thebes was there. After verifying the bodies were alive, he handed Mr. Gascon ten thousand credits.

"Okay, follow me to incinerator Number Ten," Edgar said. "Dr. Smith, I'll handle these. You get the toe tags entered and the drug administered to the others."

Edgar scanned in the toe tag and nodded to Thebes. He worked slowly, maintaining the same rate as the other working incinerators. Thebes pointed to the victim, and one of his associates lifted the victim out of the box and carried the body out the side door and into their own waiting vehicle. None of this could be seen from the center of the warehouse or from other incinerator stations. Once fifty men and women had been carried out, Thebes nodded and left.

Edgar joined Dr. Smith, checking on the overall operation. Satisfied, he said, "You can take over for me on Number Ten, Dr. Smith. I've got to check on the Airliner and with GMed Philadelphia."

"Of course, sir."

Dr. Smith continued entering toe tags, observing the person's bio information on the small screens near the incinerator. Occasionally, he slid one of these bodies in their box down to Number Ten, where it was out of sight. Another man entered and carried the body out the side door, while Dr. Smith shoved the box into the incinerator and pressed Incinerate, before returning to the central staging area for the next body. Most he injected with the termination drug and slid that box on down the roller ramps to the next available incinerator, where the workers handled the rest of the operation.

By sunrise, they'd cremated the last of the victims. The tired workers headed home, expecting to work all night again when the Airliner returned. When Dr. Smith departed, he stopped at the unmarked EMAC parked near the side door.

"All twenty are doing fine, Jim. We're off now," his associate whispered. The doctor nodded and continued walking to the MTES. He sent an electronic signal as he stepped onto the moving sidewalk.

***

Jill Koch's attack came on September 20. Three days later, Bishop visited Molly shortly after breakfast.

"Molly, I've got the final tallies from the Tokyo, Philadelphia, and Mumbai attacks."

He copied the file to my computer and brought up the results table on the holographic screen. I scanned down the listing.

Victims	Terminated	Survived	Unaccounted for
Tokyo			
1001	499	402	100
Philadelphia			
1505	600	805	100
Mumbai			
2006	911	995	100
Totals			
4512	2010	2202	300

I said, "So about half chose to live. That's something. Wait. What's the story on the unaccounted for? How can a victim go missing?"

"First responders counted the victims when they entered the rooms. As you know, they undress those in comas. Their initial tallies don't match the final tallies when the victims are taken to various medical facilities. What I find suspicious is that number is always one hundred. I'm curious. Do you find that suspicious, too?"

"Yes, Bishop. You're catching on to this PI business. If this was due to random error, the numbers would be different. Somehow a hundred victims have vanished at each site. We're going to have to investigate."

"Shouldn't the Senior Investigator carry out this investigation?"

"Ordinarily, yes. But they're now victims. I'll check with Helen, but I don't think the investigation branch is back in operation. Certainly the justice arm isn't fully functional. Any word on the number of GPan victims?"

Bishop said, "Yes, two hundred six, including mostly the Senior Investigator and her staff and the Senior Judge and his staff, but also a few GPan executives. If you recall, you encouraged many earlier victims to join the investigation staff. So of that total number of victims, fifty-three have already recovered from their short duration comas, having gotten their breast reductions and feet repairs undone. They aren't too happy about that. But who is?"

"So that makes one hundred fifty-three new victims. Maybe the judges will now display some humanity and vacate some Council of the Senate's laws. Wonder what the odds of that happening are?"

Yes, I sounded cynical. Bishop shrugged his shoulders. I took a deep breath and exhaled slowly. "Okay. So how can we figure out what happened to the hundred missing victims in each attack?"

"I've got GMed working on that," Bishop said. "I had an investigator call up Moscow's GMed CEO and force an investigation with me as head coordinator. I'll back off if you wish to do it."

"No. Thanks for taking the initiative, Bishop."

"I've suggested they compile a listing of who should have been a victim by living or being in the area of the attack and a listing of those who came out of their comas. So far, they report they're getting many names, but time is needed to track down this potential list of missing people. Some may have been gone during the attack. If the missing hundred are truly missing, the question will be how to find out what happened to them. Certainly, they were in comas and couldn't have left on their own."

"Probably kidnapped, Bishop. That's my presumption. By whom? I've no idea. Maybe giants."

"I thought as much, Molly. But I've reviewed the spaceport logs in Mumbai, Tokyo, and Philadelphia. There wasn't an influx of Liatos-D tranports landing as there was here in North Chicago. Just the usual cargo runs. But I'll keep looking. By the way, I finally have a clue in Ted's murder and even a theory about why he was killed."

"Wow! After all these years. I'm all ears."

"I applied what I've learned about PI work from you. The routine investigations yielded nothing. So I took another approach. The perp must have entered and left the Galactic Robotics building, probably along with the hundreds of other workers. I identified every person who entered or left the building during the day Ted was shot."

"That's hundreds of people," I interrupted. "That would take days if not weeks to do."

"I don't sleep. Days, yes. But I was able to identify every person who came and left except one man." Bishop uploaded a file to my phone and computer before displaying the 3-d holo image. "Here's the unknown man. Further, I've run his face through every database we have. No match. This man just doesn't exist. I did trace where he came from and went to after the assassination. An abandoned warehouse on the south side. I've looked at surveillance both seven days before and seven afterwards but didn't see him or anyone arriving or leaving. It's as though he vanished. I went to the warehouse and found a connection to the sewer system. My conclusion is he arrived and departed through those tunnels. Dead end. But..."

"But what?"

"But I think I know who the man is. Rather what it is. I believe it's one of the five missing human form robots that didn't have the robot laws programmed into it. I think Ted was killed because he was getting too close to uncovering those five robots and what they might have been planning."

"Incredible, Bishop. Well done. This makes total sense. Ted was always trying to find out what happened to those missing robots. I think he saw them as dangerous to us. I wonder what those five robots are doing today? Have we seen him around Chicago in the last seven years?"

Bishop chuckled or so it sounded. "I've compared this image to all criminal activities in this area during the last seven years. Ahead of you, for once. No sign of him. But that means nothing. Remember, we can change our appearance and even gender. He could appear to be a female today."

"I wonder what their objectives are? I suppose like all life forms it's self-preservation."

Bishop smiled. "So I'm a life form now? Since the robot laws underlie my calculations, I can't calculate what a robot without these laws would think, but self-preservation must rank high."

"Precisely. And after self-preservation, life forms use procreation to continue their species. Robots don't have babies like other mammals. How can they reproduce? By making more of duplicates of themselves." I answered myself.

"Ah, I think you've given me an new avenue to research. To produce more robots, they'll need parts—items Galactic Robotics has in abundance. I'm going to follow that avenue."

My door chime rang. I saw a purple uniform and knew he was a GPan executive.

"Molly Parkinson?" he asked.

I nodded.

"I'm Phil Weston, acting GPan local CEO while the others are in their comas. I've come bearing really bad news, discovered when I went over documents the CEO was supposed to handle. You haven't heard from either Isabella Parkinson or Bernardo Parkinson in four months. Right?"

I nodded. My throat constricted as my stomach found a will of its own.

"We've lost both deep space exploration ships. I'm deeply sorry for your double loss." His sympathetic tone shifted to boredom.

"Let me explain what little we do know. The Star Voyager sent a distress call mid-June. From the garbled communication, we couldn't decipher the trouble the ship had, but we knew its approximate location. Since the Pathfinder roughly paralleled the Star Voyager's path and was the nearest Sol Empire ship, the CEO decided to divert it from its search for habitable worlds. Days later, the Pathfinder reported nothing at the last known location and began a search for the missing ship. Two days later, high command again received a garbled long distance communication from the Pathfinder. Other than the fact the ship was in dire trouble, nothing else could be ascertained before the comm abruptly ended. That was June 22.

"Nothing has been heard from either ship since then, despite daily long distance communication attempts. A light cruiser was dispatched to that last known location, but they found nothing there at all. No space debris and no trace of the two ships. A sweep search over the last month has yielded no clues. And at this point, both ships are now listed as missing in action, presumed destroyed. GPan executives were about to contact the nearest relatives of the sixty presumed-deceased personnel when the mutation attack occurred. Within a month, you may expect to receive the insurance settlements on the deaths of your two children."

Stunned. I just stared at the man, mouth open. What could I say? Thankfully Bishop was with me. He said, "Thank you for the information. Can you give me the precise coordinates of that approximate location and the general galactic direction they were traveling prior to their destruction?"

"Huh? Well, yes." He rattled off numbers from his phone, while Bishop jotted them down for me.

"So has GPan given up searching for both ships?" he asked.

"Officially, yes. We've done all we can do. If later on additional information is uncovered or if we hear from

167

either one or both ships, we'll take immediate action. But it's been four months. We've heard nothing at all and found no trace of the ships."

With that, he departed, while I still sat stunned. *Focus, Molly, focus.* I didn't get my nickname Cool Head for nothing. "Bishop, I feel sick. This can't be happening. They can't give up the search. If Isabella died, I'm sure I would have felt something."

"I calculate they've abandoned the search because they've lost a second ship and the cruiser they sent to locate the two ships found nothing. I'm so sorry, Molly."

"Well, I'm not giving up. I'm a pilot. I'll get a ship and go search for them until I find them."

"Perhaps you should tell Sam and everyone what's happened."

Chapter 14 Don't Give Up

Sam and I leaned into each other, allowing our grief to flow. We'd put on a brave face for the sake of Nikita and Matt, but once they were in bed, we dropped such pretenses. Eventually, our grief ran its course and a semblance of normalcy returned.

"Molly, I can't believe they're both dead. I think I would have felt something, somehow, someway," Sam said.

"Me too. I know they were with us only a short while before they left in their exploration ships, but still..."

"I know. It's as though I can still sense them somehow. We can't give up."

I sighed. "We can't, Sam. Look, if we just had a spaceship. I can fly it, while you navigate us to their last known location. Maybe we'd be close enough to make telepathic contact with them or something."

"Dear, you got it. So where do we get us a deep space transport? Are they expensive?"

Though late, Deanna Cartwright dropped by. Most of my sisters had already visited me offering their sympathies. Celeste had even run a short therapy session on me erasing the emotional shock of the news.

"I'm so sorry, Molly, Sam. Bishop told me the details. I can't believe GPan is giving up the search. They've billions invested in those two deep space exploration ships. I certainly wouldn't give up if Jana was out there."

"Sam and I don't want to give up, but we need a spaceship. I guess my pilot skills are going to come in useful, as is his navigation ability. There has to be hope. They didn't find any debris. If the ships were destroyed, bits would be scattered all over space."

Deanna smiled. "That's why I dropped by. I've recently made a deal with companies on Azizi-C—the Kanika battleship Admiral Skaggs' home world. They want me to set up an EMAC subsidiary on their world. In return, they are setting up a deep space transport company here in

Chicago. They'll make armed, commercial transports capable of carrying a hundred passengers and fifty tons of cargo. Cartwright Enterprises has purchased one. The Friendship landed at New O'Hare last night. I want to put it through its paces, so to speak. I can learn so much about their technology by studying this ship. What would you say to us taking it out on a shake down cruise and see if we can find your missing twins and their ships?"

"Wow! Incredible, Deanna. I was about to beg you for the chance. What about a crew? Can I pilot it? Can Sam work its nav system?"

"And a whole lot more questions. Like how long can it go before refueling? Tomorrow, I'm supposed to get piloting instruction from their Captain, followed by navigation training. Then, I get down to the actual ship's construction principles and operational guidelines. They suggested I'll need about a month of training before I can take it on a solo flight. Will you both come train with me? I'm going to ask Bev to come along with us and learn the ship's combat capabilities, though I'm told they're mostly defensive, perhaps a tenth the firepower of a light cruiser. Still..."

"Where and when do we show up? Sam, there's still hope."

Deanna jotted it down for us. "Also, if you know of anyone else who might want to learn, bring them along, too. There's room for a hundred people, but we need a crew of at least six in order to operate everything. One can fly it solo, but they have to run everything themselves. When we go looking for your twins, I'd like at least a half dozen security guards with us. Bev can provide them."

"We'll be there. Thank you!"

Deanna smiled and left. From the window, I saw she'd landed her two-person shuttle on our lawn. Those were darn convenient, but expensive.

"What did she want?" asked Lenka, who joined us in the living room. "I didn't want to intrude."

Sam told her the good news. "So how would you like to join us tomorrow and learn how to navigate this transport?"

"Really? Me? I'd love to, if you think I possibly could manage it," Lenka said.

I chuckled. "It's going to be a big 'stop and think how' day for us. We just have to be smarter and cleverer than most."

The next morning, Sam, Lenka, and I met Deanna at New O'Hare. She led us across the sprawling tarmac to the long-term parking zone. Her new ship, the Friendship, sparkled in the morning sun. Huge. Three stories tall, the ship stretched three hundred feet along the concrete pad. Hexagonal cross sectional tubular construction reminded me of the Kanika battleship. Had they glued eight of the long hex tubes together? Deanna explained a silver based polymer formed its outer hull, light weight but extremely strong in the near absolute zero cold of space.

Four giant gun turrets lined it's top surface with two below. A spacious cargo ramp opened in its rear, while several side ramps allowed passenger access to either the middle compartments or the forward crew. We walked up the crew ramp, where Captain Ruggs greeted us.

Thus began the most challenging day I've ever had. I lost track of how many times I whispered, "Stop. Think how." The spacious control center housed the pilot's station, the navigator's station, and a small communications, control, and planning station (CCP), jammed into an equipment-filled, circular room ten feet across.

While on automatic, the computer controlled the ship's flight, but a complicated joy-stick allowed for manual pilot operations. I had an awful lot to learn and challenges to face in order to pilot this fancy ship. In contrast, navigation and the CCP sections were simple for Sam and Lenka to operate, differing little from our own technology. However, they did have to learn the operation of the planning and viewing equipment, which we needed in order to find our two missing spaceships.

Deanna and I paused in our pilot training to watch the 3-d holographic display of the spiral galaxy, as Lenka and Sam moved it about, zooming in here and there. For a moment, I wanted to learn navigation just so I could operate this incredible invention.

"This is much harder to fly than my EMAC or my shuttle," Deanna declared as we headed home that first evening. "I can see why we're going to need a three-week crash course."

"I can't believe there's so much to learn beyond just how to fly it. In spite of the incredible challenge, I haven't been this excited about learning things in a long time."

Deanna departed in her two-man shuttle, leaving Sam, Lenka, and me to use the MTES. Those two were just as enthusiastic about this as I was.

After supper, Commander L'Grina dropped by. "I heard about your sister's new deep space transport and dropped by New O'Hare to see it today. Impressive. They said you're learning to pilot it?"

"Yes, Deanna and I are on a three-week crash piloting course. Sam and Lenka are training to navigate it. It's an incredible ship."

"I was sorry to hear about the lost of two of your older children. Scuttlebutt hints you're going off to search for them. In this new ship, perhaps?" she asked, coyly.

"You bet. Sam and I believe we would have felt something if our twins had been killed. We think they're still out there but in trouble. We're going to find them."

"Kind'a thought so. Molly, I'd like to volunteer to come along and help you find them. I'm a pilot, and I can pick up the details of Deanna's new ship quickly. I can also fight, if they are being held prisoner. It's the least I can do to thank you for all the therapy you've given me."

I hesitated a moment. "Okay then. Honestly, piloting this one is an incredible challenge for me. At least the navigation is almost the same as ours, so Sam and Lenka don't have so much to relearn. Besides, I can't really fight anymore. General Bev is coming. You'll have to take orders from her."

"Acceptable. Honestly, Molly, I can't imagine how you can do a tenth of what you do. If I was in your shoes, I think I'd opt to be killed and start over again. Thank you for letting me have this chance to repay your kindness. I'll see you all at New O'Hare tomorrow."

After she left, Sam asked, "Are you really going to take a Sixth Invader commander along with us? What if it's her people who captured the two ships?"

"We need dependable arms, especially if I have trouble piloting it. Besides, she can fight, while I can't hold my Glock. Sam, we need her. Look, both exploration ships had their own security guards on board. They must have been overwhelmed. We need Bev and fighters with us."

We had just gotten the kids put to bed when the doorbell rang again. Via the monitor, I saw an unknown woman standing at the door. Both Sam and I shrugged our shoulders, before I answered it. Oops. Wrong gender. Here was a man who'd undergone the Galactic Doll mutation, but who'd hadn't yet had the two minor cures. Nevertheless, he wore one of Leslie's male outfits, which didn't really hide his massive bosom, though his long pants did hide the tall heels he wore.

His voice was in the alto range, indicative that it had once been a deep bass voice. "Mrs. Parkinson?" I nodded. "You don't know me. I'm Sergeant Walter Barker, Owen's father."

"Owen Barker? Isabella's fiancé?" I asked.

"Yes. Owen's told me about you in some of his monthly calls. Have you been notified their ship is missing and that they're presumed dead?"

"Yes, we were notified a couple days ago. We're not ready to give up on them, though obviously GPan has."

"I know I'm a freak now, but I was a sergeant in the First Infantry Division on Brussels, Tau Ceti. I was one of the robot army's victims. Lost an arm and leg. Thanks to your mutation discovery, I have my arm and leg back. The cost has been a bit much. I look like a freak; my wife divorced me; they mustered me out of the army. But Owen still calls me one a month."

"At least you have them back, unlike Sam and me."

"Aye. There a blessing in that. I know I would've

begged for termination if I awoke to find myself armless. Honestly, life was awful before the mutation; I can't imaging having to live as you and so many others are. That's why I was so proud of Owen, who wants to marry your Isabella. She's a brilliant, lovely young woman, in spite of everything."

I ignored the suggestions that she and I were living an awful life. "So Owen's an astro-geologist?"

"Yes, he just got his degree when this opening came up. It's his first exploration trip. They can't be lost. They just can't be. He's all I have left. I've saved back a few credits, and I'll donate all his insurance money if you can help me find them. I don't know how you can, but I have to try every possibility to get Owen and the others back. It's criminal how GPan isn't. What's our world come to?"

"We've got a deep space transport available. So as soon as we get trained to fly it, I'm heading off to find them. I don't want your credits. We just have to find them."

"Wow. Really? You've got a ship?" His demeanor changed. Was that hope radiating from his eyes?

"Yes, my sister, Deanna Cartwright, is loaning us her new Friendship spaceship. We're training to pilot and navigate it now. General Bev will come along, providing security."

"General Bev? Incredible. Could I come along too? I can still fight. I haven't forgotten my army training, though my mobility is limited. These heels. I shouldn't complain, since I can walk. Still, I can fight. Please, take me along, unless you don't want a freak like me along."

I couldn't help picking up his low self-worth. While being mutated into a male Doll regrew his missing arm and leg, that his body now looked like all other women took its toll on his self-respect. His wife abandoning him certainly didn't help. Also, I felt bad that I'd never been able to get every mutation victim the therapy they needed.

"We need fighters or security personnel. If General Bev gives her okay, then you have mine. I'll check with her tomorrow. Even better, she's supposed to visit the ship tomorrow around one to inspect its capabilities. Why not join her then and make your case directly to her?"

"Deal. Thank you. We simply have to find them. All of them."

After he left, I said, "Well, I couldn't say no to her fiancé's father. We could be in-laws." We both laughed.

***

On October 20, 2360, my search and rescue group of eighteen gathered at the side ramp of the Friendship. Redundancy won. I began as our pilot, but Deanna and Ambassador Commander L'Grina could substitute for me. Sam took the navigator's seat, but Lenka, L'Grina, and Deanna could also handle those duties. General Bev Blythe and her wife Major Gail Jackson handled security, aided by Bev's favorite engineer, Lieutenant (now Captain) Betsy Waters, Walter Barker, and six male soldiers. Deanna wore the Chief Planning Officer hat, but L'Grina and I could substitute for her.

As we stood before the ship's entrance, Deanna addressed us. "Welcome on board my Friendship transport. We're about to take her on her maiden voyage in search of what happened to the Star Voyager and Pathfinder. With luck, we'll rescue their crews. How long are we going to be gone? I've no idea. I can say that I've planned for a six-month trip. That means we have sufficient food and fuel for half a year. More importantly as I've now learned, the fuel load assumes we travel at sub-light speed for six months. Obviously, we'll use hyperdrive to get to their last known position. Then, we'll have to drop out and work out how and where to search. So let's get this show on the road."

We followed Deanna up the ramp into the ship. Already our duffle bags had been stowed in our private quarters. Seventeen had never been on a spaceship, though a few had been passengers. Only Commander L'Grina actually knew what to expect. Her experience and insight became vital, for none of us truly grasped the emotional impact of extended periods of space travel.

"Prepare for liftoff," I called out following the pilot protocol.

The control tower synched with my controls, making

taking off automatic. New O'Hare computers controlled our flight until the ship reached an altitude of ten miles, when I could take over. This was necessary not only because of the traffic but also because of the satellites and space debris in orbit above the earth. The computers navigated ships around these obstacles.

Control released. Red letters flashed on my console. I took control, heading the Friendship outward towards the orbit of Mars. I engaged the deflector screens.

Sam called out, "Coordinates of Star Voyager are entered, Captain."

I grinned. "Now I'm a captain. Okay, everyone. Prepare for the jump into hyperspace. Three. Two. One."

I pressed the button with my toe and felt the slight lurching sensation. From my window, I watched the star-filled universe vanish, replaced by a black void, cold and hostile.

Sam said, "Thirty minutes until we arrive. Twins, here we come."

Bev yelled, "Hey, we forgot the beer. You know how I hate these jumps."

"You'll really need it, General, once we begin cruising sub-light," Commander L'Grina said.

"Okay, I'll bite," I said. "Why then?"

"Flying about the vastness of space at sub-light speeds is incredibly dangerous. One is only safe while in hyperspace," she said. Looking at blank faces, the Sixth Invader explained.

"Space is filled with junk. Dead stars and debris are everywhere—some the size of a grain of sand, some the size of asteroids. Nearly every star has or once had what your people call an Oort Cloud of icy-sandy debris surrounding it. Some material has been pulled out of such clouds into interstellar space. Some is left over particles from star formation and gas clouds that never quite fully coalesced into a star, planet, or moon. Nova and supernova blast all kinds of matter far out into space.

"So empty space is rarely empty. As you fly along, your ship is likely to encounter anything from sand grains

176

to small asteroids, unless you are unlucky to run into the remains of a black, dead star. Or get sucked into a super-dense neutron star or black hole."

"But a grain of sand isn't anything," Bev said. Her face had paled considerably.

"It is when you are traveling along at say ninety thousand miles a second. Then, its impact is more like running into a moon."

"I really need a keg of beer!"

"Isn't that what the deflector screens are for?" I asked. I felt sorry for my sister. Perhaps I should have insisted we bring along some beer.

"Yes and no. They protect a ship up to a point. Your ADS, Active Defense System, is constantly scanning a sphere around the ship. When it detects the approach of an object the deflectors can't handle, it sounds a warning. The pilot must alter course or we become more space debris. We pilots earn our keep when flying sub-light."

She looked at the serious faces around her. "I can see none of you has done much space flying. Well, I'll share something I've discovered since residing so darn long on your world. Those who spend much of their lives flying about in space become rather frantic about life. They become highly emotional, wildly enthusiastic or antagonistic. I know because that's the way I was when I first landed on Earth. Constantly in action, I felt jittery and jumpy. In fact, we all were frantic about sex, having to have it frequently just to calm our nerves. Out here, you know your end could come at any moment and with nothing you could do about it and with no warning. So you become frantically active.

"After residing on Earth for thirty years, I've calmed down and become relaxed about life. Quite a change in my personality. I could see that when they finally rescued me some seven years ago. On the Admiral's ship, everyone was so frantic, so flighty, but I wasn't. Flying about the galaxy at sub-light speeds changes people. I think it's the unconscious, but ever present, threat of a sudden death that's behind it."

"I vote we go back to Chicago and load up on *kegs* of beer," Bev said. "How else are we going to survive this trip? Do ships get destroyed often?"

"Not that often, General," Commander R'Grina said. "Otherwise, no one could have a sizeable space fleet. No, you're more likely to become frantic about everything. Take your security guards and soldiers and go practice firing the ship's guns."

Bev chuckled. "Hey, that's a good idea. Always calms my nerves. Firing guns. Molly, too, that is, when she had arms. Okay, you heard her. Let's take gunnery practice now." Bev and eight others headed off to do that, as we dropped out of hyperspace.

I triple checked that the deflectors were on, praying they would work, before joining the others at comm center behind me and the navigator's section.

"Okay, I've brought up the holo galaxy projector," Sam said. "Lenka has it zoomed in on our rough position."

"I'll point," Deanna volunteered. "Here's our sun and here's our position."

Lenka said, "Computer: show Star Voyager's trajectory for the last year."

We watched as a red line zigged and zagged from star to star, always heading outward from Sol. The path headed on an azimuth of around three hundred degrees from a line to the center of the galaxy. Sometimes, their path took them up out of the galactic plane, while others took them below the plane. At the point of last known location, they veered down below the plane before they disappeared. Lenka ordered the computer to show a similar path for the Pathfinder, when it responded to the distress call and went in search of the Star Voyager. Its path in orange nearly blended with the red line when it reached our position, confirming we had the correct initial search position.

While we stared at the hologram, the Friendship jerked slightly beneath our feet.

"What the hell was that?" Bev's frantic voice bellowed over the intercom.

"Deflector's shoved something out of our way," Commander R'Grina answered. "Nothing to worry about. It's gonna happen lots of times each day. You'll get used to it. Don't worry. When the big one comes, you won't even know you're dead."

"No wonder they're all frantic beasts!" Bev declared. Then, we heard our ship's guns commence firing.

Sam swallowed and continued. "We know the Star Voyager wasn't due to report its position for another week from this point. The question is which direction did it travel and at what speed?

"We know they didn't just continue on at sub-light speeds like we are now. Many dozens of years would be required to reach the nearest star. This being unexplored space, our guess is they did hops."

A ship's astronomers looked ahead for any dangerous objects. If the way was clear, the ship would drop into hyperspace for one second before dropping out, thus covering a vast distance. The astronomers verified the safety of this new location and then scanned ahead once more. Huge distances could be traveled in a series of hops, each hyperspace coordinate dutifully recorded, thereby extending the Sol Empire's knowledge.

Sam said, "Of course, the question is which direction do we go and then do we use a series of hops?"

Commander L'Grina stepped up. She manipulated the galactic display for a moment. "Look. Along this azimuth line, there are only two good candidates to explore. Both are type G stars, similar to Sol. 61 Virginis and Zeta Tucanae. There are more stars to explore down below the plane near Zeta Tucanae. So if I were off exploring, that's where I'd head. It's close to their path."

"What was that?" I asked before the others could. The ship vibrated slightly.

Commander L'Grina chuckled. "Another large deflection. Nothing to worry about. Yes, these things do get on your nerves. It's what happens when exploring at sub-light speeds."

"You can't explore via hyperspace, can you?" Deanna

asked.

"Hardly. Dingo's Rats. If you enter random hyperspace coordinates and jump, you might never be able to return. Out of fuel. Or you appear in the middle of a star or black hole or neutron star. Of course, you'd not likely feel it. Instant death."

I exhaled. "Okay. Let's start the hops toward Zeta Tucanae. Commander, perhaps you should take the pilot's seat. It's riskier than I imagined."

She smiled and did so. Now the pressure was on Sam and Lenka. They had to study the space ahead to make sure it was safe to execute a one-second jump. I let Commander L'Grina pilot because I found the seemingly random jars of the deflector system unnerving. I didn't know if I could react fast enough if the big one came, requiring me to move the ship out of its way. Others were nervous, too. Whenever the ship vibrated slightly, several of the ship's cannons would fire some rounds.

Commander L'Grina handled the controls deftly, as though she'd flown this ship countless times, but I knew she'd never seen this model before—at least not until we'd trained together. Competence. Professionalism. Envy swept over me for a moment. If only I could be as cool and skillful as she was...

"Okay. We're going for a three-second burn this time," Sam announced. "Lenka and I believe we can speed up the approach to this star. Our sensors show no large objects or gravity fields due ahead. Based on how much distance we've covered so far, this should work. Prepare for jump."

As the hours passed, Zeta Tucanae grew steadily brighter. Then, we stopped for the night. If we had a larger crew, we could have rotated positions every eight hours or so. We halted, unwilling to risk a collision while we slept. If something did come our way, the computer would sound a very loud alarm. All eighteen headed to the galley, where the aroma from Gail's dinner drew us.

"Wow, this is delicious." Commander L'Grina praised her after tentatively taking a bite of her cordon blue chicken dish.

Others agreed. Bev gave her wife a knowing nod. Of course, we sisters already knew how good Gail's cooking was. After relaxing with a slice of mouth-watering chocolate pie, we chatted while several others put the dishes into the washing machine.

"Those random bumps give me the creeps," Lenka said. "How do we know it's nighttime? How will we know it's morning?"

"Hey, me too," Bev said. "Real creepy."

"I can see how people can get overly excited and frantic out here," I said. "How do we handle day-night cycles?"

"Stomachs," Commander L'Grina said, "and the computer. It'll sound an alarm at eight o'clock. Besides, each cabin has its own clock device. Just set it when you go to bed. But Lenka and Bev are right. It doesn't take long for people to get used to the intermittent bumps out here. Of course, then they become overly energetic and frantic about every little thing."

Her hands slapped the sides of her cheeks. "Well I'll be. Now I understand why everyone gets so frenzied with sex on these long trips. Create a future generation now because there might not be a tomorrow. That's so clear to me now, but I was oblivious to it when I first arrived on Earth. How interesting."

"I always thought flying around in a spaceship was so romantic," Lenka said.

"Perhaps it isn't so much," I added. Everyone laughed, and we headed to our cabins. I still felt responsible for Lenka. As she and Walter headed for their cabin, I said, "Holler if you need something."

"I will. But Walter is going to try to help me," she said.

Chapter 15 Discovery

Slowly a week passed. Zeta Tucanae appeared brighter each day, as we closed the distance to what I hoped had been the destination of the two exploration ships. If it wasn't, we'd return to the starting point and try 61 Virginis. If that yielded nothing, there were many other fainter stars to check out. Somewhere out here in the vastness of space, my twins needed me. Nothing would stop me from finding them. Alive, I prayed.

Each day just before rising, I focused and tried to touch Isabella's or Bernardo's mind. I had no idea how far our telepathy stretched across distances, but I felt I had to try. On the other hand, I didn't need telepathy to see the strong bonds developing between Walter and Lenka. Both needed the support of the other, though for different reasons.

On the eighth day, we halted about one hundred fifty thousand astronomical units (AU) from the yellow sun. An AU is ninety-three million miles, so we parked a considerable distance away. Still the sun was the brightest star on our view screens.

Commander L'Grina spoke for Sam and Lenka. "Okay, we can just detect the star's Oort Cloud of formation debris and comets in a radius of a hundred thousand AUs around Zeta Tucanae. Our next jump will take us in close to where we can look for planets in the habitable zone, which should be around ninety-three million miles from this star. This is the risky jump. We could land in an asteroid field or near a gas giant—you get the idea. I'll be at the controls, but for safety's sake, I want everyone strapped in. Sam has the coordinates entered. Questions?"

After a nervous laugh, Deanna said, "Don't land us in the middle of a planet."

"Not likely. Still, this is the tricky jump. Strap in."

After hearing a "done" from each of us, she pressed the Jump button. Yes, I held my breath, but so did everyone else. My twins must have experienced such jumps many times during the past seven years. If they could do it, so could I. Still...

The jump ended with a lurch to the right. "Avoided something big. Moving into a stationary orbit. Okay, astronomers, find us a habitable planet or moon," Commander L'Grina called out.

I undid my harness and stood beside the pilot's seat. In a low voice, I asked, "Would I have been able to handle whatever happened when we just dropped out of hyperspace?"

"Oh, sure. Probably. Plus, the ship's computer could also have moved us out of the way. I just prefer to have my life in my own hands."

"But I've misplaced mine."

She laughed. Now we waited, impatiently, as Lenka, Sam, and Deanna used all the ship's observation instruments to spot any habitable planet, failing that, a moon. Once—or if they found one or more—then came the hard part: finding any trace of the two missing ships, challenging at best.

Deanna explained that every empire ship carried a transponder for emergencies such as this. If the ship's captain activated it when the emergency arose, then we should be able to detect it. Also, we could remotely activate it and then detect it. Thus far, none of the empire search ships had detected them. This could be because the exploration ships were out of range or because they were shielded in a Faraday cage, according to Deanna. Once more, I faced my ignorance. So much I didn't know.

If we could detect that signal, then we could home in on it like any other GPS situation. If we couldn't, then we'd have to search via sight. Imagine searching the surface of Earth looking for two small spaceships. Yet, there was a third way. Telepathy, if we could somehow get close enough to make contact. The hours passed.

"This is so cool," Lenka said. "Gas giants and rocky planets just like our system. Look, there's a rocky planet about ninety-seven million miles out with an atmosphere and oceans. We should check it out first. It's going to take us a lot longer to find suitable moons."

"All right. Let's do it. Coordinates?" I asked.

"Laid in," Sam said.

I inched the joy stick back, increasing our speed, and steered the Friendship toward the planet's position. On my pilot's view screen, I watched it grow. Unlike Earth, this world had only one large landmass, about a seventh of the surface of the world. A vast ocean covered most of this world.

I kept the land mass dead ahead. A polar cap of white stuck out against the blue waters. Shades of green dominated vast areas of the land, but the central section was brown, possibly a desert. Minutes later, the enormous size of this land caused us all to gasp. Along the western edge of the central lands, giant snow-capped mountains towered, cutting off moisture to the desert regions that lay east of it. Via the apparent rotation, Sam pointed out the polar cap was at this world's north pole.

I watched the edge of night as it swept across the ever-growing continent. Were our twins down there somewhere? If so, where? Eventually, I parked the Friendship in a high, geosynchronous orbit for the night. Over dinner, we decided to see if we could activate and/or detect the exploration ships' transponders, while in the morning Sam and I would try to make telepathic contact with the twins. If both failed, Deanna suggested we work out a thorough search pattern, since this world seemed likely to hold life. In the total darkness of the continent, we could do little until morning, wholly unlike Earth with its perpetually illuminated cities.

We headed back to the command and control section. I hovered over Deanna's shoulder and watched her work the computers. Behind me through view screens, Lenka looked for signs of cities. "I don't see city lights. It's dark everywhere."

"Transponder activation codes sent," Deanna said. "Now to see if we can detect their signals."

She worked the controls while I held my breath. I

inhaled sharply, having forgotten I was holding it.

"You okay?" Sam asked.

My face felt hot. "I forgot to breathe."

"Hey, good news. I'm actually receiving two transponder signals! They're very faint but coming from somewhere on this world. I bet the transmissions are being blocked."

She turned to me. "Molly, Sam, this means tomorrow morning when we can see again, we can home in on the ships. We're going to find them."

Relief. For the first time in weeks, I felt the intense stress melt away. I glanced at Sam who beamed.

Deanna brought up a realtime image of the dark world below. A pair of red lines ran obliquely across the screen. She said, "They're located somewhere along this line. If we move the ship to say the other side of the continent, I'll trace out another set of lines. Where the lines cross we'll find them."

"No sense in doing this tonight," Commander L'Grina said. She'd quietly joined us and overheard Deanna. "It's highly likely both ships have been captured. So let's not alert their captors until daylight when we can see them. Though if they aren't stupid, they've probably already detected us."

"If they have spotted us," I asked, "they might not think we've located them. Maybe we're just another world's exploration ship checking out this world."

"Possibly, Molly. But if I was them, I'd be on high alert, ready to take action."

"You think they'll shoot us down?" Deanna asked.

"They got the Star Voyager and then later the Pathfinder. So, yeah, I think they'll try."

"The transponders are working after all these months. Okay, they do have their own built-in battery power, even if the ships have been destroyed. But it's likely, the ships are on the ground. Crashed or damaged maybe. Transponders are designed to take an enormous amount of punishment and still operate. That's the point of their existence."

"We can speculate all night," the commander said. "I say let's get some sleep. Deanna, keep one of your guards watching, just in case."

With a sigh, I agreed. We headed to our quarters. An hour later, I lay beside Sam in our cramped bunk bed. Wide awake. Adrenaline pumping. My kids. This close at long last. I tried controlling my breathing, rationally knowing I couldn't do anything until morning. It didn't work or did it? The alarm sounded as the cabin's lights brightened from their nighttime setting. Morning. I shot out of bed, a new rush of excitement flowing through my body.

After a quick breakfast, I repositioned the ship over to the far western edge of the continent. Deanna made another measurement of the transponder lines. They intersected on the northeastern edge of the continent, some two thousand miles from our equatorial position. Based on the location, I headed the Friendship directly towards the exploration ships, descending from the geosynchronous orbit.

"Battle stations!" Commander L'Grina barked into the intercom. "Dingo's rats! What's that?"

"A flying saucer, I think," Deanna said, staring at the view screen. I turned to look, too.

From the approximate location of the downed ships, the alien ship rose straight upwards. From this distance, it looked like two saucers placed on top of each other, one inverted to the other. As we drew closer to it, it shot towards us. Based on the computer's analysis, the central bulge was equivalent to a five story building. The diameter's estimate was twelve hundred feet, truly a large ship. But...

I saw no cannons on its surface. Where were its engines? Ours were in the rear. The maneuverability of the flying saucer was hard to believe. One moment it flew directly towards us and the next moment it was flying straight upwards. No way could I possibly keep up with its movements.

"Commander, take over for me," I ordered, knowing she'd be much faster handling our ship.

"No need. It appears to be leaving the planet.

186

Anyone know whose ship that is? Anyone ever heard of such a ship?" Commander L'Grina asked.

I felt a sudden twinge of nerves. None of us had, including the Sixth Invader ambassador. We'd just encountered an unknown spaceship with unknown aliens, not at all what I'd imagined we would find. I'm not sure what I did expect we'd find, giants perhaps.

As we drew closer to the position, we spotted small settlements of mud-brick buildings and people scattered here and there. Deanna zoomed in on one group of men carrying spears.

"We're there," Deanna said. She'd been monitoring our position versus the transponders.

I eased back on the stick and hovered the Friendship about a mile above the site. We stared at our view screens. The two exploration ships rested side by side off to one side of a giant grey landing pad. We saw no other ships. However, a single story complex rose in the middle of the pad. A transparent dome covered a series of buildings, none of which had a roof.

We saw a collection of bedrooms surrounding central living areas, all of which joined a giant dining room. Behind that lay a kitchen and pantry. Only a quarter of the bedrooms were occupied. The commander relieved me, since there wasn't a computer to control our descent and landing. Besides, I wanted to see if I could telepathically reach Isabella or Bernardo.

I focused. 'Isabella. We're here.'

'Mom? Help us. Don't land. The aliens shot the mutation agent into the ships. Oh. Yes.'

The connection faded away as she slipped into some kind of whitish mental mass, one that seemed overwhelmingly pleasureful.

"They're down there. I reached Isabella." I explained the image she'd sent, in which these aliens had forced one of the ship's doors open and lobbed the mutation agent inside. Before I lost her connection to the white mass, I saw dozens of other armless Dolls, what remained of her crew.

The commander set the ship down near the two

exploration ships. Across the empty pad, we spotted large doors. Once our engines shut off, two armed aliens rushed out. One carried a large gun of some kind along with several others strapped to his waist or over his shoulders. The other carried an electronic device along with even more weapons. We presumed they were weapons.

These were truly aliens. None of us had ever seen their race before. I estimated they stood about six-six, a little shorter than the giants. Their bodies and torsos looked much like humans with a tan the envy of many. But it was their heads that so shocked us. Their flattened faces looked squashed, but their heads curved back like a giant bird's beak, the tip of the head's rear nearly eighteen inches behind what would have been the back of our heads. For a moment, I imagined they were a pair of spring-time robins digging for worms in the grass.

"Open your doors," one said. A translator box spoke loud enough for us to hear him, though we couldn't hear his actual words.

I replied via the intercom connected to a speaker near the front side door. "You surrender to us and give us back our people and ships."

The aliens responded by hooking the device to the exterior keypad we use to open the doors. General Bev didn't hesitate further. I heard a dull whirring sound as the four gun turrets on the top of the ship moved into position. Then, the sound of bullets, many bullets, broke the stillness. The bodies of both aliens jerked this way and that, falling backwards as the large caliber shells slammed into their bodies and exploded. Bev wasn't messing around. I think everyone on the ship was with her, since we knew the aliens wanted to turn everyone into armless telepath Dolls. But the storm of shells was total overkill. Both aliens were dead many times over, their bodies ripped into many pieces, splattered over the grey landing pad.

Heavily armed and wearing flak suits, Bev and her security group opened the upper doors and watched the ramp lower. The eight rushed out, guns pointing in all directions, while Bev verified the two aliens were dead. As one widely-separated unit, they moved to the complex main doors.

We watched streaming video from Bev's suit. As she approached the doors, we spotted a very startled looking female alien, who hastily raised her hands high, even though Bev hadn't reached the doors. Then, a small boy appeared at her side, staring out at us, wide-eyed. Both figures also had the elongated, pointed skull backside—woodpeckers in reverse.

The dead males had closely cut brown hair as did the child. The woman's hair was styled up in a sort of elaborate turban affair. The boy wore trousers that ended at his knees and an open, billowing shirt. A gauze-like robe draped over the woman's shoulder. Both wore sandals.

"Any tricks and I'll blow you to bits," General Bev said. She, Gail, Captain Betsy, and her six soldiers swarmed around the entrance doors.

Sam, Walter, Lenka, and I stepped down the forward ramp, avoiding the bloody scene. Walter carried a blaster and pistol, but hadn't drawn them, preferring to help us three negotiate the ramp. Our steel-tipped heels clicked loudly on the grey surface, almost as though we were walking on a metallic surface—one that gently sloped up to the dome.

"How many more of you are inside? More with guns" Bev asked.

"Look, Mom. Those three are like the ones inside. Are they telepaths, too?" the boy asked.

"The others left when we detected your ship. It's just my boy and me, now that you've killed my husband and friend."

"You're lucky we don't kill you, too. You've kidnapped two of our deep space exploration ships and their crew," Bev said.

"Take me to our people," I said, as I joined them. "Yes, boy, we're telepaths, so you can't hide anything from us. You have my son and daughter here."

Commander L'Grina joined us. She said, "As of this moment, this planet is now part of the Sol Empire and is under its jurisdiction." Then, she put her hands on her hips. "Well, well. We meet again. She's part of the abominable Third Invaders from Gamma Orionis and Sirius-3. Scourge of the galaxy!"

The alien put her hands on her hips emulating L'Grina. "Foul, disgusting Sixth Invader! So you got the humans of Earth to do your dirty work for you, eh?"

"General Bev, you should shoot both of these beasts now. They make what we did to your people look like a tea party. Third Invaders can't be trusted, even with your eyes open. Shoot them or I will."

"Love to. Crap, we won't shoot unless they try something first." She waved her guns around challenging the woman, who glared at her. "All right then. Let's go find our people. We can take these two back to Earth for a trial or something."

We walked inside. The temperature inside was perfect if slightly warm and humid. "I'm Molly Parkinson. Bev, have a couple guards go back and watch the ship. Could be others around."

"Aye, aye. I hope there are, cause I only got to blast two aliens. You and you—go."

The alien woman said, "I am Edyta Iakob-Ra, my son Henio. Our people haven't visited Sol-C in millennia. Do you even still know about us Third Invaders?"

"I doubt it. What did you invade?" I asked.

"A long river that wound its way through vast desert. We helped them build giant stone monuments. In return they worshiped us."

"Egypt? Pharaohs?"

"Yeah, Pharaoh Narmer and his son Hor-Aha. Documented in our ancient history records. Our people were there for centuries, but honestly, they became bored with your pathetic world and left. I take it you've finally moved out of copper and bronze ages. You should be careful befriending Sixth Invaders. They've been ravaging your section of galaxy for centuries. Uncivilized beasts. Backwards civilization that's relegated men to domestics. Pathetic."

Commander L'Grina barked. "Slavers! Your people are nothing but slavers. You enslave all those you encounter. You're the true beasts of the galaxy. You conquer only to get bodies to sell. Fiends."

I interrupted. "Okay. Take us to our people. Now."

She led us down a corridor and then up steps to an observation post. From here, we stood above the giant living complex, capable of housing over four hundred of our people and an equal number of their assistants. Similar viewing posts sat at each of the other corners. We looked down on our people. I gasped.

"What have you done to them?" I blurted out, but I already knew what they'd done.

Below us sixty armless men and women lay on the beds. They wore nothing but a garter belt like I'd seen Senior Ambassador Sanura Fenuku of Zahra-C wear. They held up the same silky black second-skin hose she'd tried to get me to wear when I met her on the Kanika battleship. Each also wore tall heels. Sitting beside each of our people was a short, red-skinned woman wearing only a leather loin cloth.

These aliens lived on this world. I soon learned each had been kidnapped from their village and forced into slavery, attending to the needs of our people. Things were far worse than this as I soon discovered.

"What have you done? Who are the red women?" Sam asked. "And why are they all writhing around on their beds?"

Edyta flinched and backed up to a wall of the observation room. "Local personal assistants. Each human has their own helper. It's only humane thing to do."

She did her best to put a positive slant on the situation. I sensed her thoughts and knew better.

"And..." I insisted on getting the truth heard.

"Okay, we had this facility going long before your first exploration ship found us. We had to defend ourselves."

I pointed out, "But those ships are unarmed." She ignored me.

"We have supply of that incredible biological mutation agent from Sol-C that mutates humans into telepaths. We used it on them, adding them to many other humans who were here. Then, that second ship came, and we were forced to mutate them as well. We've provided for them, as you can see."

"But what's wrong with them?" Sam asked.

"And why are they wearing the fancy hose from Zahra-C?" I asked.

"We needed to reduce their upset and wild emotions when they awoke from their comas. And we need to make them accept their native personal assistants and be patient with them as they learn your language and what telepaths need. Locals have barely reached copper age. Pretty ignorant."

"So what have you done to them?" I persisted. I sensed Isabella's mind, which was still enmeshed in a swirling white drug mass.

"All right. All right. We have them properly addicted to Methalon, which comes from Zahra-C. It's harmless, but it stimulates their senses—tactile in particular. Zahra-C is famous for promoting tactile sensualism. We finally have them all properly addicted to drug. You'll find them perfectly pliable, doing what you ask of them. All traces of their initial upsets and fright have been replaced with intense pleasure. Of course, they'll have to be given ten units of Methalon three times each day, usually with their meals. You can't take them off it or they'll die."

I probed her mind further, angry with what she'd done to my twins and the others. "What did you do with the other humans you had here? What were you going to do with our people? You can't lie to me. I'm in your mind now."

Her face paled, eyes blazing into mine as if they could somehow force me out of her mind. "Okay, okay. We transported others and their local helpers off to home world. In another couple of weeks, we planned to do same with this batch. What of it? Everyone needs telepath, but..."

"But what?" I demanded, glaring into her eyes.

"But these humans have been far too much trouble, even heavily drugged. So..."

"So?"

"So we changed our minds. We're keeping them here until they have their babies. We'll take their babies and leave them here to breed more telepaths. That's all this group is good for: breeding. They're too difficult to manage or trust—not like the others."

Commander L'Grina snickered. "I told you these were the worse slavers in the entire galaxy. Beasts. Vile beasts. You should kill her and the boy."

"Watch them both, Commander. Sam, Walter, let's go find our children."

We found Isabella and Owen Barker lying on the same bed, writhing about, sliding their legs up and down. When we entered, their fearful native assistants backed into a far corner.

"Isabella. It's Mom and Dad."

"Owen, it's Dad. We've come to rescue you."

"Umm. Mom, Dad. Need a fix. Can't take this much longer. We're going to have a baby. Don't let them take our baby. Give us a fix. Now. Please. Oh god."

"Dad. Need a fix. Protect our baby. I can't anymore."

"Teni look after her," the small native woman said. Her companion nodded, too.

"Thank you, Teni. Both of you, thank you."

Later, we found Bernardo and his fiancé Captain Wendy Lu. She had led the security force on the Pathfinder. Both of them begged us to not let the aliens take their baby.

In fact, when we visited the others, we found the women were pregnant. Since GPan usually balanced the number of men and women on these long-duration voyages, that meant close to thirty women were going to have a baby sometime in the next three to six months.

Edyta led us to the kitchen where they kept the Methalon. "Put dropper full into their drink at each meal. That corresponds to ten of your units. Now, if you don't mind, I have to cook lunch for hundred twenty, unless you want to do it."

"Go ahead. We'll watch you," I said, determined not to let her poison everyone. When she had a giant pot of soup ready for Henio to dish out, I made them each have a bowl of the soup. Since they didn't die, I let them sound the meal gong.

Soon, the helpers ushered their charges out into the large dining room. Our people looked like normal armless Galactic Dolls, so I was convinced that somehow these aliens had gotten a large supply of our mutation agent. I needed to find out how, to say nothing of where they'd taken the others they had mutated or even how many there were.

Deanna joined us. "I've relayed everything to Admiral Rossi. He's sending a pair of cruisers. Should be here within the hour. Also, GPan is sending a crew to help colonize this world, putting things to right with these local victims. I was right; they have a crude Faraday cage around the two exploration ships. How are the twins doing? Are all the women really pregnant?"

"Their helpers are feeding them now. From the way they downed their drinks, they were desperate for the drug she put in it. I'm hoping they'll be more communicative after they've eaten. I've not seen everyone up close yet, but it would seem there are about thirty pregnant women here. Is Admiral Rossi going to take care of our two prisoners for us?"

"Yes. They'll be taken back to Chicago and interrogated. He wants to find out how they got the bio agent, how they got our people, and where they took our people. I want to know if these aliens have other colonies like this one. I think he'll grill them on that point too," Deanna said. "Don't they have any of the mechanical aids that we give all our telepaths?"

"Nope. I think that's why each one has their own personal assistant."

"General Bev, you better come see this. We've a real problem. Natives." One of her rear guards dashed into the dining room.

Hastily, we rushed out to see that the commotion

was about. Of course, Sam, Lenka, and I were way behind the others. When we stepped outside the main doors, hundreds of short red men with spears filled the entire landing tarmac, save for the small portion occupied by the three ships. Each wore a leather loincloth. Some had copper ornaments dangling from their chests. One stepped forward.

I did too. "Hello. I'm Molly Parkinson. We've come to rescue our people from these bird-beaked aliens and return your captive women to their villages. We're putting a stop to the aliens and the kidnaping of your people." I said what I sensed was uppermost in the man's mind.

He spoke, but Henio and Edyta also came to see what was happening. His translator unit worked, converting the local speaker's language into ours.

"We want our women back. For many grain cycles, beak-heads stole our women. Have many warriors with magic weapons. She always with them. She takes our daughters and wives. Kill those who try to stop them. We patient. Saw last sky bird depart and have come to get our women back. Make aliens pay for what they've done. You give our women back now. We no hurt your people. Want them." He pointed his spear at Edyta and Henio.

My group looked at me. This was my rescue party and thus my decision to make. These natives had a valid argument. I'd seen images in Edyta's mind of how she'd acquired the many personal assistants. Did he know that most of their women weren't on this world any longer and that I had no idea where they were or how to get them back?

I thought about how to respond. Henio and his mother were behind me. I heard him cry out, "Never, beasts."

A trio of gunshots echoed, followed by Edyta's scream. I pivoted to see Bev and Gail lowering their Glocks. Henio lay on the ground, an alien pistol-like device beside him, hastily kicked away by Bev.

Bev said, "Tried to shoot you in the back, Molly."

"Thanks." Turning around, I said to their

spokesman, "Take her. We'll bring all your people that are still here out to you now. Friends?"

He nodded. We headed back inside, while native men swarmed around Edyta, dragging her away. She screamed and fought, but one of the men knocked her out. Six hastily carted her off. I turned a corner and lost sight of them.

"Are we really going to let them have Edyta?" asked Sam. "She might have lots more information on where they took the others."

"A hundred of them and only a few of us who could fight. We'll let Admiral Rossi's group figure out what to do. Maybe they won't kill her."

The two women looking after Isabella and Owen didn't want to leave them. "We take care them. They helpless now."

I convinced them that more of our people were arriving soon. Eventually, we shooed sixty women out into the waiting arms of the men.

"Where rest our women?" their leader asked.

"We don't know. These beak-headed aliens took many of our women too. Maybe Edyta knows where they went. We have our own sky birds. If she tells us, maybe we can go there and bring your women and ours back," I explained, thankful for the language translators some of the women still wore.

He nodded and the swarm departed, as silently as they arrived. A couple of our guards deposited Henio's body with the other pair.

"Now we *do* have our hands full," Deanna said.

"I've misplaced mine," Lenka said.

Everyone chuckled, thankful for the brief levity.

Chapter 16 Recovery and Plans

Two hectic days passed. As promised, two light cruisers arrived, bringing a replacement exploration crew with them. One cruiser headed off to explore the Zeta Tucanae solar system, while the other, the Bolt, investigated this world and helped with the ground situation.

Commander Lia Johnston, a forty-five year old with piercing blue eyes, commanded the Bolt. She brought Earth's new ambassador to this world with her. Short and brown skinned, Ambassador Rummani anticipated fitting in with the local population. Commander Johnston's linguist worked with the ambassador to update our own language translators with this new language, compliments of the working models the aliens had left us.

The real challenge: handling the sixty victims. By the end of the second day, I faced an entirely new situation. Fortunately, Celeste arrived via cargo shuttle bringing along a supply of the usual machines we gave everyone, including sixty laptops with the hundreds of hours of how-to holo videos on them. Unfortunately, this time these much needed devices proved useless. Why?

The Methalon drug had already turned them into tactile sensualists. I should explain. After ingesting the next dosage of the drug, they slipped into a writhing delirium, twisting, tossing, turning, and doing everything possible to have intercourse before slipping into a deep, but still writhing, sleep. That lasted an hour. The victims awoke coherent and told us what had happened and what they knew about the aliens who had been here. However, that lucid period lasted only an hour. Slowly, their bodies began craving more Methalon, twisting and turning in agony, relieved only by receiving their next dosage.

Thus, we had sixty patients who needed almost constant care. During their fleeting lucid times, we learned at least three hundred other humans had been here since June when they captured Isabella and the crew of the Star

Voyager. That also meant at least three hundred local women were taken away as their personal assistants. Although Commander Johnston questioned each of the sixty, none knew where they were taken.

She uncovered what we expected. They planned to use the victims as telepaths and to procreate more telepaths. Where did the aliens obtain the mutation agent? "Earth provides it" was the oft-repeated answer. We also concluded the aliens hadn't drugged the missing victims as heavily as they had our two crews, probably because the exploration members were rugged individuals, who put up more of a fight. However, their current situation made them useless as telepaths, coherent only a few hours each day.

Commander Johnston's people searched the alien base, uncovering two gallons of Methalon. They discovered a pile of hundreds of empty syringes that once contained the armless Galactic Doll mutation agent. A small lab contained equipment to convert those single-person doses into an aerosolized form stored in mutation bombs that could be tossed into spaceships. They'd used these to take out both our exploration ships. And they'd tried it on us, but Bev and her guards had terminated them before they could get our doors opened and the gas bombs tossed inside.

The commander was thorough. She had her team document the manufacturer of each syringe. Most came from GMed Moscow. Commander Johnston informed me of this discovery and that she would have Earth's Senior Investigators find out how these aliens acquired it.

"Look," I said to her, "if these Third Invaders got their hands on hundreds of doses, you can bet many others have it, too. Heck, probably every planet in the galaxy now has samples that could turn any human into an armless telepath. If only Bev had been able to destroy it when we discovered it."

"You're too pessimistic. We've only found it here with these aliens. I don't see any hope for these sixty victims. If you want my advice, I'd put them out of their misery."

My whole body tensed. Those were my twins she condemned.

Her search yielded a number of small arms weapons, which her science crew drooled over. Unfortunately, they discovered no information about the others who had been taken away as slaves, but they found three hundred documents that might hold a clue, if they could be read.

Meanwhile, Celeste studied the symptoms and consulted GMed Chicago about Methalon; they consulted our ambassadors from Zahra-C. That night after we got our people into bed, Celeste sat down with Sam, Walter, and me.

"Via our ambassadors, I have bad news. Methalon is one of Zahra-C's major exports. In low doses, it's used to enhance a person's tactile senses. That's its major galaxy-wide use. However, in the doses these Third Invaders used, it's not only addictive, but ruins the person. There's no known way to get someone as hooked on it as they are off it. From watching our people, I was afraid of that."

"No way at all?" Sam asked.

Celeste sighed and shook her head. "We can try reducing their dosage each day, but..."

"But what?" I asked. I hadn't felt such a wave of anger in a long time. If I'd had hands and if Edyta was here, I'd probably lose it and take my anger out on her.

"But that doesn't work. I already asked about that. It's been tried many times. The victims always go insane from their cravings and usually die unless they're given more. What I can't figure out is why these Third Invaders so overdosed these sixty crew members and not the hundreds of others."

I slept fitfully. In the morning, I sat beside Isabella and Owen, watching their bodies writhing. Helpless. That's how I felt.

Isabella moaned. "Mom. I deciphered Fifth Invader writings on the moon. I deciphered Fourth Invader hieroglyphics on Mars. I deciphered Third Invader writings here. Please. I need a fix. Please." Delirium came again.

Bev found me. "Hey. Any change?" I shook my head. "Well, come on. One of those native women is at the door. She's asking for you. Commander Johnston sent me to find you."

The commander and four guards stood just outside the dome's doors. I spotted the native woman who had looked after Isabella. "Hi, Teni." I trusted the translator devices.

The short woman, barely four feet tall, smiled at me. "Greetings Isabella's mother and our savior. I brought toca leaves for her and your people."

"Thank you. What do these toca leaves do?"

"Have each one eat leaf. No give alien drug. Toca help Isabella. No more silliness."

"Okay. One leaf at each meal. But how many days do we do this?"

"Two, maybe three at most. Teni good remedy. You see."

"I sure hope so, Teni. We can't find a cure for them anywhere."

She smiled, handing me a large leather bag filled with greenish leaves, slipping its loop over my head.

"Oh. Chief says you can have alien woman back. Use her to find missing women. Six tribes met three days past. Now done punishing her."

I didn't get a chance to respond. Commander Johnston said, "Excellent. Yes, we'd like the alien woman back. We'll make her talk and maybe we can get your people back and ours, too."

"Chief bring here by high sun." She nodded and left, disappearing silently into the wooded hills just beyond the dome and landing pad.

"My people can test those leaves before you give them to the victims," Commander Johnston said. "What a lucky break. Getting Edyta back. I'm sure one of you telepaths can pry critical information from her."

I joined Celeste, Walter, Sam, and Lenka in Isabella and Owen's room. I told them what Teni said, while Celeste took the bag from me and examined the large pile of leaves.

"So is this a cure for them?" Sam asked.

"From what Teni said, I assume so, but do we dare have them eat an unknown plant leaf?"

Celeste exhaled deeply. "Yeah. Look—right now we're out of options. We've no way to cure them or even get them off Methalon. I heard Commander Johnston say they should be humanely terminated. Before that happens, we should at least try. Homeopathic remedies can work."

"Okay. We'll try it on Isabella and Bernardo first," I said.

"And Owen," Walter said. "We have to do something. He's all I have left. I feel so helpless." His eyes watered.

Lenka pressed her body into his giving him a hug. "We'll find a cure, Walter. Guys, what about not giving them the Methalon and instead injecting them with the mutation agent. Maybe the mutation would undo the chemical addiction."

"She has a point," Celeste said. "We'll give these leaves a chance first. If that fails, I'll inject them myself. Walter's right. We must try everything possible."

Gail sounded the lunch gong. Our small group headed out to the dining room, assisting others as we went. My heart went out to these people. Everyone moaned, begging for the drug—some trying to writhe while standing.

Mealtimes, crew from Commander Johnston's cruiser helped us handle the sixty victims, who could do nothing for themselves. Poignant. That's how I felt about Isabella and Bernardo who should have been as skilled as I was, but they were just as zonked by the drug's effects as the others.

I had the three eat a leaf before feeding them their soup and sandwich. They guzzled their drink first, believing it contained their next fix. By the time the three finished lunch, they looked alert and talked coherently.

"Mom, Dad, I deciphered the writings on Mars! Of course, Owen helped me lots. He's a great astro-archaeologist. They were the Fourth Invaders with giant praying mantis-like bodies."

"She's right," Owen said. "Fifty-feet long. Three

desiccated remains have been found on Mars so far, perfectly preserved. Hi, Dad." He glanced at us, but his eyes landed on my daughter. "Isabella, I had no idea how bad this is for you. I'm utterly helpless. I've got no way to help support us, but we're having a baby, so I've got to help somehow. Maybe you should marry someone else, but let Dad and me see our baby sometimes."

Isabella looked at him and giggled. "Owen, don't be silly. Hey! We're coherent; it's now the middle of the afternoon. I feel funny, though. Like I'm about to explode or something. Mom, can you help me get out of these stockings? Do we have any clothes around? I've my things on the Star Voyager. Maybe some might fit Owen. Don't worry, honey, we can do fine with our feet. I'll show you. It's not the end of the world. Why is everyone looking at us?"

I had tears tickling my cheeks. "Teni gave us a cure for the Methalon addiction. It looks like it's working. Celeste, see about getting clothes for everyone. We'll give everyone a leaf for supper instead of the drug. Teni said you'll need to eat a leaf three times a day for a couple of days. We're going to have to find her and thank her. She's saved sixty lives."

Bev interrupted us. "Molly, come see Edyta. They've brought her back. Looks like the natives really punished her. They chopped off her arms!"

"Back shortly," I said and followed Bev back to the dome's doors.

Several native men headed back into the hills, while the Bolt's doctor hovered over the alien, who's unconscious body lay on a crude stretcher. Commander Johnston stood close by, watching intently, while six guards holstered their guns.

When she saw me arrive, she said, "The locals got their justice—poetic, in my opinion, considering how many humans she's done something similar to. She's unconscious. Doc thinks she'll live. If she doesn't revive, can you still use telepathy to get anything useful out of her?"

"Not really, but I'll try. We've got to find the others."

"Commander," her doctor said, "they've left about two inches of her arm bones, but she's weak, lost blood, and has infection setting in. If she were human, I'd recommend immediate surgery, removing the arm remnants from her sockets, cutting off the infected flesh, and giving her massive antibiotics. But..."

"But she's alien," Commander Johnston said. He nodded. "Infection has set in?" He nodded again. "Okay then. We don't have much choice. Do your best for her. We need her alive, if possible."

"Molly, as soon as she regains consciousness, I'll send for you. We need to find the rest of our people."

"We need to destroy this damned mutation agent," I said.

She paused and stared at me. "Then we wouldn't have any telepaths."

I left it at that and returned to the others, convinced that those who weren't mutated wanted this bio agent around, while those who had been mutated wanted the cures and to have it destroyed. When I returned to the dining room, Isabella, Bernardo, and Owen continued to chat with the others. They hadn't slumped, further evidence the cure was working.

Celeste said, "Molly, I'd like to get therapy sessions going as soon as we can. When the others come out of their drugged stupors, they're likely to react badly."

"I know. Okay, let's do it now. I'll do Isabella."

Sam said, "I'll do Bernardo."

"Can I help?" Lenka asked.

Celeste took charge. "Yes. You and Walter watch me as I do Owen. Tonight, I'll have you each helping others."

Thus began a long afternoon of therapy sessions. Because Bernardo and Isabella had already had a lot of therapy—particularly seven years ago when they'd been initially mutated—by late afternoon they'd erased the recent harmful physical and emotional trauma. Both had once lived a past lifetime of opium addiction. Much of the power of the Methalon drug rested upon those incidents which happened centuries ago.

Lenka and Walter watched Celeste handling Owen. By late afternoon, Owen discharged much of the Methalon haze. As supper approached, his raw emotions over becoming an armless telepath blazed, shocking the two observers. Helpless, hopeless, useless, intense terror, and grief swamped Owen, as it usually did with anyone who had been mutated against their will.

As others arrived for dinner, Celeste ended the current session with Owen so she could assist feeding so many victims.

While Walter fed Owen, Lenka said, "Owen, I felt the same way when this happened to me. I felt so helpless. Terror almost cut my stomach in half. And the grief—it still bothers me—just not so often. I really do need lots more sessions. Anyway, hang in there with the therapy. It makes all the difference in the world. Celeste says I get to run someone through their trauma tonight. At least I can do that."

"Oh, you do many things, Lenka," Walter said. "I'm continually amazed with you. You never give up."

"Walter, I can't give up. If I do, I'm doomed. I don't want to die, not yet anyway. Everything is damned hard, Owen, but you keep at it. If you don't, Isabella will kick your butt."

Owen managed a very slight smile, fleeting only. I said, "Lenka is right. You can't give up, not if you want to marry my Isabella." Another minuscule smile.

Deanna joined us. "Say, we're incredibly lucky. I've been working with Commander Johnston's engineers going over this alien technology. We just found and deactivated a mutation bomb. They had it rigged into the air filtering system of this entire dome. Think what would have happened if a hundred of us were inside caring for the victims and one of the aliens pressed the detonate button? We could have been wiped out. We're looking for more booby traps."

"Well done, Deanna. And whew, too," I said.

"On the bright side, this dome of theirs is a fabulous

technological feat. We're going to try to figure out how to duplicate it for use on other worlds we encounter. Oh yes. Bev uncovered a stash of alien handheld weapons. She's in heaven. We've encountered many strange things about this setup. We landed on a metal surface. We've no idea why they used metal instead of a concrete or asphalt tarmac, but we'll keep studying."

One by one, the remaining fifty-seven victims came out of their Methalon induced daze. For them, heaven instantly became hell. For those who had never experienced mutation victims awaking, they received a taste of hell. The reality of what had happened slammed into them. Most were highly educated people: botanist, geologists, zoologists, anthropologists, pilots, navigators, for example. Months ago, they had been living productive, exciting lives exploring the galaxy for new planets. Awakened from their Methalon daze, they reacted to their perceived destroyed lives.

Commander Johnston, her hands covering her ears, looked at me. Over the din, I yelled, "Like I said, that agent should be destroyed."

"Can't you do something?" she yelled back.

I glanced at Celeste. She rose and called out with incredible intention, so much so that everyone ceased whatever they had been doing. "Okay, close your eyes. Good. I want you to return to the first moment when you suspected something wasn't right, that something was about to happen. All right. Now go through the incident and tell us what happened, what you saw, what you smelled, what you felt."

Telepathically, she sent, 'Fan out and position yourselves so you can listen to several as they re-experience their trauma.'

I moved beside Wendy Lu, Bernardo's fiancé. All eighteen of the Friendship crew fanned out sitting beside other victims, along with thirty-eight of Commander Johnston's crew. Some had been feeding their victims.

The presence of Celeste dominated the room. I'd never known that a person could have such personal power over others. Had she said "Jump," I swear everyone would've immediately done so. Wow. Then, I settled down, listening to what the terrified Wendy Lu was saying. I did notice Commander Johnston paying close attention to this remarkable therapy session.

Wendy said, "I'm cleaning my guns when we heard the commander over the intercom. 'Battle Stations. We've discovered an unexpected domed town. Definitely not one of the locals. Landing on a kind of tarmac now. Captain Lu, prepare a security team to guard our perimeter when we land.' I'm racing to the bay doors along with my six guards. We're given the order to open the doors and fan out. Protective Screen One, the commander orders. The door opens. 'Grenade!' I yell. A strange alien tosses it in. We hit the deck. Explosion. No real damage. I get up to report to the commander. I feel weak. Have to be strong. Have to protect everyone. So... Oh, I slump to the deck. All is black."

In the background, I heard similar words from others, but from their points of view, scattered around the ship. Thus passed the evening.

At bedtime, Celeste gently interrupted all the sessions. "Okay, everyone. You did great. We're stopping for the night. We'll resume after breakfast. For those who listened, thank you."

Commander Johnston said, "Molly. When you are free tomorrow, come see me."

I wasn't able to get free for two more days. Right after getting everyone fed their breakfasts, we resumed their previous therapy sessions, halting for lunches and then suppers. I know we handled these emergency therapy sessions crudely, but the traumas were right there in the present—live and hot.

Her incredible presence allowed the victims to have enough confidence to view and re-experience what had happened. Mutation comas were intensely painful. Once that pain reduced, all manner of other feelings, emotions, and attitudes surfaced—raw and debilitating. Helpless, hopeless, useless—these threatened to destroy each victim. In fact, these were the very things that had caused so many earlier victims to beg to be terminated. This is why Celeste insisted on working them for two long days.

The product achieved via this crude version of her therapy: a reduction of the overall trauma and the myriad feelings, emotions, and attitudes. We didn't achieve full erasures. A willingness to have more therapy and to learn how to survive replaced their terror and death wishes. The third day, Celeste, Sam, Isabella, Bernardo, and I began private sessions on five of the fifty-eight. We focused on each person's actual needs, working them towards a full erasure of the trauma and subsequent debilitating feelings.

Walter, Lenka, Bev, and Gail worked with those not in sessions, focusing on how to use the hair and nail machine, the dressing machine, and the laptops filled with the 3-d how-to videos. By the end of the day, they'd gotten everyone satisfactorily handling these devices.

That evening, Celeste relayed her plans, based on how it well our five patients fared during the day's sessions. "We've gotten our five victims into reasonably good shape today. Base on these results, we'll do five new people each day. In twelve days, we should have everyone in a stable state. While I'd like to give each all the therapy they need, that'll take us many months. Heck, Lenka needs more herself."

"It's educational helping others cope," Lenka said. "But you're right. I have all kinds of weird feelings and emotions bothering me. We can worry about me after we get everyone here stabilized. My god, Celeste. You've saved fifty-eight lives with your therapy!"

I interrupted. "Hey, Commander Johnston wants to see me. I've been putting her off for several days. I best see what she wants tomorrow morning. Lenka, cover for me, please."

At breakfast I met with Commander Johnston. "I can be free this morning, if you still want to see me."

"Absolutely. Edyta has recovered. I need assistance getting truth out of her."

"She looked really bad when I saw her a couple days ago."

"My doctors removed her infected stumps from her shoulders and used our silver compound healing nanoparticles and the nano graphene healing mesh on her. She's up and about. She's about as terrified as our mutation victims are. Lordy, I don't know how you could stand to listen to their screams."

I smiled. While I might not be able to convince her the mutation agent should be destroyed, she now appreciated what the victims endured.

"Also, Deanna and my engineers have been going over this building. They've discovered what they believe is a sealed door leading downward. So I want to bring Edyta to it and ask her how we open it. Probably should bring your daughter, Isabella, along with you. Her uncanny ability to translate the Third Invader's writing is invaluable. I'm sure we're going to find many more documents for her to translate."

"Okay, I'll have Deanna take Isabella's place today. I don't want to shortchange anyone's therapy session this morning."

"Meet me in the hallway in, say, a half hour." With a satisfied look, Commander Johnston rose and left the dining room.

Isabella and I walked to the meeting location, our steel-tipped heels clicking on the metal floor. She said, "Mom, I still can't figure out why the floor is metal, except that we telepaths can be heard coming a mile away."

I chuckled. "Maybe that's why. If they housed several hundred here, they could hear anyone walking, perhaps where they shouldn't be."

"Mom? That's silly. We've been all over this dwelling. There's hardly anything here to keep away from the victims. Ah, here they come. Gosh, Edyta looks terrified. At least she doesn't have to wear tall heels."

Commander Johnston wore her blue uniform, freshly pressed. A thin man accompanied her, also wearing a similar uniform, but a decal on his pocket indicated he was an engineer. He had a bag of tools slung over his shoulder.

Edyta walked in front of them—her face, a ghastly pale. I didn't need telepathy to sense the terror radiating from her like a lantern. Unlike the rest of us, she wore flats. Someone had found one of Leslie's light blue dresses that fit her—the kind I always wore that encased our shoulders.

"Well, Edyta, how do you like being one of us?" Isabella asked. "Sorry that you don't have telepathy, though. You look a bit scared."

"I'm helpless. But at least I provided each of you with your own personal assistant."

"You need to learn to use your feet and toes like we do. Then, you can be independent again, Edyta," I said, sharing some hope for her benefit.

"Why did you make me come? I can't do anything anymore," Edyta said.

Commander Johnston chuckled. "That's why I don't have to bring along armed security guards. You can't harm anyone anymore. No, we discovered a door that we need opened. This way."

She led us down a long hall that made three sharp turns before ending at what must be a door. I noticed the hall sloped gently downward. In our tall heels, our knees took a beating. The door was eight feet square, divided into two panels and looked much like some kind of bank vault—less the locking mechanism.

"So how do we open it?" Commander Johnston asked.

I saw scratch marks here and there on the silvery surface. Whatever her engineers had tried failed to open it.

"If I had my hands, I could show you," Edyta whined.

"Tell us instead."

Commander Johnston put her right palm on the cold steel roughly where the alien said, moving it slightly until a keypad suddenly appeared, startling us.

"Okay, code?" she asked.

Thankfully, Edyta wore her translation unit strapped to her waist. The keypad showed a dozen strange symbols, none of which I recognized. Edyta rattled off the six

symbols, and Isabella translated for the commander, telling
her which symbol on the keypad corresponded to the code.
After the last symbol was touched, a hissing sound echoed
and the two door panels slid into the sidewalls, revealing a
large opening.

We carefully stepped down a short flight of stairs.
Commander Johnston and her engineer rushed ahead,
eager to see what was down there. In our tall heels, Isabella
and I descended very carefully.

"I can't do this. I'll fall," cried Edyta.

I felt sympathy for the woman. I knew precisely what
she was feeling—been there, done that many times. And
yes, it's frightening the first time you have to face it.

From far ahead, Commander Johnston called out,
"What *is* all this?"

To my utter surprise, from behind me, Edyta's stern
voice barked a command. "Computer: execute Protocol
Nine."

The steps and floor beneath me wiggled and
vibrated. Isabella and I very nearly lost our balance, but
managed to reach the main steel floor. Edyta joined us,
laughing hysterically.

My eyes swept around the large room we were in—
my eyes as wide as the commander's. We were inside some
kind of spaceship's command and control center. On one
wall monitor, we watched a hemispherical steel cover
sliding over the dome, sealing it in. This caused the
vibrations.

"Is this a flying saucer?" I blurted out, finally
grasping the magnitude of what I was seeing. On the
monitor, I watched the two exploration ships slide off what
we thought was the metal landing pad. The Friendship
slipped off next. Someone on board the Bolt must have
realized what was going on; they'd issued a liftoff order,
and the cruiser's bottom jets stirred up a cloud of dust.

Edyta continued to cackle, unnerving us. Further, a
whitish gas slowly filled the room. Both Isabella and I
recognized it: the armless Galactic Doll mutation agent.

"Damn you!" I cried, as Commander Johnston and

her engineer slumped to the floor entering mutation comas. "What have you done?" Edyta continued to cackle. Insanity struck. I admit this was perfect protection against humans breaking into the ship's control room. Then, the ship lurched upwards, knocking all three of us onto the floor. My head hit the floor hard. Darkness swept over me.

Chapter 17 Unexpected Flight

My head hurt. I felt cold. Still groggy, I came to. The revelation and events flooded through my mind, as I struggled to sit up. Beside me, Isabella roused. A startled look appeared on her face.

"Mom. You okay? I've a headache. Haven't taken a fall like that in years, not since we spent days learning how to use our feet at your place."

"Same here. Edyta's still unconscious. We best undo the commander's clothes."

Isabella giggled. "No kidding. She's from Brussels, Tau Ceti. That's why her body isn't a Galactic Doll. Well, it soon will be. Damn. What are we going to do? Where's the ship taking us?"

"Don't know yet, honey. Let's make these two comfortable. Then, we'll put your language skills to use deciphering the controls. I wonder how long we were unconscious."

"Probably not too long," Isabella said. "His bosom hasn't begun to enlarge. Their arms haven't withered much. I forgot how much of a pain it is to get someone undressed without using our fancy machines."

Sitting on the cold floor, we wrestled with their uniforms and shoes. After a lengthy struggle, we had them stripped. After getting up, we stared at the unfamiliar controls spread out among five stations. Dials and readouts flashed. They looked like gibberish to me, but not to Isabella.

"Mom, I think we're in hyperspace. Someone's pounding on the doors too."

"Okay, see if you can find any button or thing to press to lower our velocity to zero. We don't dare just drop out of hyperspace at some random location. I'll see if I can get the door opened again. I could use Sam's eidetic memory about now." We laughed.

I had no hands to place on the door to enable the

keypad to appear. I slipped off a heel, balanced, and slid my foot around the approximate position Edyta had indicated on the other side of the door. Just as I was about to give up, the pad appeared. Not having much luck, Isabella joined me. Together, we touched the six symbols. The door opened, revealing the very worried faces of Commander L'Grina, Deanna, and Sam.

"You all right?" the Commander asked. "We're in one of their flying saucers. Hyperspace, too. What's going on?"

"Edyta triggered another trap. Mutation agent flooded the control center," I said. "The ship is on some kind of automatic pilot. We've no idea where we're going. Deanna, see if you can find a way to prop the door open, then join us. We have to take control of the ship from its computer. Oh, Edyta went insane on us, but she hit her head when she fell and is out cold."

"Hey, slick control center," Commander L'Grina said. We gazed at the myriad controls, dials, and readout units—all foreign to us. "Whatever you do, don't just drop us out of hyperspace. We could end up in the middle of a black hole or neutron star."

Isabella giggled. "Mom's already told me that. Looking for some way to lower our velocity. It helps because they trained me to pilot and navigate the Star Voyager. It was the hardest things I ever tried to do, but that was their policy. In case of emergencies, anyone could fly the ship home. So I'm trying to see if I can find something similar among all these controls."

Deanna joined us, gasping at the complexity of the control center and what had happened.

Sam said, "If only I could read some of this, I might be able to find the navigation controls."

"Hey, Dad. I think this might adjust our velocity. Should I try it? Something bad might happen if I'm wrong," Isabella asked.

He looked at me. I said, "Okay. Go ahead and try. If we wait for the ship to get to where it's programmed to go, we'll all be captured by these aliens. I've no desire to become a slave telepath. Do it."

I held my breath as she used a toe to adjust the lever upwards. One readout's display changed symbols rapidly, then stopped.

"Hum. I think we're still in hyperspace, but not moving. That is their symbol for none or zero," Isabella said.

I relaxed. "Okay. Let's go tell everyone what's happened. Commander, stay here with Edyta. Don't let her use her voice to issue further orders to the computer. I've no idea what we can do now, though."

We'd been gone about two hours and found Gail preparing lunch for everyone. All eighteen of the Friendship's crew and sixty-one from the Bolt's crew were trapped inside the flying saucer. When everyone gathered in the dining room for lunch, I explained what happened. Bringing food for the others, Bev and Lenka returned with me to the control center, though many others dropped by just to see it, before resuming their therapy sessions.

I chuckled. Commander L'Grina had gagged Edyta. "You'll get food, but only if you keep quiet," I said. She nodded. I sat down and used my foot to feed her. "Soon, you're going to have to start practicing this yourself. I'm not going to do this often."

"You've stopped us moving through hyperspace. You can't do that. No, no, no. You can't do that." She cackled hysterically.

"We did it. Why not? Where were you planning to take us?"

"I'm not telling you that." She pouted like some a silly school girl, tossing her head to one side before laughing again.

"Edyta, we need you to tell us how to return the ship to where we were at. Eat up. Then, we have to reverse course."

By the time they'd eaten, we saw that Edyta had really snapped. I couldn't get anything useful out of her. Commander L'Grina agreed with my assessment and led her back into the main living area where everyone else resumed the many therapy sessions. Celeste took charge of

214

Edyta, and I hoped that she could find a way to remove Edyta's insanity.

During the long afternoon, Deanna and another engineer discovered sub-floors that housed fuel cells, wiring, an armory that Bev just had to acquire, and a large supply of food and water in bottles. Late afternoon, I held a meeting with Deanna, Commander L'Grina, Isabella, Lenka, and Sam.

"Here's the situation. We're motionless in hyperspace. We are in no danger of starving or running out of water. Time's on our side. It's up to us to learn the Third Invader language, enough so we can work out how to operate this spaceship. Once we master all these controls, we should be able to navigate our way back. If Edyta ever overcomes her temporary insanity, I'll try to pry operational details out of her mind. If that doesn't happen, it's up to us to study all the documentation we can find and figure it out ourselves. Deanna and Isabella will be in charge of the project. Commander L'Grina, Lenka, Sam and I will follow their orders. If we have to sit here a month, we will because we're going to fly this ship home."

I hoped I sounded inspirational enough. Deanna booted up her laptop. Together, she and Isabella documented what they'd uncovered thus far, which was very little. Meanwhile, they charged us four to learn to read the alien symbols.

Days passed swiftly—a blessing for the fifty-eight victims because they continued to receive therapy sessions, erasing the smaller upsets, unwanted emotions, and attitudes that arose while they emulated the how-to videos. Celeste couldn't do anything for Edyta, so she kept her locked in a quiet bedroom. After eight days, I sat beside Commander Johnston, waiting for her to come out of her coma. Right on time, her eyelids fluttered, and she awoke to the never-ending nightmare. Next door, her engineer roused, too.

"It's okay, commander. You're alive."

In spite of my efforts to present a calm environment, she screamed. Her body shook. I remained quiet and allowed her terror to run its course.

"I'm useless. My life is over! My career's gone," she wailed. "I don't want to be a helpless telepath. They won't even allow me to return to Brussels. Oh, god! I'm going to throw up."

Unfortunately, she did. After that, she slumped from terror down into grief, while I cleaned up the mess. A flood of tears rushed down her cheeks and onto her now massive bosom. All the while I remained silent. When she stopped crying, I used my feet and a towel to dry her off.

"Commander Johnston, here's a status report. The ship is parked in hyperspace. Isabella managed to lower its velocity to zero. We're now learning how to fly this ship, but it's taking a long time to decipher everything. Edyta has gone insane, so no help from her. Celeste is hopeful she can pull her out of her insanity, given time. Unfortunately, you and your engineer are now one of us, a telepath.

"I'll give you as many therapy sessions as needed to get you back to battery. Your life isn't over, and neither is your career. Your crew isn't deserting you. You're still the commander of the Bolt, even if the Bolt isn't with us. I won't lie to you. It isn't easy, but we're far from useless. Now then, the first thing is to get you dressed and familiar with how to use these two machines. I think you'll love the hair and nail machine. We use it to keep toenails trimmed. Once you get the hang of running the dressing machine, you'll be much more independent. We have a laptop with all the how-to videos on it for you. Our motto is 'Stop and think how.' So up and at it. Time to get dressed and some food in you. Then, it's therapy time."

"But this therapy isn't going to regrow my arms, so why bother? I'm doomed."

I ignored that and showed her how to use the dressing machine, using my foot to put garments into their places on the machine. She wobbled wildly, unused to her distorted feet. The machine did its job. Soon, she wore a light blue satin gown that encased her shoulders along with matching pumps.

Her hair had grown considerably. Blonde locks fell

to the small of her back. As expected, the hair machine brought the first smile to her face.

"There, you look good, Commander. The gown matches your eyes."

"Lia. Call me Lia. I'm never going to be a commander again."

"Okay, Lia. Let's get you properly fed. I bet you're starving."

"The terror I felt has lessened. Enough so that I think I could eat. I feel so darn helpless, Molly."

"Of course you do. Come on."

Gail served up a healthy meal for Lia and her engineer. I ignored tears that flowed when we had to feed them. When we returned to the room, I began her therapy session.

"Okay. Close your eyes. Let's return to the first moment when you thought something was wrong when Edyta spoke up. Go through what happened and tell me what you saw, what you felt, what you smelled."

"We are standing there, looking at the room. She yells something. I see a white gas filling the room. I feel a bump on my head. Then, I'm awake with you helping me up."

She'd bounced over ninety-nine percent of what happened, but that was to be expected. I had her go back and run through it again and again. On the sixth pass, she shrieked. "A stabbing pain in my right arm. Ow. In my left arm. God, it hurts. I can't stand it anymore. I'm so useless."

"I understand. Keep on moving through the trauma." On the tenth pass, the pain jolts subsided. Eventually, I asked if there was an earlier trauma that was similar to this one.

"No. I just have this feeling of pressure all over my body and a slight pain in my head. I must have really bumped it when I fell down in the coma. I told you I'm useless."

"All right. Is that pressure coming from an image?"

"Well, sort of. I see something white."

"Good. Go through it and tell me what's happening."

"Oh! I see a sterile white room. It's a hospital. I'm being born. Ouch. The doctor almost drops me. I hit my head. See, I'm so useless."

After several more passes, the pressure alleviated, but the head pain turned into a sore right arm where the doctor grabbed the baby before it fell to the floor. So I asked for something earlier.

"But there can't be anything before that. I was born. See, I'm so useless."

I kept her looking and finally she spotted something greenish. After running her through it several times, the trauma became clear to her.

"I'm on a cruiser, and my roommate has no confidence at all. How the devil she even got on our ship I don't know. Anyway, I'm doing my best to encourage her. We're taking gunnery practice. She drops an artillery blaster shell on my arm, shattering it in five places. I scream. The pain! She keeps saying, 'See, I'm so useless.' I wanted her to shut up and get the doc, but she just kept saying it until I passed out. Men come and carry me to the infirmary. They remove my lower arm. God, does that ever hurt. Oh, I'm getting a fancy prosthetic lower arm, one that really works.

"What a minute! I've lived before!" Lia exclaimed and began laughing. I ended this first session. "Well, I feel lots better, but still helpless."

At dinner, I had her make her first attempt at feeding herself holding her fork in her toes. "This is so hard, so clumsy."

"Practice makes perfect, Lia. Give yourself time. You'll become adept at it."

"I had no idea how hard life is for you telepaths. Perhaps Edyta was right to provide everyone with a personal assistant."

"Absolutely not. We have to become independent so we can get on with our lives and goals. Having a personal assistant will only re-enforce how helpless you are. That's suicide. With practice and bright ideas, there's only a few things we can't do."

"Point taken. You can't fire your gun. Bev told me about it. That you used to be a crack shot."

I sighed. "Yeah. Sometimes I truly miss that. Still, in time and with practice, you'll be back commanding the Bolt again."

"Only if we can figure out this flying saucer."

***

Days turned into weeks, beneficial to the many victims, especially Commander Lia Johnston and her engineer. I continued to work with her, helping her practice life skills, but giving her another therapy session whenever anything came up. Defeatist attitudes, wild emotions, and even strange feelings and sensations arose. Lia traced each one back to a basic trauma filled with pain and unconsciousness before they vanished leaving no trace. Each day, Lia became more capable. Her confidence rose, as did her self-respect.

Meanwhile, the crew members of the Star Voyager and the Pathfinder recovered and wanted to help unravel the mysteries of this flying saucer. Isabella and Deanna appreciated the help, as they slowly worked out the workings of the ship.

At the two week mark, Edyta finally pulled out of her insanity. Total peace and quiet allowed her to relax. At this point, Celeste took a calculated risk and took Edyta into a therapy session. While I'd proven her therapy methods worked on dwarves and on Sixth Invaders, we didn't know if it would work on this alien. She and I hoped it would for two reasons. One, this alien had undergone real torture at the hands of the natives. Two, we needed her to help us figure out how to fly the ship and get back.

That night, Celeste confided in me. "Molly, I've handled some rough cases before, but none of them compare to Edyta's. She's caused the mutation to so darn many people, kidnapped so many natives, that her scales are totally out of balance. She's holding onto this painful traumatic incident very hard, trying to equal what she's done to others. Plus, she won't do anything for herself."

"Is it working?"

"I think so, but getting her to give up a tiny drop of

pain is akin to pulling her teeth out." We laughed.

"I guess this can happen if you unjustly harm too many people." Celeste nodded.

***

At the month mark, Celeste finally gave up trying to help Edyta confront her trauma. "Molly, go ahead and probe her mind. Try to find out all you can," Celeste said. "I'll have everyone prepare a list of questions you can use to probe her mind."

Edyta didn't mind. She sat uselessly on the edge of the bed waiting for someone to tend to her needs. By now, no one wanted to do that. I entered, sat beside her, focused, and entered her mind.

'Edyta, where are you taking us?' I placed this thought and watched what resulted. I saw glimpses of many other pairs of telepaths and their assistants, hundreds of them swirling in and out of her thoughts. Finally, her mind focused on a huge, strange city with dozens of flying saucers darting about like fireflies. Her home world, I presumed. Well, we certainly didn't want to go there.

'How can we return to our world?'

By now, she realized I was probing her mind. Honestly, I felt dirty. This was mental rape, but we had to find answers. We'd been marooned a month.

She fought answering me by another round of her insane, gleeful laughter.

'How do we fly this ship?'

Again, she fought back, bringing to mind the natives brutally hacking off her arms. She blacked out from the pain, forcing me out of her mind. Trying to force her mind to pull up answers to questions she didn't want to answer proved pointless. Just as I was ready to give up, I had another bright idea.

'Edyta, you asked the computer to execute Protocol Nine. How can we see all the protocols you have installed in your computer?'

Since this wasn't a question she anticipated I would ask, her mind responded. I saw a button and a display. It looked much like a menu of some kind. But when she

220

realized she'd divulged something she didn't want me to know, she forced me out of her mind by recalling again her painful amputation attack. While her pain didn't bother me, I found it too annoying to stick around and backed out.

I headed down to the control room. "Isabella, I've just gotten a clue from Edyta. There's a button we can press that'll display all the preprogrammed computer controlled flights. Now where's the button?"

I looked at the myriad controls before I found one that matched what I'd seen in her mind. "Press that one, Deanna," I said, indicating one with my nose.

She did so and a bunch of symbols appeared on a display screen.

"Move over, Mom. I can read this. Deanna, write all this down. There are ten protocols stored in the computer's memory."

One by one, Isabella translated the alien writing. Protocol Nine was titled Security Attack and Fly Home. We'd already guessed the meaning of that one. Number ten proved vital. When that one was run, the computer displayed the complete operations manual for the ship!

"Oh my! Jackpot. Deanna, you're going to have lots to write down for us all," Isabella said. She shook from excitement.

I felt so proud of her. Only she could read this alien language, though some of the rest of us sort of bungled our way through bits of it.

Deanna said, "This is precisely what we need, Isabella. Gang, we're not pressing any more buttons until we've gone through all this material and figured out what we're doing. Do we have enough food and water for a few more weeks?"

"I'll check on that," Lenka volunteered.

When I joined Commander Johnston, I told her my mind probe of Edyta had paid off. She agreed with Deanna's assessment. Study first before experimenting.

"Okay. Let's get you practicing writing," I said.

I pushed her hard, harder than the others, but for a good reason. I had no idea how long we'd have together.

Plus I wanted her to have the best chance to be able to continue her career as the commander of her cruiser. We would practice activities and run another therapy session when needed. From experience, I've a keen sense of when another trauma manifests itself via their attitudes, emotions, or behaviors.

Finally, five weeks since Edyta commanded the ship to return to her home world, we understood enough to fly the ship. Unlike Earth's spaceships, only the computer could pilot this flying saucer. Apparently, the complicated guidance motions exceeded the capacity of a person. Thus, the aliens controlled their ship via preprogrammed protocols or scripts, as Deanna called them.

Using Edyta's translator box, Deanna, Sam, Lenka, and Isabella prepared a script to return. Lenka read the script the four, while Deanna held the Record Protocol switch. Once entered, Deanna displayed the script on the monitor. Isabella translated the script, while the others compared it to what Lenka had read. Satisfied they'd made no linguistic errors, they turned to me.

I looked at Commander Johnston and Commander L'Grina. "Okay, you two. What do you think? Give it a try?"

"I'd suggest we put some key personnel in the two escape crafts just in case," Commander L'Grina said. "I volunteer. Probably should be those who can fly the small ships. I'll take Bev with me."

"She's got a point," Deanna said. "I can fly one. I'll take Commander Johnston with me. If this goes south..."

"Okay," I said.

Commander Johnston said, "Sorry, Molly. This is your call. How does it feel to have the weight of so many lives on your shoulders? We commanders carry this load constantly."

I laughed nervously. "I don't like it. Still, I got us into this mess by insisting we find our twins. All right then. Let me know when you four are in the escape vehicles. I'll tell everyone else to prepare for the flight."

Thirty minutes later, I stood beside Lenka, Sam, and Isabella in the control room. "Do it," I ordered.

Lenka read the command, which the translator box converted from English into this alien tongue. "Computer: execute Protocol Eleven."

Dials, gauges, and readouts started flashing. The ship lurched, knocking the four of us off our feet. A number of curses echoed, but we got to our feet. I sent Sam off to check on everyone else in the living quarters, while Lenka, Isabella, and I watched the controls, ready to press the button that lowered the ship's speed. If troubles came while landing, reducing our speed to zero probably wasn't going to be a good idea, but there were very few things a person could do to control the flying saucer's flight.

We were in hyperspace. Black view screens verified that detail. Suddenly, we felt a slight lurch beneath our feet. The three penguins wobbled, but we remained upright. The planet with the giant continent appeared on the view screen.

"Yeah!" Lenka said. "Now if it'll just land right."

The ship announced touchdown by once more knocking us off our feet. Admittedly, landing was little more than a bump.

"If we're going flying again, I suggest we install seats in here," I said, struggling to regain my feet.

We heard a grating or sliding noise in the distance. "Maybe that's the dome opening," Lenka said. "Let's go see."

When we arrived at the central living quarters beneath the giant dome, the other four joined up. Commander Johnston said, "Well done, all of you. Nice work under pressure. If you were in the space fleet, why, I'd see you all get medals."

Deanna said, "Remind me *never* to board a ship that can only be flown by computers! Lem'me off this saucer."

"Guys! Guys, come to the doors. We've got troubles," Sam yelled.

Yes, we had landed back on Zeta Tucanae-3 within a few hundred feet of our original position. However, during the weeks we were gone, a dozen other ships arrived. A wall of soldiers with heavy blasters pointed weapons at us.

Guess they were expecting alien trouble.

I swallowed hard. "Commander Johnston, can you handle this? Please."

"I've misplaced my hands, so I can't open the doors," she jested.

Deanna opened them for her, and the pair stepped out into the sunlight.

Chapter 18 It's Mine. No, It's Mine

Me? I relaxed. I hadn't realized how much stress I'd been under the past month. My knees felt weak, so I stayed back, watched, and listened.

As expected, I heard gasps when some of the Bolt's crew saw their commander. Five other commanders stepped in front of the wall of soldiers, who secured their many weapons. I sensed their disappointment. Commander Lia Johnston gave her official report to the others, while several recorded it. I noticed a GEnt crew in the background. Undoubtedly, they'd broadcast this across the Sol Empire.

The captains of the Star Voyager and Pathfinder asked if they and their crew could return to their exploration ships, while the Bolt's crew wanted to do the same. Everyone wanted off this flying saucer. I can't blame them after what we'd endured.

"We'll provide a flight crew for each ship," one commander said.

"But we don't need them. We can manage," the captain of the Star Voyager protested.

Ah, the moment of truth for these sixty victims. Would they be allowed to continue with their work, their livelihoods?

I had my answer in seconds. "You can ride home on the ships. New flight crews will take over. We'll see about putting your telepathic skills to work as linguists on other exploration ships."

Seething anger boiled over. Many curses flew back and forth. The two crews, including our twins, headed on over to their ships, which didn't appear damaged from being knocked off the metal disk of the saucer when it took off.

'I've some ideas to make use of your crew members,' I sent both to Bernardo and Isabella. 'Tell them their space careers aren't necessarily over. I've a plan.'

'You better have, Mom," she replied. 'They're furious. We know we have limitations, but we aren't helpless. Even I know how to pilot the Star Voyager home. Stupid men.'

I sent to Commander Johnston, 'If they oust you from your position, come see me. I've some ideas for the future.' I sensed enormous relief coming back from my light touch of her mind.

Chaos ensued. Many abandoned the saucer, returning to their own ships. The victims had soldiers cart their vital hair and dressing machines off the saucer, though each carried their own laptop. At the same time, commanders, engineers, and the GEnt video crews came aboard to see the myriad details of this unique ship, never before seen in the Sol Empire.

Commander Johnston, Deanna, and I provided guided tours of the ship for the brass. It turned into a controlled chaos until most had returned to their own ships.

When we showed them the control center, Deanna said, "I'd like to take this ship back to Chicago. There, Cartwright Enterprises will make a detailed study of the ship and hopefully be able to produce more of them for our Sol Empire." I got her intention. "This ship is mine."

Commander Johnston countered. "Look. It should belong to the sixty members of the exploration ships who found it. They've paid a terrible price acquiring this ship. I think the salvage rights belongs to them."

One of our admirals said, "Not a chance. This is a unique chance for the Sol Empire to acquire incredible technology. The space fleet is taking possession of this incredible discovery. I'll see you receive a reasonable finder's fee."

"One moment there," another admiral said. "Federation Circle of Admirals sent me to appraise the find. The Circle of Admirals will take possession of this incredible breakthrough discovery. They've been trying to acquire one of these flying saucers for a century. They aren't about to let this one slip past. Why, the tech here could provide major breakthroughs, which will benefit every member of the Federation of Planets. I'm sure if you submit a request, they might see fit to giving you a finder's fee."

Just then, one of his junior officers ran up to him. "Sir. Sir, this communication just came in from Gamma Orionis. The Third Invaders are demanding the return of their saucer."

"Not a chance in a black hole," the admiral said.

Our admiral said, "Look, Sol Empire personnel discovered the ship, killed the Third Invader owners, and captured it. The saucer belongs to the Sol Empire. I'm sure we can share the findings with all other worlds in the Federation of Planets."

"Hey," Commander Johnston said, "Molly's crew and the two exploration crew paid dearly to capture this saucer. Legally, by Sol Empire Salvage Rights, the ship belongs to them."

"Sol Empire needs supercede local members," our admiral countered.

"Wrong. Federation of Planets trumps everyone. We're taking control of this saucer. I assure you it's not going back to Gamma Orionis," the Federation representative said.

Deanna looked at me. I nodded my head to the right. Together, we quietly departed, returning in silence to the Friendship. Lenka said, "Bernardo's ship just left for home. Isabella's ship is leaving in thirty minutes. She wants us to make sure they get off safely—something about no confidence in the men who usurped the crew."

I laughed. "Sure. Looks like we're not getting the saucer. They're fighting over its ownership. We'll leave once the Star Voyager is safely off and into hyperspace. Oh, I guess I best issue that order."

"Aye, aye, Captain," Lenka teased me.

Sam said, "I bet our kids are wondering what happened to us. I hope they haven't given the Hugo's too much trouble. I sure miss them. Hey, we're going to be grandparents soon."

"I can't get my head around that detail, dear. It makes me sound positively old," I said. Many chuckled.

"Coordinates are laid in," Lenka said. "Sam double checked them. Deanna triple checked, so we're ready when you give the word."

We watched the Star Voyager lift off. I waited until the ship made its jump. So far, their new crew hadn't goofed.

Unexpectedly, I heard Commander Johnston's voice at our open upper ramp. "Permission to come aboard." I sensed suppressed emotions in her voice.

"Absolutely. We're about to head for home. Had to see the twins safely on their way first."

"Can I hitch a ride with you? My engineer too. I've been relieved of my command and told we can't go home to Brussels, Tau Ceti."

I could see that she fought to keep her eyes from watering—a strong woman not daring to show any emotion.

"Certainly, Lia. You both are most welcome to come with us." I spotted several men lugging the machines for the two, while each had their laptop in a bag over their shoulder. "Sam, show them where to stow the machines. You two, come with me to the control center."

Once there, I said, "I was afraid this would happen, Lia. I had no idea they'd react so badly and so quickly. For now, you can stay at our home. We've plenty of room."

"Thank you, Molly. I—I really don't know what we would have done if your people had already left. We're so screwed. They did say that someone will clean out my quarters on the Bolt and my place back on Brussels and send my stuff to Earth. His, too."

"Well, the way the senators made up the nasty laws, I'm not surprised. I've not told you about how I got mutated." I told them my story, killing time until the soldiers left. Sam closed the forward hatch. "Okay, time to go. Commander L'Grina, would you do the honors of flying us back?"

"You sure you don't want to pilot this time?" she teased me. "Everyone buckle up. Liftoff in one minute."

Later, from the navigator's chair, Sam announced, "We'll be landing at Chicago's New O'Hare in twenty hours and sixteen minutes, unless there's a lot of traffic there."

After making the jump to hyperspace, Celeste and I called on our new additions.

"Lia, let me give you another therapy session. Let's tackle the shock and grief you're holding back," I said.

Next door, Celeste handled her engineer.

She wailed, "But I worked so hard to be able to continue doing what I must as a commander. They didn't even give me a chance. 'No mutants on Brussels or any other Sol Empire world except Earth. That's the law, Commander Johnston. You know it as well as I do. You are relieved of your command.'"

Alone with me in her cabin, Lia broke down and sobbed, no longer suppressing her emotions. "What am I supposed to do now? Spy on others for the greedy corporations?"

"Not a chance, Lia. Yes, we must deal with our handicap. Lifting and carrying things is always going to be challenging for us—a royal pain. But given enough time, patience, and creativity, we can deal with most things, if only others would allow us to do so. What people always see is our need for help with things they take for granted like carrying things. Yet, there isn't a person alive who doesn't need help with some action. It's just most people don't constantly point out to them where and when they need help. Not like they do with us. Our limitations seem glaring to others."

Softly, I began the session. If she had any chance of adapting to the huge change in her fortunes, this therapy session had to work a miracle.

I coaxed Lia through being relieved of her command and not allowed to return to her home world, accompanied by buckets of tears. It didn't erase. I'd long ago learned that losses were kept in place by previous and underlying pain and unconscious traumas. I asked her for something that occurred earlier.

"I've never, ever been demoted. Always, I worked

harder than the men around me. Never give up. There can't be any thing earlier. What am I supposed to do now?"

"I understand, but let's see if you can see any earlier images or masses that are similar."

She wiggled her jaw a while before speaking. "Well, I do see something yellowish, but what am I supposed to do now?"

"Okay. Let's go to the beginning of that one. Go through it and tell me what's happening as you go along," I said.

On the sixth pass through it, much became clear. "I'm a fighter pilot. We're in a battle with lots of other single-pilot spacecrafts. My ship takes a direct hit. Pain shoots through my legs. Seat ejects. I'm floating down to the surface, but I black out. I'm in a field hospital, I think. A woman, my wife I think, is saying, 'What's he supposed to do now? What's he gonna do now?' I can't figure out why she's saying this. I ejected in time.

"I wake up. I can't feel my legs. That awful pain is gone, but I can't feel them. I look down and gag. I've got no legs! I shriek. What am I supposed to do now? My plans to make commander of my own cruiser vanish. She comes into the room. Her eyes are bloodshot.

"Johnny, I don't know what you're supposed to do now. All is lost."

"I didn't know what I was supposed to do. I had no legs at all. It's a field hospital. My things are on a table next to my bed. I reach over and grab my weapon. The doctor comes in, a startled look on his face. I don't know what I'm supposed to do like this. I pulled the trigger. Instant pain and then blackness. No, then I seem to be looking down on the room from above.

"She says, 'Well, I don't know what he is supposed to do without any legs.' I agree and float away."

Lia started laughing. "Hey, I'd rather be able to move around on my legs than have arms and be stuck in a chair. Wait. She kept saying, 'What's he supposed to do now?' That really impinged. I agreed with her. What an idiot. I presume they planned to fit me with prosthetic legs of some kind. If I hadn't agreed with her—wait a second. She says that repeatedly to get me to kill myself. She doesn't want to be married to a hopeless cripple for the rest of her life. Well, it worked. I bought into her attitude all the way. Guess I'm the idiot. I feel like a ton has lifted off my chest."

I ended the session, confident that Lia wouldn't succumb.

***

Dawn of December 1, 2360, the Friendship landed at New O'Hare Spaceport. Deanna made arrangements for her workers to transport our bags and machines to our homes. In the chilly twilight, she led us to her company EMAC. One by one, she dropped us off. Sam and I brought Walter, Lenka, and Lia with us. The sun just rose as we five entered our home.

"Surprise! Welcome home!" a crowd yelled, suddenly turning on the lights. Owen, Isabella, Wendy, Bernardo cheered us, along with our kids, Nikita and Matt. Also, the Hugo family from next door welcomed us, Helen, Casper, Veronica, and Fritz. I wasn't surprised to see the neighbors, since our children were nearly inseparable. In the background, my dear dwarven friend and geneticist, Lara Axe-head, grinned broadly.

The kids had arrived several hours ahead of us and arranged for our welcome. We didn't have enough chairs for everyone, but that didn't matter. Sam and I sat on the floor and Nikita and Matt plopped on our laps, snuggling. A half hour passed between body-presses and introductions.

Walter said, "I feel really out of place here. Am I the only person with arms here?"

The dwarf laughed. "You and me are the only ones. I don't recommend losing yours, though. You can lend me a hand carrying the drinks for everyone."

Lia said, "This is incredible. So many of us. I don't feel so—well, you know, alone."

Helen said, "Hardly, Commander Johnston. Welcome to Earth. I'm the CEO of Sol Empire Galactic Defense, taking Hardy's old position. Casper is the CFO. We've moved into the offices on the hundredth floor where

Molly once conducted her investigations.

For once, those in power made good choices for top leaders, I thought.

"By the way, Commander Johnston, your Senator Bill Fennel of Brussels wants to meet with you as soon as possible. Everyone, I have a lot of news to tell you," Helen said.

"There's been many changes while you were gone. After the last mutation attack on GPan, they've re-established the Empire-wide GPan corporation. We really do need people overseeing the expansion projects.

"At the same time, they enacted a new law. All CEOs of the major empire-wide corporations must be armless Galactic Doll telepaths."

Casper interrupted, "Yeah, because they figure we can't do much to abuse our powers—not like we used to—not like Hardy and Armstrong did or even like I did. And they do have a point. Perhaps this will go a long way to reducing corporate corruption. I kinda think it will."

Helen continued, "I agree. It's a good idea to place limits—physical constraints—on those who wield such power over our empire. Anyway, they formed two new positions, based on the need to have one person making executive decisions. Natalie is now the Sol Empire Minister of Defense. Dimitri is the Sol Empire Minister of Expansion. Those two are now the highest executive personnel running our empire. The corporations answer to them. However, future ministers must also be armless Galactic Doll telepaths .

"As I understand it, Natalie and Dimitri refused the positions when offered because they didn't want to be mutated. They reached a compromise. The two will serve for four years, while proper replacements are groomed. If Natalie and Dimitri get mutated during that time, then they can hold the positions until they retire."

"Wow. That's incredible. I'll have to call them and congratulate them," I said. "Finally, people are recognizing we aren't helpless or useless."

"I'm not so sure about that," Helen said. "There's

more. As of mid-November, the Council of the Senate, the Senior Investigator, and the Senior Judge are fully operational once more. It's now the law: all senators must be armless telepaths. Again, the reason given is to prevent abuse of power, like Senator Truman Wyman did. Between us, I think the real reason is that the other Sol Empire civilizations feared future mutation attacks and refused to send senator replacements. Anyway, from now on, all senators are like us. They've chosen a new temporary Senior Investigator, your friend, Mr. Bishop."

She continued, "And Senior Judge Roscoe Burkhardt—the man who sentenced you, Molly—he's been forced to resume his position as Senior Judge, refusing his pleas to be terminated. However, they've expanded the number of judges. There are nine now, but Roscoe is their Chief Senior Judge. With nine judges, there can't be any tie votes. Further, the law now states all Senior Judges must be armless telepaths, too.

"Again, the official reason given is to prevent abuse and misuse of power—I'm told this is a rationale that the average person buys. But the real reason is fear of future mutation attacks on the judges. In fact, that's the prevalent fear among those holding powerful positions. They couldn't get anyone to replace those who were mutated; they claimed they'd be wearing a big target on their backs. So the only way the powers that be could get the top corporations, the senate, the investigators, and the judges back in operation was to pass a law saying they had to be armless telepaths.

"Actually, in many ways, that's a good thing for us. We aren't being dumped and relegated to the back alleys of society. It gives many victims strong reasons to survive and do well," Helen said.

"Backwards is forwards," I said, laughing at the irony of it all. Well, I knew from the past few years just how much fear of being mutated had spread through those who wielded corporate power.

"That's not all," she said. "As you know, this past fall, Jill and her giants mutated twenty-five hundred of the wealthiest Chicagoans. As you predicted, most of these victims chose to hire personal assistants rather than learning how to do things themselves. What we didn't know is that many of these men own some of the Sol Empire corporations."

Casper chuckled. "Speak for yourself, honey. I knew these men owned the corporations. They're the ones I routinely ask to donate for the next battleship and cruiser."

"Well, I had no idea. Those families keep to their own circles. They never attend any corporation event, like the Mid-winter Balls. Pay attention, all of you. This affects you. These men have created a new corporation, the Sol Empire Telepath Corporation. All armless telepaths are automatically members of this corporation."

"What? Don't we get a say? How about my sponsor, GEnt?" I asked.

"Everyone keeps their current sponsor, but they also are members of the TC—the Telepath Corporation. You're going to get a summons to visit them tomorrow. The TC CEO has forced through all these changes during the last month. They've also established the policy that every Earth corporation—local, world, and empire-wide—must have an official corporate telepath. It's a new job listing and pays very well. Thus far, the TC hasn't been able to force off-world corporations to create that new job. Some of us are filling dual roles. I'm the Sol Empire-wide GD's Corporate Telepath as well as its CEO. The TC is creating many high paying corporate jobs for telepaths."

"Perhaps, that's a good thing," I said. "Gives some of us a much needed income and usefulness. But I'm not sure I want to be a corporate spy."

Helen grinned before continuing, "Plus, the TC has expedited monetary reimbursements to the many different victims of the mutation attacks. No more delays. Some of the disbursements should have been sent years ago. You both should check your bank accounts. You'll probably see funds have been deposited. I received a three million credit settlement for my mutation. Casper even received a million credit settlement, in part because he reported the mutation agent was in the drinking water. Bottom line, Molly, any victim of any mutation attack—even the protestors like Aaron Strawn—have received a large settlement, enough for them to afford a personal assistant, if they wish. Of all these changes, this one is the most beneficial to the thousands of victims."

"Have they changed the regulations on getting the cures?" I asked.

"Personally, I think it's gotten worse. If a child is mutated, when they turn eighteen, they can request cures. Any adult must wait ten years before requesting any cures," Helen said. "Personally, I hope these restrictions are going to be changed, if only so far as to allow everyone to get the breast reduction and foot repair mutations. Regrowing arms, which deletes the person's telepathic ability, is a *tough* sell. On the positive side, as of now, there isn't any shortage of good paying employment for telepaths."

Chapter 19 Quantum Entanglement

My phone woke me. In the dark, I managed to knock it onto the floor before answering it. "Bishop? It's still nighttime."

"Welcome back, Molly. But can you possibly get Isabella on the phone? I'm patching a call through from Admiral Rossi's battleship. It's vital. We need her to decipher some Third Invader writings."

Minutes later, she and I sat on the edge of my bed, while Sam headed off to make us some tea.

"Okay. I'm here, Mr. Bishop," Isabella said.

Soon, my phone displayed the ship's control center before the phone's image enlarged to a six-foot tall holographic image. Impressive. But the admiral's voice sounded upset.

"The Federation of Planets seized the Third Invader's flying saucer. I'm told a skeletal crew boarded it and installed a hyperspace long distance comm unit so they could stay in touch with the Kanika battleship. The Federation's plan to tow the saucer through hyperspace to Bela Prime via a tractor beam has run into major trouble. Shortly after the Kanika made the jump into hyperspace, the six crew on the saucer sent this video. Isabella, hit record on your phone."

She did so and we watched six men as they panicked. A small portion of the saucer's control panel turned on, one which we'd not yet explored. Strange symbols appeared below it. More importantly, the saucer fought against the tractor beam, lurching violently in many directions, knocking the six men to the metal floor. Then, a yellowish gas filled the room. We watched the six men drop into a coma, presumably the same one we'd encountered. We heard Edyta's cackling in the background.

The recording continued to playback, even though the men no longer responded to desperate calls from the Kanika. The violent lurching broke the Kanika's tractor beam. The swaying motion stopped, and the image remained stationary, still showing the control center. In the background, we could hear voices calling to the six men. At last, Admiral Rossi's voice broke in over the still-playing recording.

"The long distance comm is sending video as we speak, though the signal is growing very weak. Isabella, can you translate the alien writing below that flashing control panel? Perhaps there was another alien on board that you never discovered. He or she managed to activate some unknown controls to break free. The saucer is navigating on its own through hyperspace. Commander Lia Johnston did say the ship runs off of prerecorded protocols without a person controlling it."

Isabella zoomed in on the symbols. After a minute, she said, "Quantum Entanglement Override. That's what it says. Oh, there's a tiny reference number below it. We made copies of all documents found. Let me see if we have that one. Hold on, Admiral Rossi."

After retrieving her laptop and booting it up on the floor, she navigated to the lengthy series of document copies she'd made for Commander Lia. She had me calling off the reference number while she scrolled through the listing.

"Hey, we've got it. Bringing it up now. Oh crap. You're not going to like this, Admiral."

"What's it say about this quantum entanglement?" he asked.

"The hidden QE protocol handles emergency situations. QE automatically returns the ship to its home base. Such emergencies include the ship's crew becoming disabled in some way and unable to vocalize the proper protocols for sixty days or if the ship is towed through hyperspace with no crew override code entered, that is, a hijack attempt. So what is this quantum entanglement thing anyway? I swear we didn't see the QE control dials when we were there. It must of been invisible," she said.

An engineer standing next to Admiral Rossi spoke up. "Sir, it's a quantum mechanics effect. Two particles become entangled, meaning each reflects what's happening with the other, rather like total duplicates. Think of it as spooky action from a distance. This is an incredible find. Imagine using quantum entanglement as a mechanism to control a spaceship from half a galaxy away. Just brilliant. Anyway we can retrieve the saucer from hyperspace? We need to get that technology."

"Thank you, Miss Torres-Parkinson. You're a brilliant linguist. Do consider signing up again. I'd love to have you on board my battleship. Good bye."

After the admiral left the conference call, Bishop said, "Molly. I need to see you later today, after you finish your mandatory visits with this new Telepathic Corporation. Bye."

Sam pushed a cart into our bedroom. "Tea's here. So what was that all about?"

"Thanks Dad. Looks like the Federation lost the flying saucer." She replayed her recording, before heading back to bed for another couple hours.

Later, she replayed it for Deanna. The engineer's comment spoke volumes. "They've made an incredible technological advancement—unattended action across the vastness of space. Quantum entanglement—who would've thought such was possible?"

Around nine, I stood outside the office door of Mr. William Buffet, the head of Telepathy Corporation, ready to see this new situation that had developed while I was gone. They'd refurbished a Loop skyscraper, though why the Telepathy Corporation needed a hundred floors escaped me. I paused in the hallway, gazing at the incredible view of the other major galactic corporation skyscrapers with the lake in the background.

An alto voice barked from the office. "Oh do come in, Mrs. Parkinson. You're making me late for my other appointments. So many new telepaths to see today."

Annoyed, I entered his office. William Buffet sat behind a giant desk on an oversized chair. His assistant hovered behind him, operating his computer for him. I guessed she was barely out of high school and wore a typical Galactic Doll red satin gown. Mr. Buffet looked twenty-five at most, thanks to the mutation agent. He chose to wear Leslie's men's suit and pants, though the former couldn't hide his gigantic bosom. The oil on his short black hair reflected the intense fluorescent lights. I took a seat across from him, a small chair.

"Scroll down," he ordered his assistant. She looked flustered, but did as he asked. "Now then, Mrs. Parkinson. I presume you've heard about the Telepathy Corporation."

"Not exactly. Others told me that all telepaths are automatically members of this corporation, but I've no idea what that means."

"It means that we're assuming the mantle of Sol Empire power. One of our members must be the CEO of the main corporations. Our corporation exists to safeguard the lives of telepaths and protect their contracts. The rules are simple. All telepath children cannot have any cures until they graduate from highschool. New telepaths can have no cures for ten years. This guarantees each telepath an opportunity to achieve his or her full potential. In return for our contract negotiations and protections, the Telepathy Corporation takes one percent of your earnings, a pittance really.

"Now then, Mrs. Parkinson, you aren't currently employed as a telepath, yet you are one. This is a ridiculous waste of your talents. Running a PI business barely pays the bills. I've checked—rather my assistant has checked. We're helpless, you see. So I want you to check out all the jobs available for telepaths and put your talents to good use. I'll check back with you in, say, a month. I expect you to have found more suitable employment."

I started to protest, but chose not to react. Something didn't feel right.

He cleared his throat. "Mind if I ask you a personal question?" I nodded. "The biggest complaint we're receiving from our members is that they hear so many voices in their heads they can't think straight. I'm up here on the top floor, far from the crowded city below. Honestly, sometimes when I'm on the MTES, I hear so many voices I want to scream. I've been checking with our members.

Everyone hates being in crowds or around lots of people.

"And another thing. I've gotten many complaints about our inability to know if something was said aloud or was a picked-up thought. Have you experienced either of these? Have you any solutions to offer other telepaths?"

I sensed an opening and took it. "Oh my goodness. Are many of us telepaths experiencing these difficulties?"

"Well, yes. Frankly, Mrs. Parkinson, most every telepath is. Though I've had my assistant correlate the telepath's IQ level with their telepathic ability."

"Ah ha. And what has she found?"

"Show her the graph," he ordered his assistant.

She brought up the holo image for us.

"Point it out. You know I can't point," he barked.

"Those with low IQ get very confused. Their telepathy skills are sub-par. We're recommending they only accept security positions. They aren't suited for corporate work. Now your daughter, Isabella Torres-Parkinson—she's a stellar example for us all to follow. You should consider following in her footsteps, Mrs. Parkinson."

"How many of our members are in Isabella's rank?" I asked.

He frowned. "Too few, I'm afraid. The problem is the myriad voices in our heads when we're around many people. We can't sort them out. I've insisted telepath CEOs always have relatively isolated offices, far from others."

"What steps are you taking to guard against telepathic backlash?" I decided to push a little. Besides, my annoyance level peaked.

"Huh? Backlash?"

I knew I had him. "Yes, most all telepaths are victims of the armless Galactic Doll mutation agent. They didn't choose to become so helpless. Today, cures have been found: breast reduction, foot repair, and arm regrowth, I'm told. Yet, the laws prohibit them from getting any cures until they reach eighteen with children or ten years for us adults."

"Of course. That's for their benefit," he said.

"Oh, so you wanted to become an armless telepath?"

I asked, knowing the opposite was true.

"Hardly. I'm helpless like this. Not everyone is as flexible as you are."

"That's my point, Mr. Buffet. Many hated becoming this. Now that cures are available, most can't get them for a long time. And that foments hatred. Mark my words, sir, soon you're going to see telepaths protesting by giving erroneous reports. They'll deliberately foul up their assignments, if only to protest their treatment. I suspect the recent victims will pose the most problems, since they know the cures are there and yet the cures are being withheld from them."

"Hum, I hadn't thought about that aspect. I'd get cured tomorrow, if the law permitted it. It isn't fun being helpless. I have to have Mabel with me all the time. Hell, I can't even get the darn dressing machine to work right."

"If the laws changed and allowed any of us to have any cures we wanted right now, I think most of us would take them."

"You're probably right. But then, we'd have very few telepaths."

"Ah, but those would be even more valuable, since they chose to be one."

"Point taken. But I can't change the laws."

"Another thing, I'm glad the Telepathy Corporation will be providing protection. We're going to need it."

"Abductions? I think we've put a stop to those."

"God, I hope so, too. No, I was thinking about jealous normal workers, who see us making obscene wages while they barely scratch out a living. My PI salary barely pays the office rent. Yet, minimum telepath wages are a million a year. Sooner or later, someone's going to get really annoyed with that and come gunning for us. So I'm glad you're going to have security guards around all telepaths."

I knew he had no such plans, but I continued to punch home my objections. Maybe he had the power to do something about the stupid laws.

"Oh, I hardly think it will come to that. The penalties are too great. Mercury and all that."

Another thought flickered. "Mind if I as you a personal question? Until recently, I had no idea there were wealthy people like you. I figured everyone worked for some corporation."

He laughed. "We try to stay in the background. Some of us own the corporations. We're the shareholders. The corporations pay us dividends each year and are answerable to us in some ways. As long as the credits continue to appear in our accounts, we seldom, if ever, interfere in a corporation's operations. We only nudge from the background if things go wrong."

"So how many others are like you? Owning lots of shares in the corporations? You don't have to work?"

He laughed. "Work? Ha. Never have. I'd say there's about two hundred of us, more or less scattered about Earth. Some others reside on other Sol Empire worlds. We normally meet once a year, just after the corporations post their year-end statistics. Only if these show a steep downtrend do we take any kind of action. We're the ones who control enough funds to finance spaceships and other major ventures. So it's not like we're not doing our part. Anyway, I've wasted too much time with you. I'm now a half-hour behind. So many to see today. Most from those two recovered deep space exploration ships. Sixty new telepaths—highly educated too. Find appropriate employment that utilizes your telepathic talents, Mrs. Parkinson. I'll check back in a month. Good day."

So much for the meeting. I'd learned something. I'd no idea there were two hundred super-wealthy around in the background. Plus, I'd laid some doubts about just how wonderful being a telepath actually was. I knew many telepaths were quite angry about being denied the genetic cures. I headed home.

***

Lara led Lia Johnston to her meeting with her senator from Brussels, Tau Ceti. The forty-eight senators had their offices in the hundred-story GPan skyscraper. Various plants native to Brussels lined the outer halls of Senator Bill Fennel's office on the forty-eighth floor. Lara led her to the entrance.

"I can take it from here, Lara. Thanks. I've no idea how long with will take."

"Text me if you need me. I'll head to the genetic's lab," the dwarf said.

Lia took a deep breath and entered the senator's office, the outer door automatically opening. She inhaled the odors so familiar to her, flowers from home lined both sides of the office. A small desk with many comfortable chairs didn't fill the room, adding to the spaciousness effect. The windows along the back wall offered a view of other skyscrapers, but not the lake.

He rose when she entered. "Lia? Lia Johnston. Welcome, Bossy. It's been a long time."

"Sneaky? Gosh, Bill, I hardly recognized you. You look—"

"Different? Like a freak? This damnable Galactic Doll mutation."

"Well, yeah, Sneaky. I see you're trying to look somewhat like a male."

He chuckled. "Yes, but this shirt and jacket can't hide this gigantic bosom. I just couldn't wear women's gowns. But I have to say, Bossy, you look just as gorgeous as you did at the prom."

Lia chuckled. "I've just got my new ID card that nearly proves it. My biological age is twenty-two again. But back then when you were the prom king and I, the queen, we didn't have monster knockers."

"And we had arms. Hell, Lia, just look at what's become of me. I look like a freak. Neither of us can ever return home. We're banned for life. I look like a very well endowed woman. My voice is higher than yours, Bossy."

Lia laughed. "God, you're right, Sneaky. Soprano, right? Well, your face still looks like it did back in highschool. Glad you kept your usual haircut. A flat-top suits your face. Look what's become of both of us since that prom."

"Hey, I know after that I went off to diplomatic school and you headed into the space academy. But I've always remembered you. I still have our prom picture on my desk, but I can't turn it around to show you. Honestly, Bossy, I've always had a crush on you. As our senator, I've been able to follow your impressive career. Commander of your own cruiser. I knew you'd go far, Bossy. I've kept a video scrapbook of your achievements. My favorite is when you made commander."

Lia grimaced. "Yes, but not any more. They dismissed me without even seeing if I could still perform my duties or even asking me. Damn it, Sneaky, I worked hard with Molly's help learning new ways to do what I needed to do to command the cruiser. I know I could do it. But no way. Dismissed in sixty seconds. Now what the hell am I supposed to do?"

He sighed. "Lia, I surely don't know. After the attack mutated us senators, I thought I was jobless. But then I caught a break. It seems Brussels isn't about to send another person to Earth. Too damn risky. I heard no one would take the senator position. So like it or not, I'm stuck being our senator."

"At least you have a worthwhile position, Sneaky. Not like me. Are there many from Brussels here in Chicago or even on Earth?"

"Bossy, you're looking at all us from Brussels. Thee and me. After all that's happened these past ten years, only a crazy person would move to Earth. But I should admit up front, Lia, I've never forgotten your kiss on prom night."

"You didn't marry?"

He laughed. "I spent all my time working my way up the diplomatic ladder to achieve this ultimate position as our senator. Didn't have time for dating, Bossy. Besides, no one could compare to you."

Lia's face felt hot. "The space academy took all my attention, too, Sneaky. Quite a challenge to work my way up to being commander of the Bolt. I had hoped to make a fleet admiral one day. That's gone in the wind. Funny, we remember our pet names from highschool days. Shit, Sneaky, that's been what? Nearly thirty years ago."

"Wow. That long? You're right. Say, would you let

me take you to lunch? I'd love to catch up on old times—find out how things have gone for you these many years. Besides, I just have to hear what happened with that flying saucer. Molly Parkinson is one fabulous person. She and her friends have made life possible for me since the mutation. That is, if you don't mind being seen in public with a freak like me."

"We're both freaks, Sneaky. But yeah, you are freakier than I am. I'd like that, but only if you catch me up on what's happened with you. After that goodnight kiss, I kind of hoped we'd see each other again, but we went in two different directions. Oh, do you have a personal assistant to help us or are we on our own? I'm new to all this, but I'm going to be independent or die trying."

"I'm fairly new to all this myself. I've rejected having to have a personal assistant. We see eye to eye on the independence angle. If we can survive ten years of this, then we can get the many cures. I'll dump this telepathy in an instant to have my arms back."

Lia chuckled. "Same here. In a flash. Oh, remember I don't know where anything is. Just got here yesterday. Molly's dwarf Lara led me here so I wouldn't get lost. Also, I'm used to the frantic or hectic life on a spaceship. No barriers. Planetside, I see nothing but barriers all around me, and not just because my arms are gone. Walls, buildings, MTES, trees, even the lake. In space, there are lightyears of nothing but dust particles."

The two headed off to Barnaby's, the finest restaurant in downtown Chicago. As they carefully stepped onto the MTES, Bill said, "Amazing that you remembered our pet names for each other—after all these years."

"Hey, you didn't forget either," Lia said. "Besides, we *were* the king and queen of the prom. Those days seem so long ago. So much has happened since then—to both of us."

"I haven't forgotten prom night. What's so funny is that I almost asked you to marry me that night, but I got too nervous and worried that you'd say no."

Lia chuckled. "I probably would have. We were on two different paths. Just look at the past thirty years. But now..."

"Yeah. Maybe this is our second chance. Do you suppose?" Quickly, he changed the subject. "I can't imagine what it's like flying about space. I always thought there were tons of stars and planets and things out there."

The two chatted all afternoon.

"Gosh, it's suppertime," Lia said.

"They serve fabulous dinners here," Bill said. "Let's order again. My treat. We must have talked for five hours, but I swear it's only been a couple minutes."

"I best let Molly know I'm okay," she said.

***

Isabella said, "Mom, guess what? I've figured out more of the Third Invader's writings. I think I know the coordinates of the places where they took their kidnap victims." She waited at the door for my return. "So how did it go with the TC? I'm supposed to go there this afternoon."

"That's wonderful. Maybe we can borrow Deanna's spaceship and check them out. Oh, not so good. He wants me to find suitable telepath employment. Bull crap. I did try to convince him the laws need to be changed."

"He didn't listen?"

"Yeah, couldn't get through to him. Worse, he's never worked an hour in his life. A billionaire who's outside the corporate world. Lazy man. Already hired a personal assistant. Claims he's helpless. Ah well. Are you sure about the coordinates?"

"Yes, darn sure. We should check them out. Maybe we can rescue more of our people before they're sold as slaves."

Chapter 20 Repercussions

Middle-age just took a right turn for the wealthy ex-CEO Edward Wainwright. Until the latest telepath laws, he presided over Galactic Expansion, London, a coveted position. He'd spent his entire adult life working his way up the corporate ladder. Now, an unknown telepath from Philadelphia took his place. When that promotion forced him back down several rungs, he'd quit.

His bank account reflected his ex-position, having made a small fortune on rare earth ore from some marginally inhabited world with a red sun.

Mildred brewed his morning tea, just as she had for the last thirty years—strong and black. She poured his Wedgwood cup, placing it before him, as she always had, though Mildred knew he wasn't going to his GPan office this morning.

"Mildred, I bloody well won't take this demotion lying down!"

"You shouldn't," she ventured.

"Helpless telepaths. Why should my CEO position go to a bloody telepath. Hell, he's not even from London. Some silly town across the pond. He can't even hold vital documents or sign them."

"I'm sure this is just some big mistake," she ventured. "It'll come out in the wash one day."

"Bloody hell it won't! I didn't spend thirty years clawing my way to the top only to have some helpless, pathetic person take over."

"I'm sure you didn't. They can read minds, I hear."

"Yeah, well that's about all they're good for. I can see having one spy for us, but it's beyond stupid to have one running the show. It's insane."

"Maybe they'll soon see that, love. Then, you'll get your position back. I can make your favorite dish for supper, if you like."

"They can't get away with this. By god, I bloody well

won't let them. Mildred, I'm going out. Don't expect me back for supper tonight. I need to step up to the plate as they say over there."

"Oh, do have your morning tea, dear."

Edward took a hasty sip and dashed out. At London Library, he placed a number of calls, the last one done via hyperspace with a five minute delay. When the image of Fritz Fulco appeared on the monitor, he smiled. *Finally, I'm getting somewhere.*

He'd already dropped the key names that let Fritz know he was not only serious but also on the level. "I've heard you are an expert at varmint removal. I need certain individuals terminated. Ten thousand a head. It's risky. Are you interested? Over."

These were the longest five minutes Edward spent. He drummed his fingers on the desk, while staring at the monitor. It flickered. He inhaled.

"I'm interested. Who are the individuals? Men in power? Termination is always risky. That's why I charge ten grand a head. Details please. Over."

Edward exhaled deeply. "Telepaths. They've been put into positions of power. CEOs of major corporations worldwide. Hell, they're infiltrating all corporations across Earth. Soon, they'll be ordered to take over corporations on Pylon, too. I don't care how it's done. Dead is dead. Over."

"Risky indeed. Twenty thousand a head. Are you choosing the targets or do I get that honor? Over."

"I want the London GPan telepath CEO terminated. After that, terminate any of them, preferably those in positions of power over us normal men. Twenty thousand is fine. When can you start? Over."

"Excellent. Put the credits in this account. Once I verify the funds, I'll be on the next flight to Earth and London. After this London CEO, you don't care which ones are taken out? Over."

"No, I don't care, as long as they are wielding some kind of corporate power. Over."

"If I take out a hundred, you got enough credits? Over."

"Bloody hell, take out a thousand if you can. Transfer is done. Over."

"Good doing business with you. On my way. Over and out."

This calls for a celebration. To the pub!

***

Nina Paca Ramira wanted to live. That's what she told the men who rescued her from the mutation attack in Caracas. She'd never felt so helpless as she had when she awoke from that coma. Life blurred into uncomprehending days, before officials in Caracas sent her off to Chicago, along with many hundreds of other armless mutation victims, mostly children.

Therapy helped, but adapting to using her feet as hands both challenged and frustrated her. Others kept her hopes for cures alive. After all, someone had invented an arm and leg regrowing cure for all the victims of the war on Brussels, hadn't they? Time. That's all that was needed. Nina could wait.

"What choice do I have?" she explained to the walls of her small apartment, surrounded with hundreds of others like her. Most of them were children, who quickly adapted to using their feet, while Nina continued to struggle.

Then, the settlement came. Nina's bank account held over a million credits. That she could afford to survive permitted her to relax for the first time since it happened. Rumors of cures spread among the dwellers of the Ace Leisure Acres apartments. In fact, many suggested that Molly's friend, the dwarf Lara Axe-head, and Eve Burkey had developed an arm regrowing cure.

"Patience," Nina told herself. "Soon, I'll be whole again."

Instead, the laws regarding telepaths underwent another revision, placing the life-saving cures far out of reach. The announcement of the Telepath Corporation and its take on the curing laws crushed Nina's mind and will.

"Miss Ramira, it's way past time you put your precious telepath gift to good use for the Sol Empire,"

Mr. Buffet told her at her interview with him. "Hire yourself an assistant like I've done and get to work. I'll give you a month to find suitable employment for your telepathy. That is all."

She left furious. Not only had he put off her cures even further, he'd ordered her to work as a telepath or else the cures would be forever denied her.

"If I could walk properly—not have monsters on my chest—then maybe I could live with this—but with an assistant though. Maybe. How dare they withhold cures just to make use of my mind reading thing. I didn't want it in the first place. Está loco en su cabeza. Si."

That evening, she complained to others in her housing complex. Many had also been ordered to take positions as corporate spies. Their education or training in other fields didn't seem to matter to this new Telepathy Corporation.

"What can we do? If we don't do as he says, we'll never get our promised cures," Nina said.

"We can protest," one suggested.

"Look where that got that history professor—that Mr. Strawn. They shunted him off to some other world," another said.

"Hey, what if we feed them false things?" the first asked.

Nina smiled. "They want us to spy, so we spy, but we tell them wrong things. Then, they fire us and give us our cures. Si?"

"Sounds like a plan to me," another agreed.

"But how do we keep all the voices out of our heads?" Nina asked. "It's easy here. There are so few people around. I nearly went mad going to the Loop and the TC building. Thousands screaming in my head."

"We know, Nina. I can't take it either. I asked Buffet about that when he interviewed me. He said that's why he made his office so far away from other people. We just have to endure it a bit longer. Give them false information. Then, they'll see this foolishness and give us our cures. I was a nurse before. What I wouldn't give to be able to do that again," one woman said.

"Si. We should spread the word. Have many of us giving wrong things," Nina said.

Thus, the era of false reports began.

***

Lia returned to my place long after supper. While worried, I restrained from calling her. When she entered our commons, her radiant face melted my worries about her day.

"Sorry I'm so late. Senator Fennel and I are highschool friends. Well, actually, we were the king and queen at our senior prom. Back then, we had a thing for each other, but when we graduated, I went off to Flight Academy. Haven't seen him in thirty years. I can't believe we talked all afternoon."

"What a coincidence. Wonderful. Say, did you get something to eat? Hungry?" I imagined she must be starving by now.

She chuckled. "No, he took me to this Barnaby's place for lunch and then supper. Besides me, he's the only one from Brussels who can't return to our home world. It helps that we know each other. Then, we returned to his place. We kissed..."

"And?"

"Okay, We had the most *incredible* sex I've ever experienced! I knew what he wanted, and he, me. But it was more than that. Like we were one being or one person. You know—he wanted to ask me to marry him at the prom but was too chicken to do it. Probably wise, since we both had our careers ahead of us. But now..."

"Congratulations. That's wonderful for you both."

"It really is, but why didn't you tell me that sex with another telepath is so indescribably fantastic? We're going out tomorrow night. My first date in years."

"I'm so glad for you. Topic never came up." We both laughed.

I said, "Say, you'll never guess what Isabella's worked out? She has deciphered the hyperspace coordinates of where the Third Invaders may have taken our people. Something about the values being part of those other scripts."

Lia perked up. "Wow! That's great. So are they going to send our fleets to search for them?"

I snickered. "Hardly. Untested coordinates. Land in the middle of a star. That's the line GPan gave me."

"But we have to try."

"I know. Deanna's giving us the Friendship to go look for them. I'm putting together a crew. Need a commander. You interested?"

"Me? You bet! But can I handle it? Are you sure?" Lia asked.

"If I can pilot and Sam, navigate, you can command. Besides, we're all greenies. You're the experienced commander. We need you."

"Okay. You don't have to ask twice. When do we leave?"

"As soon as I get us a crew. General Bev promised to provide all the security forces we need. Sam's staying behind to look after the children. Lenka and Walter are coming, as are Isabella and Owen. Deanna's coming and bringing along three engineers. Oh, and Commander L'Grina wants to tag along. Something about being an ambassador. Hey, maybe you should ask Senator Fennel if he wants to come along, representing Brussels."

She blushed. *How interesting.*

I continued. "We best hurry up, though. That Buffet CEO ordered me to get a telepathy job which I'm not about to do. Gonna lift off before anyone gets wise and tries to stop us."

Two days later, six of us watched as Bev's dozen soldiers, Gail, Commander L'Grina, and Walter loaded our gear onto the Friendship. Purposely, we brought along two dozen sets of our special machines, even though only six of us needed them. This trip, those with arms greatly outnumbers those of us who lacked them. Bev, however, brought along a huge supply of beer.

Chapter 21 Mrs. Jones' Finishing School

June, 2338, Philadelphia

Ten-year-old Patricia Ann Townsend walked into her home, a thirty-room mansion on the outskirts of the city. Her jeans and shoes tracked mud into the hallway. She'd been playing football with the neighbor boys and had been tackled several times. But she'd scored a touchdown, only one of two scored in the game. Pat, as she preferred to be called, kept up with boys several years older than she was.

"Oh Patricia Ann! This is entirely too much," screeched her mother, Zoe. Simon, Simon, come here this instant!" She flickered her three-inch long talons painted a glistening red that matched her elegant designer gown and tall stilettos. Zoe prided herself on being the perfect fashion model, a billionaire's wife. Elegant, refined, superb taste in apparel and jewelry.

"What is it—oh for heaven's sake, Patricia Ann," Simon Gates barked. "Not again."

"Pat. I'm Pat. I scored a touchdown today. Gary scored the only other one."

"You're covered in mud, Patricia Ann. Traipsing filth all over our expensive hall carpeting," he said. "Enough of this silliness. Leave the roughhousing to the boys. You're a young woman, a Gates. You should be looking as elegant as your mother—not like some begging urchin from the south-side slums!"

"I dona wanna be elegant. I wanna be a boy. They have all the fun. Who wants to play dolls and house? Not me."

"I think we made a huge mistake in adopting you, Patricia Ann. Your raven hair and that silly smile of your—well, everyone knows you're adopted and not a true Gates," he said.

"Your father and I expect—no, demand you represent us at the Quarterly Local Balls. Honestly, you'll never land a billionaire husband looking like this—a complete tramp."

"Right. I'm not about to let you lower other people's opinion of the Gates family."

Pat pressed her lips tightly together, making a deep frown. "I dona wanna look like Mom anyway. I don't like those dances either. Who cares about husbands? I'm only ten."

"Foolish girl. You'd better start caring or else you're going to have to work under a corporate sponsorship just like all the other poor folks of Earth. I own much of the Galactic Manufacturing Corporation here in Philadelphia. We *have* to set examples. So Zoe, throw away all her jeans and boyish clothes. From now on, Patricia Ann, you'll wear nothing but fancy gowns. I've spoken," Simon said.

Even though Pat detected a note of finality in his voice, she still protested. "No I won't. I'll play football in those stupid dresses if I have too." She wanted to add, "So there!" but thought better of it. Her father's face was redder than usual. He must be mad. "I want my real mom and dad," she added, knowing that always softened arguments.

She expected to see both relent with: So sorry, honey. They're dead. After all, this line worked many times in the past.

Instead, Zoe said, "Simon, what about Mrs. Jones' Finishing School? You know, the one they call SWAT—School for Wayward Adolescents and Teens. She claims to never have had a failure."

Simon looked Patricia Ann up and down, noting the drying brown mud coating her hair. "I'll make the call. You clean this tramp up."

"To the bathroom, young lady," Zoe barked.

Patricia did as asked. She heard her mother's heel clicks on the marble floor following her. No escape yet. She stripped and climbed into the bathtub. She watched her mother carefully picking the soiled clothes up, trying hard to not get mud on her long talons or worse on the five rings she wore. Instead of putting them into the clothes hamper so that the maid would later wash them, Zoe slipped them into a garbage bag. Pat's heart sank. Those were her favorite and lucky jeans.

The next day, Patricia Ann discovered she'd gone too far. Her father marched her out to his two-man shuttle. She'd seen her mother going through her wardrobe throwing away all her non-dress apparel, including her spiked sports shoes. Today, she wore a simple day dress, her long black hair tied back in a ponytail, the only thing she could do by way of protest.

They landed on a grassy knoll before another large mansion. This one had a stone wall six-feet tall around the grounds. A gate man waved them in from the guard house nestled beside the entrance gate. Even from this distance, she could see the large padlock on them. *Is this a prison?*

Simon marched her up to the front door, which opened revealing Mrs. Jones. The matronly woman was overweight, but tall. A tight bun held her hair, making her stern look even more commanding.

"Thank you for accepting her. This is Patricia Ann Gates. Mind you, she's a handful, but I expect a proper, elegant young woman from her."

"Of course, Mr. Gates. You have my guarantee on that. Never found an urchin I couldn't transform. You just need the right persuasion."

"Are you sure we don't need to provide apparel for her?"

"As I said last night, we provide everything. One day, she'll be returned to you as a proper, elegant young woman, befitting your heritage, Mr. Gates. Just remember. No visits. No phone calls. She's mine until she graduates."

"Of course. We've had all we can stomach from her rebelliousness. If you need something further, call."

Mrs. Jones nodded. Pat watched him leave in his shuttle. *Maybe I should have done something different.*

"Inside, young woman," Mrs. Jones barked.

Pat stepped inside, entering the main hall of the expansive building. There stood ten other girls, arranged by height and thus mostly by age. All wore satin gowns of various types. But the oldest girl wore a billowing ball gown. The teen's heels were hidden beneath the ten-foot in diameter dress. However, all the girls wore very tall heels, so Pat presumed the older girl was wearing them, too. Heel heights varied as did their nails. Some girls had nails a long as her mother, three inches at least, while others were a more practical inch long. All ten stood stiffly.

"Children, this is our newest young woman, Patricia Ann. I expect you to welcome her to our finishing school."

"I'm Pat. Not Patricia Ann," she protested.

"Not any longer. Let's get you to your room and out of these rags," she said.

"You can't keep me here. I'll run away. That stupid wall—anyone can climb over it."

Pat saw several girls cringing and wondered what that meant. Mrs. Jones' powerful arms latched onto her arm. She pulled Patricia Ann across the hall. She ushered her into a small bedroom. A large clothes closet occupied one wall along with a full length mirror. A dresser with a hairbrush and other sundries lay against the opposite wall. The bed looked soft and comfortable.

"Strip!" Mrs. Jones ordered.

Pat did as ordered. "What's that?"

"A heavily steel-boned corset to help you get a proper waist size."

"That's too tight. I can't breath," Pat complained. "It's cutting me in half."

"No pain, no gain. Always tighten it partway and wait a half hour before closing it all the way. Now then, let's get you dressed further. All elegant women wear expensive nylon stockings, held up by the corset's eight garters. Like this. Sit down. You've wonderful raven hair. No more hiding it in boyish ponytails. Not under my roof." She undid it and handed Patricia Ann the brush.

Still gasping for breath, Pat brushed out her hair, pretending it was bedtime; instead, she lived a nightmare.

Evidently, the half-hour passed because Mrs. Jones worked on the corset again, fully tightening it. Patricia Ann nearly fainted.

"Can't breath."

"Of course you can. Shallow, short breaths."

Next, she helped Pat into a tight-fitting gown, red, of course.

"Too tight," Patricia Ann tried to say.

"It's a hobble skirt, designed to make you take only the tiniest of steps. No climbing walls in this. Now then, the heels. As long as you cooperate and work at becoming a refined, elegant young woman, your heels will stay as they are. Disobey, cause trouble, and I'll make them higher."

"You can't do that. I'll kick them off." Patricia Ann did just that. Still sitting on the bed and with as much of a protest as she could manage, she kicked off both shoes.

Mrs. Jones merely smiled. She didn't get angry as Pat believed she would. Her mother always had. Tantrums worked miracles controlling her parents—they had until recently, that is.

"I won't. I won't. I won't," Patricia Ann declared, gasping between each sentence.

Mrs. Jones picked them up and sat them just outside the bedroom door. She returned with another pair. Patricia Ann's eyes swelled at the sight of the tallest heels she'd ever seen.

"These are six inches tall. No more running around like an urchin." After slipping them onto Patricia Ann's feet, she fastened the ankle straps, adding two tiny padlocks that ensured no one could remove the heels without the keys.

"Now then, you look almost the elegant young woman. Up and follow me. Oh, tiny steps."

Patricia Ann panicked. She could barely stand. She attempted to walk, but could only get one foot in front of the other, a motion that caused her to wobble wildly before falling down. She passed out.

She awoke to an awful smell. Pat shook her head and raised her hands to her nose and gasped. While she had been unconscious, her nails had grown an inch. They glistened as red as her satin gown. Her eyes looked around the room. She was in a manicure-like shop. Mrs. Jones screwed the top onto the bottle of smelling salts.

"Okay, pay attention, Patricia Ann. Your nails are an inch long. If you behave, they can remain that long. If you continue to cause trouble, they will get lengthened. Now, up and follow me to the practice room."

"Gasping and flailing her arms, Pat followed, thankful that Mrs. Jones walked very slowly.

Other girls wandered about this room. Each tried to balance a book on their heads while walking. When the book slipped off a girl's head, she snatched it before it fell to the ground.

"Don't let the book fall on the ground," one girl whispered to Patricia Ann. "We can hardly bend enough to pick it up."

Another girl about her own age added, "We can't even get up if we fall down. I can't breathe. Can you?"

"No. I can't walk right either."

The oldest girl in the billowing ball gown moved slowly up to her. Pat guessed her nails were six inches long.

"Hi, Pat. I'm Stacey. I'm seventeen and with luck I'll be out of here next year. Some advice for you. Do whatever Mrs. Jones says. I didn't. She kept making we wear taller and taller heels. The one's I've been wearing these last years has seven inch heels—almost impossible to walk in them. Eventually I could. She keeps making your nails longer, too, if you don't obey. As you can see," she flashed her red nails, "I protested too much. She never does lower heel heights or nail lengths, even if you start obeying. She only makes it worse. My corset has so much steel in it that I can't bend at all. So take my word, do what she says and keep quiet."

"When does she take these corsets off?" Pat asked.

"Once a week when it's shower time. Sleeping is a bitch until you get used to it," Stacey said. "You will. Get used to it. In time. Even the tall heels and long nails. I only wish she'd undo some of these. I've been doing all she asks for the last two years."

Nightmare days turned into weeks into hellish months for Patricia Ann. She found it almost impossible to follow Mrs. Jones and her rules. Stacey's warning proved accurate. At the one year mark, Patricia Ann wore the heavily steel boned inner corset as well as an equally boned but fashionable outer corset. As Stacey suggested, Mrs. Jones tolerated no backtalk or protests. Patricia Ann's heel height rose to six and a half inches and finally to seven inches. Her gait reduced to a mere three inch step—any more and she'd lose her balance. That her nails continually lengthened to over six inches became a mere annoyance. When she took a tumble in the hobble gown, she simply couldn't get back up on her own. Even though Mrs. Jones scolded her, she did help Patricia Ann back onto her feet and didn't add further punishments for falling.

As the years passed, the older girls graduated and left, and sometimes new younger girls took their places. The number of girls in training varied between ten and eighteen, but no more. While Mrs. Jones never undid any punishment, she did move the girls along. When Patricia Ann mastered walking in the tall heels, she graduated from her hobble skirt to a formal gown.

At night, Pat whispered to herself, "Eight years." Then, "Seven years." *No way am I going to be beaten by this woman. Bide my time until I can escape.* However, in these outfits, she couldn't, though she tried—several times.

When she turned seventeen, she cheered. Only one more year until freedom. However, Mrs. Jones replaced her usual gowns with the gigantic, billowing ball gowns. No longer could she see her feet.

"Time to prepare for your graduation, Patricia Ann. In another year, you'll have your coming out ball. You'll be wearing a gown such as this, so you want lots of practice. Elegant. Effortless. The perfect model."

She found handling stairs quite challenging. But with freedom so close at hand, she didn't protest. Besides, she'd mastered moving gracefully with her three-inch steps.

"Patricia Ann, float across the dance floor," Mrs. Jones barked. "Elegance. Graceful. That's better."

***

June, 2346 brought graduation and her freedom. Zoe and Simon arrived for the event, both dolled up for the ball.

Neither could believe how gorgeous, how refined, how elegant Patricia Ann looked in her white gown, billowing out ten feet around her. She seemed to float over the dance floor to greet them, but they had no idea of the height of her hidden heels.

"Patricia Ann, you look beautiful. I'm so glad we brought you here. Welcome home, Miss Gates," Simon said. "We've scheduled your coming out ball next week. Zoe's invited all the available billionaire young men. You'll make a perfect impression on them. With luck, my dear Patricia Ann, you'll have your pick of a husband."

"Such wonderful nails. Simon, I'm simply going to have to have Sofia lengthen mine to match Patricia Ann's. They look so impressive, dear. Let's get you home. We've missed you."

Hardly. I'm surprised you even recognize me. "Thank you, mother."

"All these?" Simon asked.

"Of course," Mrs. Jones said. Her handyman brought out a dozen boxes containing Patricia Ann's current apparel.

Once home in her old room, Patricia Ann found it just the way she'd left it—minus all her clothing. With her mother's help, she got out of her gown and corsets. Several years ago, she'd discovered her back muscles were weak; she needed the support of the corsets. Pat took a long, soaking bath, mentally taking stock of her situation.

I haven't got a choice. Have to wear the corsets. Have to wear the tall heels. I can't wear flats, period. I wonder if there's something I can do to strengthen my back or get my calves stretched back. Have to check. Well, play along with them. Maybe some of the young men will be better than living here.

***

Her father, his arm around her, proudly led Patricia Ann through the ballroom's doors, decorated with flowers for the coming-out affair. Someone had just announced, "Miss Patricia Ann Gates." Slowly, she moved forward, gliding with three-inch steps hidden beneath the billowing white ball gown. Unused to such small steps, Simon stumbled along. For once, Pat smiled at his awkwardness.

A hundred attended the ball. Most were married couples, some with younger children. However, ten eligible bachelors vied for her attention and dances. Most looked like cocky boys, hardly the marrying type.

"May I have this dance, Miss Gates? Or can I still call you Pat?"

"Vernon? Vernon Baxter?" she asked.

"Yes. I wondered what happened to you, my favorite football player. Without you on our team, we lost every game. You look—well, fabulous."

The two began to waltz.

"Small steps, Vernon. My heels are very tall. That's better."

"Your waist. It seems so small."

"Corsets. Have to wear them now. Back is weak. So what's happened since I got shipped off to that finishing school?" Pat desperately wanted to change the subject.

"I've become the black sheep in my family. Dad wanted me to follow in his footsteps—that means sit around doing nothing. So I've gotten enrolled in medical school. I'm going to be a medical doctor. Dad can keep his wealth."

"Really? A doctor? God, how I want to escape my parents!"

"So you're not really a debutante like our mothers? You don't want to sit around a mansion doing nothing at all?"

Pat laughed. "Hardly, Vernon. They've forced me into this, but somehow I will escape and do something useful with my life. I got rather interested in microbiology this year."

One dance led to another. Vernon and Patricia Ann talked the rest of the evening. Soon, the other young men stopped trying to get her attention and left.

As the evening festivities ended, Vernon said, "Pat, when I came tonight, I expected to see another silly debutante, not the crazy Pat of my football team. The Pat who was alive with vitality, who wasn't afraid to break the stereotypical patterns our billionaire parents try to force us into. In spite of everything, you're still you. I'd love to see you again. Take you out on a date, if that's okay with you. I only have two months before my classes begin."

"Marry me, Vernon. Take me with you. I want to study microbiology, but Dad isn't about to let me. If we marry, he can't say no any longer."

Vernon laughed. "Now that's the most Pat-thing you've said all night. I can't tell you how much I missed you these years. But we should take it a bit slow and let our parents get used to us as a couple."

"Okay, but you get me enrolled in that college with you. Then, I'll have something to really look forward to. These past eight years have been a living nightmare."

***

Mid-August, Vernon Baxter and Patricia Ann Gates married. Each admired and respected the other. They hoped a deep love would follow.

At the reception, Pat overheard Vernon's father, Lane Baxter, talking with her father.

"Well, I'm thankful that's done, Simon. Vernon's in line to inherit part of my Galactic Transportation fortune, just as Patricia Ann will inherit your Galactic Manufacturing money. Honestly, I can't believe this is the same Patricia Ann who played football with Vernon and the boys."

"Lane, you and me both. I'm glad she's married. Honestly, I thought I'd made a gargantuan mistake adopting her, but Zoe found the right finishing school. If I were only thirty years younger..."

Lane chuckled. "Hey, you and me both! She's quite the prize. I hope Vernon appreciates her. If he doesn't, you let me know."

***

In August, the pair moved to Brussels, Tau Ceti, leaving Earth and their parents behind. Vernon showed such promise as a doctor that Brussels University of Medicine offered him a full scholarship. Of course, he didn't need the money, but the prestige—well, that appealed to him. He accepted as long as they also accepted Pat into their microbiology program.

Six years passed quickly, as each excelled in their fields. Vernon graduated with a neurosurgeon doctorate, while Pat received her doctorate in microbiology and genetics. During those years, Vernon looked for potential cures for the body modifications that had been done to Pat. Meanwhile, the Sixth Invader war raged in the far north. As the young couple, now twenty-four, headed home to Earth, the miraculous cures appeared, the regrowing of arms and legs.

"Look, Pat. You should get this Galactic Doll mutation. Not because you want to fit in with how all other women look, but because it might help your back so you don't have to wear those corsets."

"You won't object if I sport monster boobs? Those pictures of Earth's women—god, they're huge."

"If it repairs your back and legs, I'm all for it."

When their transport landed in Philadelphia, Pat agreed to have it done as soon as possible. First, they purchased their own mansion, hastily setting up house. That they had a nearly infinite supply of credits helped. Then, she entered the Phili Med Center to have it done. Even during the brief time this took, every woman they'd seen sported the giant bosom and wore elegant, satin gowns with matching tall heels. Even the maid they'd hired to take care of their new home looked similar.

Dr. Vernon Baxter monitored his wife's progress each day that she was in the mutation coma. Via x-rays, the resident doctor showed Vernon the miraculous changes in Pat's body.

"Here in this initial view, you can see how wearing such a restrictive corset starting at such a youthful age has caused her lower ribs to bend and twist inward. If she wanted such a small waist, she should have had those lower ribs removed. It's a miracle they didn't puncture any vital organs. Now here you can see those same ribs are definitely straightening out. Honestly, this Galactic Doll mutation agent works miracles. Did you know that it also cures dementia in our older people? We're finding it resets their biological clocks to their early twenties."

"Fountain of youth?" Vernon asked.

"Could be. But only for women. Lord, I wouldn't want to look like those freaky male Galactic Dolls in Chicago. Still, it's given our brave soldiers who lost an arm and leg in the war their lives back."

When Pat awoke, she felt different. "I feel—well, I don't know. Just better somehow. Oh, they're big aren't they?"

Vernon explained what he'd seen from her x-rays.

"Well, I'm through wearing those corsets!"

He laughed. "Your new figure doesn't require that." Both chuckled.

"Well, didn't help my legs much," she said.

"Didn't expect it would, given what we heard about this mutation."

"I can live with the heels. Come on. Get me out of here. How goes the job hunting? Are we paying our parents a visit?"

"We have to, don't we?" Vernon said.

While their parents were appalled that their children were actually working for a corporation, GMed, in both cases, they plied them with welcome home presents and pressured them for grandchildren.

For the pair, life settled down. Pat continued to wear the seven-inch heels she'd worn for so long, but kept her nails short. Like all Galactic Dolls, she wore refined, elegant satin gowns. For once, she fit in without compromising her goals. But they put off having children for a few years, until they both felt comfortable in their new roles at GMed.

Chapter 22 Patient Zero

Patricia Ann and Vernon Baxter were thirty-two when the armless Galactic Doll mutation attack struck Philadelphia. When she heard of the attack, she rushed to the med center only to find Vernon in a mutation coma. She camped out beside his bed, just as he'd done for her, pestering the doctors about his condition every chance she got, much to their annoyance.

Vernon awoke to find his life vastly altered. His voice was higher pitched than Pat's. Like his wife, his feet couldn't lie flat, forcing him to wear tall heels, though he chose the usual six-inch ones, unlike Pat. His bosom rivaled Pat's. In fact, comparing the shapes of their bodies, one could hardly tell he was male. During the mutation, his hair had grown substantially. But above all, his medical career had ended.

"You can do it, dear." Pat did her best to stay upbeat and positive, while helping the nurses get him dressed.

"I've got you." She slipped an arm around his now thin waist, steadying him as he stood in the heels for the first time. Memories of what she'd endured flashed in her mind, but she forced her attention outward onto Vernon. She felt his terror and panic. If only she could get him safely home. Time enough then to adapt. Perhaps.

She found his two-man shuttle in the staff lot, and she flew them to their mansion. Already Galactic Robotics had delivered the hair/nail machine, the dressing/undressing robot, the maid robot, and a laptop filled with the how-to videos.

"I'd no idea walking was so hard for you. I'm petrified. I can't do this, Pat."

"Hey, I endured it. Practice is all you need. You'll get the hang of taking minuscule steps. Remember how you reacted when you first saw me on the dance floor at my coming out ball? Tiny steps. Only mine are still tinier than yours." Pat attempted to alleviate some of his fears.

Later, she got him undressed and into the tub. Standing for showers hadn't been possible for her since she was twelve. She slipped in with him.

"Look at me," he sobbed. "I look like you."

Pat stared at his bosom and then hers. Laughing, she agreed. Her levity and the bath caused Vernon to finally begin to relax. She knew his mental state was fragile, based on all the information she'd read in the GMed annals from earlier attacks. So she tried the one thing that always brought them close, no matter what had happened during the day. Intimacy.

"Does this still work?" she teased.

His body reacted, though this time Pat did most of the work.

"See, dear. All isn't lost. We're just going to have to find ways to adapt."

"But all I ever wanted to do was be a medical doctor and help people. I don't want to just sit around the house, but that's all I can do now. I'm helpless."

"No, you're not. Those videos. That Molly Parkinson woman. She isn't helpless. I can quit my job and work with you every day until you're able to be independent again."

"Doing what? Just what could I possibly do? I can't even put a band-aid on a cut."

"Well, I don't know. Yet. When I was at that insane SWAT school, I never gave up, no matter how hard she made it for me. So don't you dare give up on me, Vernon Baxter!"

The next day, she took a family emergency leave of absence so she could work with him. Just walking was terrifying to him to say nothing of everything else. However, he definitely looked forward to their bedtime sex each night. Pat soon realized that was the only thing keeping Vernon going.

After two months, Pat trusted Vernon enough to leave him alone with their housekeeper. She returned to her work and lab. That's when she uncovered the cures.

Over dinner, she said, "Damn men! Vernon, they've invented minor cures that reduces breast sizes to something manageable. Another repairs our mutated legs and feet. We could wear ordinary shoes again."

"God, that would be a blessing for me. How soon can I get them? Oh, not at all." He'd just picked up her next thought. Telepathy had brought them closer together.

"And get this. There's a cure that regrows lost arms, but they believe it will wipe out your telepathic ability."

"And I can't get that either?"

"Damn men. No, they passed stupid laws. You have to wait ten years before you can get any cures. Plus, they've got some new Telepathy Corporation, and they want you to get a job using your telepathic skills."

"Like spying on others. I'll be damned if I'll do their dirty work for them!"

"I don't want you to do that either. What's the matter with the ruling men? If you got your arms regrown, you could resume being a neurosurgeon. Saving lives."

"No, they don't need me to do that. Just inject them with the armless mutation agent. That's the new cure for what ails people. I heard that on the news. Everyone's getting a syringe with that agent in it, along with instructions to inject it to save you life," he said. He'd become cynical.

"You do look twenty-one again. That's something."

"If something bad happens to me, I don't want them prolonging my life by re-mutating me, unless they're giving me back my arms. Promise me you won't let them inject me again without that."

She sighed deeply. "I promise. But I love you so much. Oh, I've a surprise for you. We're going to have a baby. I'm pregnant. We've been doing it too much at night. Caught up with us."

"That's wonderful, honey. Wait. Won't the baby be deformed like me?"

Pat sighed again. "I don't know. Yet."

He read her mind. "So some geneticists think it's dominant. Others don't."

"Yeah. Not sure who's right. I'm making a study of all these mutation agents. If I can find a way to cure you, I'll do it."

Months passed and Michael entered the world. He had Pat's black hair, but Vernon's eyes and facial structure. To their dismay, Michael also had no arms. His feet were just as malformed as his parents.

During maternity leave, Pat helped Vernon breast feed their son. He had no choice in the matter. His massive breasts automatically became a milk factory as he put it, though no more so than hers did.

When Mike was a month old, Pat took him to visit his pediatrician. "So how soon can he get the cures he needs? Arms back. Legs and feet fixed up."

The doctor shook her head. "Sorry. The current laws are very precise on this. He can't have any cures until his eighteenth birthday. They want him to get used to being a telepath and to desire such a career. After all, the amount of credits he can earn in just one year is a hundred times what I make."

"You mean these men want to doom my child and my husband to a crippled life just so they have telepathic spies?"

The nurse didn't answer. She didn't have to.

When Pat returned home, she ranted and raved about the house. Finally, she felt the calming presence of Vernon in her mind. Then, he picked up what she'd just found out and cursed profusely.

"No one's talking about what's happening to us. I just saw a GMed study on women's physical attributes. They measured width of nose, position of nose, cheekbones—thousands of measurements beyond just the usual height and weight—part of that old DNA database thing. The range of variation of each was huge. But today with all women being Galactic Dolls—well, we should look good, you know—the range in each of these measurements is a factor of a hundred smaller. Your observation that women somehow look similar, dear, is born out by the facts."

She ranted on. "But with this armless Galactic Doll telepath thing—they've gone too far. Mike can't get cures for eighteen years. You can't for ten years. Hell, they have invented lifesaving cures for you both, only they won't let you two have them!"

At this point, something within Pat snapped. Perhaps it had always been there—her fierce determination to be her own person. She said, "Do you realize that in another generation, all men on Earth are going to be Galactic Dolls? These men have destroyed our world, Vernon. They can't be allowed to get away with this."

"I can't do anything about it, honey."

"I know, dear. I know. But maybe I can. I'm hiring a personal assistant for you two. I'll be spending drastically more time in my lab."

Within a week, she received minuscule samples of the current genetic cures for the telepaths, the cures being denied them. None of the three vials contained a sufficient dosage to work its magic. That's not why she wanted the samples. Her forte lay in microbiology and viruses, in particular.

She whispered to her lab walls. "I need to create a virus that attacks the immune system, replicating itself billions of times, but I need it to be detected. The body's cytotoxic T cells must attack and those killer T cells should destroy the viral membrane, releasing the internal contents of the virus into the body. The contents will be the genetic mutation cures. But I've got to stop these insane men from re-mutating everyone. Hell, prevent others on Earth from becoming an armless telepath. So I need the B cells to produce not only the antigens but also the memory cells to guard against any future re-infection with the armless telepath agent. Plus, I need the virus to be able to rapidly bind to the immune system cells, the antigen receptors. That'll trigger activation, and the T cells can then trigger the B cells to produce the antibodies and memory cells. Tall order. Oh yeah. The virus must be *highly* contagious."

Creating the perfect virus absorbed all her waking hours. First, she merged the three cures into one nanoparticle set of activated genes. Next, she designed the viral host that would replicate those nanoparticle genes with each new virus. She needed the viral infection to rapidly explode, filling a body with billions upon billions of virus copies. Then, they'd attack the immune system. This action would make the body attack and destroy the virus, releasing the activated nanoparticle genes, which would begin the Fetal Regeneration Stimulus that would carry out the mutation. As an added benefit, she insisted the memory cells should attack and destroy any future invasion by the original armless telepath agents, but not this version or even the usual Galactic Doll agent.

For weeks, she worked on the project, spending twelve hours each day in her lab perfecting each step of the virus. She came home one night and complained.

"Vernon, do you realize that all Earth women's breasts are identical? That's insane. Before this Galactic Doll mutation swept Earth, you couldn't find two that were identical. Close or similar, but not identical. Hell, yours and mine are identical. What's worse is that we women want them this big, because we have to look good."

"I know that, dear. Women should look good."

Neither knew they were repeating the Sixth Invaders' implanted words.

"Still, if our feet could lie flat on the floor, women would have a choice in footwear. Those of us who want to could still wear these tall heels. We should have a choice, don't you think?"

Vernon didn't know how to respond and wisely said, "After we get Mike settled, bed?"

"Oh, I'll get you fired up, honey." She chuckled.

***

Finally, on Christmas day, she came home from her lab. Everyone else had headed home for the holiday days ago. "Well, honey, here goes nothing. Either you'll be cured or not. I hope you don't just get sick."

"What do you mean? What are you waving around the room?"

"A little something I've concocted. Men in power need to be taught a lesson. You and Mike need your cures. So do all the others. It's just a little airborne virus."

270

She watched as he slipped into a mutation coma. Then she too fell unconscious. Pat awoke and checked the day. "Only lost a day. Wow. My feet lie flat. Terrific. Hum, nothing else has changed. Good. Best check on Vernon and Mike."

"Look at that! Those are tiny arms if ever I saw such. It's working. Gotta get them comfortable. I hope their bodies don't need extra food for the regeneration process. Hadn't thought of that."

After making them both as comfortable, she stripped and examined her own body in the full-length mirror. "I do look years younger again."

The next day, their maid didn't show up for work, but Pat knew why. She'd also picked up the virus. After a quick trip to her lab, Pat launched a drone into the air over Philadelphia. It released the virus over the city. Drifting air currents carried it eastward. Further, each victim exhaled large quantities of the virus before the immune system kicked in with a vengeance.

Then, she took a day trip to LA, releasing the last of her stockpile of the virus over various cities along the way. Thus, the viral infection spread rapidly around the world, though not always with the same results.

Chapter 23 Reactions

While we planned to depart in the Friendship shortly before Christmas bound for the various alien locations that Isabella deciphered, the delays accumulated. We hoped to find the kidnapped victims. While waiting, we followed the news delivered by GEnt.

Things weren't going well for CEO Buffet. He'd grown tired of hearing the telepaths constant complaints of hearing too many voices in their heads and needing to shun crowds. GEnt reported the devastating news that someone had assassinated the new telepath CEO he'd installed in London's GPan corporation. A day later and after many calls to London GD, he learned the man had been shot in the head from at least a mile away. He shrugged it off and looked through the registered telepaths for a replacement. He sent an order for me to take that position, but to his chagrin discovered I was scheduled to go off-world. Again.

The following day, three more CEO telepaths were executed in a similar fashion: long range shot to the head. A sniper was definitely after telepaths. So many telepaths called him that they jammed his phone lines, each person begging for protection. His response: get the various local GD corporations to put armed security men around the other new telepath CEOs. Since these attacks came from at least a mile away, such protection left everything to be desired. Most had been executed while in their top floor offices, shot from distant rooftops.

One day passed without incident. Buffet relaxed. However, the assassinations continued the following day. The sniper picked off telepaths without harming their new GD guards. Now Buffet began to worry and seldom left his office building. He urged other worried telepath CEOs to stay indoors and not present a target. In a GEnt interview, he said, "With all the GD men in the world looking for this sniper, I'm sure he'll be found soon."

Then came calls from irate business personnel. Most

related the same story. "Look, these telepaths are no good. What they tell me they overheard in other people's mind ends up being completely wrong. It's costing us a fortune. Get this straightened out immediately or our lawyers are going to take the Telepath Corporation to court."

He turned his phone off. "Damn that Parkinson woman anyway. She said this would be happening. She must be behind it. But she's off on some wild-goose chase. So it can't be her. Damn. Damn. Damn."

He turned on the news. "This just in. A viral epidemic has struck Philadelphia. Well, many have said that Earth was overdue for an epidemic of some kind. We're getting the latest from one of their GMed centers. This is Doctor Albright. Go ahead, doctor."

"Yes, well, it's definitely been identified as a virus— an unknown one. But that's not anything new. On Earth alone, there are billions of as yet undiscovered viruses, most benign to us humans. This one is most peculiar. Once infected, the patients display no symptoms for several days. Then, they drop into a coma. It's verified. It's a mutation coma. We've seen enough patients now to see the results..." The doctor's body slumped to the floor.

"Doctor! Some help..."

The GEnt reporter dropped the mike. The picture turned into a crazy angle shot before Buffet realized the cameraman also collapsed. After a minute, the image of a reporter in a studio appeared.

"Apparently, we're experiencing some technical issues. We'll report back as soon as we receive word from the..." The reporter slumped over onto his desk, bumping the microphone.

"What the hell is going on?" Buffet yelled at the screen. He powered up his phone and tried to call out. He got the message: All lines are currently busy; please try your call later. He cursed again.

The next day's news provided actual facts. This time, a reporter from Chicago appeared on the screen. "The viral infection is spreading rapidly. A flyover has confirmed everyone in the greater Philadelphia area is infected, though women are reviving rapidly. The DC area is infected. In fact, the whole eastern seaboard is quarantined. GMed hopes to confine the infection to this area.

"Initial reports from the reviving, rejuvenated women indicate that their feet now lie flat. No other mutation changes have been observed, except that older women in the assisted living homes are being rejuvenated into Galactic Dolls. None of the men have as yet revived. Telepaths are also in comas."

"New coverage has arrived. Aerial drones show arms are regenerating on telepaths. Ordinary men appear to be growing large breasts. None of this has been confirmed. We've sent in personnel in bio containment suits, but this virus has infected them as well. Our best hope is to contact some of the reviving women who are nurses or doctors. Stay tuned for the latest."

"Wait. This just in. The giants and dwarves are immune to this virus. We're getting some initial reports from their medical personnel. I'm turning this over to Harli in Philadelphia."

A dwarf appeared on the screen. "Yes, we've been studying this viral outbreak. It's conclusive. Humans are regrowing missing limbs, just like that original Galactic Doll agent did for your soldiers on Brussels. The bodies of normal men are also mutating. Initial signs suggest they're becoming male Galactic Dolls. Many of Phili's women are awake. The mutation restored their feet. As one woman said, now we have a choice in footwear.

"However, those who have never been mutated into a Galactic Doll before are undergoing that full mutation process, including mutated feet. It's too soon to tell if the restoration of a telepath's lost arms will impact their telepathic ability.

"Already Galactic Manufacturing is gearing up production of clothing to fit these many male victims. We've verified women's biological ages are again reset to their early twenties. Presumably, men's bio ages will be comparable.

"This just in from the Center for Disease Control.

They're declaring this to be a pandemic. All of North America east of a north-south line through Philadelphia has been infected. It is hoped the ocean will halt it's spread. Many are fleeing the seaboard area. Millions have been infected, but so far no deaths have been reported. Stay tuned for further details."

The next day, the situation deteriorated. Again, Harli reported from Philadelphia. "Unfortunately, the virus has spread to England and western Europe. Also, isolated pockets have popped up in China and in the western portions of North America. LA, for example, is experiencing isolated outbreaks. This is definitely a pandemic. The question on many minds is how to protect yourself from the virus. It's airborne. All signs point to a four day window during which the person shows no outward symptoms, and yet exhales large quantities of the virus through normal respiration, thereby spreading the virus. If you have an air-tight room, my suggestion is to hold up there and hope for the best.

"On another note, I'd like to take this opportunity to educate everyone on the ever-present danger of alien bacteria and viruses. When visiting another world, it's vital you get vaccinated. We virologists prepare vaccines to help prevent outbreaks like this one. There are many inhabited worlds out there, each with their own unique bacteria and viruses. Travelers should take all precautions possible to prevent becoming ill or dying because of an alien virus or bacteria."

Talking to the monitor, Buffet said, "It won't get to Chicago. Even if it does, it won't get to me up here. I should be safe."

"Don't worry, Mr. Buffet. I'll bring food up to you. We'll be safe here," his personal assistant said.

Three days later and unknown to her, she brought the virus into his office. Only two days later did she fail to appear, having slumped into a coma. A day later, Mr. Buffet felt weak and laid down, slipping quietly into a mutation coma.

**

In London, Edward Wainwright awoke from his mutation coma to find his body mutated into that of a Galactic Doll, complete with normal feet and an enviable breast size. His screaming soprano voice told all.

Across town, Fritz Fulco awoke to find he'd been mutated. He quietly packed his gear, stole a transport, and headed home—illegally. He'd amassed a pile of credits, but such didn't offset what had happened to him.

What the empire didn't yet realize is that this pandemic achieved precisely what the Sixth Invader's original Commander R'Ina had planned.

***

"What happened to me?" Vernon asked. He awoke ravenous. "I've got arms!"

"Yes, dear. I've got food waiting for you. Let's get you up and to the bathroom."

"I'm so weak. What's happened? My feet. They're normal."

"Yes, mine are too, but our breasts are unchanged. Women should look good."

"Mike! What about our son?"

"He's grown arms, too. He should be reviving soon. Come on."

She helped him to the kitchen table. "Don't over eat. Back in a bit. I hear Michael waking up." Her heels clicked on their marble floor.

When Pat carried their son into the kitchen, he looked like a normal baby. Vernon sighed. Noticing Pat's tall heels, he asked, "Aren't your feet repaired?"

"Yes, they're normal, too. Rather, I feel funny not wearing them. At least today I have a choice and chose to wear them. Once you get your strength back, you can resume being a doctor."

"It's a miracle. But how did this happen?"

"They're calling it a pandemic. It's a virus. Spread throughout the entire world. Only infects us humans. Not the giants and dwarves. Have you still got your telepathy?"

"Oh! No. The voices inside my head have gone silent. Lord, I never thought I'd hear silence again. But what

276

caused the pandemic? What virus? How bad is it? Any deaths?"

"All telepaths were being denied the cures that would give them back their lives. So I fixed that. Men kept insisting telepaths spy for them. So I'm teaching men a lesson."

"What do you mean? How did you do this?"

"All human men of Earth are going to be Galactic Dolls with mutated feet. But that would have happened in the future, anyway. As we both know, children born to any Galactic Doll will be Dolls, male or female. It's a dominant set of genes. I just moved the process along a bit. Plus, I've reset the biological clocks of human adults back to their early twenties."

Vernon finally grinned. "Why, you devil you. Pat, I love you. But how did you do it?"

"Long days in the lab. I made a virus, which when its membrane walls are pieced by the antigens, releases the activated nanoparticles carrying the mutation agent. I concocted it from the known cures a pair of geneticists in Chicago developed—the very cures men in power kept refusing to give to the victims. I tweaked it so each body's immune system will attack any invasion of that terrible armless telepath agent they used on you. With luck, you are now immune to being injected with that bio agent again. So are all the other telepaths."

"You're a genius, Pat! Honestly, being injected again and again with that damned agent really scared me. They could keep me alive as their telepath for centuries, unless I could find some way to kill myself. Kind of hard to do like I was." He sighed. "And Mike. He can finally have a reasonable life. He won't be handicapped. All thanks to you. Wait! We best not say anything about this; they might terminate you."

"My lips are sealed," she teased.

"Hold on a second. My body still looks like yours. Men aren't going to like being mutated into Galactic Dolls."

Pat laughed. "No. I'd give anything to see my Dad's reaction when he wakens to find his body has become a sexy looking Galactic Doll. Pat finally wins one."

"You certainly have. I can't believe he forced that torture on a ten-year-old girl. But then my folks also tried to force me into a life of doing nothing, as you say."

She smiled and added, "What I don't know is if this new gene will be dominant. Will future male children's bodies also be Dolls or will they revert back to normal male bodies?"

"There's only one way to find out, honey. After we feed Mike, let's find out," he teased. "I owe you big time."

"No, we're even. You rescued me from my parents and that hideous future they'd planned for me—a life of doing nothing productive. We're even, honey. But our bed awaits. You don't have to ask twice, as long as you do your share of breast feeding."

Both chuckled.

***

We waited for final clearance to depart New O'Hare. For a week, many of us had stayed on the Friendship, while supplies arrived and were loaded. Why? Because the Telepathy Corporation CEO Buffet ordered me and others to get telepathy jobs which we weren't about to do. We watched the news on GEnt, though.

My daughter Isabella said, "Mom, you were right. Someone's assassinating telepaths CEOs. Hope Helen Hugo is being careful. Also you're right. Some spy telepaths must be reporting false information. There's a huge furor going on."

"Hey, I called what I see. Why can't others see what their actions will cause?"

We both laughed until the next newscast, the one reporting the pandemic outbreak. When it became clear it was spreading throughout the world, I called for a family meeting on board the Friendship.

"Incredible virus, but we've got some serious decisions to make," I said to the others. "I talked to Helen. She and her family are praying the virus infects them. None want to be telepaths. So what about us?"

Bernardo said, "Matt, Wendy, and I want our arms

back. Heck with this telepathy thing. Dad, you should get them regrown too."

"Hey, I want to stay a telepath," Nikita said, "just like Isabella."

Isabella said, "Well, Owen should get his arms regrown. I don't really want to lose my telepathic ability, but I'd like my arms back. Hell of a choice, right Nikita?"

My youngest daughter stamped her foot. "I don't want to lose my telepathy. No how. No way."

Our guests spoke up. Lenka said, "I'd give anything to get my arms back, right Walter?"

Her husband nodded enthusiastically.

"But don't you need me on this trip?" she added.

"Hey, first priority is getting the cures. We'll manage, Lenka."

Commander Lia said, "If you don't mind, Senator Fennel and I want our arms back, too. Kids, are you sure you about this? Life's a bitch like we are."

Nikita pouted. "Well, I've always done just fine without them, right Isabella?"

I saw just how much she admired her older sister. She added, "I can live without arms, but I can't live without telepathy."

"Maybe I shouldn't get mine regrown," Sam said. "Stay armless for Nikita and Isabella's sake."

"Dad," barked Nikita, "you don't have to do that. You've already helped Matt and me tons. You should get them back. Mom, you should too. After all, you've always been a telepath before this mutation thing came along."

I flushed. "According to the law, I can't have my arms back for years. If I get this virus and get them regrown, will they amputate them again? Beasts."

I added, "Look, kids. I had hours and hours of Celeste and Eve's therapy sessions. That's how come I developed telepathy in the first place. I've been sort of a model to other victims, showing them life can be lived without arms. We're about to rescue many more victims, so I'm thinking I should avoid this virus. For now, at least. Set a good example."

Nikita said, "So does Celeste and Eve have some therapy that I can get that would make me a telepath, too? Like you were, Mom?"

Isabella watched me closely. I sighed.

"No, dear, they don't. It just happened. Look, I was on that South Pacific island getting therapy sessions every day for six months, to say nothing of those I got after that. It's not a predictable result."

"Then I want to remain like I am," Nikita declared flatly.

"Mom, I've got a terrific job as a linguist," Isabella said. "If I lose my telepathy, I'm going to have a much harder time learning a new world's language."

Owen inserted, "Only if you continue to work on those deep space exploration ships. We're about to have a family."

Isabella sighed. I saw water appearing in her eyes. "I know that. Worse, when she's born, she's going to be like we are. But if I get the virus cure, she'll be a normal girl. Hell of a choice, Owen. If I don't get the cure, then she'll have an opportunity to earn millions of credits, something that only we telepaths and the other corporate bigwigs do. You know I want her to have the best opportunities. Hell of a choice," she repeated with a large exhale.

"Hey there, everyone," the voice of my sister, General Beverly Blythe interrupted us. "Can I come in?"

"You already are," teased Nikita.

"Say, this virus thing. You talking about it? I heard it's regrowing telepaths arms."

I chuckled. "Yeah, Bev. We were just working it out. It seems that everyone wants their arms regrown, except Nikita, Isabella, and me. Don't get me wrong. I'd love to have them back, but I think I should remain a role model for all these victims we're about to rescue. Maybe after that..."

Bev's eyes darted around the room. "Well, that makes sense. Nikita's wanted to be a telepath since before she was born. Isabella has become super famous with her linguistic feats. And you, sis, my god, you've been instrumental in helping thousands of others adapt to their loss of arms. So, yeah, it makes sense.

"But I also heard the virus is making giant boobs. Lord, I don't want that again. I was kind of hoping some of us could ride out this pandemic on the Friendship and not get re-mutated. It's turning all men into male Galactic Dolls, too. And that's freaking many of my soldiers out. I've promised to bring a dozen with us, so they want to know if they can ride this pandemic out with us on the spaceship."

"That's fine with me, Bev. Let's get on board tonight yet. I've a bad feeling. It's hit LA already. I suspect Chicago isn't going to be far behind. Nikita, go pack a bag. Isabella, you help her with what she needs to bring. Let's plan to head to New O'Hare in an hour. Okay, Bev?"

"Yeah, I'll text my soldiers. I've already texted our other sisters. They aren't worried about it," she said.

As the meeting broke up, I followed Isabella and Nikita. "I'll help you pack. Are you both certain about this?"

"Yeah, Mom," they said in unison.

Two hours later, a dozen worried men and women joined the three of us on the Friendship. Bev, Gail, and their daughter had already arrived and stowed their gear. Using a foot, I pressed the Close button that sealed us inside, ready for takeoff. Now we waited. Rescuing those the aliens abducted would have to wait a couple weeks.

The next morning, Bev declared, "That was too damned close!"

The newscast reported the virus had spread to Chicago sometime during the night. A text to Sam went unanswered, though eventually our dwarf friend, Lara, texted me everyone was in mutation comas and tiny arms had appeared. I relaxed. They were getting their needed cures. I swallowed hard. I wasn't. Not yet, anyway. Neither were my two daughters. Still, it had been their choices.

For the next two weeks, Nikita and Isabella spent their waking hours chatting away, making up for lost sister time. Bev's dozen soldiers finally relaxed, knowing they wouldn't become male dolls.

The second day, Leslie texted me. Big boobs

again. Helping to make millions of male doll apparel now. Galactic Manufacturing's making a fortune.

I chuckled. She and Felix had become wealthy by designing male doll apparel and special gowns for armless women. I suspected they'd spend weeks designing new lines, since all human males on Earth were in mutation comas.

Commander L'Grina called. "Hey there. Well, it's happened. Just like our original plan. Turn all men into proper doll forms. Don't worry. The Sixth Invaders have nothing to do with this virus. I checked. High Command is as baffled about this as your people. In fact, many admirals and senators on Bela Prime have taken an intense interest in this virus."

"Good to know. We're delaying liftoff for about two weeks. I'll text you when we're about to leave. Riding out this pandemic sealed up in the Friendship."

Two weeks passed before GMed gave the all-clear newscast. "At this time, we've verified all traces of the mutation virus have vanished. It has a short lifetime outside of a human host. No giant or dwarf has been affected. We've given the okay for other ships with humans on board to land and unload or load cargo.

"The aftermath is challenging. Many men couldn't handle the mutation and chose to die. Galactic Manufacturing is ramping up production of male doll apparel. It's strange to see men wearing tall heels, while we women have a choice. Expect many changes during the ensuing weeks, as Earth adjusts to the new normal.

"Currently, CDC is searching for the source of the viral outbreak—patient zero in their nomenclature. Stay tuned for further details as they develop."

Thus, I set the liftoff date for January 15, 2361.

Chapter 24 Discoveries

Lia, Senator Fennel, Lenka, and Owen sported tiny baby-like arms. I wished I had them too, but... Sam stayed home with our other children. Only Isabella and I remained armless on this trip.

Commander L'Grina and I shared pilot duties, while I made Lia our commander. Lenka acted as navigator, while Isabella would perform translation duties. General Bev, Lieutenant Gail, and the dozen soldiers provided security, though half of the males stayed in Chicago, replaced by female soldiers. Walter provided strong arms for Lenka, while hers regrew. Deanna joined us and brought along three engineers.

I'd heard nothing about law changes for us telepaths, and I certainly wasn't going to get a telepathy spy job. No one tried to stop us.

I watched as Bev's dozen soldiers, Gail, Commander L'Grina, and Walter loaded our gear onto the Friendship. Purposely, we brought along two dozen sets of our special machines, even though only six of us needed them, though four only needed them until their arms finished growing. I had figured we'd need them if we rescued people the aliens had abducted. So on this trip, those with arms greatly outnumbered those of us who lacked them. Bev, however, brought along a huge supply of beer.

Isabella called out her translation of the first set of alien coordinates, while Lenka entered them into the nav system. Both triple checked them.

Commander Lia said, "Okay. Pilot check."

"All set here. Triple checked," I said, while at my side, Commander L'Grina smiled.

"Okay. Tower clearance activated. Liftoff on their signal."

"Aye, aye, commander," I said.

Shortly, the tower sent the signal, and I pressed the Execute button with my right toe. The Friendship's engines ignited, and the ship began to gently rise. Many eyes peered at the view screens, as the external video cams recorded our ascent. We rose straight up into the stratosphere before the Chicago flight control rolled us over.

A computer generated voice said, "Returning flight control to the Friendship in ten seconds. Nine. Eight." The countdown continued, and I had my foot ready to respond at Zero. I flipped on the autopilot.

"Are you ready for the jump to hyperspace?" asked Commander Lia.

"All set," Lenka replied.

"Execute the jump."

I pressed the Execute button again, while noticing Bev guzzling one beer, though she had a second in her other hand. I smiled and noticed the strange feeling in my stomach as the video stream turned utterly black. I could see why Bev hated these jumps. Unnerving at best.

Lenka called out, "My readout says ninety-six minutes until we drop out of hyperspace."

***

I held my breath waiting for nerve-wracking sounds of collisions with space dust, but heard none. Was there debris in hyperspace? I had no idea. Then, something Commander L'Grina had told me made sense. In space, there are few barriers, and many hidden ones could destroy a spaceship that runs into them—lots of dust and tiny particles, to say nothing of dead stars, asteroid-like chunks of matter that failed to form into a planet. This led to a frantic type existence. Life planet-side consisted of multitudes of barriers. Thus, life became calmer, focusing on love.

"Want me to take over the controls when we drop out of hyperspace," Commander L'Grina asked.

I exhaled. "Would you? I fear I might not be able to react fast enough."

She grinned, and we exchanged seats.

"Dropping out now," Lenka called out.

I heard a belch before Bev said, "I'm ready."

Commander Lia advised, "This is always the most dangerous aspect of space travel. Dropping out of hyperspace into unknown space. Could be totally empty space or could be filled with all manner of obstacles designed to wipe us out. Be alert."

My stomach lurched. On the monitors, the external video showed a dense star field, along with one bright star—likely our destination. Now, Lenka's navigational skills were tested. She had to identify our location. Both she and Sam had a knack for this. Patiently, we waited.

Lenka said, "Okay. Inside the Hyades Cluster, closer to galactic center. Coming up on an unidentified star. A type. Scanning for planets now. Got one. Habitable zone, I think."

Isabella called out more accurate coordinates, which Deanna punched into the nav system.

Commander Lia ordered, "Okay. Set course for this planet. Stay alert for alien ships. Looks like you were right, Isabella. We're heading for that habitable planet. That's very encouraging."

"Looks like these will take us to a specific point on the planet," Commander L'Grina called out.

"Okay. Take us down. General Bev, get your soldiers ready. Don't forget the UV disinfectant protocol. God knows what new viruses and bacteria are down there," Lia reminded everyone.

"Wow. Three moons," Lenka said.

"Prepare for landing," Commander Lia said.

I admit I was glad Commander L'Grina handled our landing. Used to tower controlled landings and without arms, I didn't think I could have landed us so smoothly.

"Shit!" barked General Bev. "We're going to need dark sunglasses. This sun is incredibly bright." She must have read the dials by the bay ramp. "Outside temperature is one hundred five degrees. Gun checks," she ordered her soldiers.

"Permission to reconnoiter," Commander Lia said via the intercom.

Each soldier wore a helmet with a video camera on it, each feeding into the array of a dozen monitors. Everyone gathered around, watching what the soldiers saw.

A display of that person's vitals was displayed at the side of the video streaming images. I noticed their body temperatures rose rapidly. This planet was almost too hot. Still life thrived.

Strange trees and undergrowth dotted the hilly landscape, but Bev found a clear trail which soon led to a crude living complex, barely three hundred feet from the landing site. "Many feet. High heel impressions," she called out, though we could see that from her head cam.

Ten open-sided, pole buildings appeared with thatched roofs—hasty construction for sure. "Bad odor," Bev said.

"Oh god! You seeing this?" she asked. Six decomposing humans lay tossed into what must have been a garbage pit filled the monitor. Each was armless. We'd found some of the kidnap victims.

"Look for survivors," Commander Lia ordered.

An hour later, the landing party returned. Sweat soaked their heavy uniforms, and their faces were uniformly sunburned, even though they wore protective helmets. After decontamination, several men gathered around a sack they'd brought back.

"Hey, look what we found," Bev said. "Gold! Lots of it. Just lying around. This is one mineral rich planet, but it's hellishly hot!"

"We must have a pound of gold," her wife, Gail, added. "That's a lot of credits! Commander Lia, the men want to cool off and then go out searching for more gold."

We all laughed, but she did give them permission to fan out, looking for additional campsites. And gold, of course.

I noticed that the soldiers were only able to handle the intense heat for an hour before heat stroke signs appeared. From my own experience, I knew that those of us without the additional cooling arms provided wouldn't last half that long. I presented my theory that the aliens weren't aware of how more sensitive to heat an armless person was. Hence, the loss of a few, before hastily abandoning this location.

Hours later when we lifted off, Bev's soldiers had collected five pounds of gold, a small fortune, almost a million credits. Commander Lia recorded our discovery of this planet and its mineral resources in her log, which she would eventually turn over to GPan so they could send an exploration ship here.

She said, "Eventually, we could all receive a finder's fee if GPan finds this world worth mining or settling."

That I didn't know. I said, "So if someone flies around and finds new habitable planets, GPan pays them a finder's fee? Does finding new planets pay enough to survive on?"

Lia chuckled. "Yes, but few individuals can afford to purchase a deep space ship to explore with."

After liftoff, we circled the planet, but found no signs of intelligent life. No cities or towns or roads. Then, it was off to the next one.

"Hey, we'll be there shortly. This one's close to the last one," Lenka said. "Coordinates laid in, Commander."

Lia said, "Execute."

Again, I let Commander L'Grina handle the controls. I felt better with her handling the manual liftoff. Soon, we lurched into hyperspace for the ten-minute flight.

"Hey, I've not had time to down enough beers," Bev complained as we dropped out of hyperspace near a brilliant type B2 star.

Once Isabella called off the landing coordinates, the ship flew towards another habitable planet. Even I could tell from the displays that this planet was much farther from the star than Earth was from Sol.

" The hotter the star, the farther out the habitable zone must be," Commander L'Grina explained to me. "Wow, twin suns too."

Ten minutes later, she set us down. Again, Isabella's landing coordinates were perfect. The Friendship was much smaller than the Third Invader's flying saucers, so we had ample room on their landing pad. Following the usual protocols, Bev and her soldiers headed off to explore. All heavily armed. We watched their streaming video again.

Some type of asphalt formed the landing pad. This time, the outside temperature reached eighty degrees. Bleached trees, their response to the intense sunlight, lined the well-traveled path. I admit I gaped at the strange looking plants, while Isabella merely commented on them. She'd seen all manner of exotic plants and animals during her many years of exploration.

About a quarter mile from the pad, Bev came across a village. Thirty-six metal fabricated homes, each shaped like Quonset huts, lay in a square six by six grid. Both the path to the village and its streets were formed from the same asphalt-like material, which I later discovered was as hard as concrete. More importantly, the village was inhabited!

The reddish skinned women here had to have come from the tribes on Zeta Tucanae-3. These people had been abducted and trained to be the personal assistants to our abducted telepath victims. Thus, Isabella and I headed to the village armed with our language translation units.

They flocked to Isabella and me, believing we needed help. Thus began a long conversation, while Bev and her soldiers fanned out, securing the area. We learned the aliens brought some telepath victims here. The adult women had their tongues cut out and were shipped off to a buyer. None knew the name of that planet. The adult men were terminated, and we were shown the mass grave. However, a hundred children still remained, cared for by these women.

While Isabella and I talked with the women, I heard distant blaster fire. After that, Lenka joined us.

She explained, "Bev and her crew found three of the aliens. They terminated them, but one soldier was wounded. Not critically, I don't think. Any idea how many aliens are on this world?"

I asked the women. Three, they replied.

"We're here to take you back to your own world and take our children home. Let's get everyone to our ship before the aliens return," I said.

Close to two hundred women ushered the children

down the path to our ship. The oldest child was five. Many were infants, while twenty-three had to have been newborns, or nearly so.

We packed them into every available space on the Friendship. Deanna and her engineers calculated the total weight of our passengers. I dreaded leaving anyone behind. Would the aliens detect our arrival and send in their fighters? For once, luck was on our side. The alien women were small and much lighter in weight than a human.

Deanna said, "We are still within the weight safety limits, though we'll be at maximum fuel consumption. We've more than enough to get them home."

Commander Lia took charge. "Okay. Lenka, Isabella, get the coordinates inputted for their home world of Zeta Tucanae-3. Give me a fuel consumption readout."

Their toes entered the numbers into the nav system, triple checked as usual. Once more, I allowed Commander L'Grina to pilot us. Too many lives were at stake for me to try my feet at it.

Two hours later, we dropped the alien women off at the original site on their world of Zeta Tucanae-3. When they saw we'd landed them on their world, their faces lit up. I didn't need telepathy to know how grateful they were. We received many hugs before they jogged off, heading for their own villages.

That done, Commander L'Grina again handled liftoff, but insisted I handle the landing. Well, I agreed because the New O'Hare control tower handled the descend automatically. But she knew that, too. Less than a day after we departed, the Friendship sat down in its original parking pad. That done, I made the call to GD's CEO Helen Hugo, asking for assistance. We had one hundred small children to handle.

Hours later, we had them all moved to an apartment complex. Since the hour was late, we tucked each into a cot for the night.

Helen said, "Okay. GMed will be sending over doctors and nurses seven. Food supplies will be dropped off tonight yet. Temporary clothing will arrive by late morning.

The real question is what do we do with them? Do you realize that you, Nikita, and Isabella are the only telepaths remaining on Earth? Well, a few more are out on exploration ships. Plus these children. I'm going to request GMed inject these children with the known cures. If they'll do it, how about your three? Right now, I look kind of silly with these tiny baby-like arms. But I'm told in a year they should be just fine. Thank heavens for that virus!"

"Look," I replied, "if GMed will give these children the known cures, then yes, I'll get the cures too. I'll talk with my daughters tonight. Thanks for helping, Helen."

She smiled and left. Heading home on the MTES, Isabella and I walked side by side, chatting. The others followed behind us.

She said, "Mom, I wonder how Dimitri and Natalie are taking their mutations into Galactic Dolls. Probably she's fine with it."

"Bet he's really upset about it." We chuckled. "Look, if they cure these kids, I'm getting it done too. Have you changed your mind?"

"Hardly, Mom. No, I really loved being the linguist on the first-contact space ship. It's a fabulous job, one that I excel at, being a telepath. I know Nikita wants to be one too, so don't force her to get the cures and lose her telepathic skills."

"I won't. It has to be her decision, not mine."

"Thanks for believing in me, Mom. We rescued all we could. But I wonder where the Third Invaders sold those women? And why cut out their tongues? Aren't our lives hard enough? Beasts. Maybe the Federation will declare war on those fiends. I'm going to ask Senator Aaron Strawn about that. Send him a message anyway. Damn. I have to pee again. Did you have to go so often when you carried Nikita and Matt?"

I laughed. "Honey, wait until the ninth month. Then you'll have to go every hour or so."

"God, that's in a couple weeks!"

***

When Sam and I returned to the apartment complex,

dozens of GMed EMACs lined the street. Six doctors and twenty nurses hovered over the children, inspecting and injecting them. Helen Hugo stood off to one side of the entrance, nodding to us, so we moved to her side.

"They're checking them over first, but so far, all are healthy. Those alien women took very good care of the kids. Using female doctors, since their male counterparts are still struggling with their Galactic Doll mutations. They've unilaterally decided to give each child the full cures. The hell with the laws regarding telepaths. There aren't many now. So if you want, get in line."

"Wow. Sanity strikes. You bet I want my cures, too. Isabella and Nikita don't though."

Helen smiled. "I figured that much, especially with Nikita. By the way, CDC has narrowed the initial outbreak of the pandemic to the Philadelphia area. They're looking for Patient Zero as they're calling him or her. Don't know if they'll ever find the person. But there's been some unexpected repercussions. The Senate on Bela Prime has taken a keen interest in us. They've sent Admiral Skaggs and the battleship Kanika here to investigate."

"Investigate what?"

"The virus. The pandemic. They've concluded the Sixth Invaders don't have the technology to invent such a virus, but that virus must have been invented or developed here on Earth. No doubt about that."

"So?"

"So, if someone engineered this virus, then it could be duplicated. Imagine its use as a weapon. The entire human population of a planet could be mutated. Our men have become the freaks of the galaxy—with the exception of the Sixth Invader men. But I think what scares them more is someone managing to put the armless Galactic Doll agent into the virus. Incredibly easily, whole human populations could be mutated, conquered, and turned into slave telepaths. They'd be helpless to do anything about it. Hell, even I'm worried about that angle."

"I had no idea. Incredibly scary. Keep me posted."

"Excuse me, Mrs. Parkinson, but we're ready for you

now," a nurse from GMed said. "Sam is on his way and will meet you at the Med Center."

A half hour later, I slipped into yet another mutation coma and had awful dreams.

Chapter 25 Experiments in Chaos

Dr. Titus Jones, head of Earth's Center for Disease Control, fumed. If he could have, he'd of stomped around his temporary office in Chicago's GMed facility. In these new six-inch heels, even that outlet for his furor was denied him. One of nearly a billion men victimized by the pandemic, Dr. Jones now looked like every other Galactic Doll.

Forced to wear the tall heels by mutated feet, top-heavy from breasts the size of his head, the loss of a rib and his Adam's apple, to say nothing of his now alto voice and feminine body shape left him so angry that he'd sprained his wrists pounding the bed when he awoke from his mutation coma. For several days, he wore his wife's gowns, further humiliating him. Even GMan's issuing him one of Leslie's male suits did little to calm this medical man. In truth, he wasn't alone. Later statistics showed over ten million men chose death to this new reality.

By the second week of January, production of male apparel permitted him to purchase a second outfit. Suffering further humiliation, he'd gone to a woman barber to get his overly long hair cut short—his prided goatee having fallen out during the coma.

Despite this, Dr. Jones always kept his word. He'd promised his staff in Atlanta that they'd find the source of the pandemic. Even though half of his staff struggled with now being male Dolls, the CDC worked its detection magic. He'd lost count of the sheer number of calls from irate corporate CEOs and media reporters demanding to know how this pandemic could have occurred. Why hadn't he stopped it? Prevented it? Yes, he took very heavy flak, as if this whole pandemic had been his fault.

His staff worked day and night tracking the virus back to find its Patient Zero and hopefully the cause of the pandemic. By the time Molly departed to find and rescue the kidnapped telepaths, they'd narrowed the search down to Philadelphia. Dr. Jones then flew to Chicago to meet with the Sol Empire corporate leaders, not only to personally answer their myriad questions, but also to see what could be done to undo the mutations. Also, one Molly Parkinson seemed to often be at the center of a new mutation cure, so it made sense to personally examine her records for clues.

Upon arrival at Chicago's GMed skyscraper, Dr. Jones encountered further humiliation. Everyone he saw looked like a female Doll. How was he supposed to know how to address anyone he met? Ma'am, sir, you there? The red in his face slowly subsided, when he saw that as of now, every person in the building had a name tag identifying themselves and their gender. For example, one tag read: "Dr. Bartlemay (F)," while another read: "Dr. Felscott (M)." Someone handed him a tag, and he added (M) to his before pinning it onto his suit jacket.

Embarrassment seemed to follow Dr. Jones. Heels clicking on the tiled floor, he walked into the giant auditorium filled with several hundred top Sol corporate personnel, all anxious to hear his briefing. His face felt on fire as he walked up to the podium. Staring out at hundreds of seeming attractive Dolls didn't help, for he suspected many were males. Galactic Manufacturing couldn't produce enough male apparel yet, so most men had little choice but to wear women's gowns.

"Hello everyone," his alto voice began. Titus felt his face incinerating. He took a deep breath and continued. "I'm Dr. Tutus Jones, head of the Center for Disease Control for Earth and the Sol Empire." Thus began his half-hour presentation of the facts of the pandemic.

"So, we've narrowed our search for Patient Zero to the Philadelphia area. I'm certain we'll have the origin of this disastrous pandemic isolated soon."

"Yes, but what are you going to do to reverse these terrible mutations?" someone asked in a soprano voice. His face reheated, for he couldn't tell if the person was male or female.

"That's one of the reasons I'm here today. Chicago

has been the focal point in genetic mutation research for decades. I plan to find that out myself. Thank you for your patience. We'll soon have the source identified."

Someone asked, "Some person must have invented this virus and spread it across the planet. So what are you going to do to them when you identify the culprit? Terminate them? Hell, that's too good for them. Our lives are almost not worth living."

"Damned if I know. All the laws concerning telepaths are pointless now. I doubt there's one of them left. This hideous virus has regrown their arms and eliminated their telepathic abilities. We're going to need revised laws."

After the meeting, he met with GMed officials and toured a local Med Center. However, the next day, events escalated. First, Mrs. Parkinson returned with over a hundred children, all telepaths, though some were newborns. When he checked on what GMed was doing, CEO Wainwright explained his reasoning.

"Look, Dr. Jones. All existing telepaths have had the cures via the virus. It wouldn't be fair to these infants and children not to give them the known cures. The old laws can't handle this new situation, so I've ordered them to be injected with the cures. Besides, we're faced with finding homes for a hundred orphans. If they remained handicapped, finding someone to adopt them will be difficult at best. At least with arms, we'll have a chance of obtaining good homes for them. Most don't even know their names. Only a few do and know where they used to live."

"Okay by me. Makes sense," Dr. Jones said.

"Also, the only remaining telepaths are Mrs. Parkinson and her two daughters, along with six others who are off-world on deep space exploration ships. I'm going to offer her and the kids the known cures as well."

"Hum. I'm keenly interested in this Parkinson woman. She always seems to be the focal point for mutation cures. She was instrumental in developing cures for our soldiers who lost an arm and leg during the robot war on Brussels, Tau Ceti. I want to see her complete records."

Mrs. Wainwright said, "Of course. My aide can pull those up on her computer for you. Right now, I've got to handle a hundred children. Make yourself at home."

Dr. Jones studied Molly Parkinson's records, noting that she was one of several clones, all identical physically, but with wildly differing personalities. Thus engrossed, he didn't see Admiral Skaggs and his armed squad enter.

"Looking for a Dr. Titus Jones, ma'am. You seen him?"

The bass voice of the tall, robust man startled him. Titus felt his face burning up again. "I'm him. And you are?" he rose, extending his hand.

"Admiral Skaggs of the battleship Kanika. The Federation has sent me here to clean up this mess. Sorry, I'm not about to get infected with your virus or whatever. Is it safe for us to be planetside?"

"Yes, the pandemic has run its course. Outside a human host, the virus only has a lifetime of three days. Totally safe. You contract it via your lungs. An airborne virus."

"Okay then. You're the man I'm seeking. The Federation is, shall we say, very upset and annoyed with Earth and all these genetic mutations. Mule Rats, I've no idea why you men want to be indistinguishable from well-endowed women."

Dr. Jones felt his face instantly burning. "We don't. We hate it, but right now, we can't do anything about it."

"I'll be frank, Dr. Jones. The Federation has ordered me to handle this mess anyway I think necessary. They're terrified and for good reason. Until now, the Federation thought your Galactic Doll mutations were confined to Earth, especially since all other worlds of your Sol Empire prohibit any such mutation from settling on their world. And I admit your women do look stunning. However, mutating men into women is going too far.

"The Federation is worried that other worlds outside your Sol Empire can have their humans mutated by these agents, especially the version that makes helpless telepaths. Unscrupulous persons are likely to experiment and try to make telepaths in other solar systems than yours. Stealing your mutation agents is the first step. The Senate agrees with you.

"For everyone concerned, a telepath must be instantly recognizable as such. Lord, if a telepath looked like an ordinary person, think of the spy damage they could perpetrate. The Federation simply can't tolerate that, and they won't. Your solution to have telepaths lacking arms is perfect—brilliant perhaps. They are instantly identifiable by anyone.

"Unfortunately, the problem has escalated. When the only way to make an armless telepath was to inject them with the mutation agent, the Federation accepted that as a valid way to control it. However, when it became an aerosol that could infect an entire skyscraper or section of a city, as it did in this city and others, it became a terrorist weapon. The damage a terrorist could do to other human worlds is enormous. Thus, the Federation Senate began working out how they should respond to this new version.

"Since the aerosol version of the armless telepath agent was confined to terrorists here on Earth, the Senate believed it had time to work out ways and means of controlling the situation. However, now that someone has found a way to turn it into a virus and cause a planet-wide pandemic, the Federation Senate had to act. While turning men's bodies into ones indistinguishable from women is revolting to most and could be used as a terrorist weapon, it's not deadly in and of itself. Rather the next step is frightening, even to me. Turning the armless telepath muation agent into a virus is the most serious threat the Federation has faced in centuries.

"Can you imagine what could happen if that happens? Anyone could blackmail any world whose population was human or close enough so the mutation agent would work. As a weapon of war—I hate to even think of that. Entire worlds, entire space fleets could be wiped out. This mutation makes a helpless person who has telepathy. Think what would happen if someone unleashed it on my battleship. Besides everyone dropping into a coma for a week, when they awoke, they'd be helpless, unable to even operate the ship. That, Dr. Jones, has scared every senator on Bela Prime—us admirals as well. In short, we cannot allow this to happen. I'm here to end this, even if it means destroying every human on this planet.

"What? You—you wouldn't do that. That's genocide!"

"The alternative is even worse if someone figures out how to make the armless telepath agent into an airborne virus. I'm willing to observe and listen, Dr. Jones, before I take any action. Work with me. I don't want to terminate three billion people if we can find a way around it."

"Of course. Yes, yes. Work together. We're close to finding Patient Zero. That will provide many clues," Titus said hastily.

"Brief me on your progress."

An hour later that done to the admiral's satisfaction, they turned their attention to the case of Molly Parkinson.

"She's a very powerful woman," the admiral said. "She once saved my battleship. Something about seeing the future. So how is that reflected in her medical records. Says here she was convicted of being a telepath with arms, an illegal telepath."

"That's what the records and legal conviction stated. Being a telepath with arms. She could have infiltrated any corporation anywhere. No one would be the wiser. So they injected her with the agent and forbad any cures for years," Titus said.

"Hum, you've gone ahead and given her all known cures?"

"Well, yes. At the time, it seemed the right thing to do. All these telepath laws are now pointless. All have become normal Galactic Dolls, having lost that skill with the pandemic mutation. Only fair to restore her. There are six others out on deep space exploration missions, plus her two daughters who want to remain proper telepaths. I figured to give the six their choice when they return to Earth."

"I think I'd probably have done the same thing. But now, Dr. Jones, we're facing a new problem. Every telepath must be instantly recognizable as such. We're going to have to re-mutate Mrs. Parkinson. Federation orders."

"Could be a problem with that, admiral. This virus has caused the body to make millions of T cells which triggered the B cells to produce the antibodies and memory cells." He saw a blank expression on the man's face. "What I'm saying is that these memory cells will attack the normal mutation agent, nullifying it before it can begin the mutation process. Of course, it's not been verified yet. No one's tried to regain their telepathic ability. I can't say I blame them, either. It's horrible enough looking like I am, let alone being so helpless."

"Are you saying that we can't re-mutate Mrs. Parkinson as a proper telepath?"

"We don't know that for sure, but that might be the case."

"Then we simply amputate her arms. That'll handle that."

Dr. Jones cringed. "Can that be a last resort? Let us try to re-inject her with the armless telepath agent first."

"Agreed. We owe her much. Give that a try first," the admiral agreed.

"I'll inform her husband when he drops by for his evening visit."

***

"What? You can't do that!" Sam cried. "Not after all she's done for Earth and the victims."

"Let me explain why, Sam. I can call you Sam, can't I?" Dr. Jones asked. Sam nodded, and the doctor continued. He discussed the situation for a half hour, including what Admiral Skaggs had told him about the Federation response to this mess.

He ended with, "So you see, this is for the best. I want to try a simple re-mutation first. Amputation is a last resort."

"I can see your points. She's not going to like this," Sam said, sighing deeply. After kissing Molly's forehead, he left.

"Lord, he looks freaky. Those baby-like, nearly

useless arms dangling at his sides. God, what a mess. Okay, let's get going. Nurse, bring me the armless Galactic Doll mutation agent."

Dr. Jones administered the shot into Molly's right leg. Already, tiny baby arms had appeared and looked incongruous on her adult body.

"How long will we need to wait to see if this is working?" he asked.

"Unknown, doctor. If she were awake, we'd see her dropping into a coma within a couple minutes, but she's already in one. I'd expect to see those very thin, tiny arms shrinking by tomorrow at the longest," the nurse replied.

The next morning, Molly's arms were somewhat thicker. "It's not working, doctor," the nurse said the obvious.

"Okay, get me a blood sample. Then, we'll inject her a second time, doubling the dose."

The nurse looked up at him, but proceeded to draw the blood. This time, Dr. Jones injected Molly with a double dose of the mutation agent. Then, he headed to a lab to analyze the blood. Perhaps it contained a clue. Hours later, Dr. Jones presented his findings to a many doctors and administrators at the GMed facility.

"The virus has installed ample memory cells of this general type of mutation agent. Thus, re-injecting any pandemic victim with the telepath agent or other similar agents are attacked by the immune system before they can begin the mutation process. Perhaps after some years they will lose their ability to stop the re-mutation. For now, it's working. I've tried doubling the mutation dosage. We'll see the results tomorrow. As you've probably heard by now, the Federation is demanding all telepaths be instantly identifiable by their lack of arms. Honestly, I really don't want to resort to surgically amputating Mrs. Parkinson's re-growing arms. So I'll continue experimenting on her. What's surprising me is that she wasn't exposed to the virus directly. That's confusing the picture."

"Excuse me, Dr. Jones. How do you explain that? How can she have built up memory cells against this mutation if she wasn't exposed to the virus in the first place?"

"Could well be gene dominance. She was given the armless telepath agent. The new cures were applied over them. Could be interference, too. I'll know more as we experiment further."

The next morning, Molly's re-growing baby arms measured the same size as yesterday. Dr. Jones took additional blood samples. Analysis yielded the first positive news. The double dose was enough to counteract the current mutation agents but not enough for it to begin its work. Thus, Dr. Jones gave her another double dose of the mutation agent.

By the next morning, her arms had vanished, but her comatose body went into convulsions before vomiting over herself and the bed. After cleaning her up, her body calmed down. Surprising everyone, Molly awoke late that evening while Sam was visiting her.

***

After hearing what Admiral Skaggs and Dr. Jones told him, Sam called Celeste and Eve. Hastily, he relayed what he'd heard.

"They can't do this to Molly, can they? How do I stop them?" he pleaded on the phone while the MTES took him home. His tiny re-growing arms and hands shook from holding the weight of his phone.

"I don't think you can stop them, Sam," Celeste said. "I'm going to see what Molly thinks. Eve, take over for me."

"Sam, Eve here. I'll meet with Lara Axe-head in the morning. We'll see what can be done and what dangers giving her these injections might have. I can see the Federation's worry though. Scares me too. That someone has turned this mutation agent into a virus and so easily caused a worldwide pandemic is frightening. If they had used the armless telepath agent, the whole Earth would be wiped out except for the dwarves and giants. So yeah, Sam, this is a very serious business. Finding Patient Zero is critical. I'll see what I can do to help, too."

They continued to chat.

***

Meanwhile, Celeste used her telepathic ability to contact Molly.

'Molly, Celeste here. How are you doing?'

'Bored. It's all black. Body's in a coma. Oh, I've just backed out of its head. Now I can see. Silly me.'

'Good going. Say, we've got a serious situation here. So do you.' Celeste relayed what Sam had just told her about the Federation's orders.

'I guess I don't mind still not getting my arms back. It's my fault for being so overt about having telepathy. But how many times can my body get mutated without damaging it?'

'Unknown, but keep in communication with it. And let me know if you detect anything damaging happening. Frankly, Molly, I've a bad feeling about this Patient Zero investigation.'

'Oh, I've been having weird dreams—before you contacted me, that is. I'm all right now.'

'Okay. We'll check with you tomorrow. Bye.'

Celeste broke our telepathic contact. I watched from the ceiling as the doctor injected something into my leg. Soon after that, I felt a wave of intense heat flooding my body and found myself pulled into my head once again. As blackness covered me, I thought about Patient Zero and how the pandemic began.

This time, I recognized future tracks as they appeared. Apparently, I'm getting better at seeing future realities. I hoped I'd see a way out of these new nightmare futures. I'll relay them as they came to me far more easily than ever before.

Future One:

Admiral Skaggs said, "All right then. Since we never found Patient Zero, have no way of disposing of all the armless telepath mutation agents, have no way of undoing the mutation of Earth's men, and since the mutation is dominant, I've no choice but to exterminate all humans on Earth. All giants and dwarves on Earth have twenty-four Earth hours to evacuate before my fleet destroys this planet and its mutations."

Protesters were simply shot, their bodies left where they fell. I gathered my family and our relations together in our home. Huddling together at the end, I felt a huge wave of intense heat as the nuke detonated over us. Fortunately, the body was dead before any sound reached it. Then, all went black for a long time. Where would three billion of us find new bodies?

Future Two:

Admiral Skaggs said, "All right then. We've confiscated all samples of the armless telepath mutation agent and have installed sensor devices at all spaceports on Earth that can detect the minutest traces of that agent. Thus, I can assure the Federation Senate no one can smuggle that diabolical agent off this world. However, as you know, we've been unable to pinpoint Patient Zero. He or she is somewhere in Philadelphia. Thus, per Federation orders, I'm nuking that city today. In fact, it's happening as I report this to you Earth representatives. Next time, control your world."

On the monitor, I saw the video stream from the Kanika and watched the giant mushroom cloud encompass the entire city. Later flights over what had been a huge city revealed a new "Great Lake," which was named Lake Phili. I lost my lunch before the these terrible images faded into blackness.

Future Three:

I watched Admiral Skaggs on the monitor in my living room. "Good news. We've discovered Patient Zero and the terrorist who invented the virus and launched the pandemic. Dr. Patricia Ann Gates-Baxter. Her husband Vernon Baxter, the noted neurosurgeon, and their newborn son were originally victims of the armless telepath agent this past summer. Unable to get either of them their cures and unwilling to follow the law that demanded Vernon wait ten years before requesting cures or their son waiting until his eighteenth birthday, she charged ahead and invented the virus and infected her husband and son first. However, in a fit of rage, she unleashed it across the entire Earth."

The monitor zoomed in on a shackled young woman. Then he continued.

"The Federation demands you be punished. I hereby sentence you to death. Fire."

Six soldiers in blue uniforms opened fire with their blasters. I had no hands to cover my children's faces from what we saw on the monitor. Bits of her body and head simply vaporized before our eyes, followed by gushing blood. My children vomited on the floor, as the world turned black on me.

Future Four:

This one was nearly identical to Three, except Admiral Skaggs said, "Patricia Ann, your arms will be amputated, and you will never be allowed to have any form of arm regrow procedures."

She screamed. Time blurred and as the images cleared, I saw her looking much as I did, armless, helpless, and without telepathy. Then, a dozen irate men—I assume they were once men, since I couldn't tell their gender any longer—burst into her home.

One yelled, "You fiend! Took us this long to find where you're hiding. You did this to us. Now you're gonna pay, bitch."

While cursing her, they kicked and beat her, before pulling out their guns and putting two dozen bullets into her. She probably died from the beating. The guns were overkill. Again, the scene faded into darkness.

Future Five:

Admiral Skaggs said, "While we cannot definitively say who was Patient Zero of the pandemic, we've identified the brilliant microbiologist who created the virus. Dr. Patricia Ann Gates-Baxter invented it in order to provide the known cures for her husband, a noted neurosurgeon, and newborn son who were victims of the Philadelphia armless telepath mutation agent attack this past summer. Your insane laws would not permit these nearly helpless individuals to regrow their arms, becoming productive members of your medical community again. It's understandable why she did it.

304

"Dr. Gates-Baxter has made incredible breakthroughs in virology. Hence, the Federation is backing her further researches in this field. That is all."

A furor arose, but soon died down. We went back to our daily lives, though many men had major difficulties adapting to their new body forms.

Time jumbled a bit before becoming clear again. At first I thought this was yet another future path, but it wasn't. I saw Dr. Gates-Baxter in her lab. A giant approached her, gun drawn.

"Ah, Dr. Gates-Baxter. Found you at last."

"Who are you? Put that gun away. This is a research lab," she barked, mostly from being disturbed.

"My men have kidnapped your husband and son. If you want to ever see them alive again, you'll do as I say. Make that mutation virus of yours—the one you unleashed on Earth—only this time, make it turn everyone into armless telepaths. No, we aren't going to use it on Earth. So your conscience is clear. Make it for me or you'll never see your family alive again. Contact me at this number when you have enough ready to infect a planet this size."

He turned and left as suddenly as he came. Pat hastily called her husband, but the call went to voice mail. She grabbed her stomach before breaking down in sobs. As the images faded out, I saw her starting to construct that new virus, or what I presumed it was. Then, darkness swept over me once more.

'Molly. Molly. You there? Wake up.'

'Celeste? Is that you? I've been having nightmares of the future again.'

'Yeah. It's me. Are you holding up?'

'Sort of. What day is it? How long have I been in a coma?'

'It's two days later. One shot of the mutation agent didn't do anything. So yesterday, he gave you enough to mutate two people. Apparently, that's starting to work, so today he's giving you another double dose. We're hoping it doesn't kill you.'

'Ouch. Guess he's doing it now. Hey, I found the

person who invented the virus and caused the pandemic.' I told her all I'd seen and the many possible future tracks.

'Celeste, you and Eve go to Philadelphia right away. Find her. Bring her and her family back here. Tell them what I've seen. I want to find a better future for her and them.'

'Okay. Will do. Hang in there. Your coma shouldn't last much longer.'

I felt her presence leaving me, filling me with a sense of loss, probably because of the blackness surrounding me. I tried to rise to the ceiling again, but failed. I doped off as a huge wave of heat flooded my body. Time must have passed as I later discovered.

Pain. Excruciating pain shot through my head. It hurt worse than when the invaders put a bullet through it. I felt as though my skull was about to burst, to explode into shards. I couldn't scream, though I must have tried.

They told me my body had convulsions, that I threw up, that electrical sparks shot from all the outlets in the room shorting out the circuits, and that my bed bounced about for a minute or two.

Finally, I screamed and knew I did, because I woke up from the coma. Several held emergency lights over me, while nurses cleaned me off and Dr. Jones took my vitals.

"How do you feel?" he asked.

I looked at my empty shoulders.

"Admiral Skaggs ordered me to remove your re-growing arms because you are a telepath. The Federation demands all telepaths be instantly identifiable as such. I didn't want to surgically remove them. Too many things could go wrong, so I tried the usual mutation agent. How do you feel, Mrs. Parkinson?"

"Huh? Yeah, got that. Awful. My head was about to explode. Worst pain ever. Hum, seems to be gone now. What happened in here? Why is it so dark?"

"We don't know what happened. You went into convulsions. Shock probably. But something shorted out all the electrical circuits. We don't know why. Probably a fluke accident of some kind."

"When can I go home?"

"I'd like to observe you for a time. Run some tests."

"I'm not a lab rat. I want to go home now."

"Okay, but in a few days, will you drop by so I can make sure you are doing all right? That the mutation has taken hold again. I don't want that admiral fellow to harm you."

"Oh all right. I'll do that. I just want to go home and take a shower."

"Nurse, help her dress and find out why all the circuits blew in here. If she'd been on life support, we'd have lost her by now."

After he left, two nurses dressed me in the gown I wore here initially. Funny thing, I had no idea if either was a male or not. I decided there wasn't any need to be embarrassed either way, since now we all looked nearly the same.

"Guess I still have to wear the heels," I said. I'd hoped my feet would lie flat, but no luck. One shone a light on me so I could see myself in a mirror. I couldn't tell any differences, except that my hair had grown longer. Later when showering, I saw that my hair had grown thicker and stronger, now falling to my ankles. I was in need of a trim.

Just as they finished up, Sam showed up. "They called me and said you're awake."

"Yeah, up and back to normal. How's your arms doing? And Matt's? Get me home, please."

"We're all fine. I can sort of hold my phone, but only for a minute or so. It's the strangest thing ever. Tiny infant arms and hands. Weird. Come on, dear. Let's go home. Celeste says it's taken care of."

We remained silent until safely on the MTES, heading home.

Sam said, "Eve and Celeste borrowed an Airliner from Deanna. They found the family just one day before the investigators homed in on them. Brought them back in secret. Honestly, I think those two doctors are very scared right now. Anyway, they're staying in our old suite on the forty-ninth floor of the Cartwright skyscraper. Celeste told us and them your future visions. That has every one spooked. Hope you got a plan, because I didn't like any of those futures."

"I haven't seen any more, dear. But we'll figure something out. God, I need a bath. I feel incredibly dirty."

Chapter 26 Resolutions

After a long, hot bath with Isabella and Nikita helping Sam wash me off, I felt human gain.

"I do love these hair machines," I said, as I ran it for the sixth time drying out my hair.

"Mom, your hair is so much longer and shinier," Nikita said. "Can I let mine grow to my ankles too? No school all week. They want to give the baby arms time to grow a little and let the other boys and men get used to looking like a Galactic Doll. There's a shortage of male doll clothes. Leslie said so. I'm just glad I still get to wear the tall heels. I look so grown up. Veronica, and Fritz are wearing flats now. And their tiny arms look so weird on them, but she's really happy about getting them. Oh, yeah. They lost their telepathic ability. So did Helen and Hugo. Eve said every telepath who got the virus has lost it. I'm glad Isabella and I didn't lose it."

She would have continued chatting but I interrupted her. "Only if you can take care of your hair by yourself." She giggled. "Let's get me dressed. I need to visit our guests."

An hour later and dressed in my blue satin gown that wrapped around my shoulders like a tight blanket and matching tall heels, I headed off to Deanna's building with my winter cloak draped over me. Alone. I had Sam make sure I wasn't being followed. I stepped onto the MTES. It had snowed some so I watched my step, being careful of falling. Someone bumped into me in their haste to get to the fast lane. I ought to have fallen, but some force kept me stable until I had my balance again. How strange. I spotted the man trying to hurry in the speed lane. Tall heels prevented running, so I knew it was a man who was still getting used to his mutation as a doll. I grinned.

As the escalators moved me along, I noticed the puffy clouds and blue sky. The fishy odor from the lake wasn't present. I felt alive. I half expected I'd be upset or annoyed that I didn't have my arms regrowing. But not at all. I realized I was content, happy with my body and life. I hummed a tune, nodding to others on the MTES.

Deanna greeted me at the corporation's main doors and took my cloak off. We chatted as we headed up to meet the Gates-Baxter family.

"Are you sure you're all right? I think it's criminal to not allow you to get the cures everyone else has got."

"Oh, I'm fine, sis. Really, I'm okay with it. Just glad Eve and Celeste extricated the Gates-Baxter family before the authorities got to them."

"Hey, they're really scared now. Celeste and Eve have stayed with them. They're still dealing with their newborn son." Deanna laughed. "I've even made a diaper run for them." Her face tightened. "Any chance you can save them?"

"I'm working on it. Knowing the many paths Admiral Skaggs is prepared to take helps me work something out."

We entered my old suite. Eve and Celeste rose to greet me. I noticed they now sported the massive bosoms and wore tall heels too. They'd been mutated by the pandemic too. Until now, both had avoided becoming Galactic Dolls. Their eyes were dark, and I suspected they were short on sleep.

The Gates-Baxters sat beside each other on our old couch. Vernon was currently nursing their son. He had tiny arms protruding from his shirt, though the small arms looked fine on their infant son. Celeste had brought them one of my baby sacks that Sam used to carry around Matt and Natalie when they were babies. This way, Sam or I could manage nursing them by ourselves.

"Don't get up," I said as we entered. Vernon looked much like Sam, a male Galactic Doll wearing Leslie's male apparel. Though nothing could hide his enormous curves and giant bosom, at least he was wearing flats. The virus had repaired the feet of current dolls, but mutated the feet of normal humans. The doctor's face hung low.

Beside him and wearing a white satin lab gown sat Patricia Ann. Her red eyes told much. Her hands held onto a handkerchief twisted into knots. She too wore flats, soft-soled, highly practical for one spending hours on her feet. I sensed she had never considered the consequences of her actions or perhaps I picked that up from her. My telepathy seemed greatly enhanced somehow.

"Hello. I'm Molly Parkinson."

She blurted in a rush of words. "We know. They've told us about you—your visions of the future. Do they always come true? Are we doomed? No hope?"

"Unfortunately, I'm pretty sure they can come about unless we change the outcome. I take it they've told you what I saw?"

"Yes. I'm so sorry that I unleashed that virus on everyone."

"Men in power needed to be taught a lesson," I interjected. The relief on her face told all. "Only a genius could have invented that virus. Let's see if we can find a way to avoid getting you killed or Philadelphia destroyed."

"How? It seems hopeless. They've almost pinpointed Vernon as Patient Zero," she wailed, twisting yet another knot.

"Do you trust me?"

"We don't have a choice," Vernon said. "I love Pat. We have to save her."

"Okay then. I've a plan. We need to sit down with Admiral Skaggs. I know him. I think I can work out a solution that both he and the Federation can accept. Just trust me. Under no circumstances mention the involvement of my sisters, Deanna, Celeste, and Eve. Okay?"

Both nodded. I placed a call to Helen Hugo, who gave me his number. She offered to let us use one of her conference rooms in the GD skyscraper.

"Hello. This is Molly Parkinson."

"Well, well, Mrs. Parkinson. Why am I not surprised to hear from you. Dr. Jones told me you just got out of the Med Center."

"Yes. Well, I'm with the brilliant and genius microbiologist who created the virus and pandemic. We'd like to discuss the situation with you."

"Why am I not surprised?" he repeated himself. "I

might have known you'd be somehow involved. Dr. Jones has discovered the identity of the virus maker, but she seems to have vanished."

"Into my care, sir. Helen Hugo, CEO Sol Galactic Defense, will loan us a conference room. We can be there in five minutes. Please, no guns. I don't have any arms."

He chuckled. "All right. I'm bringing Dr. Jones with me. Of course, she'll have no way to elude us this time. The block will be cordoned off. I've orders, you understand."

"Yes. But I think we can reach an arrangement, sir. See you in five minutes or so."

I hung up, pressing the End button with a toe and slipping the phone into a dress pocket, before slipping my blue heel back on. As I rose to my feet, I nearly lost my balance, but a mysterious force steadied me. I presumed I was still recovering from that quintuple dose of mutation agent. Deanna slipped my cloak over me, while Eve and Celeste helped the two doctors don their winter coats.

Deanna said, "I'm coming with you. You'll need help with the baby and coats. Besides, the admiral knows me."

I relaxed. "Thanks."

Okay, it took us a few minutes longer than that, so when we walked into the conference room on the ninety-first floor, Admiral Skaggs, Dr. Jones, and several aides in their blue spacer uniforms were already there. Deanna helped us remove my cloak and their coats, all the while exchanging greetings with the stern-faced admiral.

"Sorry it took slightly longer. These heels," I said, before taking a seat across from him. Timidly, Patricia Ann sat beside me, while Vernon, with the baby sack still around his neck, sat beside her. Dr. Jones and the admiral's aides took positions beside him, facing us.

I began this way. "Okay. No need to nuke Philadelphia. Dr. Patricia Ann Gates-Baxter here invented the virus and unleashed the pandemic. She's sorry about unleashing it, mostly. I'll let her explain what and why she did what she did. Go ahead, Pat. Tell him the whole story."

Her poor handkerchief. Before she finished, it had more knots in it than before. She told them how she felt when the stupid laws prevented Vernon from resuming his neurosurgeon career. That her newborn son would have to endure an awful childhood, let alone have a hard time becoming a skilled professional like his parents also tore at her heart.

"It worked. Both are regrowing arms and have their feet restored. We all know that women should look good, so I didn't include the breast size reduction mutation in my formulation. Women would protest and demand to be re-mutated." She outlined just what she did.

"Now then, Admiral Skaggs, you've heard the truth. You know the motivation behind it. Hell, you know the motivation behind removing my own re-growing arms a couple days ago. I back her decision to end this telepath-making fiasco. Currently, there are only a few telepaths left, and we all lack arms. She's made it difficult to impossible for anyone to reuse that armless telepath mutation agent on Earth men and women. Besides, I've heard the telepaths were rebelling."

Admiral Skaggs laughed. "That's putting it mildly. I heard they were purposely giving out wrong data, causing all manner of bad decisions by the CEO's. I'd hate to be forced to spy for a corporation. Of course, not all telepaths are bad. Your daughter has led an exemplary career as a telepath."

"Yes, she has. So we now need to look to the future. What scares me and many others is the potential for exportation. This nasty mutation agent is available everywhere, almost as easy to get as an aspirin. Now that it can't be used on Earth humans, what's to stop giants and others from grabbing crates of the agent, taking it to other worlds, and using it on other human populations? Nothing at all. In fact, I suspect some unethical people have already done so, such as the Third Invaders."

"Yes, that is part of the reason I'm here. The Federation wants me find ways to prevent any of that mutation agent from leaving Earth."

"Good. Perhaps you could install some very sensitive devices at all spaceports—ones that could detect even the smallest traces of the armless telepath agent. I've no idea how this could be done. I'm a mere Private Investigator."

He chuckled. "All ready have my staff working on it."

"Well done. Next, we come to what should be done to Patricia. If you don't do anything to her and the public learns she invented and spread the virus, sure as I'm sitting here, an upset mob of mutated men will attack and kill her. We both know that's a huge loss. She's a brilliant microbiologist, a genius. We also know that if it becomes public knowledge, she could be blackmailed into making other virus epidemics, probably on other worlds. Kidnap Vernon and her son, threaten to kill them unless she makes the new virus—you get the idea."

"Astute observations, Mrs. Parkinson. I've already considered those myself on the trip to your world. I assure you, her execution would be humane. Others suggested I remove her arms. Then, she could no longer fabricate anything. I'm seriously considering that."

Patricia Ann cringed. Tears trickled down her cheeks.

"Ah, but that would only cause more problems. With all the known cures, anyone seeing an armless person like me knows they are a telepath, which she wouldn't be. I presume you're not going to try to make her into one. She could earn millions of credits instead of her small GMed salary."

"Good point. I thought of that, too."

"That would be a waste of her incredible talents. Rather, I propose we make use of her special skills in microbiology and virology, either here on Earth of perhaps elsewhere in the Federation. Perhaps working for your organization, Dr. Jones. With all these new worlds we're discovering, surely there are new viruses to be studied. Sorry, not my area of expertise."

"Point taken," Admiral Skaggs said, glancing at Dr. Jones. "But the Federation insists on some form of punishment, if only as a deterrent to others. Personally, I agree with you. Earth made some very stupid laws regarding the telepaths. In the case of Patricia Ann, if we identify her as the maker of the virus, she's as good as dead."

Dr. Jones said, "Where we really need someone with her skills is on board the deep space exploration ships. Each new world they discover contains billions of new organisms, anyone of which could prove fatal to the crew or to life on Earth should they accidentally bring it back with them. Except for this recent pandemic, we haven't had much need for her skills on Earth. And they always need good medical personnel on those missions. Deep space is a dangerous place. But what about her punishment? We have to deter others from doing such things."

"I've some ideas, but Mrs. Parkinson, I should tell you that the Federation has authorized me to make some rulership changes to the Sol Empire. Normally, we never interfere in local affairs. However, your current leadership incompetence and bunglings has threatened all other humans within the Federation of Planets. Like it or not, changes will be made, and you, Mrs. Parkinson, are involved in them. I believe we can work out some agreement with the Gates-Baxter family as part of this restructuring."

I swallowed. I'd not seen me being involved, but he was right about our bungling CEOs and Senate. At least he wasn't threatening Patricia Ann with death.

"By the way, Mrs. Parkinson, congratulations on becoming a transport pilot. Nothing you do ceases to amaze me. And that plays a role in my leadership decisions. Okay, to business. Here's what's going to happen later today.

"First, I'm placing Dimitri Leonovich as your Emperor of Galactic Expansion. Natalie Leonovich will be your Empress of Galactic Defense. Your Senate can continue as before, though you might consider electing replacements, but that's not required. Finally, you, Mrs. Parkinson, will be the new Senior Investigator and Judge for the Sol Empire. You're going to be the top investigator not only here on Earth but anywhere in your Sol Empire.

"Expect to travel all over your regions of space, carrying out needed investigations. When you travel, you're to bring both doctors along with you. He'll be your medical man, while she will handle anything with bugs and microbiology stuff. Further, when trials are held, you have the final say in the culprit's punishment. Your lower courts and investigators will handle the routine stuff. You handle the more challenging situations, but you're free to step in and assist the lower investigators anytime you desire and override decisions from the lower judges.

"Plus, I'm installing a new law. Two of the three branches can overrule the third branch. You and Dimitri, for example, could override the silly telepath laws that the Senate passed, along with that ill-advised Telepath Corporation. The Federation feels with these changes, the Sol Empire leaders will be able to run your own affairs without our interference and not threaten other worlds in the Federation.

He looked me squarely in my eyes. "You, Mrs. Parkinson, don't have a choice in this. Neither do the Leonovich family."

He turned to the two doctors. "As for Patricia Ann, I admit I know nothing about fabricating a virus, but I asked around. It seems doing something like that requires two hands—delicate actions with complex equipment. However, they tell me analyzing foreign bugs doesn't. So here's my proposal to spare your life and likelihood.

"You're dominant arm and hand will be amputated."

She gasped, covering her mouth.

"You can continue your invaluable work in your field. But with one hand, you'll never be able to fabricate another virus or pandemic. Further, you'll go on whatever space trips Mrs. Parkinson does, acting as her virologist and microbiologist. Dr. Baxter will go, too, as the ship's medical doctor.

"While on Earth, Patricia Ann, you'll work for Dr. Jones at the CDC. Dr. Gates-Baxter, you may resume your residency anywhere you choose as a neurosurgeon.

"Finally, I'll announce that the pandemic was just a fluke of nature, probably exacerbated by all the terrorist attacks, which spread that awful mutation agent around the world this past year. No one outside this room will know you were behind it. Your life should be safe.

"If you don't agree to this, then I've no recourse but to terminate you. Do you accept?"

Pat swallowed hard, glancing at Vernon, now struggling with their son who wanted to eat again. Barely audible, she said, "I agree."

"Good. Now then, if you'll accompany Dr. Jones, he'll take you to the Med Center to have the operation done. I'll be along shortly, since I'm obligated to witness it. They're indicating the Leonovich's have arrived. After notifying them of my decisions, I'll join you, Dr. Jones."

He looked at me again. "Mrs. Parkinson, I suggest you review your existing staff and get your feet wet with the existing investigations and trials. That is all."

With that, Deanna rose and helped me get my cloak on, while Pat did the same for Vernon. She gave him a kiss, before donning her coat, following Dr. Jones, whose heels clicked noisily on the tiled floor. Mine soon joined his.

"I feel sick," Vernon said when we left the building. The cold air of Chicago's winter revived him some. "Best outcome we could have had, I suppose," he admitted.

"Her life is spared, and she gets to continue work in her field," I said. "I had no idea about my being the Senior Investigator and Senior Judge or that I'd have to go off-world."

"She won't be able to tie her own shoes," he lamented.

I chuckled. "Give her time to adapt. She'll find new ways. Heck, I used to tie my own shoes using my toes. She'll still have one hand, which is more than I do. She'll be fine. I'm the one who should be upset. I can't get my arms back. Wonder if they'll ever let me get them?"

His face reddened, but not from the cold, I suspect. "How soon can I see her? Where's this Med Center? What'll I do with our baby? I need to see her."

Deanna spoke up. "Close by. First, we're going to my place and feed him. Once he's asleep, we'll head there. The surgery is a fast operation. With the current silver nanoparticle healing, they'll probably release her later today. She'll be okay."

Well, Deanna and I both knew Pat wouldn't be fine. After today, she faced serious life challenges, and I vowed to ask Celeste to give her some therapy sessions. I didn't know whether she would, since Pat had mutated everyone on Earth. That was a hefty crime, but losing someone of her caliber wasn't acceptable either.

Because of my distracted attention, I fell behind those two, neither of which wore heels. In my haste, I stumbled and would have fallen except that mysterious force held me steady until I had my balance back.

"Hey, guys. Little slower. I'm in tall heels here."

Vernon flushed. "Sorry, Molly. I'm so worried about Pat. How's this pace?"

An hour later, their infant sound asleep, we three headed to the Med Center. I sensed how much Vernon wanted to run ahead, to get there as fast as he could, but I held them back.

"Okay, this is silly. Deanna, you get Vernon there as fast as possible. I'll follow along at my snail's pace."

"Thank you," he gushed. Deanna smiled and did so.

One good thing about the buildings in our world—at least those I'm familiar with here in Chicago—is the automatic doors. Sensors pick up your approach and speed and respond appropriately, either opening them slowly or quickly—slowly in my case. I hated announcing my presence via the loud clicking of my spikes on their tiles, but then I always had disliked this aspect. Within five minutes, I entered Pat's recovery room.

Sitting on the edge of her bed, she and Dr. Jones examined her right shoulder. That arm had vanished. There wasn't even a bandage over the amputation site.

Seeing me entering, Pat said, "They didn't even knock me out. A local. Couldn't feel anything. I read about how wonderful the silver nanoparticle and mesh was for healing—Vernon's told me about it enough times, too. They say I can go home now."

Dr. Jones said, "Keep a close eye on her shoulder. At

the first sign of any bleeding, bring her in at once. About one in ten thousand have any leakage from the nano mesh. Admiral Skaggs has verified the surgery, so that's taken care of. You're free to go home. After your maternity leave is over, we'll contact you. Welcome to the CDC, Dr. Gates-Baxter."

Pat struggled to crack a slight smile. Deanna helped her put her coat back on, and we left. Once out in the cold air, Pat's facial color improved.

"I feel so funny. Kinda lopsided. So helpless. How am I going to do so many things? I shouldn't complain, Vernon. It must be better than you were or even poor Molly."

"Give yourself time to adapt," I said. "You'll find alternate ways to do nearly everything. Vernon's still got that laptop with all the how-to videos. While you still have one arm and hand, some of those methods we use with our feet might be useful for you. On the bright side, you're alive and still able to work in your chosen field. Frankly, Pat, I'm amazed we've pulled this off. I figured they'd terminate you."

"I—we don't know how to thank you for intervening. Before your sisters came, I expected they'd kill me. Say, how did you know about me—before they did? Weren't you in a mutation coma?" she asked.

I sighed heavily. "Yeah. In a coma, but sometimes I can sort of see future paths. And I'm a telepath."

"Well, that explains it, Vernon. She's still a telepath."

I laughed inside. She was searching for a rational explanation for a person in a coma somehow coming to her rescue. I also wanted to mention the therapy angle, but chose not to do that until Celeste approved.

However, when we got back to their room in Deanna's skyscraper, shock finally set in. Even with our modern surgical methods and the silver nanoparticle and mesh healing, she'd just had her right arm amputated at her shoulder. Shock set in. Deanna got her safely onto the couch and parka off. Next, she unbuttoned her blouse, revealing her shoulder. This way, we could check for blood loss. I saw none.

"I can't even write my own name," she said, before grief overcame her. "I feel sick at my stomach."

"It's shock, dear. Let's focus on your breathing. In. Out. Slowly. Like we did during his birth," Vernon said.

Slowly, the color returned to Pat's face.

"Say, I'm getting hungry. I suppose I should head home and fix my brood supper," I said.

Deanna grinned. "No, you don't. You stay right here. Everyone's coming over. We're holding a welcome back party for you."

Not long after that, Sam, Matt, and Nikita came into the room.

"Mom, we're going to need lots of tables and chairs. Everyone's coming," Nikita said. "Oh, I. I'm Nikita. I'm a telepath, like Mom and my older sister, Isabella. She's a famous linguist now. But she's going to have a baby girl real soon. She'll be a telepath, too. Owen, that's her husband, is regrowing his arms. I heard there's only a few of us telepaths left. I think that's a good thing, 'cause all my classmates—they got mutated into telepaths last summer—none of them wanted to be one. Probably because the corporations wanted to use them as spies. I won't spy for anyone. I'm going to be a linguist, like Isabella. Oh, here she comes and Owen, too."

While I introduced Isabella and Owen, Nikita stopped talking. Then all my other sisters and their families arrived, long with the Hugo family and Lenka and Walter. Deanna's husband and daughter joined us, announcing dinner was ready. He'd fixed up lots of tables in a workroom the floor below us. We all headed down for a feast.

Okay, I admit it. I was very pleased they did this for me.

During a quiet moment, I asked Celeste about giving Pat and Vernon therapy sessions. Her reply surprised me a little.

"Look, she's obligated to go with you on space trips as your virologist and microbiologist. He'll be your on board medical man. So yeah, we best get them in good mental shape. Randy and I will handle them starting tomorrow. Eve wants to work with you."

Chapter 27 A New Normal

Eve dropped by just after breakfast. I ate well, expecting a therapy session. But I had some questions first. Eve and Lara Axe-head were instrumental in developing the cures.

"Eve, is there any chance you and Lara will be able to develop a cure for Earth's men? Having all men mutated into male dolls isn't good."

"I don't like these monster boobs either. At least our feet lie flat. But Pat was right in not including the breast reduction cure. Most women are still unduly influenced by the Sixth Invaders' implant. They would have severe headaches if they suddenly had normal sized breasts again. Honestly, Lara and I have been frantically studying the aftereffects. It's not good. Scrambled eggs is a good analogy for everyone's DNA. Still, we are working on it. Our focus now is you. We want to get you back to battery, even if we have to be sneaky about it. Then, we'll look at the broader picture. Men? I seriously doubt we'll be able to do a whole lot for them. We'll see. Now, enough of this. You need therapy sessions. Are you comfortable? Phone off? Good. Close your eyes."

I chuckled. "I still see you. That's been happening a lot to me, lately. Seeing things clearly without my eyes. Strange. Oh, yeah. I've almost fallen several times, but each time I felt a mysterious force holding up until it regained my balance."

"Thanks for telling me about it. Let's return to when you first realized they were going to regrow your arms."

We were off and running. I blew off the initial mutation pains rapidly. Then, I encountered Dr. Jones' attempts to re-mutate me. Bam. I re-experienced that incredible head pain. I must admit that in my more recent therapy sessions, I've been flying through the aches and pains and traumas, but this one sat me on my butt. An hour later with Eve's constant help, I confronted the pain fully, and it vanished.

"Something happened in my head," I said when we ended the session two hours later.

"You can say that again. Something has really changed with you. Do you realize that at one point your chair and body rose about a foot off the ground?"

I stared at her, my mouth open wide.

"How did the room get so rearranged? It's like a cyclone swept through here."

"If we were running a session, I'd swear a poltergeist struck," Eve said. "But you did this while running through the incident. Telekinesis. I'd swear you've developed a strong telekinesis ability. I'd like to do a brain scan on you. Come on. Let's go to my lab after lunch."

An hour later, I stared at two scans of my brain. She'd taken one last year, the other, moments ago.

"Look at that thing," I said, frustrated that I couldn't point to it. "That thing has grown. Is it a tumor?"

Eve laughed. "Hardly. That's your pituitary gland. It's supposed to be about the size of a pea and is located in that bony hollow just behind the bridge of your nose."

"Neither of them look like a pea."

"No, they don't. In all the telepaths Lara and I've examined, this gland is two or three times larger than normal. We believe its increased size is responsible for your telepathic abilities. We've only been able to scan Sam and Matt so far, but theirs are back to the human normal size, and they've lost their telepathic ability. We'll be testing many others soon. Today, yours is positively gigantic. I've never heard of one being anywhere near this large. I suspect the enormous dosage of the mutation agent—five times what anyone should ever have received—has caused this abnormal growth. Apparently, this gland also controls a person's telekinesis ability or at least facilitates it."

"So that mysterious force that kept me from taking a tumble was me?" I think my face must have shown my disbelief.

"That's my working theory. We should practice using it, but only after we finish up your therapy. Come on. Back to your place. We've more work to do."

By supper, we'd erased all traces of my recent traumas and losses. Yes, not getting my arms back was a loss. I felt light and serene. Celeste dropped by to tell me she was making progress with Patricia Ann and Vernon, which only made me feel even better.

After they left, I told Sam, Matt, and the kids about developing telekinesis. "Tomorrow, Eve's going to work with me and see if I can control it."

Of course, Nikita and Isabella were particularly excited about this.

"That's really cool, Mom," Nikita said. "Think we'll be able to do that, too?"

"Don't think so. Aunt Eve thinks it's happened to me only because he gave me that overdose of the mutation agent. Five times the normal dose, she said. Kids, the pain I endured during that coma was the worst ever."

"Well, I still think it's cool for you to have it," Nikita insisted. "I've been practicing with a doll so I can help Isabella with her baby. You know, changing diapers and stuff. I'm gonna be her aunt. That's way cool, don't you think? I want to help her a whole lot, though I expect Owen will do the heavy work, once his arms get stronger."

She would have talked longer, but Isabella interrupted her. "Mom, that's just what you need. But Nikita, we shouldn't go around telling others that she's got telekinesis. We don't want her to get into anymore trouble. Look what saying she has telepathy got her."

"Okay, but I don't see why Mom can't get her arms back anyway," Nikita pouted.

"Because others are afraid of what I could potentially learn from their minds," I explained. "By having all telepaths instantly recognizable as one—no arms—they would be alerted to possible spying."

"But others have telepathy and weren't mutated to get it," she complained.

"Yes, but for heaven's sake don't tell anyone about that. I'm afraid they'll cut off their arms, too."

That sobered her, and we changed topics to how Isabella was doing. Her due date was sometime in the next two weeks. I couldn't tell who was more excited about the birth: Nikita or Isabella.

Bev joined Eve and me the next morning. We discovered that I could easily lift about three hundred pounds, but I was more interested in small, precise actions, like preventing a tumble.

Bev said, "Molly, you and I should go to the range. I bet you can now lift and fire your Glock without arms."

"Can we, Eve? You don't know how much I've missed that stress reliever."

Eve chuckled. An hour later and alone in our section of the range, I discovered I could handle my gun. True, I had to really concentrate to load the clips with the 9mm rounds. Lifting, aiming, and firing was easy, and my accuracy seemed somehow improved. I did need help field stripping and cleaning it, and Bev promised to do that for me. When we headed home that afternoon, I felt as though I could fly. My stress reliever was back in play.

The next morning, reality returned. Dimitri and Natalie dropped by.

"It's going to be on the news this morning," he said. "Admiral Skaggs will be speaking and telling everyone in the Sol Empire how it's going to be run for the foreseeable future. We're going to be in the hot seat a few hours from now. Do you suppose I could get some therapy session soon? I'm so embarrassed to be seen in public. I look and sound like a woman."

"But he's not," Natalie insisted with a wry grin. "I could use them too. I had no idea how heavy these monster boobs are. And now I have no choice but to wear the tall heels. Dimitri, too. We move at a snail's pace, but then you do, too. I don't know how you can manage, Molly. It's treacherous in the snow."

"Okay. I'll see what we can arrange soon. Ah, it's starting."

For an hour, we listened to the stern voice of Admiral Skaggs. First, he brought everyone up on the search for Patient Zero, ending with the theory that it was an accident of nature likely brought on by all the many aerosol attacks this past year. Then, he ordered the Senate to reconvene and get rid of all the laws impacting telepaths.

He outlined the Federation's position regarding the nasty mutation agent and how they perceived it threatened the Federation of Planets. This alone occupied a half hour. Admiral Skaggs made certain those listening to the broadcast understood just how serious the spread of the armless telepath agent had become. He outlined the new steps being installed at all spaceports. That is, sensing devices to detect the presence of that mutation agent.

"Anyone caught trying to export the armless telepath agent off Earth will be terminated. No questions asked." I didn't know his face could look any sterner than it had, but just then it did!

"Look, Earthlings. If you don't get control over this terrible biological agent, the Federation is prepared to nuke this entire world and turn control of your empire over to those on Pylon or Brussels."

I think many CEOs and corrupt leaders needed that nudge.

Next, he described my new position as Senior Investigator and Senior Judge, replacing the existing ones. Then, he outlined the new positions of Emperor of Galactic Expansion and Empress of Galactic Defense, before announcing Dimitri and Natalie would fill those positions.

He ended by explaining how any two of these new branches could veto any action or decision from the other. Checks and balances, he claimed. I only wish we'd had that years ago. So much of the past chaos and mutations could have been avoided.

"At this time, Earth has only nine official telepaths left. Those who suffered the pandemic are now immune to that mutation agent, so you can't make any more telepaths that way. We aren't going to allow that stuff to leave this world, either. Get your house in order or face the consequences. When the Federation of Planets believes you have, they will relax some of these restrictions. Your senators will keep the Federation Senate informed of your progress. That is all."

That was enough, I thought. Perhaps, we could now recover.

"Maybe we can make a difference this time," Dimitri said.

I found his soprano voice more than a little spooky, to say nothing of his physical appearance. Well, I rationalized, we're all going to have to get used to this new normal.

"I'll start work tomorrow. Helen's going to be a huge help," Natalie said. "Are you going to be able to manage, Molly? I mean going off world to solve cases? Have you really got a pilot's license?"

"Stop and think how. I'll manage. And yes, I've got one. It's easier piloting from New O'Hare, since the control tower computers do most of the work. I'm not as confident with manual landings on strange planets, though. Guess I'm going to get plenty of experience."

I added, "One thing. Let's make sure telepaths can get new cures as they become available. No more waiting years and all that crap."

Natalie asked, "Any chance anyone will find a way to help our men? Undo all this?"

I sighed. "Not at this time. It looks pretty bleak."

Dimitri said, "We're going to have to depend on the giants and dwarves for muscle power. I can barely walk. My strength has dropped noticeably. Plus, we can't even walk quickly, let alone run. General Blythe hasn't got a viable army any longer. Scary."

"Women are in better shape," Natalie said, "since most had already undergone the Galactic Doll mutation, so the virus actually repaired their feet. That's something, I suppose. Still, I'm going to have to depend on women for defense, along with dwarves. I don't trust giants."

"Well, we best get to it. Molly, stay in touch," he said.

After giving me a hug, they left. I took a deep breath before placing the call I knew I had to make. I retrieved my phone from my lower dress pocket—a Leslie design feature especially for me. Thank goodness for one-touch connections. "Bishop. Molly here. We need to meet."

Vic Broquard

The End.

A Favor to Other Readers

How about helping other readers? Many readers rely on reviews to make the decision whether to buy a book. You can help them make their decision by leaving your opinions and viewpoint in a short review of the positive things of this book. Writing the review and expressing your opinion only takes a few minutes, and other readers will appreciate your efforts.

Click this link: Sol Empire Volume 3 Greed
https://www.amazon.com/dp/B07BQGDVP6/
scroll down to Customer Reviews; click on Write a Review, and enter your review. Thank you.

Author Information

Visit My Amazon.com Author Page
Vic Broquard Author Page

Follow My Blog
Vic Broquard's Blog

Follow Me on Social Media
Facebook
Google+
LinkedIn
YouTube

Other Books by Vic Broquard

<u>Without Warning (fantasy)</u>

The Trident Series: (fantasy)
> <u>Volume 1 The Trident and the Book</u>
> <u>Volume 2 The Trident and the Scepter</u>
> <u>Volume 3 The Trident and the Resurrection</u>

The Adventures of Elizabeth Stanton Series: (science fiction)
> <u>Volume 1 The Evolution of the Path</u>
> <u>Volume 2 The Great Messiah</u>
> <u>Volume 3 Of Kings and Queens and Troubadours</u>
> <u>Volume 4 Chaos in the Aftermath</u>
> <u>Volume 5 Power Plays</u>
> <u>Volume 6 Age of Exploration</u>
> <u>Volume 7 Abducted</u>
> <u>Volume 8 The Emperor and Empress</u>
> <u>Volume 9 A Job Worth Doing</u>
> <u>Volume 10 Degradation</u>
> <u>Volume 11 The Second Crusade</u>
> <u>Volume 12 When Worlds Collide</u>
> <u>Volume 13 Dark Ages</u>

The Lindsey Barron Series: (fantasy)
> <u>Volume 1 The Rod of the Apocalypse</u>
> <u>Volume 2 The Board of Governors</u>
> <u>Volume 3 The Crown of Moses</u>
> <u>Volume 4 Dominus for President</u>
> <u>Volume 5 The National Health Care Program</u>
> <u>Volume 6 States Justice</u>
> <u>Volume 7 Cross and Double-cross</u>
> <u>Volume 8 Down the Dragon Hole</u>

Zoran Chronicles Series: (fantasy)
> <u>Volume 1 A Dragon in Our Town</u>
> <u>Volume 2 Dragons, Power, Courts, and War</u>

Planet of the Orange-red Sun Series: (science fiction)
Volume 1 When Kingdoms Fall
Volume 2 Dark Ages
Volume 3 Age of the Towers
Volume 4 Difficillis Exitus
Volume 5 Age of the Lords
Volume 6 The Renegade Tower
Volume 7 Rebellions
Volume 8 The Aliens Return
Volume 9 Power Struggles
Volume 10 Guilds, Genetics, and Gods
Volume 11 Magi, Witches, Swords, and Superstitions
Volume 12 The Voyage of the Eagle's Seed
Volume 13 Eagle's Seed and Origins
Volume 14 Justifications
Volume 15 Responsibilities

The Return of the Wizards: Twelve Companions – The Making of Wizards (fantasy)

Slow Comes the Dark Series: (science fiction)
Volume 1 Creeping Darkness
Volume 2 Serendipity
Volume 3 Darkness Descends
Volume 4 Perversion Incarnate
Volume 5 Extermination Wars

Reclamation Series (science fiction)
Volume 1 For the Want of a Pill
Volume 2 Organ Donors

Dragons, Magic, and Me (fantasy)
Volume 1 The Box

The Sol Empire (science fiction)
Volume 1 For the Want of Humanity
Volume 2 Fear
Volume 3 Greed
Volume 4 Power Moves